Egg Drop
Dead

·LAURA CHILDS·

Egg Drop Dead

BERKLEY PRIME CRIME
New York

BERKLEY PRIME CRIME
Published by Berkley
An imprint of Penguin Random House LLC
375 Hudson Street, New York, New York 10014

Copyright © 2016 by Gerry Schmit
Excerpt from *Pekoe Most Poison* copyright © 2016 by Gerry Schmitt & Associates, Inc

Library of Congress Cataloging-in-Publication Data

Names: Childs, Laura, author.
Title: Egg drop dead / Laura Childs.
Description: First edition. | New York : Berkley Prime Crime, 2016. | Series:
A Cackleberry Club mystery ; 7
Identifiers: LCCN 2016027522 (print) | LCCN 2016034338 (ebook) | ISBN
9780425281703 (softcover) | ISBN 9780698197435 (ebook)
Subjects: LCSH: Women private investigators—Fiction. |
Murder—Investigation—Fiction. | Women detectives—Fiction. | BISAC:
FICTION / Fantasy / Short Stories. | FICTION / Mystery & Detective /
General. | GSAFD: Mystery fiction.
Classification: LCC PS3603.H56 E34 2016 (print) | LCC PS3603.H56 (ebook) |
DDC 813/.6—dc23
LC record available at https://lccn.loc.gov/2016027522

First Edition: December 2016

Printed in the United States of America
1   3   5   7   9   10   8   6   4   2

Cover art by Lee White
Cover design by Sarah Oberrender
Book design by Kristin del Rosario

Acknowledgments

Major thank-yous are owed to Sam, Tom, Amanda, Bob, Jennie, Troy, Susan, Dan, and all the designers, illustrators, writers, publicists, and sales folk at Berkley. You are all such a wonderful team. Thank you also to all the booksellers, reviewers, librarians, and bloggers. And special thanks to all my readers and Facebook friends, who are so very kind and supportive. I truly love writing for you!

Egg Drop
Dead

CHAPTER 1

IT was an autumn of particular intensity. Of riotous colors and delft blue skies, cool nights and smoke curling out of chimneys. Halloween was barely a week away and Suzanne Dietz was feeling mighty pleased with herself as she glanced at the puddle of black silk lying on the car seat next to her. She'd just picked up the wicked witch costume that her neighbor Laurel Kennedy had sewn for her. The woman was a creative genius when it came to three yards of fabric, six yards of black scalloped lace, and a Singer sewing machine. Suzanne, on the other hand, managed to impale her finger every time she picked up a needle to sew on a button or whipstitch a hem. Which is why she was congratulating herself for out-sourcing such an odious task and looking forward to her role as a well-stitched witch at the Cackleberry Club's upcoming Halloween celebration.

Changing lanes, Suzanne caught her own reflection in the rearview mirror and thought, *Correction, make that a modern-day witch.*

Just a hair past forty, Suzanne was lean, square shouldered, and still golden brown from puttering around her herb garden in the summer sun. Her hair was a shoulder-length silvered blond, her eyes a deep cornflower blue. Today she wore a white blouse, nipped tightly at her waist by a silver concho belt, and a pair of slim-fitting jeans. She had on her favorite cowboy boots, the well-worn brown ones with turquoise leather steer heads inset at the ankles.

Suzanne was the self-appointed purveyor of foods and the driving force behind the Cackleberry Club, a cozy little farm-to-table café she ran with her two BFFs, Toni and Petra. She was also recently engaged to Dr. Sam Hazelet, who had to be the most handsome and skilled doctor in the small Midwestern town of Kindred.

Suzanne smiled to herself as she drove along, the noon sun lasering down upon the windshield of her Taurus. Sam was quite a catch, she mused. Four years younger than she was, great sense of humor, and, most important, in love with her. (Okay, truth be told, he might even be a little besotted with her.)

If she hadn't hit the boyfriend jackpot, she probably would have (horrors!) been forced to venture onto one of those Internet dating sites. Then her character sketch might have read something like, *Overworked café owner, dog mom, and curiosity seeker hopes to meet fun-loving guy for wine dinners, occasional trout fishing, and long-term mischief.* And after a few sketchy responses, someone like Sam would have popped up. Or not.

Suzanne drank in the scenery as the blacktopped country road dipped down and the woods closed in on either side of her. Late October meant the oaks and maples had erupted in a riot of crimson and orange, and every time a puff of wind came along, leaves fluttered down in perfect golden swirls. It made her think of bonfires and pumpkin spice muffins, and, of course, Halloween.

Coming up out of a valley onto a slight ridge, the road sud-

denly hooked right and ran alongside a rustic fence of silvered, weathered wood. That fence marked the property line
for Mike Mullen's dairy farm. Mike was Suzanne's go-to guy
for the homemade wheels of tasty cheddar and Swiss cheese
that she served and sold at the Cackleberry Club. Tapping her
brakes lightly, Suzanne coasted along until she spotted Mike's
familiar tilting mailbox up ahead. This behemoth of dented
metal was surrounded by a tangle of bright red bittersweet
and sat beside a hand-painted sign that read Cloverdale
Farm—Farm Fresh Milk and Cheese.

Suzanne turned into the driveway and crunched her way
down a narrow gravel road. A quarter of a mile later, her car
rolled to a stop in Mike's farmyard. The place was picture-
perfect, an old-fashioned farm built in the early nineteen hundreds by hardworking German immigrants. Off to the right
was a classic *American Gothic* farmhouse complete with finials,
balustrades, and a rambling old front porch. Straight ahead
was a faded red hip-roofed dairy barn. Several smaller buildings that housed bales of hay and farm tools were scattered off
to the left, and a large, woodsy pasture butted up close to the
house and barn.

Suzanne slid out of her car and scuffed a toe of her boot
into the gravel.

"Hey, Mike," she called out. "It's Suzanne." She let out a
breath. "From the Cackleberry Club."

The big sliding barn door stood wide open and she expected
to see Mike's broad, grinning face appear at any moment.

When, after a minute or two, Mike didn't duck out and
greet her, Suzanne decided he must be all the way back in
the barn, tending his cows. Or maybe he was in the adjacent cheese workshop, a place with a pleasant, yeasty smell
and gleaming stainless steel pipes, tanks, and tables. The
place where all the cheese magic happened.

"No problem," Suzanne said, striking out for the barn.
She'd talked to Mike a couple of days ago and told him she

needed to replenish her larder with a few wheels of his delicious cheese. He'd told her to stop by anytime. Well, now was anytime.

Suzanne ducked inside the barn, going from dazzling sunlight to a dim interior. She blinked hard a couple of times, trying to adjust her eyes, keenly aware of the mingled sharp scents of cows and hay.

"Mike?" she called again.

This time Suzanne received an answer. But it wasn't from Mike. Instead, she was greeted by a cacophony of loud bellows.

"What?" she murmured.

A few steps down the center aisle and Suzanne was confronted by the urgent, upturned faces of four dozen cows bawling unhappily at her. Cows that clearly hadn't been milked yet.

Haven't been milked yet? But it's twenty after twelve. These poor things have been waiting all morning?

Where was Mike? Suzanne wondered as she tiptoed through the barn. On either side, cows continued to blat anxiously as they stretched their necks out to greet her. To plead for help. And the farther in she ventured, the more the cows' mooing turned to pitiful moans.

Where the stanchions ended there were two box stalls. Animals moved about restlessly in there, too. Horses that tossed their heads and banged their hooves hard against the wooden walls.

What was going on?

"Mike?" Suzanne called out, trying to keep a slight quaver out of her voice. "Are you back here?" She hesitated and peered into the dimness ahead of her, where dust motes twirled lazily and worn leather halters and bridles hung on wooden pegs. Then she added, "Are you okay?"

Moving toward the wooden door that led into the cheese workshop, Suzanne felt a prickle of unease. The hairs on the back of her neck were starting to stand up straight. Really?

Now, why was that? Then her heart did a little thump-bump inside her chest and her breathing became a little more rapid. Had something happened to Mike? Or was she simply overreacting to the agitation of the cows?

Suzanne tamped down her fears and rapped her knuckles sharply against the white wooden door of the cheese workshop.

"Mike? Are you in there?"

No answer.

Gathering up her nerve, Suzanne put a hand flat against the door and gave it a shove. Instead of swinging open on its hinges, the door creaked open a couple of inches and stopped. Frowning, she pushed again, this time with a little more force.

No way. Something seemed to be blocking it.

Suzanne leaned forward and touched her cheek to the door, the smooth wood feeling cool against her skin. Then she poked her nose in, trying to peer around the edge of the door.

The first thing she saw was a green rubber boot turned sideways on the damp cement floor. That boot was clearly attached to a leg.

Mike? Something's happened to Mike?

Worry exploded in Suzanne's brain. She drew a quick breath, took a step back, and then flung her full body weight against the door. The door creaked open another foot. Suzanne eased herself into the room, where Mike Mullen sprawled awkwardly on the floor. His white hair was matted with bright red blood as if he'd sustained a dozen deep scalp lacerations, and his gnarled hands were crisscrossed with bloody defensive wounds. The blue-and-white-striped overalls he wore were completely slashed and tattered, as if he'd been existing as a castaway on some remote South Seas jungle island. The fabric was also completely saturated with blood.

Dead? Mike's dead?

Suzanne's mind spun like a runaway centrifuge. *Who? Why?* A hundred questions churned inside her head. She lunged forward, somehow thinking she'd check his pulse or hopefully clear an airway. But her foot slipped in the slick pool of blood and she fell forward. If she hadn't thrust her hands out to break her fall, she would have landed right square on top of his body. As it was, her ungainly fall put her on her hands and knees, looking directly into wide-open milky white eyes that stared sightlessly into a void.

"Mike?" Suzanne said again, in a pleading, still-hopeful tone. Because she was still trying to make sense of how someone could cold-bloodedly murder this mild-mannered dairy farmer.

CHAPTER 2

IGNORING the anxious cries and bellows of the cows, Suzanne dashed back through the barn and out into the sunlight. Skidding wildly in the gravel, she pawed open her car door and flung herself inside. *Bam.* Her door locks clicked down hard. Then she fumbled her key into the ignition, gripped her steering wheel, and cranked the engine hard until it whined in protest.

In full panic mode, her teeth chattering so hard she was afraid she'd pop a filling, Suzanne hesitated for a second and looked around. And saw . . . absolutely nothing. There were no other people, no other cars. So what was the best thing, the smartest thing, for her to do in a situation like this?

Her heart still hammering inside her chest, she squirmed wildly in the driver's seat, trying to make sure a maniac wasn't about to leap at her with a shrieking, clattering chain saw. When none showed up, Suzanne pulled her cell phone from her purse and dialed the Law Enforcement Center in Kindred.

Marilyn Grabowski, the 911 dispatcher, came on the line immediately. "Nine-one-one, what's your emergency?"

"Get me Sheriff Doogie!" Suzanne hollered. "I need Sheriff Doogie right away!"

But Marilyn needed a little more information than that.

Still babbling with fear, Suzanne tried to explain the situation. "This is Suzanne Dietz. I'm out here at Mike Mullen's place on Country Trail. And Mike's been . . . well, I'm pretty sure that he's been killed. Stabbed, I think. Murdered in cold blood!"

Marilyn, who'd honed her calming skills as a first-grade teacher years ago, knew exactly what to do.

"First things first," Marilyn said. "You get out of there, Suzanne. Do you hear me? Your life could be in danger, too."

Suzanne nodded wildly into the phone. "Yeah, yeah," she said. "Sure."

"I mean it, Suzanne. Drive back to the main road and wait there until someone shows up. I'm alerting Deputy Driscoll right now. Sending him directly out your way. It won't be long. Five minutes at the most."

"We need Sheriff Doogie, too," Suzanne stuttered. "You gotta send Doogie."

"I'm putting in a call to him," Marilyn said. "But I know he's just getting out of a county board meeting."

"Okay."

"Get out of there now, Suzanne, and don't take any chances. Help is on the way."

Suzanne was just about to throw her car in gear when she decided to make another call. She had that particular number on speed dial, so she hit it and waited. Hung on tight.

Sam was on the line in a matter of seconds.

"I have a problem," Suzanne said.

"Tell me." Sam was used to calls without long preambles. He was a doctor, after all.

Suzanne stammered out pretty much what she'd told the

dispatcher, and then Sam told her pretty much what the dispatcher had told her. *Get out of there fast. Don't take any chances. Wait for help to arrive.*

Suzanne, being a self-confessed contrarian, hung up and thought about this for exactly thirty seconds. Then she did the complete opposite of what she'd been instructed. After a careful look around the farmyard (to be sure the fire-breathing maniac with the chainsaw still wasn't coming after her), she switched off her engine. Then she kicked open the driver's side door and stepped back out.

A bright golden sun still lasered down. A light breeze kicked up bits of dust and leaves and spun them toward a low pen where a trio of woolly sheep peeked out at her. Over near the farmhouse, a birdbath pattered. The scene *looked* normal enough. On the other hand . . .

Clenching her jaw, Suzanne studied the farmhouse and worried. Was Mike's wife, Claudia, at home? Did she need help? Was somebody inside with her right now, holding a butcher knife to her throat?

Slowly, cautiously, as if she were picking her way across a bed of hot coals, Suzanne walked to the house. She climbed the three creaking stairs that led to the small back porch and stared at the screen door.

Now what? Well . . . maybe just pound on the door and see if Claudia's in there.

Suzanne knocked on the door and waited. Nothing. She knocked again, a little harder this time, causing the door to rattle in its frame. It terrified her to think that Claudia might be lying on the kitchen floor, facedown in a pool of her own blood.

That single, horrifying thought compelled her to take action. She reached down, turned the doorknob, and gingerly pulled the door open a tentative couple of inches.

"Claudia," Suzanne called out. "Are you in here?" She waited, hearing nothing but the pounding of her own heart and the rush of blood churning in her ears. She called out again. "Claudia?" Then, feeling a little bolder, said, "Anybody home?"

Opening the door wider, Suzanne gazed into the Mullen's tidy little farm kitchen. She saw a silver coffeepot sitting on the Hotpoint range, a plate and coffee cup resting next to the sink. Nothing looked out of order. And yet . . .

Her curiosity amped to a frantic level, Suzanne was about to step inside the kitchen. Then she checked herself. *No, don't do this,* she decided. *Don't risk it.*

She backed away and closed the screen door soundlessly. Feeling nervous and edgy, she knew she'd completely overstepped her boundaries. This was so not a good idea, she admonished herself as she hurried back to her car. She should have followed Marilyn's instructions—and Sam's—right to the letter.

With one hand resting on the handle of her car door, Suzanne paused and looked around once more. Nothing felt out of place. And yet . . . everything had changed. Mike was dead. The cows were frantic. And she was standing here, gazing around as if it were any old stupid Tuesday on a sunny October morning.

No, Suzanne told herself, what she was really doing was looking around, *studying* the area, to see if there was some kind of clue or takeaway. After all, she'd been the first one to stumble upon the crime scene.

Correction, I'm actually not the first one. Those honors would go to Mike's killer.

Beyond the dairy barn, a stand of trees was aflame in red, gold, and amber. The sky was a rich blue, that pure, unfiltered blue that materializes only on rare autumn days when the atmosphere throbs with electricity and it seems like you can peer all the way up to the very edge of outer space.

Suzanne knew she'd better drive herself out to the main

road immediately. The sheriff and his deputies would be roaring in any second and . . . wait a minute. She blinked. What was that?

Her eyes had caught a brief hint of movement way off in the distance. What was it exactly? A tree branch swaying in the wind? She scanned the distance, trying to pull it all into tighter focus. No, it looked almost like someone's head and shoulders. Was that a person standing way out there in the woods? No, now there wasn't any movement at all, so it must be some kind of scarecrow.

Suzanne glanced away, already making up her mind that it was a scarecrow devised to scare off scavenging birds. Then she hesitated.

Wait a minute. A scarecrow in a cow pasture?

Something about that scenario didn't quite compute. She looked down at her toes, frowned, and then glanced back up, deciding it might be worth her while to take a second, more careful look. But the figure had disappeared. It was gone, just like that. Poof.

Then the high, piercing scream of a police siren rent the air. Law enforcement was rolling toward her fast, running at top speed. And layered on top of the cruiser's screaming siren was the telltale *whoop whoop* of an ambulance chasing along in its wake.

Suzanne gazed down the long driveway, where the two vehicles suddenly steamed toward her. Then all hell broke loose as a maroon and tan sheriff's car roared into the farm-yard and slewed to a stop, its tires spitting gravel like Pop Rocks. The ambulance charged in right behind it.

Suzanne immediately recognized Deputy Eddie Driscoll as he jumped from the cruiser. He was tall and lanky, late thirties, with a slightly receding hairline. This was the first time Suzanne had ever seen him move with such urgency and speed.

"Mike's in the barn," Suzanne cried, pointing toward the gaping opening in the dairy barn. "Back in his cheese workshop." She drew in a quick breath. "Dead, I think."

"Are you hurt?" Driscoll asked.

Suzanne shook her head. "Not me. Why?"

Driscoll pointed to her slacks. Suzanne looked down and saw a smear of blood.

She grimaced. "That's Mike's blood. Please hurry!"

Deputy Driscoll placed a hand on his still-holstered gun and rushed past her. Two EMTs followed some twenty feet behind him, moving at a slower pace since they were also hauling along their med kit and a clanking gurney.

They all disappeared inside the barn and Suzanne thought, *Why am I standing here like a bump on a log?* And followed them in.

The cows were bellowing again and stomping their hooves in protest, frightened once more by the appearance of strangers and the strange metal clanking thing they dragged with them. Their necks strained outward as Suzanne rushed past, their eyes rolled wildly, lips slicked back over long bovine teeth.

"Can you . . ." Suzanne slid to an ungainly stop just inches from a stunned Deputy Driscoll. "Can you tell what happened?"

Deputy Driscoll and Dick Sparrow, one of the EMTs, were standing over Mullen. Sparrow had just completed a quick life check; Driscoll was simply observing as his hand rested on his weapon.

"He's really dead?" Suzanne asked.

"I'm afraid so," Sparrow said.

Driscoll looked horrified. "There's so much blood."

"He's been stabbed," Sparrow said. "Slashed repeatedly."

"How long has he been dead?" Suzanne asked. She wondered if she'd just missed seeing Mike's killer.

"Hard to tell," said the other EMT, a young redheaded kid whose name tag said *Rickman*.

Sparrow grimaced. "Certainly not very long. It doesn't look as if rigor mortis has even begun to set in."

"Do you know . . . ?" Driscoll began. But Sparrow just shook his head.

The beat of heavy footsteps caused Suzanne, and everyone else, to turn. And there, lumbering directly toward them, was Sheriff Roy Doogie. His khaki bulk was silhouetted against the open door for just a moment, giving the impression of a large indomitable object, and then the sheriff strode with authority into their circle.

"What have we got?" Doogie growled. His gray, rattlesnake eyes shone brightly in his meaty face as he absorbed the entire crime scene in about two seconds flat. He slid his Smokey Bear hat off his head and touched a hand to his sparse cap of gray hair. "Mike," he said. "What a pity." He glared at Dick Sparrow. "What can you tell me? Anything?"

"Wrongful death," Sparrow said.

"Who found him?" Doogie asked.

It was Suzanne's turn to speak up. "I did."

Doogie turned and eyed her suspiciously. "What were you doing out here?"

"Picking up cheese."

"Did you see what happened?"

Suzanne shook her head. "No." She lifted a hand. "He was like this when I got here."

There was more loud trumpeting from the cows and they all turned to see what was causing the ruckus.

Sam, Suzanne murmured under her breath as she caught sight of him. She was relieved that he'd gotten here so quickly.

Dr. Sam Hazelet had indeed arrived. Late thirties, devastating smile, handsome with dark curly hair. Here was everything a girl could possibly want. Except, of course, for the bloody blue murder scene.

"Suzanne?" Sam asked, concern clouding his face as he

rushed to join them. "Are you all right?" He grabbed both her shoulders and spun her toward him.

"She's fine," Doogie said.

"I'm fine," Suzanne said.

"She's a witness," Doogie added.

Sam's look of concern deepened. "You *saw* what happened here?" He sounded stunned. "That's not the story you gave me."

"No," Suzanne said. "I didn't really see anything. I just . . . I found Mike like this."

Sam seemed to accept this simpler version and turned his attention to Mike Mullen's remains. He knelt down on one knee and did a hasty assessment. "Nasty," he said. "Obviously, there's no need to transport him at this point." He was grim faced but his demeanor remained cool and professional.

Sheriff Doogie swiped at his brow. There was a thin film of perspiration on his forehead even though the temperature was in the low sixties. "How do you think he died?" he asked. Doogie was big on clarification.

"At first glance, I'd say he bled out," Sam said. "Although it's possible his heart gave out or his respiration was severely compromised."

"Any guess on what he was *attacked* with?" Suzanne asked. "I mean, he's all cut up and there's so much blood . . ."

Sam was just about to answer when Doogie gave a quick frown and made a silencing motion with his hand. "We don't need to go into the precise circumstances of death right now," he warned. "First things first—we need to process the scene."

"And notify next of kin," Sam said.

"That would be Claudia," Suzanne said. "But I don't think she's home."

Doogie turned and drilled her with flat, inquisitive eyes. "What exactly are you trying to tell me?"

Suzanne shrugged. "That she's not home?"

"Because you already checked."

Suzanne bit her lip. "Well, yes, I kind of did. I knocked on the back door and . . ."

"Suzanne." Sam grabbed her arm and tried to pull her away from the group. "You can go into all that later. Right now Sheriff Doogie has to focus on his investigation."

"If there's an investigation, then it means there was foul play," Suzanne said. Her voice sounded slightly shrill in the cavernous barn. She glanced down the length of the barn and out the barn door, where another deputy was stringing up a flutter of black and yellow plastic tape that said SHER-IFF DEPT—DO NOT CROSS. She wondered exactly who they were trying to keep out. Wasn't this like shutting the proverbial barn door after the . . . killer?

Doogie's eyes flashed Suzanne a warning look. "Suzanne, don't be getting in my way here. We need to take pictures and go over the scene. Then there has to be an autopsy and . . ." He glanced at Sam and said, "Oh hell, she's gonna worm everything out of you anyway, isn't she? I mean, the two of you are engaged."

Sam just raised his eyebrows.

"Yeah," Doogie said. "That's what I thought." He turned to Deputy Driscoll and said, "Eddie, grab the camera out of my trunk, will you? And you may as well haul in the rest of that gear the state crime lab sent us." He gazed down at Mullen and sighed deeply. "We'd best get this investigation rolling."

CHAPTER 3

By the time Suzanne arrived back at the Cackleberry Club, the lunch rush had petered out. Petra was rattling around in the kitchen, baking a couple pans of her trademark peanut butter scones. Toni was dawdling out in the café, flirting with the male customers and ringing up tabs on an old-fashioned brass cash register. Even though she was a shade past forty, Toni still considered herself the resident hoochie momma. Not quite divorced from Junior Garret, she favored big hair, push-up bras, skintight cowgirl shirts, and even tighter jeans. Today, she'd clipped an extra fluff of genuine Dynel hair to her ponytail and wore an eye-popping red satin shirt with heart-shaped pearl buttons.

Toni's face lit up when she saw Suzanne bounce through the front door. "Hey, Suzanne." Then, when she noticed Suzanne's slightly grim expression, she hurried over and said, "What's wrong, Suzy-Q?"

"Everything," Suzanne said. She hooked a thumb toward

the kitchen and said. "We need to have a board of directors meeting."

Toni's brows rose in twin arcs. "Uh-oh, sounds serious."

"You got that right." Suzanne pushed open the swinging door and the two of them trooped into the café's kitchen, where pots bubbled, pans of chicken breasts sizzled, and they were greeted with a multitude of delightful aromas.

"My peanut butter scones are gangbusters," Petra sang out when she saw them. "And it's all because I used that organic . . ." She glanced over her shoulder, caught the serious look on Suzanne's face, and did a fast double take. "Suzanne, why the lemon face?"

"We have a slight problem," Suzanne said.

"I'm guessing it's probably not all that slight," Toni said, crowding in behind her.

With Toni and Petra gazing at her expectantly, Suzanne gave them a straight-ahead blow-by-blow description of her terrible discovery. No sugarcoating here—save it for the glazed donuts.

Toni's hand crept up to cover her mouth. "Mike Mullen is dead? Our Mike Mullen? Dear Lord."

"No," Petra cried in a high, strangled voice. "Mike can't be dead." She clutched her hands together as if in prayer. "I mean . . . he and Claudia go to my church." Petra was a big-boned Scandinavian lady with a broad, open face and a cap of short, curly gray hair. Blessed with a can-do, no-nonsense attitude, not many things upset her. But right now she was knocked for a loop. "He was really murdered?" she whispered, as if saying the words out loud was almost too painful. "Just like you said?"

"I'm afraid so," Suzanne said.

"Oh, poor Claudia." Petra dug a hankie from the pocket of her blue-checkered apron and dabbed at her reddening eyes. "How did she take the news? I bet she was completely devastated."

"She doesn't know yet," Suzanne said. "She wasn't home when all this happened."

"Where is she?" Toni asked.

"I don't know," Suzanne said.

Petra's eyes went round with fear. "Do you think Claudia was abducted?"

Suzanne grimaced. That idea had never occurred to her. "Probably not." *I hope not.* "I'm sure that Claudia's . . . somewhere safe."

"Is Doogie trying to locate her?" Toni asked. "So he can deliver the bad news?"

"I would think so," Suzanne said. "It's part of his job, after all."

"Let's hope Claudia doesn't have to hear the news from strangers," Petra said. She shook her head, still very upset. "What's the world coming to? Mike Mullen was always such a sweet, gentle guy. He was a deacon at our church, for goodness' sake. The man didn't have an enemy in the world."

"Clearly he had at least one," Suzanne said.

Toni frowned. "You're positive Mike was murdered?"

"Pretty sure," Suzanne said.

"How do you know it wasn't some terrible farm accident?" Toni asked. "Some kind of malfunction with machinery? Or he could have tripped on a piece of equipment and fallen in his barn, cracked his poor head wide open."

"Trust me," Suzanne said. "Mike met with a very violent end. Like I said, there was a lot of blood."

Toni still wasn't satisfied. "So you mean Mike was brutally clubbed? Or stabbed with a knife?"

Petra let loose a shiver along with a muffled sob.

"I would say stabbed . . . yes," Suzanne said. "With a really large knife."

Toni wrinkled her nose and thought for a few moments. She'd gone from shocked to curious. "You mean like one of those scary, serrated combat knives? Or was it a kitchen knife?"

Suzanne threw up her hands. "I don't know, Toni. There was blood all over the place, okay? The man was stabbed, his clothes were shredded. It was an awful mess."

"Please stop," Petra said. "I can't bear to hear one more gory detail." When the timer on the stove dinged, she just stared blankly ahead, lost in thought. Suzanne grabbed an oven mitt and pulled the last two pans of scones from the oven.

"I'm sorry to break this news so bluntly," Suzanne said as she dropped the pans on the counter. "Sorry to have upset you both."

"But who . . . who would want to hurt Mike?" Petra asked. "I mean, he was this sweet dairy farmer who loved his cows. He gave them names like Birgit and Dahlia, for goodness' sake."

"Yeah," Toni said. "Who could've possibly had a vendetta against him?"

Suzanne drew a deep breath. When something like this— a murder—took place in a small community, it was bound to shake everyone to the core. And Toni and Petra were quite right. Mike had been a good, solid guy. He sold his milk to the County Cooperative for whatever the fair-market price was and made tasty wheels of cheese on the side. What had he done to cross someone? What did he do to deserve being butchered in his own barn?

Suzanne pulled herself away from her dark thoughts, clenched her hand into a fist, and brought it down hard against the butcher-block counter. She was suddenly aware that Toni and Petra were staring at her with shocked expressions on their faces. "What?" she said.

"Are you going to"—Toni made a whirring motion with her hand—"do something?"

"Me?" Suzanne said with a high-pitched squeak.

"Yes, you," Petra said. She adjusted her apron and pulled herself up to her full height. "Next to Sheriff Doogie, you're the one with all the smarts in this town."

"Thank you," Suzanne said. "I think. But where exactly are you going with this unwarranted flattery?"

"I think you know," Toni said. She reached up and adjusted her fake puff of hair, as if to underscore her sentence. "When Petra said 'smarts,' she meant investigational smarts."

"I'm not getting involved," Suzanne said.

"You're already involved," Petra said. "You found him."

Toni nodded. "It's like kismet or karma or whatever that Eastern philosophy stuff is."

"Doogie would kill me if I tried to elbow my way into his investigation," Suzanne said. *And so would Sam.*

Toni lifted a shoulder. "So be subtle. You can do subtle."

"Do it for us," Petra said, a sad expression on her face. "Do it for Claudia."

"The grieving widow," Toni added for emphasis.

"Don't you think you guys are laying it on a little thick?" Suzanne asked.

Petra gave a sober nod. "Maybe we are. But you're awfully good at ferreting out clues."

"And coming up with suspects," Toni said.

"Hmm," Suzanne said. She'd tumbled down the rabbit hole and stumbled upon a horribly violent scene. Now that mental snapshot of poor dead Mike was stuck like a burr in her brain. And it wasn't just her curiosity that was amped up. Mike's murder had her feelings of outrage and her sense of justice strumming like crazy, too. So . . . could she? Dare she?

"Come on," Toni whispered.

Suzanne still wasn't certain about trying to insinuate herself into the investigation. "Maybe if I just . . . tried to keep an eye on things?" she said. "If I asked around?"

"Good girl," Petra said, her approval evident.

Suzanne held up a finger. "But we can't let this tragedy completely envelop our lives."

"Of course not," Toni said. She suddenly looked relieved.

"Because we've got a busy week ahead of us."

"That's for sure," Petra said. "With the Yarn Truck rolling in this Thursday we'll be hosting a Knitter's Tea. And Friday night is our big pizza party."

"And then Monday is Halloween," Toni said. "We can't forget that."

"Okay then," Suzanne said. "I'll poke around, quietly, I assure you, and see if I can get a handle on possible motives or suspects." She glanced at her watch, a silver Gucci watch that Sam had given her as an engagement present. "But right now we've got to get set up for afternoon tea."

"We're on it," Toni said. "I'll put out the teacups and things."

"And I'll put on the teakettles," Petra said. She grabbed a yellow and a red kettle and started filling them with water.

"Okay," Suzanne said. For some reason she felt a little better. Maybe it was because she'd decided to poke her nose into the investigation. Or maybe it was because the three of them were in this together.

STEPPING out from the kitchen and into the café, Suzanne felt a renewed sense of energy. This place, the Cackleberry Club, was her lifeline and dream job. The whitewashed walls were decorated with antique plates, grapevine wreaths, old tin signs, and turn-of-the-century photos. Wooden shelves were jammed with clutches of ceramic chickens and '40s-era salt and pepper shakers. Besides the battered tables, there was a large marble counter and soda fountain backdrop that had been salvaged from an old drugstore in nearby Jessup.

The rest of the place, the Cackleberry Club in toto, was a homey, crazy quilt warren of rooms that almost defied description. Across the hall from the café was the Book Nook, a small space that carried bestsellers and boasted a fairly decent array of children's books. Next door was the

Knitting Nest, a cozy room packed with overstuffed chairs and stocked with a rainbow of yarns and fibers.

To Suzanne, the Cackleberry Club was everything a small entrepreneur could ask for. Not so big that she'd be swamped with problems, big enough that there were always exciting challenges.

"HEY," Toni called out, interrupting Suzanne's reverie. "How's this look?"

Suzanne glanced around. The tables were set with silver spoons and butter knives, floral napkins, and antique sugar bowls piled high with sugar cubes. The air was redolent with the scent of malty Assam tea and fragrant orchid plum tea.

"Perfection," Suzanne said. And it was. The word had long since trickled out to the community that the Cackleberry Club was the official go-to spot for high tea. When the café first opened its doors some two years ago, customers had come in wanting afternoon coffee and pie, almost a de rigueur tradition in the Midwest. But slowly, over time, Suzanne and company had changed hearts, minds, and taste buds so that the residents of Kindred actually looked forward to enjoying their tea and scones.

AROUND three o'clock, amidst the genteel stirrings of teacups and clink of bone china, Sheriff Doogie came huffing in. He crossed the café like a man on a mission, rattling some of the dishes on the antique hutch, and plopped his fat butt down on his favorite stool. He slid his hat off his head in one swift motion and placed it on the stool next to him (the better to dissuade nosy neighbors). Then he put his arms on the marble counter and leaned forward.

Suzanne was front and center to serve him in a heartbeat.

"What can I get you?" she asked. "Maybe a nice cup of Assam tea?" She was anxious to ask him about the investigation, but decided she'd better play it cool.

Doogie shook his head. "Nope. But I will take a cup of coffee. Black and plenty strong."

"Coming right up." Suzanne grabbed a pot of French roast that she'd brewed some ten minutes earlier and filled a white ceramic mug.

"And . . ." Doogie cleared his throat dramatically as he nodded toward the scones, donuts, and sticky rolls that were displayed in the glass pie saver.

Suzanne followed his glance. "You want a scone?"

"With plenty of that poufy stuff."

"You mean our Devonshire cream?"

Doogie nodded. "If that's what you call it, yeah. But it sounds awfully fancy just to dab on a sweet roll."

"You can thank those stuffy Brits for all their pesky traditions," Suzanne said. She placed Doogie's scone and a small cup of Devonshire cream on a plate and shoved it across the counter to him. "So how's it going so far?" she asked. "The investigation, I mean."

Doogie took a huge bite of scone and said, "Ungh."

"That bad?"

He chewed quickly, swallowed hard, and said, "No. I'm just getting started. But I need to ask you a few questions."

"Sure."

He took a smaller bite as his eyes bored into her. "What time did you arrive at Mike Mullen's farm?"

"I don't know. Maybe just a few minutes after noon?"

"And you were there . . . why?"

"You know why," Suzanne said. "I wanted to pick up a couple of wheels of cheese."

"And how exactly did you find Mike?"

"We've been through this already." She glanced across

the café, saw that all was running smoothly, and then looked back at him. "You're making me feel like I'm a suspect."

"Are you?" Doogie asked her in a flat tone.

"You must be short on possibilities if you're sniffing around me."

"I know you didn't have anything to do with this, Suzanne. I'm just dotting the i's and crossing the t's."

"If you're going to be cranky and evasive, maybe you should dot and cross somewhere else."

Doogie lifted his scone in a sort of hopeful gesture. "You know I always need an afternoon pick-me-up. What with my fluctuating blood sugar."

Toni breezed by. "That must mean the candy machine at the Law Enforcement Center is broken again."

"Nobody asked you, Toni," Doogie called after her. He focused on Suzanne again. "So you went out to Mike's farm to pick up cheese. You stepped into the barn and . . ."

"The cows were uneasy."

"Uneasy?" Doogie's brows pinched together. "Are you channeling Herefords now or was this just a simple observation?"

"Observation," she assured him.

"Go on."

"I started looking around for Mike, calling his name, and then . . ." Suzanne made an unhappy face. "And then I found him. I . . . I kind of slipped in his blood and fell down. It was pretty awful."

"Then you ran out to your car and called 911."

"That's about the size of it."

"And you're sure you didn't see anyone else there?"

"No. Absolutely not."

"You didn't notice anything out of the ordinary?"

Suzanne hesitated. In all the excitement of police and EMTs arriving, seeing the scarecrow in the woods had kind of slipped her mind. Now she decided she'd better mention it to Doogie.

"Actually I did see something," Suzanne said.

Doogie stopped chewing and stared at her. "What are you talking about?"

"I saw something off in the woods. Like a figure of some sort."

"A person?"

"I thought it was a scarecrow."

Doogie stared harder at her. "Pardon my French, Suzanne, but no shit?"

"Well, it *looked* like a scarecrow anyway. I saw this vague outline of a head and shoulders. But when I glanced back to kind of confirm it, the thing was gone."

"Wait a minute . . . So you're saying a *person* ran away?" Doogie was sitting up straighter now, looking keenly interested.

"Maybe. Unless my eyes were playing tricks on me."

Doogie lifted a hand and snapped his fingers. "And it disappeared just like that?"

"Like I said, I could have been mistaken."

Doogie was shaking his head. "No, I don't think you were. I think you might have actually seen someone. Hot damn, Suzanne."

"Say there!" Petra yelled through the pass-through. "There'll be none of that language in this café, Sheriff."

"Sorry, Petra," Doogie called back. He turned his attention back to Suzanne. "Can you give me a description?"

"Not really. Sorry."

"Still," Doogie said. "Your scarecrow sighting. That's the kind of information we need."

"I suppose it could have been a hunter."

"Could have been," Doogie said. "But that would make it a very odd coincidence."

"You think I might have seen a witness?" Suzanne asked. "Or maybe even the killer?" For some reason the scarecrow still felt like an illusion to her. Some kind of sleight-of-hand magic trick.

"I think you could have," Doogie allowed.

Suzanne walked to the end of the counter, grabbed a second scone from the glass pie saver, and plunked it down on Doogie's plate. "Now it's my turn to ask a couple of questions. What's going on with Mike's wife, Claudia? Do you know where she is?"

"Claudia's on her way home," Doogie said. He picked up his fresh scone and took a bite.

"On her way home from where?"

"She's been up in Minneapolis visiting her sister."

"That's where you reached her?"

"No, no," Doogie said. "Claudia happened to call her home phone, trying to reach Mike, and one of my deputies picked up. We were inside, going through the house, doing a sweep to see if anything had been disturbed."

"So you guys gave Claudia the bad news over the phone?"

Doogie shrugged. "What was my deputy supposed to do? Make up some far-fetched story and tell her we were there to rob the house?"

"I guess not." Suzanne thought for a few moments. "Was there any sign of a struggle inside the house?"

Doogie raised a single eyebrow. "You tell me."

"I did tell you," Suzanne said. "I didn't go inside the house per se, I just peeked into the kitchen."

"Stupid."

"I suppose." Suzanne dropped her voice and leaned across the counter. "So. *Are* there any suspects? Besides my scarecrow, that is?"

Doogie brushed at a tumble of crumbs that cascaded down the front of his khaki shirt. "Maybe."

"Tell me."

"Not on your life, Suzanne. This is a closed investigation."

"Come on, Doogie. Don't make me pull it out of you. Because you know I will."

"Ho, I'm shaking in my sneakers."

"You don't wear sneakers. You wear big old heavy cop shoes."

Doogie took a sip of coffee. "Whatever. Bottom line is I'm not telling you squat." He dipped his chin and stared at her over his coffee cup. "And making that grumpy face isn't going to change my mind."

"Huh," Suzanne said. Then, "Who's gonna take care of the cows?"

"We got hold of Mike's brother, Dan. He's gonna come by. Feed 'em, do the milking."

Suzanne thought about going back into that barn again to carry out ordinary chores. For her the place would feel . . . forever tainted. In her mind's eye she could still see the wet cement floor, the blank, nobody's-home-anymore expression on Mike's face, and the fat droplets of blood spattered everywhere. The horror of it all, still fresh in her mind, prompted Suzanne to ask Doogie the lollapalooza of questions.

"Do you know what kind of weapon was used?"

Doogie tilted back on his stool. "Oh jeez. You really want to know the gruesome details?" When Suzanne didn't answer, he said, "Mike was stabbed, just as we initially figured. But seeing as how he was hacked up rather badly, we're guessing the knife was really large. Oversized even. Like a machete."

"A machete?" Suzanne said. "That's not exactly your ordinary household item."

Doogie sighed. "I've never seen anybody torn up this badly and I never care to again."

Suzanne turned away, poured herself a cup of coffee, and turned back to Doogie. She put the cup to her lips, stopped, and set it down. "I just wish I could give you something more concrete that would help edge your investigation along."

Doogie was nodding. "But you did give me something, Suzanne. You saw someone who might have been the killer."

Suzanne felt a chill settle around her heart. "That's not good."

Doogie cocked an eye at her. "Why would you say that?"

Suzanne swallowed hard. "Because if I really did see the killer, then he saw me, too."

CHAPTER 4

SUZANNE had promised Sam a hands-down fantastic meal tonight that he wouldn't forget. So as soon as she flew through the door and accepted about a million zillion kisses from her dogs, Baxter and Scruff, she washed her hands, put on an apron, and donned her virtual chef's hat.

So . . . okay, what about that splendiferous dinner?

Suzanne opened the refrigerator and scanned the shelves. The rack of lamb she'd pulled from the freezer last night sat front and center. She smiled. Yes, that was going to be perfect. Savory and hearty, delicious with almost any type of red wine that Sam decided to bring along. And he would for sure bring a bottle of wine.

So how was she on time? A glance at the clock above her Wolf range told her she could manage this dinner with minutes to spare. Grabbing the frenched rack of lamb, Suzanne assembled garlic, flat-leaf parsley, thyme, rosemary, and olive oil on her counter.

Humming to herself, Suzanne decided her retinue of ingredients made it look as if she were about to go live with a TV cooking show. Huh. Or maybe someday she could have her own Internet channel? Just a simple little show where she would create great farm-to-table dishes? She leaned down and pulled a small roasting pan out of the cupboard.

That's when two pairs of beady eyes stared at her. Or, rather, at the rack of lamb.

"Let me guess," Suzanne said to the two dogs. "You'd like dinner, too."

"Dinner" was the magic word that set the dogs' noses twitching and their tails wagging. She dished up two bowls of kibble, and then, as the dogs went facedown into their food, bits of kibble spilling everywhere, she went back to work. She decided she'd kick off dinner with a citrus salad and serve herbed new potatoes as a side dish with the lamb. As she chopped, diced, and sizzled, Suzanne thought about her soon-to-be life with Sam. He'd proposed, she'd accepted. It had been as magical and as simple as that. Now they had a wedding to plan. Which everyone, especially Sam, saw as a *major event.* Of course, she'd be delirious if the two of them simply dashed off to a small-town justice of the peace and then holed up in a cozy B and B for the weekend. But Sam apparently wanted to get down to some serious planning that included a genuine white dress, buckets of flowers, a walk-down-the-aisle ceremony, and a fairly elaborate reception.

Suzanne wrinkled her nose as she turned on her oven. So much to do, so much to worry about! Couldn't she just hand him the latest issue of *Brides* magazine and let him follow the bridal checklist? There was always a bridal checklist, wasn't there?

Still, it was terribly sweet that Sam wanted their wedding to be extra special. So who was she to quibble? After all, women her age and younger still flirted outrageously with the handsome Dr. Sam Hazelet.

When the phone rang, she picked it up on the first ring. "Hello?"

"I should be there in two shakes," Sam said. "Need anything?"

"Just you," she said.

"In that case, I feel the need for speed."

"Please don't. I prefer you in once delicious piece."

Suzanne slid the lamb into the oven and then hurried in to set the dining room table. She put out place mats, tall white tapers, the good china, and Riedel crystal wineglasses. *Let's see, what else? How about some music?* Or maybe she could find something on the radio. Stepping back into the kitchen, she turned on WLGN, their local station. At this time of night their drive time show featured a nice mix of news, mellow music, and fun gossip.

But tonight the gossip wasn't all that fun.

"Two men were arrested in a methamphetamine raid," the announcer barked out. "In a hastily called press conference, Sheriff Burney of Deer County called his findings the possible tip of the iceberg."

Suzanne snapped off the radio. That kind of news she didn't need, especially after such an unsettling morning. It had taken her the better part of the afternoon to ease into a more relaxed frame of mind. Of course, she was still burning with curiosity over the circumstances of Mike Mullen's death. It seemed like something out of a contemporary thriller. A brutal murder. No witnesses. No clues. No known motive. The only concrete thing so far was Sheriff Doogie's speculation about a machete.

"Woof." Baxter, Suzanne's aging Irish setter pointed his silvered muzzle at the front door. Scruff, a Heinz 57 dog that Suzanne had found wandering down a lonely country road, hurried to join him.

There was a sharp knock, then the door clicked open and Sam came bounding in. "Anybody home?" he called out.

That was all Baxter and Scruff needed. They spun around Sam like a furry maelstrom, sniffing, nuzzling, toenails clicking against the tiled entry, making happy little dog grunts.

Suzanne met Sam at the door. "It's good to be appreciated, huh?" she asked. And she loved that he looked so casually elegant in a brown leather jacket and faded blue jeans.

Sam put his arms around her and pulled her close. "It sure is." They kissed and Suzanne felt herself melting in his arms. It wouldn't take much for Sam to sweep her off her feet and carry her upstairs. Let the lamb burn to a crisp, the potatoes wither. She wouldn't care.

On the other hand, she did want to ask Sam some rather specific questions about Mike Mullen's injuries. So a well-prepared dinner would make for a mean bargaining chip.

From behind his back Sam produced a bottle of red wine. "I figured a nice glass of Barolo would put us in the mood."

Suzanne accepted the bottle and smiled. She was already in the mood.

When the lamb and potatoes were ready, Suzanne put everything on a large platter and carried it to the table. The couple nibbled their salads, sipped wine, and helped themselves to the main entrée.

"Nothing like meat and potatoes," Sam said. "Of course, this isn't exactly your garden-variety meat and potatoes." He grinned. "I can't believe I'm marrying a gourmet cook. Lucky me."

"Maybe I should have served something more pedestrian. Like burgers and fries."

Sam was quick to counter. "No, no, this is great. Better than great."

"So," Suzanne said. "Are you going to tell me about the autopsy?"

Sam set down his fork and made an unhappy face. "Suzanne, really?"

She smiled sweetly at him. "Yes, really. I need to know

about this, Sam. I'm the one who found Mike Mullen's body, remember?"

"Well, you're out of luck," he said. "Because I'm not the one who's going to perform the autopsy. Sheriff Doogie has decided to bring in an outside medical examiner."

"Interesting."

"Not really. It's always better to have an expert. Especially in a case like this."

"You mean a case of murder."

"That's right." Sam picked up the wine bottle and refilled their glasses.

"But his body was transported to the hospital morgue, right? Can I at least ask you a couple of probing questions?"

"You can probe all you want. I endured four years of medical school, two years as an intern, and another two as a resident. Discussing blood, death, and dismemberment doesn't bother me." He jabbed his fork at his medium-rare chop. "This is wonderful."

Suzanne persisted. "Doogie said the weapon could have been a machete."

"The murder weapon?" Sam helped himself to another scoop of herbed potatoes. "I suppose a machete is a distinct possibility. We'll know a lot more after the ME does his analysis of the cut marks, depth of wounds, that sort of thing."

But Suzanne was beginning to feel a tingle of excitement. Truth be told, she wanted to get on with the hunt. "Where would you even get a machete?"

"I don't know. Army surplus store? Buy one on the Internet? Maybe somebody found a relic left over from the Korean War?"

Suzanne thought for a few moments. "There's an army surplus store out on the edge of town. I heard they carry all sorts of old uniforms and military patches. It might be smart if Doogie checked there."

Sam dangled a scrap of meat for Baxter, who immediately snapped it up in his jaws. "And maybe you should leave well enough alone and let Doogie do his job."

"Still," she said. "It's interesting."

Sam reached over and caught her hand, gave it a squeeze. "Suzanne, I want you to walk away from this."

"I'm not sure I can."

"Sure you can. You just . . . make up your mind to forget about it. Look, I know it's tempting to want to stick your nose into official police business. Especially after you stumbled upon the brutal murder of a friend. But Sheriff Doogie is a trained investigator. You're not."

"I do have some experience," she said with a touch a pride. "Remember the fire and Hannah's death a couple of months ago?"

"What I remember most," Sam said, "is that you got yourself into a load of trouble." His face pulled into a look of concern. "And I almost lost you."

"But I helped solve that case."

"Yes, but that doesn't mean you can just waltz into something like this." Now Sam's blue eyes shone with warmth and love. "Please, just try to let it go."

"Hmm," she said in a noncommittal tone as she stood up to clear away the dishes.

When Suzanne walked into the living room a few minutes later, Sam had dimmed the lights and put on music. He reached out and grabbed her hand, pulled her close. They slow-danced, cheek to cheek, while Sam Smith crooned out "Stay With Me." It should have been a romantic, magical moment, everything a girl could want. But Suzanne was still thinking about the murder.

"We have plans to make," Sam said when the song ended. He kissed her on the nose and led her to the sofa. Then he pulled out a pen and a small leather-bound notebook, obviously ready to jot a few pertinent notes.

"Big plans," Suzanne agreed, though she was still deep in thought. Her brain was working overtime, whirring crazy thoughts about Mike Mullen, the scarecrow she'd seen, and the terrible injuries Mike had sustained. Didn't the police have a term for massive injuries like that? Wasn't it known as overkill, when a body had been worked over way beyond the point necessary to cause death?

Sam clicked his pen. "Have you given any thought as to when and where we should get married?"

Suzanne blinked. "Um . . . what?"

He gazed at her. "Any thoughts on timing?"

Suzanne straightened up. "Oh sure. I was thinking next spring. A May wedding. We could maybe even have it outdoors."

Sam grinned. "I love that idea. You see, I knew there was a reason I asked you to marry me. You're thinking apple blossoms and green grass and maybe even a bower covered in flowers, aren't you?"

Suzanne hadn't been thinking about any of those things, but she said, "That's it exactly."

"Then let's try to nail down some specifics. What about Founder's Park? Or maybe that picnic grove out by Catawba Creek?"

"Those are all great options," Suzanne said, stalling.

"Or should we throw caution to the wind and have our wedding out in the country somewhere? I'm thinking rolling hills, lots of trees . . ."

"Romantic," Suzanne whispered.

"So what do you think? Let's try to sketch out a plan."

"You mean . . . now?" She was having trouble wrapping her head around this whole wedding thing.

"Am I putting too much pressure on you?"

She nodded. "Maybe a little."

"Sweetheart, it's only because I'm in love. And I'm excited about marrying you."

"Oh, Sam." She bit her lip. She felt awful, her mind was a million miles away. He deserved better than this.

"What do you think about Kopell's over in Cornucopia for our wedding reception? That's a fairly cozy restaurant, and the brass and wood and big stone fireplace give it a schlosslike vibe."

She smiled back at him.

Sam's smile slipped. "Suzanne? Earth to Suzanne?"

"I'm with you."

"No, you're not," Sam said. He sounded profoundly disappointed. "You're a million miles away."

"I'm sorry. I guess I really am."

He snapped his notebook shut. "We're not going to do this tonight. I should have known better. You're still . . . your head is still in that dairy barn, isn't it?"

"Yes," she whispered. She put a hand on his arm. "Please, I need to know a little bit more."

He let out a deep sigh. "Such as?"

"The attack against Mike must have been fierce, almost frantic. So the killer had to have sustained some injuries of his own."

Sam's nod was imperceptible. "It's a possibility."

Suzanne continued. "Did anyone come into the hospital or clinic today with unexplained injuries? What you'd call defensive wounds?"

"Not that I know of. And Doogie did put the word out, especially to all the ER personnel." Sam narrowed his eyes at her and said, "What else do you want to know?"

"Has there been any guess made as to time of death?"

"Certainly not more than an hour earlier than the time you showed up."

"So I just missed the killer."

"Looks like." Sam didn't seem happy.

"And the wounds . . ."

"Deep, slashing cuts. The lungs and heart sustained significant damage. Clearly there was a good deal of arterial spray." He gave her a cool smile. "There, are you happy now?"

"Not really."

"Look, I know how important this investigation is to you, Suzanne. But do you think you could clock out of it just for a while?" When she didn't answer, he said, "Do it for me?"

"I'll try. I really will."

Sam touched a hand to her face, then brushed back a strand of her hair. "You know how much I love you, don't you? I don't want anything bad to happen to you."

"I love you, too, Sam."

Suzanne rested her head on his shoulder and listened to the soft music that was still playing. Yet, when she closed her eyes, she couldn't shake the image of Mike Mullen's pale white face as he lay dead in the barn. She couldn't escape the sounds of bellowing, outraged cattle as they expressed their sorrow in the only way they knew how.

Yes, she could try to shelve her worries for now and enjoy the rest of her evening with Sam. But in her heart, Suzanne had already come to terms with one critical fact.

She was already deeply involved.

CHAPTER 5

STRIPS of turkey bacon sizzled on the grill, teakettles chirped and burped, and the aroma of apple bread and muffins (cinnamon, chocolate chip, and bran) perfumed the air in the Cackleberry Club's kitchen. It was Wednesday morning and they'd been open only twenty minutes, but the joint was seriously jumping.

Petra cracked eggs, flipped pancakes, and gave her scrambled eggs an occasional shuffle. Her hands worked so quickly and efficiently that she looked like a magician doing sleight of hand. Her feet, encased in bright green Crocs, did a little happy dance as she hummed along to a classic rock station playing on her old Philco radio.

Out in the café, Suzanne and Toni were taking orders, pouring refills on piping hot coffee and tea, and delivering breakfast entrées along with a dollop of sass.

As Toni slid past Suzanne, a large silver tray balanced against her hip, she said, "In case you haven't noticed, girlfriend, this place has gone plumb loco today."

Suzanne nodded. "I'm afraid all our customers are gossiping like crazy about Mike Mullen's murder. I can't tell you how many weird stories and rumors are swirling in the air."

"The Cackleberry Club has become rumor central," Toni said.

Even mild-mannered Todd Lansky, who had stopped by for breakfast before going on his milk route, jumped into the fray. "What do you hear, Suzanne?" he asked as he peered slyly at her from a table by the window. "I mean about yesterday's murder?"

"Not much," Suzanne said. She pulled out her pen and order pad and fixed him with a neutral smile. "What can I get for you this morning? How about a nice Italian sausage scramble or one of Petra's heart-healthy veggie omelets?"

Lansky held up a hand. "I'll just take coffee and one of your sticky rolls, Suzanne."

"That's it? You're looking awfully thin."

"Just watching my weight." Lansky patted his stomach, which Suzanne figured had to be washboard flat beneath his red plaid shirt.

"I'm watching mine, too," Toni called out as she breezed by. "Not doing anything about it, just watching it."

"Has Sheriff Doogie said anything to you about possible suspects?" Lansky asked.

"No, Todd," Suzanne said, her frustration beginning to boil up. He had to be the tenth or eleventh person who'd quizzed her about possible suspects. "Doogie hasn't mentioned a word to me." Actually, he'd been fairly forthcoming with her yesterday, but Suzanne wasn't about to share that with the general populace. Doogie had a class A murder investigation on his hands and there was no way she wanted to compromise it. Of course, truth be known, her curiosity was raging at a fever pitch and she was itching to dive into the investigation herself!

"Orders are up," Petra called out loudly through the pass-through.

Suzanne spun toward the kitchen, kicked the door open with one foot, and squirted through. "How are you doing?" she asked Petra. "Do you need any help?"

Petra turned and gave a wide-eyed, slightly frazzled expression. "I think I might. I'm spinning like a rotisserie chicken in here."

"Just tell me what to do."

Petra jerked her chin toward a half-dozen white china plates that were spread out across the butcher-block counter. "Those all need to be prepped for French toast orders."

"Got it," Suzanne said. She quickly arranged fresh-sliced strawberry garnishes on each plate, then added a few pats of butter along with small ramekins of warm maple syrup.

"Perfect," Petra said. She grabbed her pancake flipper and stacked four pieces of French toast on each plate, as smoothly and efficiently as if she were dealing blackjack in a Vegas casino.

"Hey," Toni said as she swooped into the kitchen. "Have you got those French toast . . ." She skidded to a stop. "Orders. Yeah, I guess you do."

"Help me deliver them, okay?" Suzanne asked. Then she and Toni each grabbed three plates and hustled them out to their waiting customers.

BY mid-morning, things had settled down to a dull roar. Customers were leisurely sipping second and third cups of coffee, breakfast orders had slowed to a trickle, and Petra had finished her baking and even found time to decorate a three-layer cake. Because of Petra's prodigious skills as a baker and cake decorator, custom cake orders were on the rise at the Cackleberry Club. And while the profit margin for selling a fancy birthday or anniversary cake certainly wasn't as good as selling a Cadillac Escalade, every dollar they earned helped to fluff the bottom line. As Suzanne liked to point out, there was a vast difference between making a living and making a profit.

"You know what?" Suzanne said as Petra squeezed out a final pink fondant rosette on the top of her cake. "I'm going to pack up a basket of muffins and take it out to Claudia Mullen."

"That's sweet of you," Petra said. She glanced sideways at Suzanne and arched an eyebrow. "Or is that *really* sweet of you?"

Suzanne shrugged. Petra was always keen at figuring out people's motivations. "Well, I did kind of want to ask Claudia a few questions."

"I thought you might have an ulterior motive. So you're definitely getting involved in the investigation?"

"I think I'm already involved," Suzanne said.

Petra gazed at her. "Well . . . I think that's good. I think you can offer a certain perspective."

"Because I was there? Because I found him?"

"There's that. And because you possess an insatiable curiosity, you're good at asking the right questions."

"I sure wasn't last night," Suzanne said, recalling her evening with Sam. "I think I blew it with Sam. Got a little too nosy."

Petra put a hand on her hip. "Then just be a lot more careful, Suzanne. Because sometimes you can be a trifle overzealous. Which lands you—kersplat—in deep trouble." She waggled an index finger. "No judgment here. I'm just offering a word to the wise."

"Okay, I get that. Now do we have enough muffins for me to take to Claudia or what?"

"I can let you have four bran muffins and four chocolate chip muffins. How would that be?"

"Probably a nice balance between healthy eating and outright decadence," Suzanne said. She grabbed a wicker basket out of the back room, lined it with a red-and-white-checkered napkin, and began stacking in muffins.

"As long as you're going to run out there," Petra said, "could you make a quick stop at the bank and deliver my cake?"

"Sure. Is it someone's birthday?"

"I think they're having some kind of customer appreciation day," Petra said.

"So people will appreciate their car loans and mortgages a little more?"

Petra shrugged. "I guess it all goes back to a tight economy." Then, "Let me box up this cake so it gets there in one piece."

SUZANNE dropped off Petra's cake at Millennium Bank and then, because she found herself on the far edge of town, out by the new Robinette Shopping Center, decided to take a different route to Mike Mullen's farm.

This alternate route wound past a bunch of newly constructed townhomes. But instead of looking charming, like a block of English row houses, they managed to look slightly tacky and low budget. The current building boom was the unfortunate result of real estate developers having discovered a cute little community (Kindred!) that was surrounded by woods, bluffs, and any number of burbling trout streams. They'd snatched up the land, thrown up townhomes and twin homes, and advertised like crazy. New home buyers, lured by the affordable prices, also fell in love with the gorgeous views and snapped up the houses. *Veni, vidi,* vista. Or maybe, if too many town houses were stacked one on top of the other, it would be *hasta la vista* vista.

Suzanne drove past the cutoff that led to the cemetery, past a City Works Garage that had a dump truck and a road grader parked in front, and finally past a gravel pit that was in the throes of being shut down. Another mile out of town and the scenery got a whole lot prettier. She wound her way past Morgan's Apple Orchard, where rows of carefully pruned apple trees stretched off toward a dip in the horizon, and then passed a couple of farms. One of the farms had a hand-lettered sign set out near the road that said Pumpkins for Sale, and Suzanne reminded herself that Junior Garrett, Toni's soon-to-be ex-husband, had been tasked with picking up a bushel basket full of gourds and pumpkins to use as decorations at the Cackleberry Club. She wondered if Junior's Budweiser-chugging, stock car–addled brain would remember to do that little chore.

Four miles on, just before Suzanne hit the turnoff for Country Trail, she spotted eight straggly-looking horses standing in a small corral. Their heads were down, their hip bones jutted out a little too prominently, and the horses looked just generally tired and run-down.

Suzanne slowed her car as her heart immediately went out to them. She was a lifelong horse lover. In fact, her own horse, Mocha Gent, and his buddy, a mule named Grommet, lived at the farm she owned just across the field from the Cackleberry Club. She and her husband, Walter, who'd passed away several years ago, had purchased the farm as an investment.

"I wonder who owns these horses," she murmured. And resolved to find out exactly who was responsible for their care and feeding. Or lack of feeding.

Five minutes later, Suzanne pulled into the Mullen farm. It was another gorgeous October day, sun shining down, golden leaves drifting on crosscurrents. Except today it felt like a slight pall hung over the place.

A sheriff's car was parked directly outside the dairy barn, and, when she rolled up next to it, Deputy Driscoll stretched his legs and got out.

"Hey there, Suzanne," Driscoll said. He groaned as he

tilted his head to one side and wiggled his shoulders. He'd obviously been assigned guard duty though there wasn't much to guard.

Suzanne lifted her basket of muffins for Driscoll to see. "I brought a gift for Claudia. Is she home?"

Driscoll nodded. "She's up at the house."

"How's she doing?" Suzanne wondered if anyone had bothered to clean up all the blood in the barn yet.

"I'd say she's still kinda weepy." Driscoll held up a ceramic mug filled with coffee. "Though she did take the time to brew up a nice strong French roast."

Suzanne walked up to the house, climbed the steps that led to the back door, and knocked. Fifteen seconds later, Claudia appeared at the back door.

"Oh my goodness," Claudia exclaimed and let Suzanne in.

Suzanne handed her the basket of muffins. "I'm so very sorry for your loss," she said. "Everyone at the Cackleberry Club sends their condolences."

"Kind of you," Claudia said as she accepted the basket. She was wearing khaki slacks and a pink sweatshirt that said I'm a 4H Grandma. Her gray hair was short and tousled, she wore not a speck of makeup, and her eyes were red and pinched as though she'd been crying. Which she probably had.

Claudia cleared her throat and, in a slightly quavering voice, said, "Could I offer you a cup of coffee?"

"That would be nice," Suzanne said. As she seated herself at the big wooden kitchen table, she was secretly delighted that Claudia had offered coffee. This would give her an opportunity to ask a few questions that had been percolating in her brain.

But just as Suzanne accepted her cup of coffee, just as she was wondering how to kick off the conversation, Claudia said, "Sheriff Doogie tells me that you were the one who found Mike."

Suzanne took a sip of coffee, allowing herself time to gather

her thoughts. "I'm afraid that's right," she said. "I stopped by yesterday afternoon to pick up a couple wheels of cheese and . . . well . . . when Mike wasn't around I went looking for him in the barn. And then I . . ." She knew she was stumbling around with her answer and felt bad about it. "That's when I found him."

Claudia gazed at her. "Sheriff Doogie said he hadn't been dead all that long."

Suzanne took another sip of coffee. "I wouldn't know about that."

"So you didn't see anyone?"

"I'm afraid not."

Claudia let loose a heavy sigh. "Sheriff Doogie mentioned that you had seen someone."

Suzanne sat up straighter in her chair. "Well, okay, yes. I thought I *might* have seen someone off in the distance. Someone kind of peering at me through the woods." A tear trickled down Claudia's cheek and Suzanne said, "You seem awfully upset—maybe we shouldn't be talking about this."

Claudia shook her head. "No, it's okay. I *want* to talk about it. I need to talk it out."

Suzanne looked around the kitchen at the white ruffled curtains, embroidered kitchen towels, and cheery yellow cupboards and thought, *Okay, here's my chance.* "I understand you were visiting your sister?" She decided to keep her questions low-key and offhand.

Claudia nodded. "In Minneapolis. But I was halfway home when I found out about Mike. I was just rolling through Mankato when I decided to call. Instead of getting Mike on the line I got Deputy Driscoll. He broke the bad news to me."

"Sorry you had to hear it that way. Long-distance, I mean."

"He was pretty gentle about it. But then Sheriff Doogie got on the phone and started asking me all sorts of questions. Like how long was I supposed to be gone? Why was I coming home early? That sort of thing."

"Were you coming home early?" Suzanne asked.

"Yes," Claudia said. "But just by one day."

"Any particular reason?"

"Not really. Well . . ." Claudia lifted a hand and idly massaged her forehead. "Maybe I had a weird sort of vibe. Like something might be going on. Not that I thought anything was wrong, mind you. Just that something might not be right . . . if that makes any sense to you."

"Kind of."

Claudia stood up and went to the stove. She poured herself a cup of coffee and carried it back to the table. "Mike didn't have any enemies," she said.

"I'm sure he didn't," Suzanne said. Though she knew there had to be at least one.

"That I *know* of. Still . . . Sheriff Doogie has been asking some very probing questions."

"Such as?"

"Like what am I going to do now?"

"What are your plans?" Suzanne asked.

"I'm going to sell this place," Claudia said. The words tumbled out of her mouth without a moment's hesitation.

"Excuse me . . . but *really*?" Suzanne hadn't been expecting such a strong definitive answer from such a newly minted widow.

"Oh, absolutely I am. Fact is, we've had a number of offers over the years, but Mike has always turned them down cold." Claudia gave a rueful smile as she glanced around. "He loved this old homestead. Loved getting up at the crack of dawn. He even loved those fool cows."

For some reason, Suzanne felt the words *loved them more than me* hanging unsaid in the air.

"I know Sheriff Doogie asked you about this," Suzanne said. "And please excuse me if you think I'm probing. But do you have any suspicions about who might have murdered Mike?"

"I'm not really sure," Claudia murmured.

"I mean, now that you've had twenty-four hours to think on it, maybe a few ideas have seeped into your mind. Maybe you remembered someone who might have had a grudge against Mike."

"Not really a grudge." Claudia licked her lips nervously as if she wanted to say more.

Suzanne reached out and gently patted one of Claudia's hands. "If there's anyone you can think of . . . if you have even the slightest suspicion."

Claudia looked slightly pained. "I hate to . . ."

"Is there someone, Claudia?" Suzanne asked quietly.

Claudia seemed to steel herself. She put her hands flat on the table, clenched her mouth tightly, and said, "I have to admit . . . I've always been a little fearful of Noah Jorgenson."

Suzanne shook her head; the name didn't ring a bell. "I'm afraid I don't know who that is."

"No, you probably wouldn't," Claudia said. "But I've been thinking about this and I'm fairly sure that Noah's the one you saw. You know . . . standing there in the woods. He lives on the farm adjacent to this one."

"He owns it?" Suzanne pounced on this newfound information.

"No, no, Noah is just a boy. Probably around sixteen now." Claudia's eyes hardened. "But he's tall and muscular for his age. And he's always been homeschooled by his mother." There was a long pause. "The boy is supposedly autistic."

"And you're frightened of him." It was a statement, not a question.

"I am now, yes," Claudia said. "The thing is . . . Mike was always very kind to Noah, so Noah tended to follow him around like a puppy. That was okay when Noah was just a kid. But now . . . now that he's a big strapping guy . . ." The expression on Claudia's face changed from one of fear to anger.

"I mean, if Noah's got a problem with impulse control, imagine what could happen? What might have happened?"

"Have you shared this information with Sheriff Doogie?" Suzanne asked. "Told him about Noah?"

"I most certainly did."

"And what did Doogie say?"

Claudia's jaw tensed and her blue-gray eyes shone like a pair of polished nickels. "He promised to conduct a thorough investigation."

CHAPTER 6

THE Cackleberry Club hummed with conversation and typical café racket. Silverware clinked against plates, cups settled into saucers, rumors were whispered and shared. It looked as if murder had been good for business.

Suzanne flew in the front door, took one look at the blackboard, and scratched her head. Toni had written out today's menu, but the printing looked like a combination of Pythagorean theorem coupled with Egyptian hieroglyphics. Oh no, that would never do. Wiping the blackboard clean, Suzanne set about correcting Toni's scritches and scratches. With colored chalk, she drew a smiling cartoon chef holding up a large baking sheet. Inside the sheet she printed *Today's Specials.* Then she quickly listed those specials: spinach salad, Chicken Pickin' Stir-Fry, beef barley soup, and a grilled ham and cheese sandwich. For dessert they were offering cherry cake bars, rice pudding, and fudge brownies.

"Oh, you didn't like my menu?" Toni grinned. She'd crept up behind Suzanne.

"I liked it just fine. I just couldn't read it."

Toni looked puzzled. "I guess nobody else could, either. A couple of people asked me to translate."

"You see," Suzanne said, happy she'd caught the problem before lunch was in full swing. "You didn't know you could speak a foreign language, did you?"

"I do now," Toni said, looking pleased. "Hey, maybe I could get a job at the United Nations."

"There you go."

Suzanne and Toni got busy then. Greeting customers and taking orders as more and more customers piled in. They did their lunchtime ballet of dodging tables, pouring water, delivering entrées, and keeping up a running patter with their guests.

Just as they were hitting maximum velocity, the front door slammed open and, like Jabba the Hutt from *Star Wars*, Mayor Mobley postured dramatically in the doorway. Mobley, who had somehow managed to get reelected to a second term, was a tower of jiggle who wore tight neon-bright golf shirts and Sansabelt slacks that barely contained his ample girth.

Suzanne had always assumed that Mobley was crooked as a creek and could be bought for a song. He always seemed to have his sticky little fingers in some shady deal and the rumor around City Hall was that he wasn't immune to accepting a payoff or two. Or three or four.

"Suzanne," Mobley bellowed as he strode across the café, enjoying his own self-importance and the slight stir he created. "I want you to meet someone." Tagging along behind him was a nice-looking man with a swarthy complexion and a mane of salt-and-pepper hair. Unlike Mobley's out-of-season golf getup, this guy was dressed in a tasteful dark blue suede jacket and putty-colored corduroy slacks. A large gold watch winked from his left wrist.

Suzanne smiled gamely and pulled out chairs at her last

available table for the two men. "Hello, Mr. Mayor. Nice to see you again." She smiled at his companion. "Welcome to the Cackleberry Club. I hope you brought your appetite."

Mobley sat down heavily and said to his friend, "This is Suzanne, she's one of Kindred's hotshot entrepreneurs." He paused. "Even though she's usually a colossal pain in the butt."

Suzanne ignored Mobley. He was a legend in his own mind.

But Mobley continued with his introduction. "Suzanne, this slicko here is Byron Wolf. He's a majorly successful real estate developer. A really top-notch guy."

Suzanne shook hands with the rather attractive Mr. Wolf. "Nice to meet you," she said. She figured if Mobley was fawning over this guy, he was probably crooked as well. After all, birds of a feather . . .

"I'm hoping Byron will start spreading some of his real estate razzle-dazzle around our fair city," Mobley said loudly.

"I take it you have some developments in the area?" Suzanne asked Wolf.

Wolf nodded. "That's right. I built a shopping center over near Cornucopia and I just finished developing Brass Gates Estates over in Jessup."

Suzanne knew the place in Jessup, she'd driven past it on more than one occasion. Brass Gates was a gated community cluttered with over-the-top mega mansions. Exactly the sort of thing she hated.

"Actually," Mobley said, looking like he was about to burst with pride, "Byron is looking to do another planned community just outside of Kindred."

Suzanne nodded politely. But, deep down, she hoped that Kindred, a picture-postcard little town, would be able to weather any additional real estate development that came its way. She prayed that the parks, towering bluffs, Catawba Creek, and the Big Woods on the outskirts of town wouldn't be mowed down in the name of progress.

"Byron Wolf is exactly the kind of go-getter this town

needs," Mobley boasted. "He knows how to kick business up a notch."

"Thank you," Wolfe said. He allowed himself a semi-modest smile. "But I like to think of myself as a community builder. That I create the kind of upscale homes that will bring in the right kind of residents. New people who will contribute their skills and talents."

Suzanne arched an eyebrow. New people, new talent. This all sounded very pie in the sky to her. "So what's in it for you?" she asked Mobley. "You're not usually this excited about residential construction." She knew Mobley had helped to spearhead the building of the new for-profit prison, that ugly pile of gray stone that hunkered on the outskirts of Kindred. She'd heard firsthand that he'd fattened his bank account from kickbacks on contracts.

"I care deeply for this community," Mobley said. He said it so fervently that beads of perspiration actually popped out on his forehead. Or maybe it was because Petra was running the oven full bore and the heater in the café was roaring like a blast furnace.

"So it's about economic development," Suzanne said. She'd heard Mobley blather on like this before. Platitudes that won him votes, ideas that never quite sprouted into fruition.

Mobley's jowls sloshed as he bobbed his head. "And increased opportunity for Kindred."

With a look of amusement on his handsome face, Wolf listened to Mobley. Finally he said, "You know what, Mr. Mayor? You'd better stop pontificating so we can order lunch. We've got a lot of work to do."

"Excellent point," said Mobley, who seemed disappointed to be cut short.

"What can I bring you?" Suzanne asked, her pen poised above her order pad.

"Grilled ham and cheese," Mobley said. "With fries if you got 'em."

Suzanne carefully wrote down, *Heart Attack Special.*

"Spinach salad for me," Wolf said.

Suzanne wrote down *Veg.* "It'll be just a few minutes, gentlemen." She hesitated for a moment, tapped her pen hard against the table and said, "Out of curiosity, where exactly is this wonderful housing development going to be?"

"Ah," Wolf said, crossing his arms and leaning back in his chair. "We're still dickering about the land, but I'm hoping to move ahead as fast as possible." He glanced across the table at Mobley and added, "Especially since the situation seems a bit more favorable now."

Something dinged in Suzanne's brain and she said, "Just whose land are you dickering for, anyway?"

Mobley flashed a thousand-megawatt smile at her and said, "Why, Mike Mullen's farm, of course."

Stunned, all Suzanne could do was turn and run for the kitchen.

"SUZANNE," Petra said as Suzanne stumbled into the kitchen. "These chicken stir-fries need to be delivered to table six. Now I just have to . . ." Her words cut off abruptly when she saw the look on Suzanne's face. "Suzanne, honey? What's wrong? You look like your fiancé just ran off with some no-good floozy."

Suzanne took a step forward and leaned heavily against the butcher-block counter. "I was just talking to Mayor Mobley."

"Old blather butt," Petra said. "Did he just try to make his problem your problem?"

"No, it's something else. He's sitting out there with this real estate developer named Byron Wolf, who's pretty much busting his buttons about putting an offer in on the Mullen farm."

"What!" Petra suddenly went cross-eyed. "Seriously?"

"That's what the man just said."

Petra fought to recover her composure. "That can't be,"

she said in a very deliberate tone. I can't imagine that Claudia would ever sell the land to a real estate developer."

Suzanne held up a hand. "Not so fast. That's the exact opposite of what Claudia told me an hour ago."

Petra shook her head in disbelief. "What? What are you saying?" She suddenly looked frazzled again.

"Claudia said that she definitely would sell the farm. That she actually *wanted* to."

"No."

"Yes. She said that she and Mike had received several offers over the years, but he'd always turned them down cold."

"And she'll turn this one down, too," Petra said.

"I don't think she will," Suzanne said. "I think this time she really means to sell the farm."

"That's . . . outrageous."

Suzanne lifted a shoulder. "Face it, with Mike gone the farm is hers to do with as she wants."

"What about the cows?"

"I suppose the cows will have to find another home. Barn."

"Does this seem strange to you?" Petra asked.

"Does what seem strange to you?" Toni asked. She'd just slid through the swinging door, a plastic bin filled with dirty dishes in her hands.

"That guy sitting out there with Mayor Mobley?" Suzanne said. "He says he's going to buy the Mullen farm."

"Holy crap," Toni cried. "Really?" Then, "Is the place even for sale?"

Suzanne quickly went over what she'd just told Petra.

"And this developer . . . what's his name?" Toni asked.

"Um, Byron Wolf," Suzanne said.

"He's going to build a bunch of humongous houses?" Toni said.

"Mega mansions," Petra said. She spat out the words like she was referring to camel poop.

"So what does all this mean?" Toni asked. Her eyes bounced from Suzanne to Petra as if she were watching a tennis match.

"Here's what I think it means," Petra spoke up. "It means that the timing couldn't be worse. It almost looks as if Mike's death wasn't an accident at all."

"Well . . . we know that," Suzanne said.

"But you're saying that maybe his murder was orchestrated?" Toni said. "By Claudia? Oh jeez."

"No, no," Petra said. "That's not what I'm saying at all."

"Then what are you saying?" Toni asked.

"I think Wolf wanting to buy the land is just a sad, strange coincidence," Petra said. "Claudia and Mike had a wonderful marriage. She would never entertain such a terrible deed as murder." They all stood there for a few moments, shuffling their feet, looking uneasy. "Would she?" Petra added.

"Let's hope not," Suzanne said.

Toni waggled her fingers. "Go ahead and dish up the orders for the mayor and his buddy. I'll run them out and see if I can worm any more information out of Wolf."

Petra hurried to fill the orders. "What are you going to do?" she asked. "Shine a bright light in his eyes? Beat him with a rubber hose?"

"No," Toni said. She reached up and flicked open a button on her blouse. "I'm going to flirt with him."

TONI was as good as her word. She sashayed out into the café, as sweet as pecan pie, and delivered the luncheon orders to Wolf and Mobley. Suzanne and Petra peered out through the pass-through, watching her.

"A spinach salad for the good-looking gent," Toni said, setting Wolf's lunch in front of him. "Ham and cheese for the mayor."

Toni's warm smile, husky voice, and eye-popping blouse

full of goodies wasn't lost on Wolf. "Say now," he said. "You work here?"

"I'm one of the partners," Toni said.

"You're not exactly the shy, silent partner, are you?"

"Honey, I'm just getting started." Toni gave a throaty little growl.

Wolf winked at her and gave her a little growl right back. "I do believe I'd like to take you out for a drink sometime."

Toni thrust out a hip. "I think I'd like that."

"Can I call you?"

"Better yet, drop by anytime," Toni said. "I'll be here."

From her perch behind the pass-through, Petra said, "I think I'm going to be sick."

ONCE the lunch rush was pretty much over, once Mobley and Wolf had departed in Wolf's shiny red Porsche, Suzanne retired to the adjoining Book Nook. This small one-room bookshop had become her pride and joy. Without a proper bookstore in Kindred, Suzanne had converted this space into a well-stocked retail getaway that featured floor-to-ceiling bookshelves, a frayed Oriental carpet on the floor, and two rump-sprung chairs to cozy up in. She stocked everything from mystery to cooking to romance, with lots of craft books, kids' picture books, young adult, and even some military history for the men.

Right now, with Halloween only a few days away, Suzanne was working the shelves, pulling out all the Halloween-themed books that she could find. There were lots of picture books, of course. *Angelina's Halloween* and *The Ugly Pumpkin*. Oh, and she couldn't forget classics like *The Legend of Sleepy Hollow* by Washington Irving and anything by good old Edgar Allan Poe.

She piled up the books and then ducked into her office, a messy little alcove adjacent to the Book Nook. She grabbed a vase filled with dried flowers and added it to her small arrangement.

Hmm. It needed something more.

Suzanne hurried into the Knitting Nest next door. Mostly Petra's domain, it was stocked with hundreds of skeins of colorful yarn, baskets of knitting needles, and stacks of quilt squares. Petra taught her Hooked on Knitting classes here and also displayed some of her homemade shawls and comforters on the walls. The place was elegantly rustic, shimmering with color and texture, and served as a magnet for their female customers.

Ah, here they were. Suzanne grabbed a trio of orange knitted pumpkins and hurried back to the Book Nook. She plopped the pumpkins atop her stack of books and smiled. Perfect.

Just as Suzanne was unpacking a box of books that UPS had delivered earlier in the day, Sheriff Doogie strolled in. He looked around, nodded at her, and picked up a book on classic cars. Doogie was a not-so-secret motorhead.

Suzanne glanced sideways at him. "I need to talk to you about something."

"Oh yeah?" Doogie was acting nonchalant. Maybe a little too nonchalant. "I heard you paid a visit to Claudia Mullen this morning," he said.

Suzanne glanced sharply at him. "Who told you that?"

"Claudia Mullen." Doogie looked pleased that he'd been able to punk her.

"Okay. So you've got your trusty spy ring operating."

"I know you've been snooping around." Doogie closed his book and set it down. "I also bet you can't wait to grill me about that kid, Noah." He focused steel gray eyes on her. "I think he's the guy you thought was a scarecrow."

"I'd definitely like to get the full story on Noah," Suzanne said. "But right now I'm more interested in hearing what you know about Byron Wolf."

Doogie shook his head, obviously not recognizing the name. "Who the Sam Hill is Byron Wolf?"

"Let me give you a hint," Suzanne said. "Wolf is the sleazy developer who put up those monstrosity homes over in Jessup."

Doogie's face was still a blank. "So what?"

"Wolf was just in here for lunch," Suzanne said. "Bragging about putting in an offer to buy the Mullen farm."

Doogie took an involuntary step backward, a look of pure shock crumpling his face. Then his voice dropped to an urgent whisper. "What did you say?"

CHAPTER 7

"I said that Byron Wolf is about to put an offer in on the Mullen farm," Suzanne repeated.

"I got that part," Doogie rasped. "What I meant was, how do you know about this? Where did this guy Wolf come from? I mean, he didn't just parachute out of a clear blue sky, did he?" He rapped his knuckles hard against the counter to emphasize his words. "How the crap did you find out about a developer wanting to buy the Mullen property, but I didn't? How do you *know* this stuff?"

"Take a look around," Suzanne said. "I run a café where my morning customers are all lubricated by coffee and jacked up on sugar donuts. Half the people are from right here in Kindred, so they stop in to gossip about everything that's going on. The other half are from Jessup, and they drive over just to get the poop on the Kindred folks." She gave a quick smile. "Small towns, don't you love 'em?"

"Don't give me a folksy lecture, just tell me about Wolf," Doogie demanded.

"Mayor Mobley brought him here for lunch."

"Whoa," Doogie said, holding up his hands. "Rewind that tape for me, Suzanne. I want to hear about the land-buying part."

"Byron Wolf is a developer."

Doogie half closed one eye and cocked his head. "Okay . . . I'm startin' to have a recollection here. Wolf is the fat cat who built those ugly McMansions over in Jessup?"

"Bingo, my friend."

"Where half the places look like cut-down versions of the White House and the rest are faced with tacky fake plastic brick?"

"Architecture for the ages," Suzanne said.

Doogie was nodding now. "And the whole place is surrounded by big brass gates and guarded by a bunch of dumb rent-a-cops. Huh. And you're telling me this Wolf guy wants to build a development just like that outside Kindred? On Mike Mullen's property?"

"See," Suzanne said. "I had a feeling this might grab your attention."

"Well, it did. In fact, it took me by complete surprise." Doogie frowned. "But what gave Wolf the idea that the Mullen farm might be for sale?"

"Because it is for sale."

"Say what?" His eyes popped again and he ran a hand through his sparse crop of hair, ruffling it so vigorously it almost stood straight up.

"You already know that I was out there this morning," Suzanne said. "Dropping off a basket of muffins for Claudia."

Doogie sucked air through his front teeth. "Yeah?"

"That's when Claudia confided to me that she'd been wanting to sell the farm for a number of years, but Mike was always dead set against it."

Now Doogie ran the back of his hand across his face. "'Dead' being the operative word here."

"Well . . . yes. That might be key."

"It's a strange thing," Doogie said. "Claudia never mentioned a word about this to me. Never said they might be selling the farm."

"Probably because *they* weren't going to," Suzanne said. "Until now. Now that it's Claudia's to do with as she pleases."

"Mike's sudden death certainly makes things more convenient for her," Doogie said. He sounded angry and more than a little suspicious.

"I hate to admit it, but that's exactly what's been going through my mind, too."

Doogie hitched his belt, setting his sidearm, flashlight, radio, and nightstick in motion. "Looks like I need to have a sit-down, come-to-Jesus meeting with Claudia Mullen."

"I think you do." Suzanne hesitated. "And maybe with Byron Wolf, too. Because I have to tell you, my first impression of the man wasn't exactly positive."

"Why is that?"

"Wolf is one of those guys who acts friendly and engaging, but probably has the personality of a pit viper. And he's got all these fancy trappings. Shiny red Porsche. Expensive clothes. And I'm pretty sure he was blinged out with a Rolex watch."

"Wolf sounds like some kind of hotshot."

"I think Wolf knows his way around a multimillion-dollar deal. And I think he's smart, too," Suzanne said. "Not MBA smart, but smart like a fox. I had the feeling this is a man who understands how to negotiate."

"Forewarned is forearmed," Doogie said. "He may be a fat cat developer, but I still gotta talk to him. This land deal with Claudia is just too much of a . . . coincidence."

Suzanne reached out and straightened a stack of books. "I was hoping you'd say that." She glanced sideways at

Doogie. "Now, if you don't mind, I'd like to hear what you've learned about Noah Jorgenson." When Doogie didn't say anything, she continued. "Claudia told me that she was frightened of Noah. Not at first, not when he was a little kid. But now that Noah has grown older and gotten a lot bigger, she said that he scares her to death."

"Yeah," Doogie said. "That's what she told me, too."

"So I have to ask," Suzanne said. "Is Noah a suspect?"

Doogie looked unhappy. "You really want in on this investigation, don't you?"

"I'd say I'm already in. I was there, remember? I found Mike's body."

"Yeah . . . well." Doogie seemed to be capitulating. Not gracefully, more like a rogue nation that had been forced to sit down at a bargaining table.

Suzanne decided the best approach was to be direct. "Do you think Noah could have killed Mike Mullen?"

Doogie mulled over her words for a few seconds and then said, "I honestly don't know. Noah certainly had the opportunity. I mean, the Jorgenson farm is right there, directly adjacent to the Mullen farm. And I know for a fact that Noah's mother wasn't home yesterday morning."

"Where was she?"

"Something to do with church. Straightening hymnals or waxing the pews, I don't remember which."

"Was she purposely vague about what she was doing?" Suzanne asked.

"No," Doogie said. "I didn't think her *exact* whereabouts were all that important so I chose not to retain that information on my hard drive." He tapped an index finger against the side of his head. "I can't keep track of every stinking little fact."

Doogie sounded stressed, so Suzanne backed off a bit. "So Noah was home by himself when Mike was killed?"

"All morning and into the early afternoon. At least that's what he said when I talked to him."

"You talked to Noah yesterday?"

"That's right."

"When was that?"

"Late yesterday afternoon. After the coroner hauled Mike's body away. Right after Claudia got home and pretty much pointed a finger at Noah."

"Let me ask you this—when you told Noah that Mike had been murdered, what was his reaction?"

"The boy acted real upset."

"Did he have trouble understanding you? Or communicating with you? Claudia told me that Noah is autistic."

"That's what she told me, too, but Noah's mother says he has Asperger's syndrome. That the boy is actually very high functioning." Doogie frowned. "Still, every time I asked Noah a question, Faith Anne, that's his mother, jumped in to answer for him. She stuck to the kid like a bottle of Elmer's glue. She obviously hated the fact that I was there, asking about Mike Mullen's murder. In fact, she said she felt like I was interrogating them."

"I would have thought she'd want to cooperate," Suzanne said. "After all, when a neighbor is murdered . . . that's a very frightening thing. A violent crime happening so close to their own home."

"Exactly my thought. But Faith Anne acted like I had no right to talk to Noah at all." Doogie stuck out his chin. "Me, the duly elected sheriff."

"What if you asked somebody from County Services to get involved? To mediate?"

"What good would that do?"

"If Noah is classified as having some sort of disability, then they could step in to help."

"To help me?" Doogie asked.

"To help facilitate your questions," Suzanne said. She figured a trained caseworker would use a much more gentle approach in questioning Noah. "Did you ask Noah if he saw anything out of the ordinary? If he saw anyone hanging around Mike Mullen's farm?"

"I asked and the kid said no." Doogie rolled his eyes. "Or rather his old lady did."

"So you talked to Noah for quite a while?"

"Not long enough. And it should have been just the two of us. Without his doggone mother constantly throwing me the evil eye."

"Does Noah really need his mother to run interference for him? Do you think he really has difficulty communicating?"

Doogie shrugged. "Ah . . . I don't know. He spoke in a kind of monotone, but he seemed like he got the gist of my questions just fine."

"Did he act frightened?"

"Not at first, but after a while . . . yeah, I guess."

"Maybe Noah was worried that you were going to arrest him."

Doogie rocked back on his heels. "Maybe I should have. Maybe Claudia Mullen's hunch is right on the money. That Noah flipped out for some strange reason and killed her husband." He clenched his teeth together, tightening the muscles in his jaw. "Or maybe it was classic misdirection on her part. Maybe Claudia hired someone to off her old man and now she's trying to pin the blame on Noah."

"You don't really believe that, do you?"

"I don't know what to believe right now."

Suzanne thought for a few moments. "Did you ask Noah if he owned any hunting knives or machetes?"

"I asked him that," Doogie said. "And he said no. At least none that he or his mother would admit to."

*   *   *

SHERIFF Doogie didn't leave right away. He followed Suzanne into the café and plunked himself down on his usual stool at the counter. The one with the sideways tilt to it.

"Look what the cat dragged in," Toni said. She slid a ceramic cup across the counter and poured him a cup of coffee. "What'll you have, Sheriff?"

"Maybe a piece of pie," Doogie said.

"We got pumpkin, apple, and lemon meringue."

"Gimme a slice of apple."

"You got it, big guy."

Toni bustled around behind the counter, pulling the apple pie out of the pie saver and cutting an extra big slice for Doogie.

"You want a scoop of ice cream on that, too?" Toni asked.

"Why not?" One of Doogie's hands crept up to his gut. "I gotta get over to the Hard Body Gym one of these days. Lift some weights."

Toni set Doogie's apple pie à la mode down in front of him and then gave him a fork and a spoon.

"You know what my surefire workout is?" she asked.

"What's that?"

"It's a cross between a lunge and a crunch. It's called lunch." Toni gave him a slow wink and spun away.

"How long is His Royal Highness going to sit out there anyway?" Petra asked. She was perched on a stool in the kitchen, working on the menus for tomorrow. It would shape up to be a busy day. Breakfast, lunch, and then their mid-afternoon Knitter's Tea.

Suzanne was in the kitchen enjoying a quick sandwich— cream cheese and roasted red pepper stuffed inside pita bread. Glancing out the pass-through, she said, "Doogie's probably going to sit there until he gets bored."

"How's he coming with the investigation?" Petra asked. "Any more serious suspects?"

"Noah Jorgenson," Suzanne said. "The neighbor kid. And you can't rule out Claudia Mullen."

Petra looked worried. "Noah's just a boy. And I still can't believe Claudia would kill her own husband."

"I don't want to believe it, either," Suzanne said. "But look at the facts. Claudia is suddenly interested in selling her farm to Byron Wolf. Maybe a little too interested."

"Maybe Wolf killed Mike," Petra said.

"Maybe he did."

"You didn't think much of Wolf, did you?"

"I think Wolf is one cagey guy. He could probably pick your pocket and sell you a parcel of swampland in Florida, all in one fell swoop."

"Remind me not to buy any retirement property," Petra said. "As if I can afford to retire." She touched the eraser tip of her pencil to her chin and frowned. "We're going to need a few groceries for tomorrow."

"Make a list and I'll run out to the Save Mart," Suzanne said.

"Thank you." Petra slid off her stool and ambled over to her big, industrial-strength oven. She opened the door, said, "Yum," and pulled out a steaming hot pan of banana nut bread.

Toni came rocketing through the swinging door. "Is that for us? I sure hope so, because I'm about ready to *collapse* from hunger."

"Didn't you already snarf a sandwich along with two brownies?" Suzanne asked.

"So what," Toni said. "I've got a very high metabolism."

"Sorry, but I'm taking this banana bread to Donny tonight," Petra said.

Her husband, Donny, had advanced Alzheimer's and lived in the Center City Nursing Home. Every couple of nights Petra drove over to visit him, feeding him cookies and sweet breads, watching TV with him, singing him songs from their past. When she was there, he responded beautifully to her. Once she packed up and left, he had no memory of her visit. Suzanne found it heartbreaking, but Petra had finally made peace with it. She was a till-death-do-us-part kind of wife.

Suzanne, on the other hand, had experienced the untimely death of her husband, Walter. His presence was still with her, of course, tucked deep within her heart. But she'd processed her grief and, surprise, surprise, had also found room in her heart for Sam. Two hearts—really three now—beating as one.

Toni reached into the Scooby-Doo cookie jar on the counter, grabbed a cookie, jammed it into her mouth, and, between bites, said, "What's the deal with that Yarn Truck?"

"It's an old truck that two women rehabbed and turned into a mobile yarn store," Suzanne said. "It's supposed to be really cute and loaded with all kinds of homespun artisan yarns."

"They're scheduled to roll in here around two o'clock," Petra said. "But I expect we'll have a couple dozen anxious knitters show up here for lunch. And then they'll hang around until the Yarn Truck arrives." She hesitated. "Toni, would you like me to make you another sandwich?"

"Oh yeah," Toni said. "That would be great. She gulped down the rest of her cookie. So . . . what time is our tea gonna happen?"

"Tea at three," Petra said. She buttered two slices of whole wheat bread, added a slice of roast chicken, and slathered on some of her homemade avocado spread.

"We'll probably be crazy-busy then, huh?" Toni asked. "Should I ask Kit to come in and help us?"

Petra pursed her lips. "The girl is what . . . almost five months pregnant now?"

"Yeah, but that doesn't make her a bad waitress," Toni said. "Just a little slow moving." When Petra didn't respond she added, "Hold the pickles, the lettuce, and the judgment, please." She was referring to the fact that Kit still hadn't married her boyfriend, Ricky.

Petra smiled a thin smile as she sliced the sandwich. "I hear you."

Toni grabbed the sandwich, took a big bite, and said, "Guh."

"I think that means 'good,'" Suzanne said.

Toni gave a vigorous nod. She chewed, swallowed hard, and said, "Suzanne, would you come with me to Schmitt's Bar tonight?"

"Oh, I don't know," Suzanne said. She was just this side of disinterested. The local dive bar just wasn't her thing. Imagine that.

"Pretty please," Toni said.

"Why? What's going on?"

"Margarita night," Toni said, beaming. "You know, Jimmy Buffett tunes on the jukebox, a pitcher of chilled margaritas on the table? Please come along and be my wingman? Wingwoman?"

"Okay," Suzanne said. "But just for one drink. After all, it's a school night."

"Oh, goody, goody," Toni said.

"Petra," Suzanne said, "does Faith Anne Jorgenson belong to your church?"

"Yes. Both she and Noah do."

"And they attend regularly?"

"I guess you could say that," Petra said. "They're always there bright and early on Sunday morning."

"Does Noah participate? I mean in the services?"

"Not really," Petra said. "At least I don't think so. And

I've never seen him attend Bible studies." She frowned. She knew exactly why Suzanne was asking. "But Noah's just a boy. You don't really think that he . . . ?"

Suzanne blew out a glut of air. "Right now I'm not sure what to think."

CHAPTER 8

BUT the afternoon wasn't over yet. At three o'clock, almost precisely on the nose, Junior Garrett, Toni's soon-to-be ex, shuffled his way into the Cackleberry Club. He was carrying an enormous orange pumpkin under each arm and looked like a street punk who'd just stepped out of a modern-day production of *West Side Story.* Junior wore pegged jeans, scuffed biker boots, and a dirty T-shirt with a pack of Lucky Strikes rolled up in one sleeve. A silver chain hooked his wallet to his belt.

"Pumpkins," Suzanne exclaimed. "We were hoping you wouldn't forget."

Toni was right there, too. "Where are the gourds?" she asked in an accusatory tone. "Don't tell me you forgot the gourds."

"I got 'em, I got 'em," Junior wheezed as the pumpkins slowly began to slip from his grasp. "Just hurry up and tell me where to put these stupid things."

"I'll tell you where to put it," Toni said. Ever since they'd separated (after Junior's lying, cheating fling with the floozy bartender with the hot pink extensions in her hair), Junior seemed to rub Toni the wrong way. Only problem was, she continued to drag her feet on their divorce.

Junior thumped the pumpkins down onto a table. "Jeez, Toni, who put a quarter in you today? Yap, yap, yap. Gimme a break, will you?"

"You got the gourds?" she asked.

"Of course I got the gourds. They're outside in my truck."

"Okay then," Toni said. She folded her arms across her chest, somewhat mollified. "Since you *finally* did what you were told, you might have earned yourself a glass of apple cider."

"And a cinnamon donut, too," Suzanne said. Sometimes Suzanne felt bad about all the grief that Toni heaped upon Junior. Sometimes.

"Can't spare the time," Junior told them. "I gotta keep moving. I got places to be."

"Where do you have to be?" Toni snickered. Junior's meager talents weren't exactly in demand. When he did land a job as a mechanic or factory worker, he rarely stayed employed for very long.

But Junior pulled himself up to his full height and preened. "I'm a businessman now. Time is money."

"Whoa, whoa, whoa." Toni held up a hand. "Run that by me again, bucko. You say you're a *businessman*? Do you think I just fell off the turnip truck?"

"Seriously?" Suzanne said. She knew that every crazy business Junior started had failed miserably. From his car cooker, to his Hubba Bubba beer, to his fried pig's ears on a stick at the county fair.

"Ladies, you are looking at the proud proprietor of the Typhoon Car Wash." Junior stuck his thumbs in his belt and grinned like a demented Cheshire cat. "In fact, I just made a small down payment this morning."

Toni was stunned. "You bought a car wash?"

"I'm the new bubble czar."

"What on earth did you use for money?"

"I got resources," Junior said.

"What?" Toni asked. "Monopoly money? You realize the yellow hundreds are not legal currency. Real money has to have a picture of a president on the front, not some old dude with a monocle and top hat."

"Maybe he's trading on his good looks," Petra called through the pass-through.

Junior puffed out his chest like a bandy rooster and said, "I got something better than good looks."

"What's that?" Toni asked. "An oil lamp with a genie inside?"

Junior flexed an arm and made a pitiful-looking muscle. "Sweat equity."

"Sweet dogs," Toni said, shaking her head. "You don't even wash your own junky truck, so how are you going to do it professionally? For actual customers with nice expensive cars?"

But Junior was far from deterred. "That's all been figured out. I talked Larry Butters into letting me fix up that defunct car wash he owns out on Highway 212, just past the old fish hatchery. We're gonna be business partners."

"You mean Buggy Butters?" Suzanne asked. Everyone called him Buggy because his main source of income was selling beer at the local golf course out of a baby buggy that he'd turned into a rolling beer cooler.

"That's the guy," Junior said. "Soon as I bring the car wash up to code I'm gonna start raking in some serious cash."

"You've never made serious cash in your life," Toni said. "You couldn't even give away a lawn mower on Craigslist. And every one of your pie-in-the-sky inventions has been a miserable flop."

Junior tapped an index finger against the side of his head. "That's because I never had an angle before."

Suzanne couldn't help herself. She was like a silly, fluttering moth drawn to the bright, hypnotic lure of the flame. She had to ask. "What's your angle on this car wash, Junior?"

"I'm gonna hire a bunch of hot-lookin' women and have them do all the vacuuming and hand drying."

"What!" came Petra's shriek through the pass-through.

"So you're basically going to be running a nonstop wet T-shirt contest?" Toni asked.

"Well, heh heh, yeah," Junior said. He looked a little sheepish, like he'd been caught with his hand in the cookie jar. "I guess you could call it that. How else am I supposed to lure customers in?"

"Perhaps with smart marketing and genuine business acumen?" Suzanne said.

"I'm afraid that's not in the picture," Toni said. "Sounds like Junior's going to take advantage of someone else's assets."

"The best part of the deal," Junior said, "is I get to handpick all the talent."

"Don't you mean employees?" Suzanne said.

Junior grinned stupidly. "I guess."

"This is the most embarrassing thing you've ever done," Toni said.

"Oh no," Junior said. "Remember the time I was driving a truckload of turkeys and the cages . . ."

Toni threw up her hands. "Stop! I can't take any more. This isn't happening."

"Sure it is," Junior said. "I'm going to hold open auditions for talent. Gonna print up some flyers, put out the call."

"Sounds more like a booty call," Suzanne said.

Junior sidled over to Toni and slid a hand around her waist. "If things don't work out here . . . if you ever need a new gig . . . I can always find a spot for you. All you have to do is wiggle your hips and whip your chamois rag like you mean it."

Toni squirted out of his grasp. "Forget it, Junior. I'm not

coming within a mile of your porno car wash." She grabbed a teapot off one of the tables and stormed into the kitchen.

Junior smiled after her. "She'll come around."

"Junior," Suzanne said. "Maybe you should just bring in the rest of the pumpkins and gourds, okay?"

"Sure thing, Suzy-Q."

Junior made two trips out to his rattletrap truck, finally hauling in all the produce they'd asked for. When he dropped the third bushel basket filled with colored gourds on the table, he said, "That's the last of 'em."

"Thanks, Junior," Suzanne said. She was already thinking about how to arrange them. Maybe scatter some of the smaller gourds in among her collection of ceramic chickens?

"No worries," Junior said. "Just doing a solid for a fellow entrepreneur." But despite his assertion of places to go and people to see, Junior didn't seem like he was in a big hurry to leave.

"Thanks again," Suzanne said, hoping Junior would take the hint. The sooner he cleared out, the sooner she could get back to work.

"So," Junior said, edging a little closer to her. "I heard you were out at Mike Mullen's farm. That you were the one who discovered poor Mike all cut up and bloody."

There it was. Junior was sticking around for details on the murder. Then again, who wasn't?

Junior's eyes had gone big as saucers. "I even heard you ran inside the house to check on Mike's wife. That was pretty risky, seeing as how there was a machete-wielding maniac on the loose."

"How did you know Mike was killed with a machete?"

Junior guffawed. "Everybody knows that. It's all over town."

"Great."

But Junior wasn't finished. "Are you gonna get involved in the investigation? Kind of like you did when Ricky was accused of setting fire to that old building downtown?"

"Probably not," Suzanne said.

Junior cocked his head at her. "I ain't buying your nonchalant attitude, Suzanne. I'll just bet you gals have been looking at all sorts of different angles. You and Toni and Petra are the original Snoop Sisters." He pulled his face into a knowing smile and added, "I bet you're taking a hard look at that freaky neighbor kid, too, huh?"

Suzanne's interest was suddenly piqued. "How do you know about Noah?"

Junior made a swooping motion with his hand. "I'm like a patch of ground fog. I slip in softly and hear all sorts of things."

"Most of it's probably gossip and unfounded rumors."

But Junior continued to press her. "I could help out, you know. I could sneak around town and ask a few questions. Scrape up some dirt and report back to you, all covert-like."

"You're not exactly a skilled CIA operative," Suzanne said. "Besides, we don't need your help."

"But I really *want* to help." In two seconds flat Junior had gone from boastful to whiny.

"Junior. Please don't . . ." Suzanne hesitated. "Just please don't, okay?"

Junior shrugged. "Whatever. But you're missing a great opportunity here."

Two minutes after the door slammed on Junior's sorry ass, a man Suzanne had never seen before came charging into the Cackleberry Club. Tall and thin, with a precise, almost military, bearing, he wore a navy blue department store suit. The clipboard he carried gave him the air of an officious accountant.

"Excuse me," the man said. "I'm here to see the owner."

"That would be me," Suzanne said.

"Oh," the man said, his dark eyes drilling into her. "A woman."

"Last time I looked, yes," Suzanne said. "I'm Suzanne Dietz. How can I help you?"

The man transferred his clipboard to his left hand and extended his right hand. "Rick Boyle. executive vice president at Claggett Foods." He hesitated for a moment, letting his title sink in, hoping to impress her. "It is *so* nice to finally meet you."

"Ah," Suzanne said. "Claggett Foods." She knew that Claggett Foods was a regional company that provided restaurants and grocery stores with so-so produce and meat. None of their products were that great and definitely didn't live up to the standards she'd set for their farm-to-table restaurant. She'd always insisted on using hormone-free meat, free-range chickens, fresh eggs, and locally produced vegetables and artisan breads. If she spent a little more money on inventory, so be it. The local producers prospered and her customers were happy. She wouldn't have it any other way.

"Mrs. Dietz . . ."

"Yes?"

"I'd like to take a few minutes to familiarize you with some of Claggett Foods' excellent products and tell you about some of the exciting changes our company has made."

"I hate to waste your time, Mr. Boyle, but I'm pretty happy with the vendors and producers I already have."

Boyle held up a hand. "Now, just a minute. I'm in charge of boosting sales for this particular region and there's nothing I like better than a challenge. Now if you'll just let me . . ."

Suzanne shook her head. "I'm sorry. But we really are pretty well set. If you'd care to leave your business card and product sheets, maybe I can . . ."

"You see now," Boyle said, "here's where we differ in principle. I haven't even begun to tell you how much money I can save you." He grinned. "I mean, who doesn't like to shave a little off the bottom line, right? It makes for a win-win situation for both of us." He winked at her. "And nobody, meaning your customers, are ever the wiser."

"Mr. Boyle, I'm sure you're very good at your job . . ."

"I'm the best," Boyle said. "At sales, service, and marketing. Which is why I'm primed to take over as your new cheese and dairy vendor."

"My new cheese . . ." Suzanne was completely taken aback. Mike Mullen hadn't even had a proper burial yet and this guy was pitching to be his replacement? Boyle's pushiness didn't just annoy her, it made her heartsick.

Boyle peeled off a sheet from his clipboard and thrust it at her. "Now I happen to know that your cheese vendor recently met an untimely end. So I took the liberty of drawing up an initial order. You see, I've even listed our wholesale prices on ten-pound wheels of cheddar, blue, and pepper jack cheese. I believe you'll find . . ."

"Excuse me," Suzanne said, feeling uneasy. "But you really do need to leave." She started to back away from him. "This isn't . . . no way is this going to work."

But Boyle was undeterred. He flashed a knowing crocodile smile at her and his eyes glittered. "You and I both know you need a new cheese supplier, so I plan to come back and pitch you again—as many times as necessary. I'm pleased to say that several other area restaurants and grocers have already jumped on board with me, so I'm not going to give up easily."

SUZANNE'S blood pressure didn't dip back to normal until Boyle's car pulled out of her parking lot and disappeared down the road. Then she turned away from the window and bit her lip. The nerve of him. Considering the awful circumstances of Mike Mullen's death—which everybody and his brother seemed to know the details about—who in their right mind would dare to swoop in and pressure her like that?

Toni popped out from the kitchen, a broom clutched in her hands. "That was pretty weird."

"You overheard some of our conversation?" Suzanne asked.

"Sure did. What a complete jerk to try and horn in like that." Toni twirled her broom like a baton, then poked it under one of the tables. "At least the smell of his Eau de Brimstone cologne went with him."

"It's awful to see the vultures circling so soon," Suzanne said just as the phone rang. She grabbed it, said, "Cackleberry Club," and smiled when she recognized the caller's voice.

It was Sam.

"You have no idea how happy I am that you called," she said.

"What's up?" Sam asked. "Are you having a bad day?"

"Not anymore I'm not. In fact, I'm just happy about your excellent timing."

"It's a gift," Sam laughed.

"So how's your day progressing?" Suzanne asked.

"Same old, same old. Man versus tractor, tractor came out on top, man required a dozen stitches. Then we had a nasty case of head lice among two third graders. And, let's see, two ear infections. Pretty run-of-the-mill stuff, actually."

"I was wondering . . ."

"Yes?"

"Have you heard any word yet about Mike Mullen's autopsy?"

"Suzanne . . ." Sam's voice carried a warning tone.

"Come on, it's just a simple question."

Sam sighed deeply. "If you must know, it's going on right now."

"No kidding." Suzanne was instantly alert. "Over at the hospital?"

"That's right. Doogie's medical examiner hit town this morning and got right to work."

"Are they going to share their findings with you?"

"Only if I ask."

"So are you? Going to ask, I mean?"

"I haven't decided yet."

"Come on, Sam, you know I've got a stake in this. You know that I'm interested."

"Maybe a little too interested for your own good. You worry me."

"I don't mean to," Suzanne said.

"Oops," Sam said. "My beeper just went off. Gotta go."

"Is that just an excuse to dodge me or is this a real emergency?"

"Suzanne, everything's an emergency these days." And he was gone.

Suzanne hung up the phone and gazed around the Cackleberry Club. Toni had finished sweeping and was setting up the tables for tomorrow's breakfast service. Now all she had to do was cleverly place a few pumpkins and gourds. *And, let's see, what else?*

Oh right, Petra had given her a grocery list.

Groceries.

Suzanne's thoughts immediately turned back to Boyle. What a jerk he'd been, coming in here and acting all presumptuous about being her new cheese vendor.

Maybe a little too presumptuous?

Boyle's visit had struck a chord with her that she didn't care for. And she wondered—could Boyle, in his haste to increase sales in his new territory, have had a hand in Mike's death? Maybe he hadn't set out to murder Mike, maybe he had just meant to scare or intimidate him. But then something went wrong?

It was a terrifying thought. But so was the fact that poor Mike Mullen had lain in his own barn, helpless and bleeding to death, with just the cows to witness his final moments.

CHAPTER 9

"IF I have a bad day," Toni explained, "I like to relax with a drink. If I have a good day, I have a drink to congratulate myself."

"Sounds like a plan," Suzanne said.

They were sitting in a battered wooden booth in Schmitt's Bar, snarfing down chips and salsa, as a rapidly growing crowd spilled into the place. Jimmy Buffett's "Margaritaville" blasted at nearly ear-shattering decibel levels, pinball machines clattered, and there was the sound of billiard balls being racked in the back room. The wood-paneled walls were covered with a mosaic of tin signs (I'm Not Lazy, I'm Just Very Relaxed was one of Suzanne's favorites), and an American flag and a black POW/MIA flag were draped above the nearby U-shaped bar.

"So," Toni said, leaning forward, "Doogie's going to let you into the investigation?"

"I'm not so sure about that," Suzanne said. "He's one territorial fella."

"Even though you've helped him in the past?"

"Mmn, I think Doogie's got a very short memory."

"Or one that's very selective," Toni said.

Freddy, the hippie-dippie bar owner, was suddenly hovering at their booth. "Time for a refreshing beverage, ladies? Perhaps a pitcher of our special margaritas?"

"Ya got that right," Toni said.

"We're serving traditional margaritas," Freddy told them. "And as an added treat, pomegranate- and raspberry-flavored margaritas." Tonight Freddy was dressed in his best Pink Floyd T-shirt, red bandanna, flip-flops, and had his long gray hair pulled back into a ponytail. In deference to the health code restrictions, his goatee was braided and kept in check with a teeny tiny gold ring. He was a stoner of the first magnitude and looked like he'd just stepped out of a Cheech and Chong movie. In fact, every time he blew through the kitchen's swinging door there seemed to be a slight hint of marijuana.

"I vote for the traditional margarita," Toni said. "I just don't get all these kooky flavored drinks that bars are serving these days. I mean, who wants a tutti-frutti martini, anyway? Yuck."

"Flavored cocktails are mostly for our younger patrons," Freddy confided. "They're big consumers of your crapple bombs, flaming Dr Peppers, B-52s, and duck farts."

"Those are actual drinks?" Toni asked. "They sound awful."

Freddy smiled. "They pretty much are."

"We also want a couple of burgers," Suzanne said. Freddy's grill was as black and crusted as the deepest pit in Hell, but still produced some of the most flavorful burgers in the tri-county area. Pink and juicy on the inside, a perfect char on the outside.

"And give us the works," Toni added. "Bacon, cheese, pickles, and fries."

"You got it," Freddy said.

Toni grabbed another chip, dunked it into the salsa, and said, "Dealing with Junior today completely wore me out. What a dim bulb. He wants to open a car wash that's staffed with bimbos wearing bikinis? It sounds practically illegal."

"Or illicit. Do you think he can actually pull it off?"

"I dunno. I hope not. I hope nobody shows up for his stupid tryouts. I mean, can you imagine it? Girls in string bikinis working for Junior? How many ways can you say 'jailbait'?"

"Or 'sexual harassment,'" Suzanne said.

Freddy slammed down a pitcher of margaritas on the table along with two salt-rimmed glasses. "Drink up, ladies. Burgers are on the way."

"Excellent," Toni said. She grabbed the pitcher and, ice cubes rattling, poured out their drinks. Then she held up her glass and grinned at Suzanne. "A toast."

Suzanne clinked glasses with her. "What are we toasting?"

"Here's to a long, hard week."

"It's only Wednesday."

"Don't remind me," Toni said. She took three big gulps. "I feel the need to let my hair down and loosen up a little."

"Honey, if you loosen up any more you're going to positively unravel," Suzanne teased.

A couple minutes later, their burger baskets arrived and both women tore into them.

"Ah." Toni lifted her bun and peered under it. "The bacon fairy has arrived." She shot a warning glance at Suzanne. "Now don't go and tattle to Petra about us eating all unhealthy. Otherwise she'll be on my case like stink on a skunk. First she wants to fatten me up 'cause she says I'm as skinny as a wet cat, and then she yells at me to watch my cholesterol. I mean, what's it supposed to be?"

"Petra means well. She just goes off the rails once in a while. We all do."

Toni gazed at Suzanne. "You don't. Look how everything always comes up sweet red roses for you. You had the smarts to open the Cackleberry Club . . ."

"After my husband died," Suzanne reminded her.

"And then you hooked up with Sam a little while later," Toni said.

"I met Sam in the ER after a crazy person tossed me through a window and I almost bled to death."

"Huh, I kind of forgot all those nasty details." Toni's eyes slid sideways and she said, "Say now. Take a look at that long, tall drink of water that just strolled in."

Suzanne followed Toni's gaze and watched as a tough-looking man slid through the crowd, all shoulders and narrow hips, and then casually eased himself onto a bar stool. Wearing tight jeans and a worn-looking brown leather jacket, he was skinny and wiry with a stubbly beard, intense eyes, and strong jaw.

"Who's the cowboy?" Toni wondered, instantly intrigued. "I mean, giddyup."

"I don't know," Suzanne said. "I don't think I've ever seen him before."

"Maybe he's new in town? He doesn't look like one of our local yokels. He looks like . . ." Toni tilted her head and thought for a moment. "Like he could show a girl a good time."

"Down, girl."

"I'm just doing a little window-shopping," Toni said, but her eyes were clearly drawn to the stranger.

The man at the bar ordered a longneck beer, rested his elbows on the bar, and sipped his brew slowly. Even though there was lots of flirting and dancing going on all around him, he seemed to have little interest in anything but his beer.

"Nobody's talking to him," Toni said. "I think he looks kind of lonely."

"Or maybe he just doesn't enjoy the witty repartee of a small-town bar."

They watched as the man tipped back his beer again, then curled a finger at Freddy. Freddy shuffled over to him and leaned across the bar.

"The plot thickens," Toni said. "Maybe he's applying for a job here as a bouncer." She chuckled. "He could bounce me on his knee."

"With a stone face like that, he might scare away the customers."

"He doesn't scare me. I think he looks like the strong, silent type."

Freddy was listening impassively as the man spoke to him. It looked as if the man was making a pitch to Freddy, trying to sell him something. When Freddy shook his head no, the man seemed even more insistent. Finally, Freddy threw up his hands and walked away. The cowboy barked something at Freddy's back and then returned to his beer.

Five minutes later, when Freddy stopped by their booth to see if they wanted another pitcher of margaritas, Toni was still twitching with excitement.

"Who's the dude you were talking to at the bar?" Toni asked. "The tall, rangy guy?"

Freddy wiped his hands on his apron. "Nobody you'd want to know."

"Don't be so sure of that," Toni said.

"But you seemed to know him," Suzanne said. Truth be told, she was a little curious, too.

Freddy ducked his head, as if he was almost embarrassed. "Aw, that's Julian Elder. He was trying to sell me some ground horsemeat."

The words "ground horsemeat" seemed to hang in the air like a malevolent thought bubble.

"Excuse me?" Suzanne said.

"Horsemeat?" Toni said, shocked. "Like actual dead . . . horses?"

"It's not a pretty story," Freddy said. "Elder buys horses, mostly old ones that nobody wants anymore. Glue factory rejects or something. He pays next to nothing for them and then sells them at auction to some guys up in Canada. There's apparently a market for that sort of thing."

Freddy's story completely horrified Suzanne. She was, after all, a dyed-in-the-wool horsewoman. Dearly loved her barrel racing quarter horse, Mocha, and her dear plodding Grommet.

"I can't believe it," Suzanne said. "Who would . . . ?" She peered through the crowd at Elder, who was still lounging at the bar, and swallowed hard. "Well, I guess *he* would."

"That little nugget of information pretty much sucked the mojo out of the evening," Toni said. She pushed her half-eaten burger away from her. "At least for me, anyway."

"Me, too," Suzanne said. "Vegan is starting to sound good."

"And that guy is suddenly so not attractive," Toni said.

"I'm sorry to upset you ladies," Freddy said. "I sure didn't mean to."

Suzanne waved a hand. "We're okay. A little bummed out, but we'll live."

Freddy nodded, as if a bit more explanation was in order. "Elder comes in here every couple of weeks and tries to hustle a few pounds of what he calls horse burgers. Of course I would never buy that stuff and serve it here. It's just not right." He tapped his ample chest. "Hey, I'm a horse lover, too." He hesitated. "So. Another pitcher? This one's on the house for you gals."

"We'll take it," Toni said.

Suzanne snuck another peek at Elder, who was still sitting at the bar. She was careful to avoid his direct gaze—she didn't need him noticing her and getting the wrong idea.

Still, she was curious about him. Especially since Freddy's comment about Elder purchasing old horses had struck her so hard. She thought back to the pathetic herd of skinny horses she'd seen this morning on her way to visit Claudia. And wondered if Elder could be the owner of those poor creatures? If so, he was a very close neighbor to the Mullen farm.

THE bar lights dimmed and a slow, torchy song played on the jukebox. Couples filed hand in hand onto the dance floor, lovers melting into each other, hips swaying on the downbeat.

"Jeez," Toni said. "Now I'm really depressed."

"About the horses?"

"No, because everybody's all paired off."

"Honey," Suzanne said, "you've got men flocking around you like bees to honey."

"Now I'm a plastic squeeze bottle. Great."

"You know what I mean. And you know darned well that if you divorced Junior you could probably be happy-ever-aftering with a really nice guy."

Toni ducked her head. "Yeah, I know. But if I wasn't there to boss Junior around, what would happen to him? Where would he go?"

"Jail?" Suzanne said.

Freddy showed up with their pitcher of drinks and a fresh basket of chips. "Enjoy," he said. "Sorry about the horse thing. Didn't mean for it to be such a bummer for you guys."

Suzanne nodded. "Thanks for the drinks." She poured out a margarita for Toni. "I think we better quit after this round."

"I hate to admit it," Toni said, "but you're probably right.

I'm not as young and nubile as I used to be. My recovery rate has slowed." She held up a finger. "And if you ever mention that I said that, I'll claim plausible deniability."

"I get it. It takes me longer to bounce back in the morning, too."

"Or afternoon," Toni said. "Considering ours is going to be super busy tomorrow."

"Petra's pretty excited about this Yarn Truck she's got coming in. She did a great job at marketing the whole event, so I think the Cackleberry Club is going to be packed to the gills."

"I just hope all the nervousness over Mike Mullen's murder doesn't put a damper on things," Toni said. "I mean, people are really scared. No one knows if they're safe in their own home. There's a vicious killer out there and Sheriff Doogie's got no suspects."

"He's got suspects. Just no actual proof."

"Still, the killer could be anyone."

"I don't believe Mike's death was random," Suzanne said. "The way Mike was killed . . . the horrific stab wounds . . . it's what a homicide investigator would call overkill. Meaning it was up close and personal." She paused. "I think Mike knew his killer."

Toni gave a little shiver. "Who do you think killed him, Suzanne? Do you think it was that neighbor kid, Noah? Even Junior thinks that kid is a little strange."

"I don't know," Suzanne said. "But I intend to do a little digging on my own. For one thing, I'd like to meet this Noah in person."

"Just be careful," Toni said.

"I will." Suzanne glanced toward the bar and saw that Elder had left. She'd gotten a vibe off him that she didn't care for and had decided to find out more about him, too. And about the herd of horses she'd seen this morning. So, a lot on her plate.

Suzanne grimaced. But no horsemeat on her plate. No horse burgers. That was just plain awful. No way would she ever let something like that happen to one of her horses, even if he was old and sick and lame. Never. Never in a million years.

CHAPTER 10

PETRA grabbed her spatula and, quick as you please, flipped over a dozen blueberry pancakes. Then she moved over to her enormous skillet and pushed around a mound of sizzling turkey bacon. Thursday morning breakfast service was under way at the Cackleberry Club and today everyone was fizzing with excitement.

For one thing, Toni was all whipped up about choosing a Halloween costume for Monday night's big party. "It's gotta be ultra sexy," she said to Petra as she set out plates. "Something that will make everybody's eyeballs pop out of their heads."

"Don't make it too sexy," Suzanne warned. She was slicing oranges and strawberries for garnishes. "Or Junior will try to recruit you for his car wash."

"The thing is," Toni said, "Halloween is the one day of the year a girl can go hog wild and let it all hang out. I mean, I could be a harem girl, a fortune-telling gypsy, or even . . . ." She arched her back and kicked out a leg. "A ballet dancer."

"I could care less about wearing a sexy costume," Petra said. "All I want is to be comfy."

Toni wrinkled her nose. "You mean, like, a stretchy waist-band?"

"And roomy through the hips."

"Ach. I bet you wear granny panties, too."

Petra squinted at her. "Hey, don't knock 'em until you've tried 'em, honey."

"Not me," Toni said. "I'm a Frederick's of Hollywood gal. I like my undies flashy and trashy."

"Not to change the subject," Petra began. Then she managed a lopsided grin and said, "Actually I *do* want to change the subject." She was suddenly serious. "Are you ladies aware that Mike Mullen's visitation is tonight?"

"Yeah," Toni said. "Are you going?"

"Well, I suppose so," Petra said. She glanced at Suzanne. "I mean, I assumed all three of us would go and pay our respects."

"Of course we will," Suzanne said. In the back of her brain, the parietal lobe area that didn't concern itself with remembering breakfast and lunch orders and dealing with a bunch of crazed knitters this afternoon, she was still wondering about the autopsy report. Had anything interesting turned up? She needed to call Sam and find out.

"I don't know about this," Toni grumped. "You guys know how much I hate looking at dead bodies that are all tricked out in a fancy casket. The whole creepy ritual bums me out."

"I don't think you should be unduly concerned," Suzanne told her. "I'm pretty sure it's going to be a closed casket."

Toni jittered on the balls of her feet like an over-caffeinated Chihuahua. "You mean because"—her eyes darted back and forth—"because Mike was all chopped up?"

"Excuse me," Petra said as she added golden brown pancakes to the waiting plates. "Can we *please* change that subject, too?"

*   *   *

BALANCING three orders, Suzanne pushed her way into the café and delivered the breakfasts to waiting customers.

Toni followed on her heels and delivered another four orders. Then she smiled, poured coffee, accepted compliments on the food, laughed at jokes, and did everything but the bunny dip to make their customers feel welcome, happy, and semi-coddled.

"You're suddenly in a good mood," Suzanne told Toni when they both found themselves behind the counter, grabbing sticky rolls and little wrapped pats of butter.

"I'm in a good mood because I just figured out my Halloween costume," Toni said.

"So what's it going to be?"

"Definitely a ballet dancer. A really sexy one."

"Interesting choice," Suzanne said. It was interesting because Toni's dance moves generally involved doing an energetic two-step at a country-western bar.

"You don't like it?"

Suzanne held up her hands, palms outward. "Hey, I'm the one who's going as a witch. Who am I to judge?"

"I was thinking of wearing a leopard-print leotard and some kind of frilly, black ballet skirt."

"And you're going to create this skirt yourself?" Suzanne asked.

"I thought maybe you'd help me."

"Oh, I don't think so. Remember, sweetie, I'm the sewing-challenged partner who foisted the design and stitching of my costume on my too-polite-to-say-no neighbor."

"Well, do you think Petra would help me?" Toni asked.

"Probably have to ask her, though she's more into quilting and knitting."

"You sure you couldn't help me with the skirt?"

"Toni . . ."

"What if I went to the dime store and bought ten yards of black netting and frilly lace?"

"And then what?" Suzanne asked. "You want me to wrap you up like a burrito?"

"It should probably be a little more artful than that," Toni said.

Suzanne glanced into the café. "We'll see, okay?" She'd just noticed a new face in the crowd. Well, not completely new, since she'd met the man yesterday. "Toni," she said in a whisper. "Don't look now, but that guy Byron Wolf just walked in and sat down."

Toni spun around like an out-of-control gyroscope. "He did? Where?"

Suzanne grabbed her and cranked her back around. "Table by the window. And don't stare at him. Don't make it so obvious."

"Are you gonna wait on him or do you want me to go over there?" Toni asked.

"I'll take care of him."

"Anytime you want to hand him off to me, that's just fine," Toni said. "Cause that Big Bad Wolf looks like he might be a big-time tipper."

Suzanne grabbed a fresh pot of coffee, pasted a smile on her face, and hustled over to Wolf's table. "Good morning," she said in a cheery voice.

Wolf thumbed something on his iPhone and then glanced up at Suzanne. "You," he said with an almost smile. "The lady entrepreneur."

"Masquerading as your waitress today." Suzanne poured him a cup of coffee and set the pot down on his table. "Have you had a chance to look at the board? Do you know what you'd like?"

Wolf lifted an eyebrow as he continued to gaze at her. "The board?"

"Chalkboard. As in menu?" Suzanne was not unaware

that Wolf was rather good-looking. No wonder Toni was so smitten.

"Why don't you just bring me what's good."

"It's all good," Suzanne said.

Wolf settled back in his chair, a smile playing at his lips. "So bring it all."

Suzanne tapped her pen against her order pad. "How about we whip up a nice mushroom and red pepper omelet for you? With a side of chicken and rice sausage."

"That sounds ridiculously healthy. How about a couple of fried eggs with a rasher of bacon?"

"Up to you."

"Hey," Wolf said. "You're kind of cute, you know that? And I hear you're smart, too."

Suzanne smiled. "Somebody's been spreading nasty rumors about me again."

"I happen to be an excellent judge of character. You have to be when you're in my kind of business."

"The kind of business where you build shopping centers and housing developments?"

Wolf nodded. "That's right, honey. When hundreds of millions of dollars are on the line, commercial real estate development is not for the faint of heart."

"How much money will it cost you to buy the Mullen farm?" Suzanne asked.

"You're very forward with your questions."

"Thank you, I am."

"The thing is," Wolf said, "we're still in negotiations."

"But you didn't waste much time, did you? Mike Mullen has only been dead for forty-eight hours. Of course, you wouldn't know anything about that."

"Say now . . ." His face clouded over.

"What did you promise Claudia, Mr. Wolf?" Suzanne asked. "And is she really and truly a willing seller or did you have to twist her arm?"

"Don't read too much into this, honey. It's just another negotiation."

"What's Mayor Mobley's part in the deal?"

Wolf frowned and his dark eyes bored into her. "What is this? Twenty questions?"

"Just a few friendly questions," Suzanne said. "I'll go put your order in. Honey."

"WHAT'D he say?" Toni asked when Suzanne came into the kitchen.

"Wolf says he's still in negotiations with Claudia."

Standing at the stove, her back to them, Petra shook her head. "I still can't believe Claudia is thinking about selling the farm, just like that."

"Believe it," Suzanne said. "I'm getting the feeling this is really going to happen."

"Claudia could stand to make a bundle," Toni said. "Unless . . ."

Petra turned and cocked an eye at her. "Unless what?"

Toni grimaced. "Unless Claudia whacked her own husband. Then Sheriff Doogie will probably figure out the whole scheme, arrest her, and the poor woman will spend the next twenty years working in the laundry of some crappy women's prison."

"Will you *stop*," Petra hissed. "There's no way Claudia could have harmed Mike. No way at all."

But Toni was unwilling to let it go. "You don't find it strange that, boom, one day Mike is dead, and the next day, howdy do, mister, the farm is on the market?"

"Yes, I find it strange," Petra said. "But I chalk it up to stress and frayed nerves. To Claudia not knowing where to turn or what to do."

"I don't know," Toni said in a singsong voice. "It looks to me as if Claudia knows exactly what to do."

"Why don't we table this discussion for now," Suzanne said. She knew she had to intervene or Toni and Petra would go back and forth all day long. Toni tossing out theories, Petra trying to shoot them down. "Why don't we go to the viewing tonight and . . ."

"Knock knock," a voice at the back door called out.

"Hmm?" Petra said, turning.

Toni flew to the door and yanked it open. "Hey," she said, a smile coloring her voice. "It's Kit. Get in here, girlfriend. Glad you could come by and help."

Kit Kaslik stepped tentatively into the kitchen and paused as Toni gave her a great big bear hug. Even though Kit had once worked at Hoobly's Roadhouse as an exotic dancer, she was a slightly timid girl. She was also twenty-two years old with long blond hair, a sweet face, and a lush figure. And now, since she was five months pregnant, her figure was positively ripe.

"Hey, sweetie," Suzanne said. "Thanks for coming. We really need your help today."

"That's for sure," Toni echoed. "We're gonna be crazy-busy, what with the Yarn Truck and the Knitter's Tea. Petra's already in a huge flutter."

"Am not," Petra said. "I'm just trying to anticipate any problems before they crop up."

"See what I mean?" Toni said.

"How's Ricky?" Petra asked Kit.

"He's good," Kit said. "In fact, he just called me last night from Afghanistan." A hand slid protectively down to her belly.

"Still have plans to get married?" Petra asked with a distracted smile.

"Petra," Suzanne said. There was a warning tone in her voice. Petra was old-fashioned and tended to be a trifle disapproving of single mothers.

"Maybe when Ricky comes home at Christmas," Kit said.

"That would be great," Toni exclaimed. "I just love a Christmas wedding. And we'd for sure throw you a great big baby shower."

"Here? At the Cackleberry Club?" Kit's eyes shone brightly. "That would be fantastic!"

"Ladies," Petra said. "There isn't going to be a Cackleberry Club if you don't get out there and start waiting on tables."

WHILE Toni and Kit hustled out to take orders from the guests that had shown up mid-morning, Suzanne busied herself at the chalkboard. She quickly erased the breakfast menu and started writing out the luncheon menu.

Today was going to be easy. Tomato bisque soup, chicken salad on pumpkin bread, muffuletta sandwiches, and shepherd's pie. With chocolate cupcakes, cherry crumb bars, and pumpkin fudge for dessert.

"Suzanne?"

Suzanne spun around to find Kit looking a little lost. "Yes?"

"Do we carry oolong tea?"

"We sure do, but you're going to have to brew it."

"Can you show me how?"

"Of course." Suzanne took Kit behind the counter and showed her how to warm the teapot with hot water, measure out two scoops of loose leaf tea, add hot water, and then figure out the steeping time.

"This is so cool," Kit said as she watched the leaves twist and dance as they brewed. "But wouldn't tea bags be a whole lot easier?"

"They probably would," Suzanne said. "But a lot of the tea that comes in tea bags is made up of pieces and stems. And tea dust. Loose leaf tea is generally fresher and more flavorful."

"How do you know all this stuff?"

"Trial and error. Lots of error." Suzanne glanced over at

Byron Wolf's table. He was still planted there, apparently conducting a full morning's worth of business. He talked on his phone, scribbled in a little leather notebook, and looked generally important as well as slightly discontent. Was he trying to hammer out a big important deal? Suzanne wondered. Or was something else going on?

She strolled toward his table, where Toni had suddenly materialized to pour him a fifth refill of coffee. Or was it his sixth?

"You've got some big business deals going on, huh?" Toni asked Wolf. She winked and fixed him with a friendly, flirty smile. "I like a man who's a wheeler-dealer. Reminds me of . . ."

"Toni," Suzanne said. "You're needed in the kitchen."

Toni spun around. "Huh? Now?"

Without giving an answer, Suzanne grabbed Toni by the arm and steered her into the kitchen.

"What are you doing?" Suzanne asked once they were out of earshot.

Toni shrugged. "Flirting. Entertaining the customers."

"You've been prancing around the café like Gypsy Rose Lee."

"So what?" Toni said. "Jiggling is just my way of saying hello. And I know the customers enjoy my friendly banter 'cause I get lots of feedback from them." She gave a contented sigh. "And you know what else? I think I'm just beginning to hit the peak of my sexuality. You ladies wouldn't want to deny me that, would you?"

Petra eyed her carefully. "You know that little tingle you feel?"

Toni turned and widened her eyes. "Yeah?"

Petra snorted. "Those are just garden-variety hot flashes."

LATE morning, Sam called Suzanne to see how she was doing.

"I'm going crazy," Suzanne said. "And it isn't even lunch-time yet. The Yarn Truck will be here in three hours and I still haven't had a free moment to think about this after-noon's tea."

"You're telling me it's business as usual?" Sam asked

"That'd be about right." Suzanne paused. "Listen, I'd love to see you tonight."

"Can't," Sam said. "I'm on call at the hospital."

"Oh right, I forgot. And now that I think about it, I was planning to swing by Driesden and Draper Funeral Home for Mike Mullen's visitation."

"We're ships passing in the night."

Suzanne dropped her voice into a conspiratorial tone. "So . . . what did you find out about the autopsy? Or did you find out anything?" She was dying for any drip or drop of news.

"Actually," Sam said, "the autopsy report came across my desk this morning. I guess our good sheriff decided to share."

"Does he usually do that? Include your name on the routing slip?"

"Hardly ever. Maybe he figured this was a sneaky way to pass the information on to you."

"Then maybe you should enlighten me," Suzanne said.

"You're sure you want to know about this one? It's fairly gruesome."

Suzanne sighed. "Lay it on me."

"Okay, let me see," Sam said. "Visiting ME is Dr. Ethan Pope, autopsy of a sixty-one-year-old . . ."

"Just cut to the chase," Suzanne said.

"My, we are eager. Okay. Multiple stab wounds, left side, right side, and the throat. Cuts two to three and one-half inches in length, diagonally oriented. Fresh hemorrhages and bruising along wound paths, estimated depth of penetration two to three inches, perforation to the lungs and abdominal walls . . ."

"So death wasn't exactly instantaneous," Suzanne said. "Mike suffered."

"I'm afraid so."

Suzanne was silent for a few moments and then she said, "When am I going to see you, Sam? I think I need a hug."

"Tomorrow night for sure. I'll circle it in red on my calendar. Or, perhaps even more appropriately, punch it into the calendar on my phone."

"There's a problem," Suzanne said. "Tomorrow's Friday, one of our busiest days. And we're also having our big pizza party in the evening."

"No problem. I'll come by your party, if that's what it takes. Just look for the cute guy hiding behind a big slice of pepperoni."

Suzanne sank against the wall. "That seems like light-years away. I'm missing you right now."

"I've got an idea—let's plan a doubleheader. I'll see you at your pizza party tomorrow night and I'll take you out for a fancy dinner on Saturday night."

"Oh, Sam, I would love that."

"And I love you, my dear."

CHAPTER 11

"I'M about ready to burst with excitement," Petra said. She was ladling tomato bisque into bowls and Suzanne and Kit were standing by, ready to add crackers and a dollop of sour cream and then hustle the entrées out to waiting customers. "Have a lot of knitters shown up for lunch?"

"The café is packed," Kit told her.

"And people are waiting in line for tables," Suzanne said. "You did a fantastic job of marketing."

"All I really did was tell Paula Patterson about the Yarn Truck," Petra said. "And then she started talking it up like crazy on her *Friends and Neighbors* radio show."

"And you did posters," Suzanne said. Petra had created a collage of colorful yarns, photographed everything, added some typography, and printed posters. Those posters had made their way onto the walls of every bakery, craft shop, sewing store, boutique, gift shop, and coffee shop in a thirty-mile radius. Hence, the huge crowd that was already starting to gather in anticipation of the Yarn Truck and their Knitter's Tea.

"I don't know if you noticed," Petra said, "but I stayed late last night to primp the Knitting Nest. I wanted to make sure we were stocked to the rafters with yarn and quilt squares and make sure our craft supplies were displayed to perfection."

"I noticed how great it looked," Suzanne said. "And so have our customers. They've already started shopping—grabbing wicker baskets and piling them full of yarn and knitting needles." She turned to Kit. "After you deliver these luncheon orders, maybe you could hang out in the Knitting Nest for a while. Help customers, ring up orders, that sort of thing."

"I'd like that," Kit said. "It sounds like fun."

"Oh, Suzanne," Petra said. "If you want to display a few knitting and craft books in the Book Nook . . ."

"Already did that."

"You're a step ahead of me then," Petra said.

"Somehow," Suzanne said, "it doesn't feel that way."

"THESE ladies may look like knitters," Toni said to Suzanne, "but they chow down like truck drivers." Toni and Suzanne were standing behind the counter. Toni was brewing two more pots of coffee, slicing a second pan of apple crumb bars, and putting cupcakes on dessert plates. Suzanne was readying three take-out orders.

"Who knew these ladies would show up in droves?" Suzanne said. "And I'm afraid we still have two larger parties waiting for a table." She was relieved that Byron Wolf had finally taken off around eleven.

"Ooh." Toni frowned as a cupcake flew out of her hand and tumbled to the floor. "I'm all fumble fingered. And I keep forgetting to put doilies on the dessert plates."

"Forget the doilies, just try to keep up," Suzanne said as she scooped chicken salad onto six pieces of whole wheat bread.

"Who's the take-out order for?"

"Deputy Driscoll called earlier," Suzanne said. "Said he needed three lunches to go, but didn't specify what he wanted. He was in a big rush."

"Maybe Doogie and his boys are making some progress," Toni said. "Maybe they're hot and heavy on the trail of Mike Mullen's killer."

"We can only hope." Suzanne glanced over her shoulder, said, "Oops, there's one table I can clear," and ran to do exactly that.

When Suzanne had the table for four all wiped down and set up with place mats, silverware, and coffee cups, she hurriedly seated Laura Benchley and the rest of her party. Laura was the editor of the *Bugle*, Kindred's weekly newspaper, and always seemed to have her finger on the pulse of things.

"We've got you hopping today," Laura said as Suzanne filled their water glasses.

"You do and I love it," Suzanne said.

"We can't wait for the Yarn Truck to arrive," one of the ladies said.

"Neither can I," Suzanne said.

FIVE minutes later, Deputy Driscoll came in. He banged open the door and strode halfway across the café before he glanced around. When he saw that the café was occupied entirely by women, he stopped in his tracks and gaped. Then his face turned pimiento red and he hustled over to the counter.

"What's going on here?" Driscoll asked Suzanne. "Some

kind of hen party?" He looked and sounded like he was out of his element. Way out, like on Mars.

Suzanne didn't know Driscoll's marital status, but based on his reaction, decided the man must still be single. "We've got the Yarn Truck rolling in here any minute," she told him.

"Yarn Truck?" Driscoll seemed flummoxed by the concept.

"It's an old bread truck that's been turned into a kind of mobile yarn store," Suzanne explained. "Yarn in a truck. A Yarn Truck."

"Why?" he asked.

"Um, because two enterprising women thought they could make money by selling hand-crafted yarns and driving their Yarn Truck around to fairs, craft shows, and other venues."

"And do they?" Driscoll asked. "Make money, I mean?"

"I'm fairly certain they do."

"Ain't that something."

"Isn't it?" Suzanne said. "I know you're in a hurry, so I have your three lunches all packed up and ready to go."

Driscoll finally showed some real interest. "What'd you come up with?"

"Chicken salad sandwiches, kettle chips, and chocolate cupcakes. All stuff that travels well."

"Sounds real good."

"You want me to put this on your tab?" What she really meant was the Law Enforcement Center's tab, since Doogie never paid for anything personally.

"That'd be great, Suzanne. Thanks."

"I take it Sheriff Doogie has all of you hopping like crazy?"

"He sure has. He's even deputized a couple of reserve guys."

"Wow. So the investigation is moving right along?"

Driscoll's hat dipped forward as he bobbed his head. "We're doing our best."

"You're looking at a number of suspects? Interviewing them?"

"Quite a few."

"Do you know," Suzanne asked, "if Doogie intends to question Byron Wolf?"

"That real estate developer? The one who's trying to buy the Mullen farm?"

"That's the guy." *And that's the tip I gave him*, she thought.

"Um . . . yes he is," Driscoll said. "Wolf and a couple of other people."

"Like who?" Suzanne knew she was pushing him and didn't care.

"I really shouldn't say," Driscoll mumbled.

"I understand completely. On the other hand, I'm already involved in the investigation. Don't forget, I'm the one who found Mike in his barn."

Driscoll made a face. "I know. And it was awful."

"It was. So I'm just wondering . . ." Suzanne let her sentence trail off.

Driscoll took a step closer and placed his hands flat on the counter. "Well, I know for a fact that Sheriff Doogie *is* investigating Claudia."

"Isn't that fairly pro forma?" Suzanne asked. "In the case of a murder, doesn't the spouse always get investigated?"

"Pretty much."

"And you're also looking at . . . ?" Suzanne gave an encouraging smile.

"That neighbor kid. Noah Jorgenson."

"I thought Doogie already talked to Noah and pretty much dismissed him," Suzanne said.

Driscoll gave a quick glance over his shoulder and dropped his voice. "Now the sheriff's circling back around," he said. "I don't know if he's got new information or if he just wants to be real thorough."

Suzanne handed over the bag of take-out orders. "Interesting."

TONI burst into the kitchen, a silly grin on her face, her fluff of fake hair bouncing like mad. "It's here! The Yarn Truck is here! They just pulled into the front parking lot and tooted their horn."

Petra threw down her ladle, ripped off her apron, and flew through the swinging door. "Hot dog!" she cried, leaving Suzanne and Toni in her wake.

Toni blinked. "I guess Petra wants to be their first customer."

But Petra wasn't the only one who was all fired up. With the appearance of the Yarn Truck, the café pretty much emptied out in one fell swoop. Their customers tossed their napkins down, jumped up from their seats, and rushed out the door. It seemed that everyone was delirious to have a look.

"This is actually kind of cool," Toni said. She and Suzanne had followed the crowd outside—trailing the stampede, really—and were gazing with keen interest at the Yarn Truck. In an earlier incarnation, the truck had served as a delivery vehicle for Red Deer Bread. Now the little dancing fawn had been painted over with a coat of mauve paint. The words Yarn Truck bounced across its side panel in bright red letters accompanied by cartoon illustrations of skeins of yarn, knitting needles, and fluffy frolicking sheep.

The truck, which had just jockeyed into position, gave a jerk and a shudder, and then a loud belch issued from its tailpipe. A side door slid open and a set of wooden steps rolled out as the crowd moved closer. Then a frizzy-haired woman in a pink-and-saffron-colored knit poncho leaned out and grinned. "What are you ladies waiting for?" she called out.

That was the encouragement everyone needed. Suddenly,

the rush was on. A line formed immediately as all the women began crowding into the truck. Even standing at the back of the pack, Suzanne could hear their chirps of excitement.

Suzanne saw the woman in the poncho looking around, so she hurried over to greet her. "You're Lonnie?" she asked. Lonnie was in her early fifties with warm brown eyes, a gap-toothed grin, and multiple ear piercings.

Lonnie grinned. "That's me." She gestured over her shoulder. "Linda, my partner in crime and driver extraordinaire, is still in the truck."

Suzanne quickly introduced herself and Toni and said, "We're so thrilled you could make it."

"Happy we could add you to our route," Lonnie said.

"Do you actually have a regular route?" Toni asked.

"We hit as many of the art fairs as we can in July and August," Lonnie said. "When autumn rolls around we start visiting different knitting and needlecraft shops, as well as a few places like yours."

"And then what?" Toni asked.

"Then we go home and die," Lonnie laughed. "No, seriously, then we put the truck in storage for the winter and work at selling our yarns online."

"And that's all you sell?" Toni asked. "Yarn?"

"Pretty much," Lonnie said. "Why don't you come in and have a look?"

"Absolutely," Toni said.

Curious now, Suzanne and Toni crowded into the truck to see what the fuss was all about. And, just as advertised, the inside had been magically transformed into a lovely yarn store. Floor-to-ceiling wooden cubbyholes were stuffed with skeins of yarn. Balls of yarn were artfully mounded in large wicker baskets. Overhead, skeins of yarn shimmered in the light as they dangled from the ceiling like bunches of grapes at an outdoor restaurant.

"This is so neat," Toni said as she looked around, practically transported.

Petra saw Suzanne and Toni enter the truck and quickly pushed her way to meet them, an enormous smile lighting her face.

"Can you believe this?" Petra gushed. "They only carry artisanal yarns. Everything they sell here is spun by hand." She clasped her hands together. "This is just . . . amazing. I feel like a kid in a candy store."

Toni fingered a skein of merino wool. "This is kitty-cat soft. What's it made out of?"

"That's high-quality merino wool," Petra said. "But just look around—they also have yarn spun from alpacas and yaks, as well as brushed mohair. And there are yarns from plant fibers, too, like organic cotton, China grass, linen, and bamboo."

"Fabulous," Suzanne said. "It's even better than I imagined." She was particularly struck by the colors of the yarns. They were subtle and pleasing to the eye. There were no gaudy reds, yellows, and greens like you'd see in a dime store craft section. Rather, these yarns were elegant shades of fawn, terra-cotta, primrose, saffron, celadon, and indigo. These were genteel, exotic colors that hinted at captivating sunsets, emerald forests, and mystical places.

"I think I might have to take up knitting," Toni said.

"You should," Petra said. "It's very relaxing. And it would be a good antidote to Junior."

"Good for my wardrobe, too," Toni said. "I mean, who couldn't use a few more sweaters and ponchos?"

"You might want to start with something easy," Suzanne advised. "Maybe a scarf or a pot holder?"

"What I need is this brushed mohair," Toni said. She fingered a skein of ultrasoft yarn. "Or maybe this thick, ropy-looking yarn. It's got some real heft to it."

"Better grab it now," Suzanne said. "Before somebody else wants it."

"You think this yarn would be easy to work with? For a beginner?"

"I don't know. Let's ask Petra."

Petra had moved to the front of the truck, where she was fingering a skein of beaded silk yarn and talking to a woman with a narrow face and long gray hair that streamed all the way down her back. In her nubby sweater and longer skirt, the woman reminded Suzanne of an earth mother type.

"Hang on a minute," Suzanne told Toni, "while I grab our resident expert." She moved through the truck, trying not to jostle too many people, trying not to get squished herself. She was just about to tap Petra on the shoulder and break into her conversation when Petra said, "I think you're right, Faith Anne, that alpaca yarn would make a gorgeous sweater."

What? Suzanne was suddenly jolted from the top of her head all the way down to her painted pink toes. This woman's name was Faith Anne? Was Petra talking to Faith Anne Jorgenson? The mother of the mysterious Noah?

"Excuse me," Suzanne said. And now she really did break into their conversation. "Are you Faith Anne Jorgenson?"

Faith Anne turned toward Suzanne, a look of curiosity on her slightly careworn face. "Yes?" she said.

"You're Noah's mother?" Suzanne asked.

Faith Anne seemed to shrink away from her. "Why do you want to know?" she asked. She looked apprehensive and her tone of voice was decidedly frosty.

"Because I think I saw your son," Suzanne said. "On . . ." There was no subtle way to put it. "On the day that Mike Mullen was murdered."

A look of fear washed across Faith Anne's face, utterly

transforming it. Her eyes turned hard and her mouth suddenly pulled into a grim horizontal slash. "No!" she cried, and promptly dropped the two skeins of yarn she'd been holding. Then she slid away, practically clawing her way through the crowd, pushing and shoving, trying to squeeze her way out the door. As if her life depended on it.

CHAPTER 12

SUZANNE caught up with Faith Anne in the parking lot, just as Faith Anne yanked open her car door and tried to hurl herself inside.

"Wait!" Suzanne called. "Please wait. I just want to *talk* to you."

Faith Anne whirled around to face her. She brought her hands up in front of her, palms facing forward, as if she meant to physically push Suzanne away. "We've answered enough questions!" Her eyes glistened like a pair of hard marbles.

"You mean questions from Sheriff Doogie?" Suzanne asked.

"Yes," Faith Anne spat out. "He came charging in and invaded the sanctity of our home. Scared us half to death. My son, Noah, was extremely upset by his actions. I'm not sure when he'll recover from the trauma."

From what Doogie had told her, Suzanne figured Faith Anne was the one who was traumatized, not Noah. But she decided not to belabor the point. Instead she said, "I'd really like to meet Noah sometime."

"Why would you want to do that?" Faith Anne snapped.

Suzanne decided to take a chance. "Like I told you, I think I saw Noah standing in the woods that Tuesday morning."

"Excuse me, but I'm sure you were quite mistaken."

Suzanne forged ahead. "It was actually just a few minutes after I discovered Mike Mullen's body in his barn. I was outside, feeling quite upset, as you might imagine, and happened to glance off toward the woods. And I'm pretty sure I saw someone standing there. At first I thought it was a scarecrow, and then I realized it was probably a person." Of course, Suzanne thought, it could have been the killer that she'd glimpsed.

"And you want to ask Noah about *that*?" Faith Anne screeched. "No. Absolutely not."

"Faith Anne, your son might have witnessed something very important that day. Something critical to the murder investigation. If you let me talk to him, I promise I'll be a whole lot more gentle than Sheriff Doogie was."

"You're the one who put the sheriff after us, aren't you?" Faith Anne sneered. "You tried to turn our lives upside down with all your nasty innuendos and accusations."

Suzanne wanted to tell her that Claudia Mullen was probably the one who'd convinced Doogie to take a hard look at Noah, but she didn't. Instead, she said, "Mike was your next-door neighbor, Mrs. Sorenson. Don't you want to see his killer apprehended? And if the killer's still out there—and the sheriff seems to think he is—then aren't you worried about your own safety? Your son's safety?"

"Just . . . just leave us alone," Faith Anne cried. She clambered into her car and slammed the door. Fumbling to jam her keys into the ignition, she stared straight ahead, refusing to glance Suzanne's way.

"Okay then," Suzanne said, stepping away from the car.

Moments later, Faith Anne revved her car's engine, threw

it in gear, and fishtailed her way out of the parking lot, almost clipping the fender of a white Jeep.

"Another satisfied customer?" Toni asked.

Suzanne turned to find Toni and Petra strolling up behind her. They both carried brown paper bags stuffed with yarn. She gestured toward the puffs of dust that Faith Anne had left in her wake. "That was Faith Anne leaving early. She completely freaked out when I tried to talk to her."

"Maybe you shouldn't have tried to talk to her," Petra said.

"Excuse me, but why were *you* talking to her?" Suzanne asked. "You know her son is a suspect in Mike's murder."

"Well, I was just being friendly," Petra said. "But it looks like you scared her half to death."

"I didn't mean to," Suzanne said. "I just wanted to have a . . . a conversation."

"I think what we have here," Toni said, "is a failure to communicate."

FIVE minutes later, Suzanne, Toni, and Petra made hard work look like an afternoon nap. While Petra scurried into the kitchen to work on her tea sandwiches and scones, Suzanne, Toni, and Kit cleared tables and then pulled out their best tablecloths and dishes for their Knitter's Tea.

Suzanne chose cream-colored lace tablecloths and napkins to set the tone and color palette of their tables and then added white milk glass pitchers filled with bright orange marigolds for centerpieces.

"Which set of dishes do you want to use?" Kit asked. She was gazing into an antique cabinet that held dishes as well as a rather extensive collection of teapots.

"Let's put out the Shelley Chintz," Suzanne said. "And the pewter silverware."

"Sounds perfect," Kit said. "Elegant."

"And we need those little glass dishes for the Devonshire cream," Toni reminded them. "And for candles, let's use those honey-colored beeswax candles."

They all worked for another twenty minutes. Then they paused in a collective break to study their handiwork.

"Everything's glowing," Kit said. She sounded a little bit in awe.

The café did look magical, Suzanne decided. Crystal glassware sparkled in the candlelight, sunbeams streamed through the windows and danced across the cups and saucers, the flowers seemed to bob their shaggy heads in approval.

Toni grinned. "We did good. This looks like a picture out of a magazine. The *Tea House Times* or *TeaTime*."

"Which is exactly what we were aiming for," Suzanne said, pride evident in her voice.

Even Petra popped her head out the kitchen door and said, "Holy moley, ladies, it looks like a Stratford-on-Avon tea shop was just plopped down in the middle of Kindred."

"Thank you," Suzanne said.

Toni held up an index finger. "We can't forget the place cards. Suzanne? Are they ready to go?"

Suzanne took the place cards she'd already hand-lettered according to her reservation list and began plopping them down on the tables, making quick, intuitive decisions about where to seat each of their various guests.

"Uh-oh," Toni said suddenly, her voice almost catching in her throat.

Suzanne straightened up. "What?"

Toni jerked her head toward the front door, where Sheriff Doogie stood outside. He was peering in, his face mashed hard against the window.

Suzanne rolled her eyes. "Somebody must have spilled the beans about our Knitter's Tea," she said under her breath. "He's probably here to cadge a scone or two."

"I guess we have to let him in," Toni sighed. "And grab some Windex so we can wipe off those smudges."

Suzanne hurried to the front door and pulled it open. "What brings you out this afternoon?" she asked with a smile. She wondered if there'd been a break in the case. Hoped there was, anyway.

Doogie removed his hat and combed his fingers through his barely there hair. "I've been thinking . . ."

"Now *that's* what I like to hear," Toni called out. "A man with a working brain that can actually formulate an idea."

Doogie narrowed his eyes. "Don't you and your smart mouth have something better to do?"

Toni shrugged. "I guess."

"Can I get you a cup of coffee, Sheriff?" Suzanne asked, stepping in to defuse the situation, wondering if her role was always going to be that of peacemaker.

"No thanks," Doogie said. "I don't have time. But I do have a sort of message to deliver."

"Yes?"

"I just got a call from Faith Anne Jorgenson."

"She was just here," Suzanne said. *And I'm guessing she wasted no time in calling you and making a big fat stink.*

"So I understand," Doogie said. "She told me she was at that yarn thing you got going outside."

"Is there a problem?" Suzanne asked. *Are you suspicious of her? Are you thinking that she might have been the one who killed Mike?*

Doogie frowned. "Faith Anne was real upset. She says you harassed her and spooked her."

"She actually said that?" Suzanne said mildly.

"It's obvious you must have exchanged a few words with her," Doogie said. "Asked her about her son, Noah, I guess."

"I did indeed."

Once the topic of Suzanne's conversation had been confirmed, Doogie switched over to being more than a little interested. "Well," he demanded. "What'd you find out?"

"Not a whole lot. Just as you saw with your interview, Faith Anne is extremely protective of her son."

"No kidding. She tells me that Noah has a hard time processing new and unusual happenings in his life. Says he's got Asperger's." Doogie paused. "She even accused *me* of upsetting him the other day." Doogie seemed to consider this. "I didn't mean to interrogate the boy, I just wanted to ask a few questions. But I guess maybe I frightened him."

"So she says," Suzanne said.

"Yeah," Doogie said. "Faith Anne acts so strange and skittish, I don't know what to believe."

"But you think something's going on."

Doogie pulled a toothpick from his shirt pocket and stuck it in the side of his mouth. "It sure feels like some sort of undercurrent. That one of them knows something but doesn't want to talk about it."

"About the murder," Suzanne said.

Doogie's eyes took on a hard glint. "Accessory to a crime is nothing to fool around with. Warrants can be issued, people can be brought in for questioning." He adjusted his gun belt. "It's my right as duly elected sheriff."

"I agree completely," Suzanne said. She glanced across the room where Toni and Kit were starting to make googly eyes at her. It was nearing three o'clock and the café still needed a few finishing touches. Suzanne decided to cut this conversation short. "Doogie, we have a tea party starting in just a few minutes, so why don't I stop by your office later today. If we put our heads together maybe we can come up with some kind of plan."

"No," Doogie said. "That's a terrible idea. The whole town already thinks you're on the payroll."

"They do?" Suzanne smiled. "As an unpaid deputy?"

Doogie looked uncomfortable.

"A consultant?"

"Maybe coming here was a bad idea," Doogie said, edging his way toward the door. "Maybe I shouldn't be talking to you at all."

"Too late now," Suzanne called after him.

THREE o'clock came with a *bing bang bong* of the old railroad clock that hung on the wall. Then the door flew open and Lolly Herron, one of their regulars, came bounding in, followed by Jenny and Bill Probst, who owned the Kindred Bakery.

"Look how beautiful this is," Jenny exclaimed, tugging at Bill's arm. "I hope you don't mind, Suzanne, but I brought my hubby along to show him what he's been missing as far as a genteel tea party goes."

"Happy to have him," Suzanne said. "Delighted to welcome everyone."

The Yarn Truck ladies, Lonnie and Linda, followed, as well as another thirty or so guests. Suzanne was frantically busy for the next ten minutes, seating guests, jockeying place settings around to accommodate Bill, exclaiming over old acquaintances. Finally, when everyone was seated and looking about expectantly, she stepped into the center of the room.

"Welcome, everyone," Suzanne said. "We're delighted to have you at our Knitter's Tea." She winked at Lonnie and Linda and said, "And thank you all so much for making the Yarn Truck's first visit to the Cackleberry Club such a rousing success."

"Hear! Hear!" Lonnie said with a grin.

Suzanne continued. "Today we'll be serving your choice of peach oolong tea or Lapsang souchong, a Chinese black tea with a slightly smoky flavor."

That was the cue for Toni and Kit to appear with steaming pots of tea and begin filling their guests' teacups.

"So choose your poison," Suzanne said. "And then get ready for a delicious first course of pumpkin soup served with crostini spread with goat cheese." She paused. "Your second course will be an apple cinnamon scone served with Devonshire cream, and your final course consists of a three-tiered tea tray laden with three different varieties of tea sandwiches. Chicken salad on cinnamon bread, ham spread on rye, and roast beef with cheddar cheese on hearty potato bread. On the bottom tier of the tray you'll find honey-custard tartlets for dessert."

From there they were off and running. Suzanne, Toni, and Kit made the rounds with fresh pots of tea, then chatted with guests, served the soup, cleared bowls, and then served the fresh-baked scones. Classical music wafted from the sound system and a lovely hum of conversation filled the room. And when the three-tiered tea trays were brought out (looking spectacular and adorned with edible purple flowers!) and presented to each table, there was enthusiastic applause. Even a reluctant Petra was coaxed out from the kitchen to take a bow. For a while, Suzanne could almost forget the hard fact that she'd practically witnessed a murder two days ago.

As late afternoon approached and the shadows outside began to lengthen, the guests drifted into the Knitting Nest, where Kit was once again holding down the fort. And then, finally, they drifted back out to the Yarn Truck.

Which gave Suzanne, Toni, and Petra a sort of breather. Dishes still had to be cleared and washed, the kitchen needed to be tidied up.

"I guess we're still going to Mike Mullen's wake tonight, huh?" Toni asked as she popped a leftover tea sandwich into her mouth.

"We said we'd go," Suzanne said. "And it's probably the neighborly thing to do."

Toni wrinkled her nose. "Ugh."

"Say now," Petra said. "That better not be commentary on my tea sandwich."

"It's not," Toni said, still munching. "Like I said before, I just hate anything to do with dead bodies."

I'm not particularly fond of dead bodies either, Suzanne thought to herself. But, instead of articulating her feelings on that particular subject, she said instead, "Are we going to be ready for tomorrow night's pizza party?"

"Just as soon as we scrape all the crumbs off the floor," Toni said.

"It's that bad?" Petra asked.

Toni shrugged. "Aw, things are a little cattywampus. But nothing that can't be fixed."

"When will you make the pizza dough?" Suzanne asked Petra.

"First thing tomorrow," Petra said. "I'll mix up a huge batch and let it sit."

"Let it toughen up," Toni said.

Petra swatted her with a pot holder. "Stop it, you. That dough's going to be nice and flavorful and mildly chewy. But definitely not tough."

"Think we're going to get a big crowd?" Toni asked.

"I'd say we're going to be jammed," Suzanne said.

"More than today?" Toni asked.

"A whole lot more," Suzanne said. "Friday night pizza is a pretty big deal in these parts. And today's *Bugle* gave us a nice write-up in their What's Happening section. So what do you think's gonna happen?"

"I guess we'll be mobbed," Toni said. She pulled a scone pan across the counter, stuck two fingers in, and helped herself to leftovers, which were basically nothing more than crumbs.

"Tell me you're not eating those," Suzanne said.

"Oops," Toni said. "I guess not." She dumped the crumbs into a brown paper bag. "For the birds. I know how much Petra loves to feed the birds."

"Now I know who to blame for my dirty windshield," Suzanne said.

"Blame away," Petra said as she sank onto a nearby stool. "But hold off until tomorrow. As of right now I'm going to put an Out of Order sticker on my forehead and call it a day."

CHAPTER 13

DRIESDEN and Draper Funeral Home looked imposing any time of year. But four days before Halloween, the place looked like the Addams Family was having an open house. A very spooky open house.

A misty fog had burbled up and now served as a scrim to dampen the glow from the streetlamps and soften the outline of the funeral home's peaked roof, riot of finials, balustrades, and corner turret.

"I don't like this one bit," Toni murmured as they approached the large wooden front door with its brass lion's head door knocker.

"Neither do I," Suzanne said. To her, the Gothic-shaped windows, with light faintly shining through, looked like old-fashioned coffins standing on end.

Inside the funeral home, two ushers were dressed for both the season and the occasion. With their downturned mouths, dull black suits, and spit-polished shoes, the men wore their titles of undertaker/usher like badges of honor.

Suzanne decided that when things were bad, business was probably good.

"This place gives me the heebie-jeebies," Toni said, gripping Suzanne's arms as if she thought her friend would protect her. "It looks like the movie set in *Paranormal Activity 3*."

"Shhh," Suzanne whispered as they stepped up to a podium to sign their names in a black leather guest book. The floorboards let out an awful creak (was it just the damp weather?) and they both flinched.

"That sounded suspiciously like a casket swinging open," Toni said.

"Try not to think about it," Suzanne said.

They gazed around the Victorian-style lobby with its maroon velvet chairs and settee, faux walnut trim, dark floral wallpaper, spindly tables, and abundance of plastic plants. Funeral music moaned from scattered speakers and Kleenex boxes were perched everywhere. The faint smell of chemicals permeated the air and mingled with the scent of fresh flowers.

"Cozy, isn't it?" Suzanne joked.

"It's not exactly where I'd want to kick back and enjoy a bottle of chardonnay," Toni whispered back.

George Draper, the funeral director and namesake of Driesden and Draper, came to greet them. He was tall and slightly stooped with a sad, hangdog face. Draper reached out and took Suzanne's hand in his. "Suzanne. Welcome. You're here for the Mullen visitation?"

"Yes," Suzanne said.

"Toni." Draper tilted his head in a cool hello.

"Howdy," Toni said. She was fidgeting like mad, clearly nervous about the whole situation.

"Mr. Mullen is resting in Slumber Room A," Draper intoned in a deep voice. He lifted a hand that looked pale and ethereal in the low light of the entryway and pointed. "Directly to your left."

"Thank you," Suzanne said as Draper faded away to greet another gaggle of mourners.

Toni's head practically spun around. "Did you hear what he said? That Mike was *resting?*"

"What's he supposed to say?" Suzanne asked. "That he's dead as a doornail?"

"I don't know. Maybe something like 'He's chilling out in Slumber Room A.'"

"It's a visitation, Toni, not a Coldplay concert."

They walked slowly into Slumber Room A.

Toni touched a hand to her chest and said, "Whew. Closed casket."

"Happy now?" Suzanne asked. "No dead bodies? No pennies on the eyes?"

"As happy as I can be in a funeral home, yeah."

"Come on," Suzanne said. "Let's go up there and say a little prayer. Light a candle or something."

"If you insist."

They slipped quietly up to the casket, bowed their heads, and stared down at the mahogany box for what Suzanne figured was the requisite minute and a half. Then they edged away from it.

"There's Claudia," Suzanne said. Claudia Mullen was standing next to a purple velvet love seat, dabbing a hankie to her eyes. There was a sort of receiving line stretching out in front of her. "We should go and say something to her."

"Like what?" Toni asked.

"How about 'I'm sorry.'"

"Oh. Okay."

They got in line and shuffled ahead slowly. When they were finally in front of Claudia, Toni stuck out her hand like a gawky child. "I'm sorry," she said.

Claudia was far more gracious. "Thank you. Thank you both for coming tonight." She snuffled loudly and dabbed at her eyes yet again.

"You have our deepest sympathies," Suzanne said.

Claudia took Suzanne's hand. "You're very kind, Suzanne. And I'm so sorry that you were the one who . . ." A tiny sob escaped her lips.

"Sorry, so sorry," Toni said again as they shuffled past.

When they were a good ten feet away, well out of earshot, Suzanne said, "Well, that was perfectly awful."

"Do you still think Claudia got up the guts to kill her own husband?" Toni asked.

"Judging from the way she's acting tonight, it feels like a long shot," Suzanne said. "She seems to be genuinely grieving."

"Unless she's a really terrific actress. You know, like Meryl Streep caliber."

"There's always that," Suzanne said. She was scanning the room, searching for Petra. "Do you see Petra anywhere?"

"Not yet. But I do see Sheriff Doogie prowling through the crowd. And he's got his trusty sidekick, Deputy Driscoll, with him."

"The Lone Ranger and Tonto," Suzanne said as she eyeballed Doogie. He was clearly there for investigative purposes only, since he was scanning the crowd like a hungry lion might study a herd of zebras. His sharp eyes bounced from one person to another, obviously trying to discern the killer in the crowd. Driscoll was doing the same.

"Get a load of Deputy Driscoll," Toni said. "If anybody looks remotely guilty, he's liable to draw his gun, fumble it, and shoot out all the lights in the chandelier."

"Law enforcement," Suzanne said. "Ya gotta love 'em."

"Do you think the person who killed Mike *might* be here?" Toni asked. The notion seemed to both thrill and repulse her.

"I don't know. He might be. He could be." Suzanne perused the room herself. It was crowded and filling up even more as people continued to pour in. She saw townspeople, business owners, and several people that she knew attended Mike Mullen's church. There were also people from the Rotary club, the Jaycees, and two farmers, Todd Lansky and Mark Schoemer, who lived out on Highway 86, several miles past the Mullen farm.

"Just think," Toni said breathlessly, "the killer could be right here in this very room."

If the killer was here, Suzanne wondered if he would be easy to spot. Would he look guilt-ridden? Would he assume a sad countenance? Then she considered the sheer brutality of the crime. No, he probably wouldn't be easy to spot at all. Anybody who could murder a man in cold blood like that was one cool character. A stone-cold killer.

Toni gave her a nudge. "Take a look at who just showed up."

Byron Wolf had just sauntered into Slumber Room A, looking like he'd strolled into a private country club to enjoy a good cigar and a snifter of twenty-year-old cognac. In other words, the man looked both relaxed and entitled.

"That's still one good-looking man," Toni growled.

"And look where he's headed," Suzanne said.

Wolf made no pretense of even glancing at Mike Mullen's coffin. Instead, he headed straight for Claudia and embraced her gently. She smiled at him and, as he whispered something in her ear, nodded vigorously. Suzanne wondered if she was acknowledging his condolences or if they were sharing a private moment.

"What do you think is going on over there?" Toni asked.

"I don't know," Suzanne said. "Maybe they're working out the final details of their real estate deal?"

"You think?"

Suzanne continued to watch the two of them. "Now they're sitting down together and he's acting very solicitous."

"So they could be coconspirators," Toni said.

"I suppose." The idea was repellent to Suzanne, but she

knew it was a possibility. She took a step back, the better to keep an eye on Claudia and Byron Wolf, and practically fell into the arms of Todd Lansky.

"Whoa," Lansky said as Suzanne stumbled, realized her mistake, and caught herself. "You okay?" Lansky was tall and lean, dressed in a freshly pressed red and yellow plaid shirt and olive drab slacks.

"Yes, sorry," she said, turning to face him. "I wasn't looking where I was going."

Lansky gave her a sad smile that seemed to emphasize the prominence of his cheekbones. "That's okay. I've been noticing those two over there myself. And I have to say there's no way I'd ever trust a guy like Wolf."

"You know who he is?" Suzanne asked, suddenly curious.

Lansky seemed to consider his words carefully. "He's a real estate developer, so he's kind of at odds with a farmer like me who wants to preserve and protect the land. And—this is just my personal opinion based on a bunch of jacked-up hearsay—Wolf strikes me as kind of a carpetbagger type. He breezes into town with his swagger and fancy car, trying to ingratiate himself, when all he's really got on his agenda is to make a shitload of money." He glanced down shyly at his well-worn brown boots. "I think our community can do better than a guy like him."

BECAUSE Toni had wandered off somewhere, Suzanne decided to circle back and talk to Claudia Mullen again. Byron Wolf was no longer bending her ear and Claudia was looking a little lost.

"Claudia," Suzanne said. "How are you doing? Really?"

"Terrible," Claudia said. "This whole thing—Mike's murder—has finally hit me like a ton of bricks. At first I thought I could handle it." She swallowed hard. "Like when you stopped by yesterday, I probably acted like I was all pulled together. But in reality I was just plain numb. And now, a day later, everything feels completely overwhelming." Tears pooled in the corners of her red-rimmed eyes. "I've got the funeral tomorrow, trying to deal with the dairy herd . . ."

"I thought Mike's brother, Dan, was going to come over and take care of the cows . . . do the milking and all."

"He is and I'm incredibly grateful to him, but he can't do it indefinitely. And it's awfully late in the season to ship all that livestock to auction, the cows, those horses . . ."

"Horses?" Suzanne said. Then she remembered. Oh yes, she had seen a couple of horses in Mike's barn.

Claudia made an unhappy face. "Mike bought a couple horses from one of our neighbors. Something about saving them from a bad end . . . I don't know. He was always trying to do the right thing, be the good guy. And look where it got him." Tears rolled down Claudia's face. "My poor Mike. He let some crazy person get the drop on him . . ."

Suzanne put her arms around Claudia and hugged her tight. But at the same time . . . she wondered about the horses in Mullen's barn.

George Draper was suddenly there, whispering to Claudia, offering his professional brand of comfort. Suzanne let him take over. Surely he knew what was best for the bereaved. Besides, Toni was waving frantically at her.

"What?" Suzanne asked once she'd slipped down a row of folding chairs and joined Toni.

"We should take off. I've hit my creep load."

"Did Petra ever make it?"

"Yes," Toni said. "She's sitting over there with some folks from her church. I think they're having some kind of prayer circle."

"Let's go light a candle," Suzanne said. "And then we'll go."

But before they could make their way to the wrought iron stand where white votive lights flickered like tiny beacons, there was an unexpected arrival.

"What the . . . ?" Suzanne couldn't finish her sentence because her jaw literally dropped.

Faith Anne Jorgenson suddenly swished her way into the room. Dressed head to toe in a nubby black sweater and long skirt, her hair pulled tightly against her head, she looked like a Sicilian widow. Following in her footsteps was a teenage boy. He had a pale face with rosy cheeks, bright blue eyes, dark slicked-back hair, and he walked with a kind of herky-jerky gait. Although that could have been because he was following so closely on his mother's heels and carrying a bulky violin case.

"Holy guacamole," Toni whispered. "You see that kid? I think that's Noah Jorgenson."

Suzanne peered at Noah expectantly. So this was the much-talked-about but rarely seen Noah. He looked much more normal than she thought he would. In fact, he looked like any ordinary sixteen-year-old kid, albeit one who'd been coddled and secreted away by his mother.

"What do you think is going on?" Toni murmured.

Everyone else seemed to be wondering the same thing. The hum of conversation died to a low buzz, chairs creaked, eyes were suddenly riveted on Faith Anne and Noah. A sense of anticipation seemed to burn through the room.

Faith Anne smiled serenely as Noah placed his violin case on a folding chair and clicked it open. Then carefully, almost reverently, he removed the violin and bow.

Was he going to give a concert? Suzanne wondered.

Noah certainly was. Once he had his violin carefully positioned on his shoulder and his bow held lightly in his right hand, he nodded to himself once and began to play.

With eyes half closed, Noah played a violin rendition of Eric Clapton's "Tears in Heaven." The notes were pure and haunting as they poured out, building with assurance as Noah continued to play.

Suzanne swayed slightly, hearing the words in her head. *Would you know my name, if I saw you in Heaven . . .*

Everyone in the room listened with complete and rapt attention. Except for the violin's sweeping notes, you could have heard a pin drop.

I must be strong and carry on . . .

Each note was sweet and sure and emotionally charged. Eyes filled with tears, men cleared their throats, nobody moved a muscle.

When the final haunting note died in the air, there was a long moment of silence, and then a wave of thunderous applause.

"That was amazing," Toni exclaimed.

"Just incredible," Suzanne agreed.

But Noah wasn't sticking around for any compliments or attention. He quickly packed up his violin and doggedly followed his mother out of the room.

"I want to talk to him," Suzanne said. She spun away from Toni and pushed her way through the crowd. She spotted Noah's head bobbing just ahead of her. Ducking into the foyer, she looked around. But Faith Anne and Noah were already out the front door.

"Wait!" Suzanne cried as she scrambled after them. "Noah!"

Outside on the sidewalk, Noah heard his name being called. He hesitated for a moment and then stopped in his tracks.

"Excuse me, excuse me," Suzanne called as she rushed up to him.

Faith Anne spun around and came at her like an avenging angel. "Go away," she said in an icy tone. "Leave us alone."

CHAPTER 14

SUZANNE ignored her. "Noah," she said. "That was just wonderful. You have an amazing talent. I hope you noticed there wasn't a dry eye in the house."

In the faint glimmer of a streetlamp a crooked smile appeared on Noah's face.

"Are you not hearing me?" Faith Anne snarled. "I said, get away from us."

"Wait, please," Suzanne said. She focused all her attention on Noah. "Noah, I'm Suzanne Dietz from the Cackleberry Club. I'm sure you've heard of me. And I'm pretty sure you know my dear friend Petra, who goes to your church."

"This is so not happening," Faith Anne said.

"And I think you and I kind of know each other," Suzanne continued.

Noah stared at her, a question dancing in his eyes.

"I'm pretty sure I saw you the other day, standing in the pasture. And I wanted to ask you about that because it's really important."

But Faith Anne would have none of it. "Get in the car, Noah," she ordered in a no-nonsense voice. And Noah, looking back over his shoulder at Suzanne, was forced to comply.

"THAT'S one weird kid," Toni said as they headed for Suzanne's car.

"I feel sorry for Noah," Suzanne said. "His mother seems to dominate his life. From what I understand, he's being homeschooled so he hardly ever gets to socialize with kids his own age."

"You think attending a regular school would be better for him?"

"I don't know, but it seems like it would be worth finding out. He's got no peer group to relate to and his mother always comes across as overly protective."

Footsteps scraped loudly on the sidewalk and Suzanne and Toni froze, both of them suddenly feeling nervous and unprotected in the darkness and shifting fog. But it was just Sheriff Doogie coming up behind them.

Suzanne touched a hand to her chest. "Oh, it's you." She exhaled slowly as she got in her car.

"Yeah, it's me," Doogie said. As Toni dropped into the passenger seat, he leaned in and said, "You ask me, I think that kid knows more than he lets on."

"You mean Noah?" Suzanne asked.

Doogie nodded.

"What if Noah saw what happened to Mike?" Toni asked. "What if he was hiding somewhere nearby and saw the attack . . . the murder?"

"And now he's too traumatized to talk," Suzanne said. "To tell anyone about it."

"Maybe," Doogie said, a harshness coloring his voice. "That's why I plan to question Noah again."

"Good," Suzanne said. "Glad to hear it." She continued, "But the thing that struck me as incredibly odd tonight is why Claudia allowed Noah to play his violin when she claims to be terrified of him?"

"I just asked Claudia about that," Doogie said. "She told me that Noah called her up this afternoon and asked if he could come to the funeral home and play his song. He said that Mike had always been his special friend. Claudia said the kid sounded so upset she just couldn't say no."

"Interesting," Suzanne said.

"Yeah, interesting," Doogie echoed. "One more dang thing to try and make sense of. Ah well." He slapped his hand down hard on the top of the car and said, "You ladies take care. Drive safe on your way home." And then he was gone, melted into the darkness.

Toni closed the car door and pulled her seat belt across. "Whew, right now I'm way too pooped to worry about everything that's going on. I can't wait to jump into my jammies and sink into a soft mattress. My alarm clock's gonna go off awfully early tomorrow morning if we plan to attend that funeral."

But Suzanne wasn't quite so anxious to call it a night.

"Toni, I have a favor to ask."

"Huh? What?" Toni's head lolled back against the head-rest. She seemed halfway to dreamland already.

"I want to make a quick stop and I'm hoping you'll go with me."

"Oh, honey," Toni said, "As much as I'd love to stop at Schmitt's for a quick bump, I'm just too tired."

"I wasn't thinking of going there."

"No?" Toni said. "Then where did you want to go? I mean, there's nothing else open this time of night, except for Hoobly's Roadhouse. And I *know* you don't want to go out there and hustle random trucker dudes while exotic dancers prance around onstage, twirling their tassels." She chuckled. "I mean, we're cute and all that, but the two of us wouldn't stand a snowball's chance against those USDA Prime babes."

"Remember what I told you about that herd of horses I saw yesterday morning?" Suzanne asked. "When I took the muffins to Claudia?"

"Herd of horses?" Toni said. "Um, maybe. But I might have forgotten."

"But you didn't forget about the horsemeat guy from last night, did you?"

"No, that still bums me out." Toni wrinkled her nose. She was starting to come awake. "Suzanne, where are you going with all this?"

"I'm wondering if the horsemeat guy, Julian Elder, is the same guy who owns those poor horses out by Mike Mullen's farm."

Toni turned to stare at her. "So what are you really asking, Suzanne? That you want me to go with you to check on those horses? To see if they really do belong to Elder?"

Suzanne smiled into the darkness. "That's it exactly."

"Huh." Toni reached up and scratched her head. "Well . . . sure. Why the hell not? I mean, who needs eight hours of beauty sleep anyway? Especially when I got all this natural beauty goin' for me."

"You certainly do," Suzanne said. "Along with a devilishly curious mind."

"No, honey," Toni said. "That would be you."

TWENTY minutes later, Suzanne tapped her foot against the brake. They were coasting along County Road 10, a blacktopped road that unfurled like a dark ribbon through the countryside. They cruised past acres of stubbly corn and soybean fields that had been recently harvested, the night preternaturally dark with fog drifting in and obscuring any possible hint of moonlight.

"Spooky out here," Toni said. Way off in the distance they could see the faint glint of light from a farmhouse.

"Yes it is," Suzanne said.

"You think the horses will be out in the pasture or stashed in a barn?"

"If this guy Elder is just warehousing them until he can move them to Canada, then they're probably just being kept outside."

"If the horses are even owned by Elder," Toni said.

"That's what I'd like to find out." Suzanne peered through the darkness. Some kind of wet crud had congealed on the windshield, making it difficult to see. And she felt disoriented. She wasn't all that familiar with this part of the county and with the October night being so dark and damp . . . well, driving was difficult at best. Still, she figured they were closing in.

"Is that a mailbox up ahead?" Toni asked. She was sitting on the edge of her seat, trying to get a fix on where they were.

"I think so. Oh yeah, and there's a farmhouse, too. Set back from the road."

"Pull up slow," Toni said. "So we can read the name."

Suzanne rolled down her driver's side window as she slowly approached a tilting tin mailbox.

"Can you see anything?" Toni asked.

Suzanne shook her head. "Not yet." She let her car continue to creep forward. "Wait a minute, I think I can . . . yeah. There it is."

"What's it say?" Toni asked. "What's the name on the mailbox?"

"It says Elder."

"Holy sweet potato," Toni said. "And this is where you

saw that herd of horses? The ones that looked kind of sick and tired?"

"That's right," Suzanne said. She was suddenly feeling a little sick and tired herself.

"So what are we supposed to do now?"

Suzanne cut her headlights and rolled forward another fifty feet, stopping only when her view of the farmhouse was obstructed by a thick stand of poplars. Which meant that Elder couldn't see her, either.

"We're going to go see if those horses are still here."

THEY climbed out of the car and stood on the side of the road. The night was dark and dreary and the chill wind rustling through almost-bare trees made it sound like bare bones clacking together.

"This is scary," Toni whispered. "Us being out here all alone. I'm suddenly flashing on visions of Jason and Freddy and all those other horror movie guys."

"Save it for Halloween," Suzanne said. "Right now we've got a job to do. We're going to take a quick look at those horses and then get out of here." Suzanne mustered her courage and squared her shoulders. "Come on." She led the way as they walked single file along the edge of the road, trying to be as quiet as possible. They passed the mailbox with Elder's name on it and, ten feet on, came to his gravel driveway. They stood there for a few moments, gazing at a small house that was hunkered thirty yards back from the road. It was a one-story affair that looked more like a cottage than a house. A dreary affair with peeling paint and a dilapidated porch hanging off one side. No flowers, no picket fence, no smoke curling up from the chimney.

"What do you think?" Suzanne asked.

"I'd say the place probably has bad plumbing and dirty

linoleum," Toni said. "Plus, I see a light on inside, so somebody's home. Probably watching TV. We're going to have to be careful."

"We will be," Suzanne said.

"Where's this pasture supposed to be?"

"Just off to our left."

They crunched quietly down the driveway and then veered off onto a patch of grass. That was better. The grass was slippery but quiet to walk on. So there was much less chance of Julian Elder hearing their footfalls and rushing out to harass them.

They stumbled through a fairly dense grove of trees. Low, twisty branches reached out, tugged at their hair, and practically ensnared them.

"What is this?" Toni whispered. "Some kind of orchard?"

"Old apple and plum trees, I think," Suzanne said. "Only I doubt any of these trees have been pruned or fertilized in years."

They ducked their way through the orchard, heading toward a rickety-looking fence of silvered wood. And just as Suzanne touched a hand to the top rail, just as she was about to pull herself up and over, they heard the faint sound of a dog barking inside the house.

Yap, yap, yap.

"Holy crap!" Toni cried in a hoarse whisper. "What if Elder lets his dog out and it's some kind of ginormous police dog? Or a man-eating rottweiler?"

"Then we climb up into one of these trees," Suzanne said just as the front porch light flashed on.

That sent them ducking to the ground, crouching low on their hands and knees, scrambling for cover.

Seconds later, Suzanne peered through a tangle of gnarled branches, trying to figure out what was going on. She didn't see a dog; she didn't see a person. So maybe a false alarm? Just when she'd decided things might be cool after all, the front door to the house flew open and a small white dog bounded out.

"Dog," Suzanne said to Toni.

Toni stared at her with wide eyes. "Should we make a run for it? If that dog comes over here and finds us we're cooked."

Suzanne raised a hand. She could see the dog and it was spinning around in a circle making a ton of noise—it really was a little rabble-rouser—but it didn't seem to be venturing their way.

"I think we're okay," Suzanne whispered. "The dog's not exactly your fierce guard dog type." Truth be told, he looked like a cute little mop.

"Yeah?" Toni's head popped up just as Julian Elder threw open the door and stepped out onto his porch.

Suzanne motioned frantically. "Down! Get down! Elder just came out and he's carrying a shotgun!"

Toni curled up and pressed herself against the damp ground. "Holy crap," she whispered. "We're gonna end up with a load of buckshot in our butts."

"Just stay down," Suzanne whispered back. "Don't move a muscle and don't make a peep."

"Do you think he saw us?"

"I don't know. I don't *think* so." Suzanne ventured another look. "He's just kind of looking around."

"Maybe he saw your car?" Toni asked.

"I think he's just reacting to the dog."

"By grabbing his *gun*?" Toni huffed. "He's a real friendly sort, isn't he?"

"Well," Suzanne said. "We are on his property."

"Please don't remind me."

For the next couple of minutes, they scrunched into tight balls like the proverbial dormouse at Alice's tea party. Finally Toni said, "What's going on now? Can you see?"

Suzanne lifted her head and peered toward the house. "I think he's going back inside."

"You think he is or he really is?"

"Hang on a minute. No, he's going in. There, he just closed the door behind him."

"Dog's gone, too?" Toni asked.

"He took the dog in with him."

"Then pardon me while I let out a very deep breath," Toni said. She sat up and brushed bits of grass off her slacks. "Poop. I think I just ruined a perfectly good pair of JCPenney slacks."

CHAPTER 15

SUZANNE and Toni hurried to the fence and scrambled over.

"Now what?" Toni asked as they tromped through knee-high grasses.

"I want to see what kind of shape those horses are in," Suzanne said.

"Where are they? I don't see them anywhere."

"Shhh."

Suzanne listened carefully for a few moments. She figured she'd be able to detect a low nicker or the faint stomp of a hoof. And, after a couple of seconds, she did. There were definitely horses in the general vicinity. "This way," she whispered to Toni.

"Which way? I can barely see my hand in front of my face. I don't know if it's this fog or if I've suddenly developed inch-thick cataracts."

"Just hang on to my coat sleeve."

They tromped their way through the pasture, which, thank goodness, had just moderate tree coverage and a few patches of overgrown buckthorn that they had to skirt around.

"There," Suzanne said. Her hand came up and she pointed straight ahead.

"I don't see a dang thing," Toni said.

"Look harder. There's a white horse staring right at us."

"Yeah?"

"See him now?" Suzanne asked.

"Oh yeah," Toni said finally. "Kind of like a friendly ghost horse."

"Come on, let's go."

"You don't think the horses will be afraid of us?" Toni asked.

The eight horses that were crowded into one section of the pasture weren't one bit afraid of them. In fact, the horses greeted them with welcoming nickers and inquisitive noses that poked at them.

"I wish we'd thought to bring along some carrots or apples," Suzanne said. "These guys look hungry."

"I've got some Tic Tacs in my purse," Toni said. "Mint flavored. You think they'd like that?"

"Probably not."

"So what do you think?"

"You mean about their health in general?" Suzanne asked as she ran her hand across the withers of a small pinto.

"Yeah."

"I'd say it's pretty poor. These horses are thin and definitely underfed."

"They seem kind of sad, too," Toni said.

"Dispirited," Suzanne said.

"As if they know what their fate might be."

Suzanne walked from one horse to another, rubbing behind its ears, under its chin, giving each horse a gentle pat on the shoulder. "This isn't right," she said. "We have to do something."

"Like what?" Toni asked.

"I'm not sure." A dappled gray horse snuffled at Suzanne, trying to stick his nose in her jacket pocket. "I'm sorry," she told him. "I don't have anything for you."

"Maybe we could contact some sort of horse rescue group," Toni said.

Suzanne rubbed the gray horse's forehead. "You know what? I think Mike Mullen was already trying to rescue some of these horses."

"What do you mean?"

"Claudia mentioned it to me tonight. When she was talking about getting rid of the livestock, she said that Mike had bought a couple of horses from one of their neighbors."

"You think he bought some of these horses?" Toni asked.

Suzanne ran her hand down a gray horse's nose and touched his rope halter. "Maybe."

"Do you think that horses somehow figured in Mike's death?"

"I don't know," Suzanne said.

Toni dropped her voice, as if she were afraid the horses might hear her. "Do you think Elder could have killed Mike?"

"I can't imagine why. Unless Mike wanted to buy more horses and Elder didn't want to sell."

"So they got into a fight?" Toni asked. "And things went from bad to worse?"

"Maybe. I suppose that could have happened." Suzanne gazed at the horses that had closed in around them in a semicircle. Horses that looked slightly hopeful, as if maybe she and Toni had come to rescue them. If horses were able to put that much together. "What I'd like to do is figure out if Mike's horses came from this particular herd."

"How are you going to do that?"

"For one thing," Suzanne said, "these horses are all wearing the same kind of rope halters. We could check and see if Mike's horses have the same halters."

Toni cocked her head. "So you're saying we're gonna sneak into Mike's barn tonight, too? The barn where he was murdered?"

"I'm afraid so."

IT was a lot easier to sneak down Mike Mullen's driveway. A few clouds had graciously parted, allowing a sliver of moonlight to show the way. And Suzanne knew exactly where she was going. She parked her car some hundred yards from the house and she and Toni quietly hoofed it in, heading for the dairy barn.

Once they hit the farmyard, they could see a dim light shining from a window in the main house. Claudia was definitely back home from the visitation, but there was no sign of a deputy on guard.

"What if Claudia comes out and catches us?" Toni asked as she slunk along, keeping to the shadows.

"Then we'll have to come up with some kind of answer."

"The truth won't work?"

"I'm not sure," Suzanne said. They'd just reached the dairy barn and she was feeling around, looking for the catch to open the door. There it was. She flipped up the lock and slowly, carefully, slid the barn door open. "Come on," she whispered to Toni as she stepped into the gaping darkness.

The first thing that struck Suzanne was the aroma of cows and the scent of fresh hay. Then the cows, subtly aware that someone had entered their domain, began to shuffle about in their stalls and utter low moos and grunts. She took a moment to get her bearings and then headed to her left, toward where she'd seen the box stalls that contained the horses. Just beyond was the room where Mike had been killed.

"Shhh." Toni gestured to the cows as she followed in Suzanne's footsteps. "Keep it down, ladies."

Suzanne and Toni tiptoed quietly through the barn. Luckily, there were a number of long, rectangular windows set high on one wall. A faint glow from the yard light shone through so they weren't creeping along in total darkness.

"Do you know where you're going?" Toni whispered.

"Just up ahead are two box stalls," Suzanne whispered back.

"Do you think the horses are still there?"

"They're in there, all right, I can hear them stomping around."

Seconds later, Suzanne and Toni peered through the wooden slats of the first box stall.

"How many horses are in there?" Toni asked.

"Two that I can see," Suzanne said. She could see the faint outline of two smaller-sized horses. Pretty little things that were probably a reddish roan color.

Toni scrambled over to the next box stall. "I only see one horse in here."

"Is he wearing a rope halter?" Suzanne asked.

"Hard to tell."

Suzanne reached up and slid open the catch on the stall gate.

"You're going in?" Toni sounded nervous.

"I'll be fine," Suzanne said as she slipped into the stall.

The occupant was a large black horse. A nice-looking stocky, blocky quarter horse that looked as if he'd been fairly well fed. He stood calmly, ears flicked forward, watching Suzanne intently as she approached.

That's good. It means he's not going to get feisty on me. No kicking or biting.

Suzanne stretched out a hand to let the horse sniff her. He took a good hard whiff and stomped a hoof, as if in approval.

"Good boy," she said. She let her hand wander up to his nose, gave it a gentle rub, and then slid her hand down under his chin. "How are you doing?" she asked him.

The horse lifted his head and stretched his neck forward. He was sniffing her more closely now, scoping her out.

"Are we gonna be friends, big guy?" Suzanne asked. She touched his cheek, then slid her hand over to his halter. It was a rope halter.

"You okay in there?" Toni called out.

"We're good," Suzanne said.

"Is he wearing the same kind of halter that Elder's horses were wearing?"

Suzanne's fingers ran along the rope part until they reached the buckle. She felt around carefully. "I'd say it's the exact same kind."

"Suzanne?" Toni called in a quavering voice.

"Yeah?"

"Crap on a cracker, girlfriend. I think I heard something. We gotta beat feet out of here."

Suzanne slipped out of the stall and locked the gate behind her. "What did you hear?" she whispered.

"A noise. Outside." Toni was balanced on tiptoes, ready to run.

Suzanne's heart did a quick flip-flop. "You mean like someone walking around?"

Toni grabbed her hand and hustled her back through the barn. "Yeah. Exactly like that."

But when they reached the doorway and peered outside, they didn't see a thing. A faint light still shone in Claudia's house, but there wasn't a soul moving around the farmyard.

"Nobody here," Suzanne said.

Toni shook her head. "Maybe my ears were playing tricks on me?"

"Maybe." Suzanne slid the barn door shut and turned to face Toni. She knew Toni was probably right about getting out of there. They'd been creepy-crawling in places they didn't belong for the better part of forty minutes. Which might be pushing their luck. "Okay, time to leave."

They padded across the soft earth, trying to be as quiet and unobtrusive as possible. But all around them it felt like shadows flitted about. Suzanne tried to tell herself that it was just her imagination. An old pump looked like a crouching figure. The corncrib hid a silent watcher.

Moon shadows, Suzanne reassured herself. Nothing to be frightened of.

And just as they passed an old hay wagon, stepping through puddles of liquid silver, Suzanne really did see a fleeting shadow. Just off to her right, slipping behind a small wooden building. As she stiffened, Toni immediately caught her reaction.

"You saw something?" Toni hissed.

"I think so," Suzanne said. At least, she was pretty sure she had.

They stopped dead in their tracks.

"What was it?" Toni clutched Suzanne's arm as if her life depended on it.

"I don't know," Suzanne breathed. But she wondered—was Claudia, fresh from her husband's funeral, capering through the woods? She thought not. Was it Deputy Driscoll? But if it was him, wouldn't he simply pop out and reveal himself? Wouldn't he demand to know what *they* were up to?

Another shadow slipped behind a tree, way off in the pasture.

That did it for both of them. Holding hands, Suzanne and Toni raced toward their car as fast as their legs could carry them.

CHAPTER 16

IT should have been Flapjack Friday at the Cackleberry Club, but on this particular Friday half of Kindred was seated in Hope Church waiting for Mike Mullen's funeral to begin.

Suzanne, Toni, and Petra had arrived early and taken seats midway between the altar and the rear of the church. Petra, of course, had wanted to be prompt. Suzanne wanted to eyeball each and every person who showed up, just in case a suspicious mourner wandered in.

Much to her annoyance, they hadn't yet.

Overhead in the choir loft, tiny Agnes Bennet cranked out "Wind Beneath My Wings" on the old pipe organ. She bent and swayed as her fingers flew across the keys, pumping the foot pedals as if she were driving an Indy car. The choir (only fourteen of the normally twenty-six-member group had shown up today) gamely belted out the lyrics as mourners continued to filter in and the church filled to near capacity. Mike had obviously been well liked and held in great esteem by the community.

"Your head is swiveling like a periscope," Toni whispered to Suzanne. "You must be on the lookout for Mike's killer."

"Only if I'm suddenly struck in the head by lightning and develop a psychic sixth sense," Suzanne said. "Or the killer hangs a great big banner around his neck that says I Did It."

Petra leaned forward and gave them a slightly disapproving glance. "I doubt you're going to find any killers here," she said rather stiffly.

"Don't be too sure about that," Suzanne said. She'd just spotted Mayor Mobley and Byron Wolf as they entered the church. They both moved importantly and presumptuously, as if this funeral service were somehow all about them.

"Look at Mobley with his bad comb-over," Toni sniffed. "Making a beeline for the front. Sheesh, the guy's wearing a crappy leisure suit with topstitching."

"I think that's his golf jacket," Suzanne said. She figured Mobley planned to sneak out after church and play a round before he headed off to join a few of his fat cat cronies for lunch. A typical day in the life of their busy, do-nothing mayor.

Still, Suzanne watched Mobley closely as he plopped down in the second row, causing the wooden pew to groan loudly. And she kept an even more watchful eye on his buddy Byron Wolf. There was something about Wolf that she found distasteful. He projected a little too much swagger and bravado, was a little too hale-hearty-handshaking sure of himself. If she had to characterize Wolf she'd say the man was definitely slippery when dry.

The *thunk* of the double doors opening at the back of the church caused everyone to spin in their seats. And, sure enough, there was George Draper, silhouetted in the doorway for a moment. Dressed in one of his Sunday-go-to-funeral suits, he hastily ushered in six pallbearers as he honchoed the rolling in of the gleaming wooden coffin.

A murmur rippled through the congregation.

"Oh dear." Petra touched a hand to her cheek. Funerals always made her emotional.

"There's Claudia," Toni said. "I was wondering when she was going to show up. Looks like she's opted to lead the casket down the aisle."

"That's a little strange," Suzanne said.

But Petra was leaking tears. "I find it very touching that she'd do that. They must have had a very loving marriage."

Maybe, Suzanne thought. *Or maybe not.*

Claudia Mullen, dressed in a sedate black dress, her hair pinned into a retro French roll, walked slowly down the aisle. She looked grim, but that could be an act, Suzanne decided. Inwardly, she could be jumping for joy at the windfall she was going to get for selling the farm.

Directly behind Claudia came Mike's casket. It had been hoisted onto a stainless steel casket carrier that was being rolled down the aisle by six pallbearers. They were a robust-looking group, all red-faced, big-boned men. One of the pallbearers looked like he might be Mike Mullen's brother and probably was. She recognized the other five guys as being local farmers as well.

The wheels of the carrier clacked noisily as they proceeded down the aisle while an immense spray of white roses bobbed precariously on top of the casket. Once the casket arrived at the front of the church, Draper seesawed it into position and Claudia and the six pallbearers took their places in the front pew.

Suzanne glanced about the church again. There were lots of friends and neighbors here, lots of folks that she recognized from last night. But there was no sign of Noah Jorgenson and his mother, Faith Anne. And no sign of Julian Elder, their friendly neighborhood horse broker.

At the very last moment, just as Reverend Strait strode out to take his place at the pulpit, Sheriff Doogie slid inside the church. He stood in back, next to the baptismal font, a large, immovable object in a rumpled khaki uniform, appraising the entire gathering with cool law enforcement eyes.

And just as Suzanne tried to catch Doogie's attention (he seemed to be resisting her glances), Sam hurried in and sat down next to her. He gave her a warm smile, then reached over and squeezed her hand.

"I thought you weren't going to be able to make it," Suzanne said under her breath.

"Didn't you want me to make it?" Sam looked dead serious but his eyes danced with amusement.

Suzanne slid closer to him so their hips and legs were touching. "Of course I did. But I didn't expect you to move heaven and earth to be here."

"No biggie," Sam said. "Just shoved a little earth to the side."

Petra leaned forward and eyed them, her brows rising to form twin arcs.

"Petra disapproves of our talking in church," Suzanne whispered.

"Of course she does."

Reverend Strait had already launched into the service. Looking dignified and handsome with his white hair, dark suit, and solemn air, he'd opened with a blessing. Then he led everyone in prayer and proceeded to deliver a short but heartfelt eulogy.

As always, Suzanne tried to keep her head in the game but her mind began to wander. She wondered why she could never seem to focus her attention at a funeral. Maybe it was because she'd buried her own husband not that long ago and was trying to block that painful memory. Or maybe because the finality of the whole thing was just too much for her. Was just too overpowering.

The other thing that worried Suzanne was that maybe she just didn't care all that much. Perhaps she'd come to the realization that life was simply a transitory trip and there was more waiting for her on the other side.

She frowned and shook her head. No, that wasn't it at all. If anything, she wanted to hang on desperately to the here and now, to grab all the earthly living she could for as long as possible. She guessed that what really pulled her away from the hard reality of the service was thinking about Mike Mullen's murder. Wondering if she was on the right track to figure it out. To solve the crime.

"Are you feeling okay?" Sam was suddenly peering at her with great concern. As if she were one of his sick or injured patients.

"I'm fine," Suzanne said.

"You don't look fine."

Suzanne squeezed his hand, prompting another look of reproach from Petra. "I'm okay. Really." She arranged her face in a look of deep concern and decided she'd have to be a lot more circumspect when it came to this investigation business.

FORTY minutes later, the service was concluded. Music and voices thundered down from the choir loft, a few rays of sunlight shot through the stained glass windows, lending a somewhat hopeful glow, and the coffin was rolled back down the center aisle. Claudia followed in its wake, accompanied by a gray-haired, middle-aged, sniffling-into-her-hankie woman whom Suzanne hadn't seen before. Was this a relative? Maybe the sister from Minneapolis? Probably.

Out on the sidewalk, people milled around, forming into clusters, breaking up, and then reforming into small groups yet again. They expressed their condolences to Claudia, chatted casually about the service with one another, and then, as usually happened, began to pull away emotionally. The funeral was over, the deceased would be hustled on his way to the cemetery, and they were more than ready to jump back into their normal everyday lives.

Sam was one of them.

"I've got to take off," he told Suzanne. "But I'll for sure catch you tonight."

"Great," Suzanne told him. "Thanks for coming. See you then." But she was already looking around, craning her neck, trying to locate Sheriff Doogie in the scattering crowd.

Finally she spotted him, cutting across the street, almost kitty-corner from where she was standing. He was heading resolutely for his maroon and tan sheriff's car.

"Doogie!" Suzanne called out.

Doogie stopped, his hand paused on the handle of his car while he waited for Suzanne to cross the street. She dipped and dodged through a string of cars, got halfway across, then was bullied back by a large black SUV. Finally she made it across.

"What's up, Suzanne?" Doogie asked. He sounded slightly resigned, as if he knew she was going to badger him some more about Mike Mullen's murder.

Suzanne greeted him breathlessly. "I need to talk to you about Julian Elder."

Doogie stared at her. "Julian Elder." He said the name as if he was totally unfamiliar with it.

Suzanne quickly enlightened him. "Julian Elder lives a farm or two over from Mike Mullen. He buys run-down horses and then sells them to some Canadian dealer for horsemeat."

"And this should concern me why?" Doogie asked.

"For one thing, because it's awful," Suzanne said.

"In case you might have noticed, I don't exactly have jurisdiction in Canada." Doogie chuckled. "A bright red Canadian Mountie's uniform isn't exactly my taste."

"Here's the thing," Suzanne said. "Mike Mullen bought three of Elder's horses. In fact, they're stabled in his dairy barn right now."

Doogie continued to stare at her. "There's no law against horse trading."

"It wasn't trading," Suzanne said. "Mike bought those horses in order to save their lives."

"That's nice. Mike was a good guy. We all knew that."

"I think there's a chance that Mike Mullen tried to buy the rest of those horses and got into an altercation with Elder."

Doogie's shoulders dipped and he rocked back on his heels. "Oh jeez. Are you trying to tell me that this horse guy Elder is a suspect? That he was the one who killed Mike?"

"He certainly could have," Suzanne said. "I'm telling you, Sheriff, this Elder is a bad apple."

Doogie stared at her. "Huh."

"Don't huh me, Doogie. What you really need to do is strap on your six-gun and investigate Elder."

Doogie reached up and slid his Smokey Bear hat back on his head. "First you were suspicious of Claudia Mullen. Then it was Noah Jorgenson. Then you jumped on the bandwagon for Byron Wolf. Now it's Julian Elder."

"Need I remind you that *you* were just as suspicious of Claudia, Noah, and Wolf?"

Doogie gazed at her. "You're really serious about this Elder guy?"

"Of course I am."

"But this is all speculation on your part," Doogie said.

"No," Suzanne said. "It's not speculation. This is based on the fact that Mike really did buy three horses from Elder. And I'm guessing he wanted to—or tried to—buy some more."

"To save their lives."

"Yes, to save their lives." Suzanne paused and took a calming breath. If she acted too upset, Doogie might write her off as a hysterical female. Not someone with legitimate and relevant information. "Can you find out if Elder has any prior arrests or outstanding warrants?"

Doogie was slightly amused. "Now you sound like one of my deputies."

"I could be one of your deputies," Suzanne said. "Because I'm good at this. I'm not exactly an amateur when it comes to investigating."

"Who says?"

"Everybody. Toni and Petra and . . ."

Doogie put up a hand. "Hold everything, Suzanne. I'm not discounting a word you just said. But for me to go cowboying in to some horse trader's farm . . . it's not exactly within the parameter of the law."

Suzanne bit her lip. That's exactly what she and Toni had done last night. Gone cowboying in. And almost gotten in trouble.

"What's your interest in this?" Doogie asked. "Aside from the fact that you found Mike Mullen dead in his barn?"

Suzanne had to think for a few moments. Finally, she said, "I guess what I'm really looking for is justice."

Doogie stared back at her. "That's funny. Here I thought that was my job."

CHAPTER 17

"I need another package of turkey bacon," Petra called out. She was standing at her grill, flipping squares of hash brown potatoes, fried eggs sizzling in her cast-iron skillet. It was ten forty-five and the Cackleberry Club had filled up the minute they took the Closed sign off the front door. Which was about ten minutes ago.

"Coming right up," Suzanne called out. She dashed into the cooler, grabbed the turkey bacon, and delivered it to Petra. "This stuff is really catching on, huh?"

"You could say that."

"I mean, people are requesting it, right?"

Petra smiled to herself. "Sometimes they are."

"Wait a minute," Suzanne said. "Are you substituting turkey bacon for the real deal?"

Petra set down her spatula. "You know what, Suzanne? I like to think I'm the good fairy for healthy hearts. That I'm doing my part to keep our male customers from dropping dead of cardiac infarctions."

"You're substituting."

"Think of it as saving lives. Just ask Sam. He's a doctor, he probably sees lots of heart disease. And the tragedy that comes along with it."

Suzanne folded her arms and leaned against the butcher-block counter. "You're something else, you know that? Especially when your idea of vegetables consists of carrot cake, zucchini bread, and pumpkin pie."

"I try," Petra said. She reached for the pepper shaker, then changed her mind.

"Are you upset about the funeral?" Suzanne asked. For all her good nature, Petra seemed a little discombobulated.

Petra picked up her spatula and poked at her bacon. "I guess I am. A little."

The swinging door slammed open and Toni rushed into the kitchen, hips swinging, ponytail bouncing. "Who's upset?" she asked.

"Petra's got a funeral hangover," Suzanne said. "She's feeling somewhat morose."

"Yeah," Toni said. "A funeral will do that to you. It makes you think about your own immorality."

Petra peered at her. "Don't you mean mortality?"

"Huh?" Toni asked. "Isn't that what I said?"

Petra smiled. "Never mind, dear."

"I think the funeral made us all a little introspective," Suzanne said. "We're sad about Mike and wondering what's going to happen with Claudia."

Toni grabbed a strawberry and popped it in her mouth. "Maybe she'll be sitting fat and sassy after she sells the farm to that hunky developer guy."

"Byron Wolf," Suzanne said. She'd been surprised that he'd shown up at the funeral.

"I saw Claudia talking to Wolf right after the funeral," Toni said. "They looked awfully chummy."

Petra furrowed her brow. "Really? Claudia was talking to him?"

"Chatting him up," Toni said. "Heck, he was practically *sitting* with her at the funeral. And then, afterward, they had their heads together, looking thick as thieves."

"I don't like to hear that," Petra said. "It's awfully . . . unseemly for a widow to carry on like that."

"Maybe Claudia's a modern-day widow," Toni said. "As in 'the times they are a-changin'.'"

"Maybe," Petra said. But she didn't look like she was buying it.

THEY buckled down then, Suzanne laying out plates, Petra serving up her brunch entrées, and Toni delivering them to customers. Then they coalesced back in the kitchen and did it all over again.

"Got the second shift delivered," Toni chirped when she came back into the kitchen. "The Cackleberry Club is humming like clockwork."

"Trying to anyway," Petra said. She'd already started mixing up her pizza dough for tonight and had just stuck two loaves of molasses bread in the oven.

"But I'm still not sure if we're serving breakfast or lunch," Toni said.

Petra put both hands on her hips and turned to face her. "Did you not check out the chalkboard?"

Toni shook her head. "Not exactly. In case you haven't noticed, I've been busting my buns out there."

"We're serving brunch," Suzanne said.

"Got it." Toni gave a thumbs-up sign. "I like that brunch always sounds so classy. Hey, Pet, are you baking molasses bread?"

"Just stuck it in the oven," Petra said. "Along with a pan of apple scones."

"So do you want me to toss out what's left from yesterday's muffins and stuff?"

"No, that's okay," Petra said. "I'll take care of it." She grabbed a large brown paper bag filled with day-old baked goods and shook it hard. It was her habit to toss the crumbs out back for the birds and squirrels. "I already crunched everything up."

Only when Petra opened the back door and leaned out to dispense her crumbs, she let out a surprised yelp. Then she threw up her arms, dropped the bag, and screamed like a wild banshee.

"What the . . . ?" Suzanne said. What was the problem?

"Holy Hannah!" Petra shrieked again, her voice rising to an even more ear-piercing octave. "There's some kind of crazy monster out there." Petra backed away from the door, fanning herself wildly as if she was in danger of passing out.

"What?" Toni was instantly alert.

"A monster?" Suzanne asked. Even though Petra's face was pinched and white with fear, as if she'd just blundered into a *Tyrannosaurus rex*, this all sounded rather interesting to her. A genuine monster in their back parking lot? Do tell.

Petra reached out and put a death grip on Suzanne's arm. "The thing . . . it reared up on its hind legs and stared at me with bright, beady eyes." She made a few more frantic fanning gestures and then sat down heavily on a wooden bench. "And then it made a nasty clicking sound!"

"You're sure it wasn't Junior?" Toni asked. She was half serious.

"Last time I looked, Junior didn't have a pink snout," Petra practically shouted.

"He might after a night of drinking," Toni cackled. "Especially if he's been hitting the Wild Turkey."

Suzanne pushed her way past Petra, ready to do battle with the monster in the backyard. But when she peered out the back door, a mangy little brown critter stared back at her. It had a humpy, dumpy body, stringy-looking tail, and a weird pink snout.

"It's not a monster," Suzanne said. "It's an opossum. The little thing is snuffling around in the dirt, obviously looking for an easy handout." She picked up Petra's bag, dug out a day-old poppy seed muffin, and tossed it at the creature. Then she ducked back inside.

"Possum, you say?" Toni said. She pressed her nose against the back window to look out. "I hear those things are good eatin'."

Petra sprang up from her bench and poked a finger at the back door. "That critter's not setting one lousy paw inside my kitchen!"

"Then I guess we're going to have to kill it," Toni said. She glanced speculatively at the knife rack. "Maybe lop off its head with a meat cleaver or something?"

Petra suddenly frowned. "Wait a minute. You want to . . . kill it?" She pursed her lips together, considering Toni's words. "Well, I can't say I approve of *that* idea. I kind of hate to bring harm down upon one of God's own creatures." She was backpedaling like crazy now. "I mean, it is a sentient being, after all." Her hands twisted nervously in her apron. "Couldn't we figure out a better option?"

"Sure," Suzanne said. "We could get it in the witness protection program."

Two minutes later there was a knock at the back door. But it wasn't the opossum nosing around for more goodies, it was Junior.

"Junior," Suzanne said as she opened the door. "What's up?" He was dressed in saggy blue overalls and had a red trucker cap pulled low on his brow. A pair of pink sunglasses, the kind a teenage girl might wear, was perched on his nose.

Suzanne decided he looked like a disreputable mechanic who'd just escaped from a carnival. Or maybe he was just plain disreputable. If he wasn't Toni's almost-ex, she never would have let him in.

Junior flashed a cheesy smile. "I brought you guys another load of pumpkins."

"Did we order more pumpkins?" Suzanne asked Petra. Toni had conveniently disappeared into the café.

Petra shook her head. "Not that I know of."

Junior hooked a thumb back to where his rattletrap truck was parked on the hardpan outside. "I got 'em for free. I put a new carburetor in Hooch Aitkin's truck in exchange for a load of pumpkins. I thought you guys might like 'em. You know, to line your driveway for the big Halloween party."

"Actually," Suzanne said, "that sounds like a very creative idea."

Junior took a step closer to her. "I gotta ask you something, Suzanne."

Uh-oh. "What's that, Junior?"

"When I gave Toni a ride over here from the funeral, she was telling me about that guy Julian Elder. And I think he might be your man."

Suzanne blinked. "Our man?" *Thanks a heap, Toni.*

Junior dropped his voice to an interested, conspiratorial tone. "You know, Elder *could* be the killer. Mike Mullen's killer."

"We don't know anything for sure yet."

"That's why you should let me help investigate."

"Oh no. No way."

"I could just kind of sniff him out a little."

"Bad idea," Suzanne said.

But Junior was not to be dissuaded. "I could hang out at Schmitt's Bar. Or over at Shooter's." His eyes burned with intensity. "I bet Elder'll come in there. Every good old boy does sooner or later."

"No, Junior," Suzanne said. "Please just leave him alone. Don't get involved."

SUZANNE joined Toni out in the café to pour refills, take orders, and update the chalkboard, since they were now plumb out of chocolate chip muffins.

"Your almost-ex just showed up," Suzanne told Toni.

Toni nodded. "Yeah, I spied his pointy little head out the front window. He's unloading a bunch more pumpkins for us, I guess."

"He says he wants to be a secret agent. Help investigate Mike's murder."

Toni snorted. "Are you kidding? Junior couldn't find his skinny butt in the hall of mirrors at high noon."

"But you told him about Elder."

Toni looked uncomfortable. "Well . . . yeah."

Suzanne put a finger to her lips. "From now on, mum's the word."

EVEN though the Cackleberry Club was serving a simplified brunch menu, they were kept hopping. More customers wandered in to eat, a contingent from the Thursday Night Mystery Readers Book Club stopped by the Book Nook, and Jan Fitzgerald, who'd missed the Yarn Truck yesterday, came in to buy two skeins of pink mohair.

By one o'clock Suzanne was feeling hungry and slightly ragged. She'd skipped breakfast this morning and was running on only one cup of coffee as well as a few secondary fumes she'd managed to snort when she brewed a pot of Kona coffee.

"Let me make you something to eat," Petra offered when

Suzanne hauled a second tub of dirty dishes into the kitchen. "How about an egg salad sandwich on whole wheat toast?"

"I'd love it," Suzanne said. "Especially if you toss on some alfalfa sprouts."

"I think that can be arranged." Petra hurriedly put together Suzanne's sandwich, slicing bread and toasting it, mounding on egg salad, sprinkling on the sprouts. As she was cutting the sandwich in half she said, "You're still looking into Mike's murder, aren't you?"

Suzanne gave her a speculative look. "Don't you want me to?"

Petra placed the sandwich on a plate and slid it toward her. "I do and I don't. I'm half scared that you're going to find out something bad about Claudia."

"I can stop. I can stop right now."

Petra placed both hands on the counter and leaned toward her. "No, you can't. When you get going on something you're like a dog worrying a bone. You can't stop. It's not in your nature."

Suzanne took a bite of her sandwich and chewed slowly. "You're saying I'm tenacious."

"Honey, you're a pit bull."

Suzanne was only halfway through her sandwich when Toni came rushing in.

"Get out here, girl," Toni cried. "There's somebody you have to meet!"

"Who is it?" Suzanne asked.

"Never mind that. Just get a move on!"

Toni grabbed Suzanne's wrist, pulled her into the café, and then led her over to one of the small tables by the window. It was occupied by a young woman who was just finishing her bowl of soup. Mid-thirties, slim, with reddish blond hair and a sprinkle of freckles across her nose, she was dressed casually in blue jeans, boots, and a light-colored suede jacket.

"This is Cassie Givens," Toni said. "Cassie, this is Suzanne, the woman I told you about."

Suzanne nodded at Cassie. "Nice to meet you." She tilted her head at Toni. "What's up?"

Toni was nearly bubbling over with excitement. "Cassie here is the executive director of Hoof-Beats Horse Rescue."

Suzanne practically gasped. "You are? Seriously?"

"That's me," Cassie said.

"Tell her," Toni urged.

"Yes, tell me," Suzanne said.

"Well," Cassie said, "as I was just mentioning to Toni, I'm here to check out some horses."

"Julian Elder's horses," Toni said. She winked at Suzanne. "I told Cassie we already checked them out last night."

"Elder's been on our radar for some time," Cassie continued. "And our organization has been raising money to try and buy several of his horses."

"You mean buy them so you can save their lives?" Suzanne said.

"That's the plan," Cassie said. "Our group despises the idea of perfectly good horses being taken to Canada for . . . well, you know."

"Yes, we do," Suzanne said. She was a little shocked that Cassie had suddenly shown up here with the intention of buying the exact same horses she'd been so worried about. Yet here she was, like a gift from the gods. "Do you think Elder will sell them to you?"

"That's the big question, isn't it?" Cassie said. "We hope he will, but you never know. These horsemeat guys—and there are more of them around than you think—are pretty weird. You never know how they'll react. Some will take your money just because it's easy pickin's. Others don't much like groups like ours because we threaten their livelihood. Such as it is."

"So you've never tried to buy horses from Julian Elder before?" Suzanne asked.

"Not from him, no," Cassie said. "But we've been aware of his activities. He's been on our watch list."

"He's kind of on ours, too," Toni said. She jabbed Suzanne with an elbow. "I told Cassie all about Mike Mullen's murder."

Cassie suddenly looked nervous. "And I'm glad you did. It freaks me out to know that Elder might be a suspect."

"'Suspect' being the operative word," Suzanne said. "Because we don't really know, one way or the other. I mean, it is kind of a stretch."

"But you obviously got a bad vibe from him," Cassie said.

"The worst," Toni said.

"You say that Elder has been on your watch list," Suzanne said. "So what can you tell us about him?"

"Not very much," Cassie said. "We know he's lived in this area for maybe eight or ten months. He doesn't own the farm, he leases it, and has only shipped out one group of horses to Canada as far as we know."

"Anything else?" Suzanne asked.

"We found out he used to be some kind of Special Forces guy," Cassie said. "Which is kind of scary. He's one of those guys who knows how to kill you with his bare hands and can probably set explosives and such."

"So he served in the Middle East?" Suzanne asked.

"No," Cassie said. "We heard he did something down in South America. Like maybe in . . . Nicaragua."

"Like jungle warfare?" Toni asked.

Suzanne kept a straight face even while she thought, *Uh-oh. Mike was killed with a machete.*

"How many horses are you going to buy?" Toni asked.

"If Elder cooperates, I'm hoping to get four from him," Cassie said. "Then I plan to trailer them to a friend's farm near Red Wing, where our volunteers will work to rehab the horses and eventually get them adopted."

"But Elder has eight horses in his pasture," Suzanne said.

Cassie looked mournful. "I realize he's probably got more horses than we can afford. Unfortunately, our group relies mainly on donations from individuals. So we can only afford to buy four horses at this point."

"What will happen to the other four?" Suzanne asked. But she was pretty sure she knew the answer. And it wasn't good.

CHAPTER 18

JUST as Suzanne slid a piece of pecan pie in front of Cassie (compliments of the house), Rick Boyle, the rep from Claggett Foods, came stomping in.

"Suzanne!" Boyle shot an index finger into the air as if he were summoning for the check. But Suzanne knew he was really demanding her attention. Which she didn't feel like giving him right now.

Instead, Suzanne headed him off like she was cutting an ornery steer from the herd. "We'll talk in my office, okay?" She didn't wait for Boyle's reply, just spun on her boot heels, headed into the Book Nook, and hooked a right into her office.

Boyle followed her doggedly, clutching his trusty clipboard, his tongue practically hanging out.

"Wait up, Suzanne. Gee, I'm glad we've got this chance to talk again," Boyle said as he huffed along.

Suzanne plopped down behind her desk, grabbed a two-minute egg timer and flipped it over. "You've got two minutes."

White sand started pouring from the top of the plastic timer into the bottom of the timer.

"Whaaa?" Boyle's face convulsed in disappointment.

"It's a busy day," Suzanne told him. "We've got a big event tonight."

"What's going on?" Boyle asked, trying to recover some of his dignity.

"Pizza party."

Boyle nodded. "Then you'll be needing mozzarella cheese."

"Already got a bunch in the cooler."

Boyle scrunched his face into a look of frustration. "Have you had a chance to study those product sheets I gave you?"

"I'm afraid not." Suzanne's glance wandered to the sand as it continued to trickle down.

"That stupid gadget is very distracting," Boyle said, pointing to the timer.

"I'm sorry, but this is one of the ways I manage to stay on track. Like I said, it's a busy day. It's been a busy week."

"You're sure not making this easy."

Suzanne shrugged. "That's business, Mr. Boyle. Sometimes you land an account, sometimes you don't. It's what you'd call a crapshoot."

"Meet me halfway," Boyle urged. He was clearly upset, well on his way to working up a big fat head of steam. "Give me a shot at this."

"I'm sorry, but I'm pretty well set as far as food vendors go."

"That's not what I hear," Boyle snarled. And this time his true colors came out. Hidden behind his benign salesman's mask was an aggressive, belligerent bully. He rose up in his chair. "I know for a fact you haven't replaced that cheese guy who got killed."

Suzanne leaned forward. "What would you know about that?"

Boyle's eyes sparkled and he pulled his mouth into a nasty smile. "I hear things. I get around."

"I'm sure you do." It occurred to Suzanne that Rick Boyle probably drove all over six different counties all week long. He talked to people, picked up rumors, probably spread a few nasty rumors himself. He was basically a traveling sales guy who slipped in and out of restaurants and grocery stores at will.

"You think you're too good for me?" Boyle asked suddenly. He leered at her, a nasty, knowing look that gave her the creeps. "You think I don't know you're a podunk operation that barely ekes out a profit?"

Suzanne gave him a cool gaze. *Show no fear,* she told herself. *Don't engage him. Pretend he's a mangy coyote groveling for a bit of crust.*

"My prices are rock-bottom," Boyle snapped. "I'm trying to give you a break here."

"I think our meeting is finished," Suzanne said as she stood up abruptly.

Boyle fumbled open his briefcase and threw an order form down on her desk. "Take a look at this," he said. "Because I will be back."

"I don't think so," Suzanne said under her breath as she followed Boyle to the door. Then, once he was outside—after muttering to himself and making a big show of slamming the door behind him—she reached up and turned the latch. There was no way she wanted Boyle to change his mind and come storming back inside. He'd just upset Toni and Petra and make a scene in front of their customers.

"Suzanne?" Toni was standing just inches from her, a look of concern on her face. "Sweetie, are you okay?"

"I'm fine."

"You don't look fine. You look like you just fought off the Prince of Darkness." Toni glanced out the window. "That food guy was bugging you again, huh?"

"He wants us to buy his cheese and dairy products," Suzanne said in a flat tone. "Wants to be our vendor of record."

"Really?" Toni said. "Because I saw the look on his face and . . . well, honey, it seemed to me like he wanted to wring your neck."

"He's aggressive, that's for sure," Suzanne said. As she said it, she wondered if Boyle really was crazy enough to try and put his competitors out of business. In other words, could he have been the nutcase who murdered Mike Mullen?

FIVE minutes later, Suzanne decided to shake herself out of her Rick Boyle hangover and show Cassie Givens the way to Elder's farm. She pulled her Taurus around front, waved at Cassie, and then slowly led her out County Road 10. She drove at an even, moderate speed, partly because Cassie was towing a horse trailer and was unfamiliar with the territory and partly because she was mulling over a lot of information.

As Suzanne drove into the countryside she tried to relax. Rays of sunlight strafed the far ridgeline where hills rose up and gave way to dark forests with sandstone bluffs and moss-crusted gullies. She passed a golden field where a flock of Canadian geese were sunning themselves and searching for stray bits of already-harvested grain. Flurries of colored leaves rained down against her windshield and red leaves on oak trees shimmered like precious jewels.

Yes, Boyle had poked at her sensibilities and tried to upset her. Actually, he *had* upset her. But was the man desperate or evil enough to have murdered his competitor? Of that Suzanne wasn't so sure.

Of course she still had her tried-and-true roster of suspects. Claudia Mullen. Noah Jorgenson. Byron Wolf. Julian Elder. She couldn't forget them. Any one of them had serious motive, didn't they? Well, maybe not Noah Jorgenson, but his mother certainly acted like she was unhinged. And that kind of strange, unpredictable behavior could never be trusted.

* * *

WHEN Elder's farm came into sight, Suzanne slowed her car. She rolled down the window and motioned toward Elder's driveway. Cassie gave an acknowledging wave back and then rolled in, the horse trailer bumping along behind her. Suzanne continued down the road, hoping Cassie would be successful. That at least four of the eight horses would be rescued and find their way to caring, loving homes.

As she turned left on Country Trail, Suzanne decided, for no reason other than her own brand of burning curiosity, to stop at Mike Mullen's farm.

Imagine her surprise when she pulled in and found two pickup trucks parked crosswise in front of the barn. She climbed out of her car, curious as to what was going on. Then she immediately recognized Todd Lansky.

"Hey there," Lansky said to her as she walked toward him. In his blue jeans, jean jacket, and boots, he looked more like a rancher than a farmer.

"I was just wondering how Claudia was doing," Suzanne said. She glanced around. "Is everything okay here?"

Lansky waved at a man who was standing on the lowest rail of a sturdy metal fence, looking over a herd of black-and-white cows. "That's Dan, Mike's brother."

"Oh sure," Suzanne said. She vaguely recognized him from the funeral that morning.

"He was just telling me that some guy over in Deer County offered to buy the cows," Lansky said. "I guess he wants to expand his dairy herd."

"Wow. Just like that, the dairy farm and cheese business is gone."

Lansky eyed her. "Kind of a tough deal, huh?"

"It really is." Suzanne glanced over at the house. "Do you know if Claudia is home yet?" She winced. "From the cemetery service?"

"Yup, she just rolled in, like, thirty minutes ago."

"Were you at the funeral this morning?" Suzanne asked.

Lansky shook his head. "I'm afraid I couldn't make it. Just the visitation last night." He gestured toward the barn. "I've been checking out a couple of large aluminum tanks. Since it looks like Claudia's going to sell the whole place, lock, stock, and barrel, I could use some of that equipment at my place. It's used but still in pretty good condition."

"You're sure Claudia's going to sell the farm?"

Lansky gave her a sad, hangdog look. "It looks that way."

"Do you know anything about the horses?" Suzanne asked.

"There are horses? No, I haven't heard a thing."

"Then maybe . . . maybe I'll just pop in and ask Claudia." Suzanne turned toward the house.

"I hope you don't mind if I tag along," Lansky said. "I want to know if she's got a price in mind for those tanks."

"No problem."

WHEN Claudia answered their knock at the kitchen door, she looked more than a little surprised. "Suzanne," she said. "Todd." She seemed to consider their presence for a moment and then graciously opened the door. "Come in."

They trooped into the kitchen.

"I don't mean to bother you," Suzanne said, "but I have kind of a strange question."

"Yes?" Claudia said. She still had on the plain black dress she'd worn to the funeral and her eyes looked dry and irritated.

"Did Mike try to buy some more horses? More than the three that are in your barn?"

Claudia looked slightly puzzled. "I have no idea."

"Because I've been kind of looking into that particular aspect," Suzanne said.

"Into the horses?" Claudia said. Now she just looked confused while Lansky looked semi-interested.

"I guess I was trying to figure out if there was some sort of connection," Suzanne said. "I mean, between Mike's death and the horses he bought from your neighbor Julian Elder."

"Interesting," Lansky said. Though it was probably said out of politeness.

"I can't imagine there is a connection," Claudia said. Then she seemed to reconsider her words. "I mean, why would there be? What exactly are you implying?"

"I'm not really sure," Suzanne said. Now she had the feeling she was upsetting Claudia. "But I did mention the horses to Sheriff Doogie."

"He's a good man," Lansky said. "If anybody can get to the bottom of this, he sure can." Then to Claudia, "Excuse me, ma'am, I wanted to talk to you about buying a couple of those aluminum tanks . . ."

Claudia waved a hand. "Name your price. I don't need them."

"Claudia," Suzanne said, edging back toward the door. "Would it be okay if I took a look in the barn?"

This time Claudia sighed visibly. "Go ahead. Help yourself."

WITH the cows out in the pasture, the barn felt empty and cold. Suzanne walked slowly down the center aisle, past the empty stanchions until she got to the two box stalls. Those were empty, too. Dan must have turned out the horses along with the cows. She wondered if the farmer who was going to buy the dairy cattle would be taking the horses as well. She hoped he would.

Pressing her palm against the white wooden door to Mike's cheese room, Suzanne pushed it open. Her eyes were immediately drawn to the exact spot on the cement floor where she'd discovered Mike's body. Where the blood had congealed around him in a ghastly sea of red.

Were those stains still there?

No, they were not.

Someone, thank goodness, had tossed down a layer of hay and sawdust. Suzanne supposed it was meant to absorb the blood, but to her it only served as a reminder that something foul had happened here. X marks the spot. A nasty deed that needed to be covered over.

Skirting around Mike's worktables, Suzanne's eyes took in the workroom. The whole place was scrupulously clean, all the aluminum vats and tables still sparkling. The only incongruous note in the whole place was Mike's desk. It was an old wooden desk that had been painted white and the top of it was heaped with papers.

Suzanne edged past the tables and went immediately to the desk. For a man who preferred his workspace nice and neat, this certainly was not very orderly. Then Suzanne remembered that Sheriff Doogie and his two deputies had probably pawed through Mike's orders and correspondence looking for some sort of clue. Obviously, they'd come up empty, since they weren't exactly hot on the trail of anyone in particular at the moment.

Picking up a yellow pencil, Suzanne stirred the jumble of papers. She didn't think she'd spot anything that Doogie had missed. Then again, you never know. She scanned order sheets, invoices, and handwritten notes. Everything seemed perfectly ordinary. Orders had come in from Busacker's Grocery and Kohn's Restaurant. There were hand-printed invoices that were ready to be mailed out. She saw no glaring problems, no brilliant clues that leapt out at her.

Suzanne heard the rumble of a big engine and glanced out a window. Lansky was just leaving in his red Ford truck. He'd probably managed to strike a satisfactory deal with Claudia. But really, it didn't matter what was sold or not. If Claudia had made up her mind to sell the whole place to Byron Wolf, then it would all be auctioned off, hauled away and dumped, or sold for scrap.

Sad, she thought, that someone's life's work could be discarded so easily.

Suzanne shoved aside a stack of dog-eared papers and uncovered an old-fashioned day minder calendar. Vaguely interested, she flipped through the pages and found them dotted with notes. A few dates (delivery dates?) were circled in red. When she came to the date of Mike's murder, she paused. There was just one word scrawled there. Gleason.

Gleason? Who was that?

Suzanne wondered if this notation could be somehow important, but didn't see how it fit in. She would ask Doogie what he thought, but decided that Gleason was probably just another customer. Someone who was waiting for their wheels of cheddar cheese to show up. Now, of course, they never would.

SUZANNE drove home the same way she'd come, passing a mail truck and then going by Elder's farm. She slowed and tried to peer down his driveway. Tried to see if there was any kind of horse trading—or horse purchasing—going on. But there were too many trees blocking her view and she didn't see a thing.

A half mile down the road, Suzanne did a double take and jumped on her brakes. A teenage boy, whom she immediately recognized from last night, stood at a mailbox.

"Noah," she breathed.

Suzanne coasted in slowly and slid down her passenger side window. She drew up alongside of him and smiled. "Hi there."

Noah turned toward her and a frown flickered across his face. Then, in an instant, it was gone. "Hello," he said. His voice sounded a little creaky, as if he wasn't used to conversing with a lot of people.

"I didn't mean to startle you," Suzanne said. "I just wanted to compliment you again on your violin playing last night."

"Oh yeah?" This time he sounded friendly enough, so Suzanne climbed out of her car and came around to talk to him.

"Suzanne," she said, touching a hand to her chest.

"Noah," he said, smiling faintly, looking a little embarrassed.

"You're very talented, you know that?"

Noah shrugged. "I just do my best. I feel the music inside my head and try to interpret it."

"Well, you're very good. I imagine you'd be quite an asset to one of our local orchestras."

"I don't go to regular high school," Noah said. "I'm homeschooled."

"That sounds very nice, but I would think you'd miss hanging out with kids your own age. A lot of fun stuff happens in high school besides going to classes. Football games, dances, class plays, band, and orchestra . . ."

"Maybe." He looked shy and a little skittish, like this might have been the longest conversation he'd carried on in a while.

"Tell you what," Suzanne said. "Why don't you come to the Halloween party we're having Monday night at the Cackleberry Club? There'll be lots of kids there. Kids your own age."

"You mean at your restaurant?"

"Actually, we're holding the party in the front parking lot. There'll be a live band, costume contests, lots of food, a big bonfire, a hayride . . . I think you'd enjoy it. You should come."

"I don't know if my mom will let me."

"Well, think about it, okay? And then ask her. Because you'd surely be welcome."

"Both of us?"

"Of course, both of you."

Then, because Noah was standing there looking big eyed and nervous, like a kid desperately in need of a hug, Suzanne bent forward and swept him into her arms. "Try to make it," she urged. She gave him a gentle squeeze and was surprised when he didn't try to pull away from her.

CHAPTER 19

"SAM was just here," Toni said as Suzanne flew through the door of the Cackleberry Club.

Suzanne skidded to a stop. "He was? When?"

"Ah, he left maybe twenty minutes ago. Dropped by to see you, I suppose. Though you'd never know it to see him scraping the last vestiges of Petra's lemon pie off his plate." She grinned. "I can see the way to that cutie's heart is through a rich dessert."

"Did you tell Sam where I was?"

Toni reached up and made a zipping motion across her lips. "No, I did not, missy. I figured your horse caper might make him a tad uneasy and I saw no reason to rock the boat. Especially with your impending marriage and all."

"Thank you," Suzanne said.

"Hey, it's the girlfriend code. We have to cover for each other, right?"

Suzanne looked around the café and saw that half the tables were occupied. "We're still busy."

"Moderately," Toni said. She'd changed from this morning's black skirt and blouse to a turquoise blue cowboy shirt and faded blue jeans that looked like they were airbrushed on. "Nothing I couldn't handle."

"How's Petra doing?"

"She's just a regular little trooper with her marching orders. She's got the pizza dough all made and a big pot of tomato sauce simmering on the stove. And now she's got three ladies coming in to the Knitting Nest at two-thirty for an autumn wreath–making workshop."

"Are these fabric wreaths or dried leaves and flowers?"

Toni threw up her hands. "How should I know? I'm the least creative in the bunch and always the last one to get any drip or drab of pertinent information."

"Toni," Suzanne said, leaning in close, "I'd watch out for that proverbial lightning bolt from above. Because you are usually the *first* one to know every pesky little detail. And, if you don't know something, you worm your way in until you figure it out."

Toni liked that. "It's like I'm my own little social media platform," she said, wiggling her hips. "Who needs Facebooking, Twittering, and tweeting when I got my own brand of twerk!"

MID-AFTERNOON brought only a few customers to the Cackleberry Club for tea. With Petra holding her wreathmaking class, Suzanne stepped in to handle the tea service. She brewed pots of Assam and Darjeeling tea, served scones, and whipped up a dozen or so chicken and chutney tea sandwiches that she cut into dainty little triangles.

Toni poked her head into the kitchen. "Mrs. Beckman requested a pot of Nilgiri tea. Do we have that?"

"We should," Suzanne said. She hurried into the café and checked her stash of tea. "Yup, here you go." She handed a tea tin to Toni.

Toni balanced the shiny black tin in her hand. "Just think, this tea is imported all the way from India."

"The Blue Mountains of India."

"That means that tea pickers probably plucked these very leaves by hand. The plants were probably growing on some ridiculously steep slope and they had to climb all the way up there to get it. Kind of amazing, huh?"

"Imagine when Chinese tea was first brought to Europe on clipper ships," Suzanne said. "It must have been quite a journey."

"Yeah," Toni said. "That had to be a much bigger hassle than just shipping it by FedEx."

"Toni, does the name 'Gleason' mean anything to you?" Suzanne asked as Toni measured out the tea.

"Not really. Oh, wait. I once knew a Patty Gleason who ran a beauty salon over near Mankato. But I think she ran away with the local undertaker. Why do you ask?"

"It's probably not important."

As the last of their tea drinkers lingered, Suzanne and Petra grabbed baskets of colored gourds.

"We've got to jazz this place up," Suzanne said. "After all, this is the kickoff for Halloween weekend."

"Are we gonna wear our costumes all day Monday?" Toni asked.

"Why not? It'll give our customers a good laugh."

"But I don't have mine done yet."

"I'll help you with the tutu part," Suzanne said. "But if you want to be a ballerina, you're going to need a pair of dancing shoes."

"I have just the thing," Toni said. "An old pair of Capezios that I bought at Milda's Thrift Shop a couple of years ago. They're like real thin black leather slip-ons and the soles are super flat."

"They sound perfect," Suzanne said.

"Except for the fact that they kill my feet."

"Nobody said being a prima ballerina was easy."

ONCE the gourds were poked into every little nook and cranny and stuck on the high shelves where Suzanne's collection of ceramic chickens reigned supreme, it was time to bring out the big guns.

"I can't wait to get the real Halloween decorations up," Toni said. She grabbed a plastic skeleton by its neck and yanked him out of a large cardboard box. "Where do you think we should hang Señor Muerte?"

"Anywhere he won't get in the way," Suzanne said. "Since he is life-sized."

"Really, death-sized," Toni cracked.

They hung skeletons, fluttering bats, and gossamer ghosts, then Toni made a big production out of stretching fake cobwebs across Petra's pass-through.

"This is really gonna bug her," Toni cackled.

"Then maybe you shouldn't do it," Suzanne said.

"No, no, this will be great. Petra freaks out if she even comes *near* a spiderweb. I once saw her stumble into a ginormous web in her garden and she looked like Marcel Marceau doing his pantomime act. Her arms were flailing and she was hopping all over the place. It was hysterical."

"As long as you're willing to suffer the consequences," Suzanne said.

"And we should have some dried-flower arrangements on the tables, too."

"Go check with Petra, see if she's got extra."

Turns out she did. So they dragged out all their vases, plopped in some colorful leaves along with dried milkweed pods, hydrangeas, and yarrow, and tied orange ribbons around the base of the vases.

"Perfect," Toni said.

The front door opened and a whoosh of cool air rushed in, setting the ghosts in motion.

"What up!" called a voice.

Suzanne and Toni turned to see who their visitor was. Only it wasn't really a visitor at all. It was Joey, their slacker teenage busboy who fancied himself a rap star. Duded out in baggy pants with chains hanging down to his knees, an Oakland Raiders jacket, and his baseball cap stuck on backward, he was here to help with the pizza party.

"Those ghosts are bumpin'," Joey said.

"Pardon?" Suzanne said.

"That means I like 'em," Joey translated.

"And I'm crazy about your costume," Toni said.

Joey scrunched up his young, almost babyish, face in protest. "No, ma'am. These are just my everydays."

"Do you always talk like that, Joey?" Suzanne asked. "Even at home?"

"Yo," Joey said. "My peeps are cool with it." He looked around again. "So . . . wassup?"

"I'll tell you what," Suzanne said. "Go hang up your jacket, pull up your pants, and wash your hands. Then you can slip into a bumpin' black apron and get to work. The mozzarella needs to be shredded, and then the long tables need to be lined up for our pizza buffet. And, let's see, maybe you could bring in the sheet cake from my car."

They all got to work in the kitchen. Slicing onions, mushrooms, and pepperoni, sautéing sweet Italian sausage, and greasing the pizza pans.

Once Joey had finished with the cheese, Suzanne had him haul out the extra tables and set them up.

"Be sure to lock the legs," Suzanne told him. "We don't want these tables collapsing on us."

"What all are you gonna serve?" Joey asked.

"Five different kinds of pizza, an Italian salad, garlic bread, trays full of relishes, and chocolate cake."

"Tasty."

"Joey," Suzanne said as she draped red-and-white-checkered cloths across the tables, "do you know Noah Jorgenson?"

"Kind of," Joey said. "At least I *used* to. We were in fourth and fifth grades together. But then his old lady pulled him out of school."

"Why was that? Do you know?"

"I don't know all the details. But Noah's mother has always been kind of freaky. She's always jacked up about something. School shootings, drugs, you name it."

"Do you think Noah has a learning disability?"

Joey scratched his head. "I don't know. Seems to me he was smart enough, but I remember somebody saying something about a problem."

"Do you think he has Asperger's? Or autism?"

"I don't remember hearing that." Joey gave a rueful chuckle. "But you know, half the kids in my class have been diagnosed with ADHD. Some of them even have a sweet little side business going. They sell their Ritalin to the other kids."

"That's awful," Suzanne said. Then, "Are there kids in your school who deal other drugs?" She knew Sam was scheduled to give a talk on drugs in the next couple of weeks.

Joey's eyes slid away from her. "I guess sometimes they do. You know, weed, poppers, that kind of thing."

"Anything else?"

"Maybe."

Suzanne lifted an eyebrow. "Maybe?"

Joey looked stricken.

"I'm not accusing you," Suzanne said. "I'm just wondering."

"Ah gee, Mrs. D. These days, there's nasty stuff all over

the place. Bath salts, PCP, meth, crack, whatever you want. I even see dealers hanging out sometimes. But I never get involved in that shit. It rots your brain."

"Good boy," Suzanne said. She hoped she could believe him.

At four o'clock they all gathered in the kitchen, ready to start making the pizzas.

"Where did you get all these pizza pans?" Toni asked.

"The Save Mart," Petra said. "They were having a sale."

"Wait a minute," Toni said as Petra suddenly brandished her rolling pin. "We're just going to *roll out* our pizza crusts? Why don't we toss them up in the air like you see those fancy chefs on TV doing?"

Petra gave her a thin smile. "Be my guest. Who am I to stifle your culinary flair and showmanship?"

"Hah," Joey said. "You mean *dough*manship."

Toni grabbed a blob of dough and flattened it out gently with her hands. When it was almost pie sized, she started spinning it on top of her palm, rapidly moving her fingers like she was playing a clarinet.

"Don't tell me she can really . . ." Petra began.

That's when it all went a little crazy. Toni tossed the dough high above her head where it grazed the ceiling and managed one full, magnificent twirl, unfurling into a flat crust almost magically. Then, seconds later, it dropped like a rock and landed directly on top of her head. *Plop!*

"Agh!" Toni screamed. Draped in dough, looking like some kind of high-gluten ghost, her voice was muffled. Then her fingers scrabbled frantically to dig the dough out of her nose and mouth. "I can't breathe!" she wheezed. Suzanne and Petra were laughing so hard they were almost choking.

"I mean it!" Toni cried out as her arms flailed wildly. "Get this crap off me."

Joey made a two-handed grab and yanked the hunk of dough off Toni's head. "You okay under all that?" he asked.

"I guess," Toni grumped. "I felt like I was smothering." She brushed bits of dough from her face, then felt around her right eye and blinked rapidly. "Uh-oh, I think my fake eyelash got yanked off with the dough."

Petra just shook her head.

CHAPTER 20

AT six o'clock the floodgates opened and customers began to pour in. Suzanne stood at the front door, a smile on her face, welcoming everyone. Business looked like it was going to be good, so blessings on everyone's head. They were going to turn a nice profit tonight.

As Suzanne directed guests to their tables, she gave everyone a quick rundown on how the pizza buffet worked. Which was basically telling everyone that they could help themselves to as much food as they wanted for the $7.95 admission charge. Petra was in the kitchen popping pizza pies into a hot oven as fast as she could pull out baked ones. Toni and Joey floated in between, pouring water, serving soft drinks, cutting the pizzas into slices, and then ferrying the still-steaming pies out to the buffet tables.

Suzanne was thrilled with the turnout—it looked like half the town had showed up! Bill and Jenny Probst, Gene Gandle, the writer and ad sales guy from the *Bugle*, Lolly Herron and a couple of her friends, and four dozen more.

The sweet scent of basil, onions, herbs, and sausage spiced the air along with the buzz of lively conversation.

"We're the hottest ticket in town tonight," Toni said to Suzanne.

Suzanne had to agree. "It's looking good." Of course, they had another couple hours to go. They needed to have, in restaurant parlance, a second seating.

"Uh-oh." Toni glanced out the door and made an unconscious grimace.

"What?"

"Look what the cat just dragged in."

Junior was suddenly standing in the doorway, grinning from ear to ear. "Hello, ladies." He rocked back on his heels and, with sleepy eyes, casually surveyed the restaurant as if he were the lord of the manor checking on his loyal subjects.

Toni leaned forward and sniffed his breath. "Junior, you miserable little weasel. Have you been drinking?"

Junior shrugged. "I might have had a bump on the way over."

"Bump or bumps?"

"Why do you have to be so snoopy?" Junior asked. "I don't see you coming by my trailer to cook dinner for me. Or pay me *any* attention for that matter."

"That's because we're getting a *divorce*," Toni snarled back. Even though she still hadn't bothered to file.

"How's the car wash coming along?" Suzanne asked suddenly. If she didn't change the subject, Toni and Junior would snipe at each other all night.

Junior immediately brightened. "It's good, Suzanne. And thanks for asking. I got my new hydrovalve installed today and it's shootin' jets of water better than a gosh darn water park. I even ran my truck through to test things."

"How did that go?" Suzanne asked.

"Got some bugs to work out," Junior admitted.

"Water bugs?" Toni asked.

Junior shuffled his feet. "Some of the mechanicals need fine-tuning."

"That means the machinery probably ripped the bumpers off his truck," Toni said.

"Just a few minor scratches and dents," Junior said. "Nothing I can't buff out." He glanced around the café. "Hey, why don't you let me play maître d' for a while?"

"Think you can handle it?" Suzanne asked. She really did need to check on a few other things.

"Sure. All I have to do is welcome folks and direct them to a table, right? It's all self-service."

"Hey, genius, a buffet is generally self-service," Toni said as she wrapped a white apron around Junior's waist. "Now just be friendly," she admonished. "Act nice and don't *breathe* on anyone."

TEN minutes later Sam showed up, as well as Reverend Yoder from the church next door. Sam came by himself; Reverend Yoder brought his Friday-night youth group.

"We're forgoing Bible study tonight in favor of pizza," Reverend Yoder told Suzanne as two dozen teenagers stampeded for the food.

"Glad to have you," Suzanne said. "Our fire-roasted peppers and green chili pizza should easily take the place of a little fire and brimstone."

Reverend Yoder, who was tall, thin, and almost Calvinistic in his bearing, just chuckled. He may have looked like a stern, Bible Belt preacher but he had a gracious heart and finely tuned sense of humor.

Sam grabbed Suzanne by the hand and pulled her into a corner. "I missed you," he said. He gave her a modest peck, but his lips still managed to convey a warm urgency.

Suzanne wanted nothing more than to throw her arms around Sam, but figured she had to restrain herself. At least for another couple of hours. Then she could drag this wonderful man back to her house and have her way with him.

"Hey, no nuzzling in the corner," Toni yelled at them.

"Sorry I had to skip out at noon," Suzanne told him.

"Business problems?" Sam asked.

"Kind of. I'll tell you about it later."

Sam moved closer to her. "I suppose I should let you get back to your pizza party."

"And you should hurry up and grab a plate," Suzanne said. *Or we could duck out the back door right now.*

Toni came hustling over and stuck a clean plate in Sam's hands. "If you don't start loading up with goodies, you're gonna miss out," she told him. "These people are chowing down like a bunch of marauding Visigoths. Especially those Bible study kids."

While Sam helped himself to the food, Suzanne grabbed two empty pizza pans and ran them back into the kitchen. Luckily, Petra was just pulling two freshly baked pizzas from the oven.

"Sausage and mushroom," Petra said. "And pepperoni and green pepper."

"They sound delicious," Suzanne said.

Joey was suddenly hovering nearby. "You want me to slice those pizza pies?" he asked.

"Go ahead," Petra said. "But cut them in smaller squares instead of triangles. They'll go farther."

The door swung open and Toni appeared. "Are there more pizzas? We're almost wiped out."

"Coming right up," Suzanne said.

While Joey was slicing the pizzas like a pro, he said, "Have you guys heard about our Haunted Forest?"

"I think I read something about it in the *Bugle*," Toni said.

"The junior and senior classes at my high school put it together," Joey said. "It's like a haunted house only we're staging it outdoors in the woods. We're trying to earn enough money so we can all take a trip to Chicago next spring."

"How's it going so far?" Suzanne asked.

"Pretty good," Joey said. "We've only been open two nights and we've already made some serious coinage. You guys should come. We're set up in the woods over near Catawba Creek."

"And it's some kind of ghost walk?" Toni asked.

"That's right," Joey said. "And it's real spooky, not just fake spooky. What happens is . . . you walk down this dark wooded path and all sorts of weird shit pops out at you. Monsters, vampires, Freddy Krueger, you name it."

"It sounds exciting," Toni said.

"It sounds too much like real life," Suzanne said.

FIFTY minutes later they were turning over their tables. The early birds had eaten, burped happily, and shuffled off. Now a second shift had arrived. These new arrivals grabbed slices of pizza and soft drinks and settled in at the tables.

Suddenly, right in the middle of all this good food and cheer, the front door flew open and smacked hard against the wall. *Whap!*

Suzanne, who was busy replenishing the salad bowl, looked up distractedly and said, "What?"

That's when Sheriff Doogie stomped into the Cackleberry Club. He glowered over the crowd until he finally spotted Suzanne. "All right, where are they?" he yelled at the top of his lungs. His belly jiggled, his jowls sloshed, even his Smokey Bear hat teetered precariously on his head.

Suzanne, who was dealing with a tumble of baby field greens, barely glanced at him. "Where are what?" she asked in a slightly perturbed tone of voice. Honestly, what was Doogie's problem? Why was he yelling at *her*? What had set off his magic twanger *this* time?

"The horses!" Doogie thundered.

That brought everything to a screeching halt. Customers paused mid-bite, the people going through the buffet line turned to stare. Petra peeked out the pass-through, gave a shrill scream, and batted away fake cobwebs.

Suzanne stared at Doogie as if he were the only person standing in the café. "Horses?" she said. What on earth was he babbling about?

Doogie spread his feet apart and self-importantly adjusted his utility belt. "Come on, Suzanne, don't play cute with me. Julian Elder just alerted me to the fact that you stole four of his horses."

Suzanne touched a hand to her chest. "He said *I* stole them?" This wasn't just confusing—Doogie had obviously been completely misinformed. "There must be a mistake. The rescue people—Cassie from Hoof-Beats Horse Rescue— she must have bought them all."

"Elder says she didn't," Doogie said. "He says she bought four horses early this afternoon. Then a few hours later, the remaining four horses that he *didn't* sell to her mysteriously disappeared from his pasture."

"Cassie *must* have bought them all," Suzanne repeated.

Doogie shook his head. "That's not how Elder tells it."

Suzanne was dumbfounded. "Then what . . . ?" She looked at Sam for help, but he seemed even more confused than she was. A movement off to her left caught her eye. Junior was easing his way into the Book Nook, tiptoeing like a cartoon bank robber, a guilty look pasted across his face.

"Junior!" Suzanne yelled out. "Did you say something to Julian Elder?"

"Who, me?" Junior halted in his tracks and made a big production out of trying to look innocent. That's when Suzanne knew he was the one who'd been running his mouth off.

"Did you talk to Julian Elder?" Suzanne asked.

Sheriff Doogie frowned at Junior. "Junior?" he barked. "How are you involved in this? What's going on?"

Junior hung his head. "I dunno. I might have said something. I ran into Julian Elder at the pawn shop this afternoon. I was looking for a good used servomotor."

"Junior," Suzanne said again. "Did you tell Elder that Toni and I were looking at his horses last night?"

"You were what?" Doogie whooped. His florid face turned an even deeper crimson.

"I might have," Junior said. He scratched his head as if he were deep in thought. "Well, I guess I probably did. But mostly I was fishing around for information, trying to figure out if Elder knew anything about poor Mike being stabbed."

"I specifically told you *not* to investigate!" Suzanne hissed.

"*Nobody* should be investigating," Doogie thundered. "I don't want *any* one of you hunyucks sticking their nose in my official investigation."

OFFICIAL or not, Doogie still insisted on having Suzanne accompany him to her barn across the back field. Naturally, she was furious over his accusation of horse thievery, but she went anyway. Sam went along with her.

Suzanne slid open the barn door and flipped on the light. Dust swirled in the faint yellow glow of the overhead bulbs, revealing a mountain of stacked hay bales. Off to the left, two polished saddles rested on sawhorses. Bridles, halters, and other tack hung on metal hooks.

Doogie strode into the barn, then stopped in a puddle of light. Hands planted firmly on his hips, feet set apart, he gazed around.

From between the wooden slats of the two box stalls way at the back of the cavernous barn, two animals stared back at him. Suzanne's horse, Mocha Gent, and her large black mule, Grommet.

Doogie's face pinched into a frown as he did a three-hundred-sixty-degree scan of the entire barn. Finally, he said, "I'll be darned."

"No kidding," Suzanne said.

Sam stepped in swiftly. "I'd say you owe Suzanne an apology."

Doogie spun around a second time, as if to make sure the missing horses weren't hiding in the hayloft or peeking out from behind a Navajo saddle blanket. Then he gazed at Suzanne. "What did you do with them?"

Suzanne shook her head. She was as puzzled as he was. "I didn't do anything with them."

But Doogie was all frothed up and wasn't about to take no for an answer. "Come on, where are they?"

"You are so going off in the wrong direction," Suzanne said. "Because I have no idea where Elder's horses disappeared to." She folded her arms across her chest and gave Doogie a challenging stare. "But clearly they are not here."

SUZANNE was still in a huff as she locked up the barn. Doogie had left in his cruiser, but her mind kept rumbling over his unfounded accusations.

"Why on earth would Doogie think that I stole those horses?" she asked.

Sam fixed her with a skeptical gaze. "Oh, I don't know, Suzanne. Let me think about this. Maybe it's because you were instrumental in helping four of them get purchased? Which I just now found out about. Or maybe because you have an enormous soft spot in your heart for homeless horses? Or perhaps it's because you . . ."

Suzanne held up a hand. "Okay. I see where you're going with this."

Sam moved closer to her. "Listen, it's just you and me

now. Nobody around except maybe an owl perched up in a tree. So tell me the truth. You really didn't move those horses somewhere?"

"No, cross my heart. I'm as puzzled about this as Doogie."

"He wasn't just puzzled," Sam said. "He was spitting mad." He peered at her again. "You're sure you don't know?"

"No, I don't," Suzanne said slowly. "But I have a couple of ideas, things I'd like to check out."

Sam caught her hand and squeezed it gently. "I think maybe there's been enough investigating for one night. Don't you?"

Suzanne smiled at him. His eyes sparkled and in the hazy light he looked like he was about twenty-two. *Mmmm,* she thought. *He really is quite delicious.* All thoughts of Doogie and missing horses slowly vanished from her brain. She stood on tiptoes and kissed Sam. "You have something else in mind?" It had been a long, crazy day that started with a funeral, segued into a nasty encounter with a food broker, and ended with a scene right out of *Bonanza* where she'd been accused of horse thievery. Now what could cap off a day like that?

"I have an idea," Sam whispered. He slid his hands around her waist and pulled her closer. "Do I ever."

CHAPTER 21

SATURDAY morning at the Cackleberry Club brought poached eggs on sweet potato muffins, cheddar breakfast strata, and blueberry puffy muffins. Petra was whistling away at the stove, wearing an oversized T-shirt that said Fries Before Guys, baggy khaki pants, and her green Crocs.

Suzanne and Toni hovered nearby, ready to grab orders and scoot them out to their customers.

"That sure was fun last night," Toni said.

Petra turned and arched her brows. "Until Sheriff Doogie came galloping in for the last roundup."

"He did make quite a scene," Toni said. She glanced at Suzanne, who hadn't said much about it. "Honey, are you okay? You look a little peaked."

"To tell you the truth," Suzanne said, "I'm still ticked off about Doogie. If he had barged in any earlier, he might have completely ruined our event."

"He certainly went off the deep end," Petra said. She placed buttered sweet potato muffins on four medium-sized plates.

"Doogie's a master at the art of overreacting," Toni agreed as she buttered two orders of toast. "He wrote the book on it." She placed little packets of jelly next to the toast.

"Still," Suzanne said, "it was wrong to come stomping in here and accuse me of stealing horses."

"He was dead wrong," Petra said. "He could have handled things much better." She scooped perfectly poached eggs from a pan of simmering water and gently plopped them atop the muffins.

"I wonder where those horses really are?" Toni asked. "Do you think actual horse thieves still exist in this day and age?"

"Apparently so," Suzanne said.

"But your evening turned out okay?" Toni asked. She had a mischievous smile on her face now. "I mean, you and Sam . . . ?"

Suzanne blushed. "Well, I guess . . ."

"Whoo-hoo," Toni whooped. "Details, please."

"Don't go there," Petra warned.

"I never kiss and tell," Suzanne said primly.

"Honey, I want to hear about more than just plain old kissin'," Toni said.

Petra placed her hands on her ample hips. "Toni, there are orders to deliver."

ONCE all the breakfast orders had been delivered to their early-morning customers, Suzanne had another mission in mind. She grabbed the business card that Cassie Givens had given her yesterday and dialed her number. When Cassie answered, Suzanne said, "Cassie, this is Suzanne Dietz at the Cackleberry Club. We have a huge problem."

"Excuse me?" Cassie sounded a little fuzzy, like she'd just woken up.

"Did you haul away all eight of Julian Elder's horses?"

"What?" Cassie sounded legitimately confused. "Um . . . what are you talking about?"

"Julian Elder's horses have mysteriously disappeared," Suzanne said. "Did you take them?"

"No, of course not," Cassie said. She was sounding a little more awake now. "I just took the four that I bought from him. Like I told you, there wasn't enough money to purchase them all."

"So you really didn't take the final four horses as well?"

"No. And why are you asking? What's going on?"

Suzanne quickly explained the situation.

Cassie was outraged at any hint of impropriety. "I wouldn't just *steal* horses," she said. "That would put our entire organization at risk. We have a group of very dedicated volunteers as well as some fairly high-test people who sit on our board of directors. Lawyers, some marketing people, a couple of veterinarians. I'd never betray their trust by pulling an illegal stunt like that." She paused. "You do believe me, don't you?"

Suzanne was 99.9 percent convinced. "Yes, I do."

"Besides," Cassie continued, "I could barely squeeze the four horses I did buy into my trailer, pathetic and skinny as those poor things were."

"Cassie," Suzanne said, "I'm sorry to bother you. Even sorrier to have doubted you."

"That's okay, that's okay. Just, um . . . well, do you have any idea where those horses disappeared to?"

"I'm afraid not. But I'm assuming our local sheriff will be hot on their trail. At least he was last night."

"Jeez. Wow. Well, keep me in the loop, will you?"

"I sure will," Suzanne said.

She walked back into the kitchen looking puzzled.

"I take it you didn't find the missing horses?" Petra asked.

Suzanne shook her head. "Nope. The Hoof-Beats lady didn't take them."

Toni had followed her in. "I didn't think Cassie carted

them away. I mean, you saw that broken-down trailer she was towing. It was a squeeze just to get four of those nags in there."

"So where did they disappear to?" Petra asked. She could tell Suzanne was still puzzled and a little upset. "Do you think Elder already shipped them off to Canada and is trying to pull a fast one? Make out a fraudulent insurance claim or just try to get you in trouble?"

Suzanne shook her head. "I honestly have no idea."

Toni grabbed a sugar donut and started munching. "Good thing we're closing at one o'clock today. And that we've got tomorrow off. I think we all need a break."

"You got that right," Petra said. "Me, I'm going to work on my new quilt. I started a star flower pattern."

"You're so dang creative," Toni said. "I was just gonna dial up some Netflix and settle in with Matthew McConaughey or Charlie Hunnam."

"So you guys think we're all set for Monday?" Petra asked. "For Halloween?"

"I think so," Suzanne said. "We're still going to serve Halloween specials all day long?"

"For sure," Petra said.

"And the little kids are invited to trick or treat from four to six?"

"And then our party for adults begins at seven."

"Hot dog," Toni said. "I guess you've lined up a band and everything?"

"I've got the Whistling Dixies coming in," Suzanne said. "And we'll have fire pits, grilled brats, costume contests, and a hay wagon."

"Who says we don't know how to throw a great party?" Petra said. She glanced at Suzanne, who was putting leftover cheese into plastic bags. "Suzanne, do you think you could carry out the trash for me? I don't want to run into that awful hissing creature again."

"Where's your sense of adventure?" Toni asked. "Maybe you could befriend that little opossum. Tame him or something. Then we could put up a YouTube video of the two of you cuddling together."

"Dream on," Petra said.

SUZANNE carried two bags of trash outside and tossed them into the Dumpster. The day had dawned hazy and cool, but a nice yellow sun was starting to peep through the clouds, promising to warm things up into the low sixties. The line of trees that stood between the Cackleberry Club and the farm fields out back was still a riot of color, and the Kodachrome reds, oranges, and russets lifted Suzanne's spirits enormously.

Sheriff Doogie may have intruded on her pizza party last night, but he wasn't going to intrude on her life. Not if she had to kick him to the curb all by herself.

As Suzanne crunched back across the back parking lot, she noticed a small, dark object leaning near the back door.

What is that? It looks almost like a child's toy.

It was toy. In fact, it was a little stuffed horse.

What on earth?

Curious now, she leaned over and picked it up. The little toy horse was a scuffed, plush animal with a mane and tail made out of yellow yarn, and little black beads sewn on for eyes. The nose was smooth and worn as if it had been well loved.

Suzanne cradled the tattered little horse in her hands. The black, beady eyes seemed to stare up at her with sweet intensity.

Who did this? she wondered. *Did someone leave this for me?*

It was puzzling at best. Maybe Petra had seen someone . . .

But when Suzanne stepped into the kitchen, there was no time to question Petra or Toni. Junior was already leaning against the counter, legs crossed, slurping a poached egg out of a ceramic mug.

"I got an important favor to ask you," Junior said when he saw Suzanne.

Suzanne smiled at him. "The answer is no."

"Whaaa?" Junior's face dissolved into a disappointed pucker. "You don't even know what the question is."

"She can guess," Toni said.

Junior set down his mug and postured importantly. "I was hoping you'd let me hold my auditions here."

"The answer is still no," Suzanne said.

"You know, auditions for my car wash girls?" Junior finished lamely.

"Are you deaf?" Toni asked. "What part of 'no' don't you understand? Now take your stupid eggs and move your scrawny butt out of here." She grabbed Junior by the arm, spun him around, and physically pushed him into the café.

Suzanne followed along. "I have a suggestion," she said once Junior had seated himself at the counter. "Why don't you hold your fantasy girl auditions at Hoobly's Roadhouse, where they already feature exotic dancers?" She ducked behind the counter to grab a cup of coffee for herself. "Maybe you can interest a couple of those ladies."

"I already explored that angle," Junior said. "And not one of those attractive young women was even remotely interested. First off, they told me they didn't *want* any kind of dumb day job. And then they told me they didn't want to get their hair wet."

"What else?" Toni asked.

Junior hung his head. "They told me they didn't think tips at a car wash would amount to very much."

Petra leaned down and poked her head through the pass-through. "Tips?" she called out. "Did I hear somebody say tips? If so, I'm available."

*   *   *

AND still Junior was harder to get rid of than a bunch of freeloading cousins at a family picnic. He remained on the fringes of the café, munching a donut and muttering to himself. Finally, when Toni zipped by him for about the fourth time, he grabbed her and said, "Toni, you're driving me crazy with that perfume you're wearing. What is it anyway? Something by one of those fancy French designers? Yves LePeu or Christian Die-orey?"

Toni glared at him like he was off his rocker. "What you're probably smelling is the faint aroma of the roach spray I used out by the garbage cans."

"Whatever it is," Junior said, "it's turning me on."

"Junior," Toni warned, "just sit at the counter like a good little boy."

"Are you still gonna come over and help me with the dishes this afternoon?" he asked. "'Cause they're really piling up. You should see my kitchen, it's a disaster zone."

"That's because you're turning into a hoarder."

"Naw," Junior said. "I just don't like doing the dishes."

He sat at the counter, staring into the glass pie saver, not saying a thing for a good twenty minutes.

"You okay, Junior?" Suzanne finally asked. "Is there somewhere else you have to be?" *Like, not here?*

"I was counting the colored sprinkles on that donut."

"Fascinating."

Junior swiveled in his chair to face her. "I've been thinking, too."

"There's a first," Toni quipped.

"About Mike's murder," Junior said. "And the disappearing horses." He made a vague spinning gesture with his hands. "The way I see it, it's all balled up together."

"And then again maybe it's not," Suzanne said.

"I still think you guys should let me put on my Sherlock Holmes hat and do some investigating."

"Please don't," Suzanne said.

Toni sidled over to join them. "Don't be rockin' the boat, Junior."

A cagey look came into his eyes. "But I know something you guys don't."

"What's that, Junior?" Suzanne asked.

Junior slid off his stool and postured like he was about to address a class of graduating lawyers. "I happened to see that Byron Wolf guy over at the County Registrar's office yesterday afternoon, when I was looking into how to get a Commercial Class A driver's license. And I know for a fact that he was doing some sort of official transaction with that lady with the jiggly arms."

"You mean Mrs. Manchester?" Toni asked. Mrs. Manchester used to teach freshman English at the high school until somebody slipped a rubber spider down the back of her dress. Then she handed in her resignation and found a new job with the county.

Junior nodded. "That's the lady. She was stamping a piece of paper, like, a million times." He cackled nastily. "Man, her arms were jiggling like crazy. Like big old tubs of Jell-O."

"You mean, like she was recording a deed?" Suzanne asked. This information was suddenly very interesting to her.

Junior shrugged. "Yeah. Maybe. Probably she was."

"Jeez," Toni said. "Do you think Claudia really did sell the farm to the Big Bad Wolf? That now it's a done deal?"

Suzanne was still processing this. "I don't know. But it would be nice to get the particulars on this."

Junior tapped his chest. "I bet I could find out."

"No, Junior," Suzanne warned. "Don't get involved."

"You'll just mess things up," Toni said.

Dismayed, Junior cried, "That's exactly the kind of sassy

disregard that frosts my butt!" Then he stomped out of the Cackleberry Club, letting the door slam behind him.

"Finally," Toni said.

"You know that Junior's going to sit in his truck and sulk," Suzanne said. "He'll wait for you to come out and prop him back up."

Toni turned up her nose. "He can sit there all day. Me, I'm waiting for my Prince Charming."

Petra came out to join them, wiping her hands on a dish towel. "Don't bother," she said. "Men never ask for directions, so your prince probably took a wrong turn and got hopelessly lost."

CHAPTER 22

AN idea had been niggling in Suzanne's brain ever since that little stuffed horse had turned up on her back doorstep.

So, against her better judgment, she drove out to the Jorgenson farm.

When she pulled into their driveway, Noah was outside, tossing a Frisbee to a shaggy black-and-white dog. He wore a tan barn jacket, blue jeans, and lace-up boots. In other words, he looked like any other teenage kid.

When Suzanne climbed out of her car, the black-and-white dog rushed over to greet her. She held out a hand so the dog could sniff her and know she was friendly.

"That's my dog, Sissy," Noah said as he came over. "I think she likes you."

"She's a very pretty dog," Suzanne said as Sissy immediately lost interest and wandered away.

"She's part Australian shepherd, which is a kind of herding breed, so she's real good with other animals."

That was the opening Suzanne needed.

"Noah, I need to talk to you."

He gave her a quizzical but benign gaze. "What about, ma'am?"

"I think you might know." Suzanne glanced around. The Jorgenson farm was a small farm, probably not a working farm since she didn't see tractors or equipment of any sort sitting around. There was just a sedate-looking white house, a faded red barn, and a detached two-car garage. "Is your mom home?"

"She's in the house. Taking a nap."

"Did you send me a message earlier today?" Suzanne asked. Then she decided this might be a little too cryptic. Noah struck her as having a more literal interpretation of things. "Did you drop by the Cackleberry Club and leave something for me?"

A faint smile played at Noah's mouth. "Did you like it?"

"I liked it very much," Suzanne said. "That was very sweet of you to leave that little stuffed toy for me. I love horses. I have one myself."

"I know. I saw you riding at the county fair last August. You were doing the barrel racing thing."

"You were there?"

"You won a third-place ribbon. Pretty good."

"I think I surprised myself," Suzanne said. "It ended up being a very wild ride." She paused. "Do you want your little horse back?"

"It's okay, you can keep him."

Suzanne smiled at Noah. "But you know the other horses have got to go back."

Noah was instantly on alert. "What do you mean?"

"I think you and I are starting to become pretty good friends. So it's probably time you start leveling with me."

Noah swallowed hard. "Yeah . . . maybe."

"Did you take those horses?"

"You mean after that lady drove off with the horses in the trailer?"

"You know about that?"

He nodded. "I see what goes on around here. I get around. There are lots of trails and paths through the woods."

"So you know that there were four horses left behind at Julian Elder's farm," Suzanne said. "And that they've disappeared."

Noah took a step backward and planted himself stiffly. "What if I did take them?"

"Well, it could be a problem." Suzanne tried to sound more philosophical than threatening. "For one thing, those horses don't belong to you. For another thing, the sheriff is out looking for them."

Noah's eyes got big. "The sheriff is, really?" He looked frightened and a little proud at the same time. "In a way, that's kind of . . . cool."

"So you did wrangle those horses?"

"Yeah, but it wasn't any big deal."

Suzanne glanced at the nearby barn. "Are they stabled here? In your barn?"

Noah shook his head slowly. "Nah, I've got a better place. A secret place."

"Where is that?"

Noah jerked a thumb. "Out in the woods where I know they'll be safe."

"Noah, why did you take them?" Suzanne studiously avoided using the word "steal."

Noah looked at her as if she just didn't get it. "To save their lives, of course. Just like Mike did."

To Suzanne's ears, Noah sounded completely logical, without any pretense or guile involved.

"But you must have known you'd get in trouble over this," she said.

Noah shrugged. "What are they going to do to me?" He didn't seem particularly worried. "Put me in jail?"

"Probably not."

"Listen," Noah said, and now his face took on a glow of intensity. "I know those horses were gonna get shipped to Canada. I know all about that. My mom thinks I'm too sensitive to hear that kind of stuff, but I'm not. I'm really not."

"Who told you about horses going to Canada?" Suzanne asked. But she already knew the answer.

"Mike did. That's why he bought the three horses that are in his barn. But I'm scared they might send those away, too. Maybe they won't be saved after all."

"I don't know," Suzanne said.

She was thinking that Mike's horses had already been bought and paid for. So maybe Claudia could be talked into just turning them over to the horse rescue group. Maybe. But for right now, there were other horses to deal with. Horses that she'd been accused of stealing.

"Will you show me where you hid the horses, Noah?" Suzanne asked.

Noah didn't hesitate. "Okay."

IT wasn't so much a horse barn as a kind of low shed. A mile out in the woods where a faint path led through a narrow gulley, sumac bushes flared red, and a trickling stream spilled merrily over moss-covered rocks.

Suzanne ducked through the doorway of the small building and looked around. The place was old and weathered, the wood worn down to a soft silver finish by the elements. But the slat roof looked solid enough and the interior felt warm and sheltering. And the horses weren't all that big, so they fit inside the shed all nice and cozy-like. It was certainly better than being left out in an open pasture.

"Where'd you get the hay?" Suzanne asked. Bales were stacked everywhere and the four horses looked perfectly content as they munched away.

"Took it out of Mike's barn," Noah said. "Even though he's dead, I knew he wouldn't mind."

"No, he probably wouldn't mind. Mike was that kind of guy."

Three metal buckets were lined up against the wall.

"And they've got plenty of water?" Suzanne asked.

"I hauled it in from the spring. I think it's a pretty sweet setup."

Suzanne had to agree. The horses looked well taken care of and certainly well fed. They were probably better off than when they were just standing out in Elder's pasture. The big question was—how long could this idyllic home last? This hidden little barn with Noah acting as loving caretaker?

Suzanne feared it wouldn't be long. Reality would intrude. Julian Elder, Faith Anne, Sheriff Doogie.

Noah put an arm around a white mare's neck and gave her a kiss on the nose. "You have to keep my secret," he whispered to Suzanne.

"I don't know if I can," Suzanne said. She felt heartless saying it. The adult telling a boy he can't have his perfect little world where all creatures are safe and loved.

A shudder went through Noah's body. "If you don't, these horses will probably get sold to the bad guy who comes with a big cattle truck and smashes 'em all in together."

Suzanne touched a hand to her face. Out of the mouths of babes . . .

Noah went on. "You should have heard that last group of horses. They were crying and whinnying like crazy when they got hauled away. Scared to death of where they were going."

"Noah, I will keep your secret. But just for a couple of days. Until I figure this whole mess out."

"Please," he begged.

Suzanne glanced out one of the small windows. "Did anybody see you bring the horses back here?"

Noah shook his head. "I don't think so. Well . . . I guess somebody could have. I heard, like, an engine roaring. Could have been a trail bike or ATV. You never know. People are always roaring through the woods on those things."

"I have to ask you something else," Suzanne said. "Something really important." She hesitated. "Do you know who killed Mike?"

Noah shifted from one foot to the other. "My mother doesn't want me to talk about that."

"I'm sure she doesn't, but it's very important. Did you see who went into Mike's barn that day and killed him?"

Noah stared at her for what felt like a good couple of minutes. Finally he said, "No. But I wish I had."

"Have you ever heard of someone named Gleason? A neighbor, perhaps? Or someone that Mike might have known?"

Noah shook his head. "I never have."

CHAPTER 23

SATURDAY evening and Suzanne was far, far away from the problems of missing horses, harebrained schemes, and snarling opossums. Sam had picked her up promptly at seven and driven her in his BMW over to the nearby town of Cornucopia for the promised romantic dinner.

Sam had definitely kept his word, and then some. Suzanne was happily ensconced in a cozy leather booth at Kopell's Restaurant and Inn, where she was being treated like a proverbial princess. She and Sam were seated in a prime spot close to the warmth of the crackling fireplace. And with the dark oil paintings, stag's head décor, dim lighting, and brass wall sconces, Suzanne almost felt like she'd been swept away to some far off schloss in the Black Forest.

And there was champagne. An icy cold bottle of Taittinger Brut.

"Here's to you." Sam lifted his champagne flute in a toast.

"And to you," Suzanne said. "For helping me weather this last week."

"It's all behind you now."

Suzanne took a quick sip of champagne. "Well, not quite."

Sam fixed her with an earnest expression. "You have something more to tell me?"

"Maybe we should enjoy a little more wine first." Suzanne figured it wouldn't hurt to get Sam relaxed. A little liquored up.

Anna, their waitress, arrived with leather-bound menus and boundless enthusiasm for tonight's specials.

"Besides our regular menu," Anna said, "Chef Affolter is offering duck à l'orange, grilled venison with chanterelle sauce, and steak au poivre." She grinned as their eyes lit up. "And each entrée comes with our house salad, basket of popovers, lyonnaise potatoes, and braised asparagus."

"Yes," Sam said. "Just bring it all, thank you."

Anna winked at them. "I'll give you some more time."

"I don't need time," Sam whispered to Suzanne once the waitress had retreated. "I need food. And plenty of it."

"Did you skip lunch again?"

"Sweetheart, I skipped everything today. Breakfast, lunch, coffee, cookies in the break room, the grape suckers we hand out to kids. You name it, I've skipped it. So I'm about ready to go facedown in that wonderful-sounding steak au poivre."

"You're definitely a meat-and-potatoes guy, aren't you?"

"And wine. If I'm having red meat I feel compelled to order an excellent bottle of red wine."

"Are you going to consult your wine app?" Suzanne asked. Sam was big into wine apps, wine clubs, and wine magazines.

"Nope, I'm just going to ask for their best cabernet." Then Sam reconsidered his words and peered at her expectantly. "Unless you're going to order the duck? In which case I'll select a lovely Pouilly-Fuissé just for you."

"I'm in complete agreement on the steak. So a cab sounds perfect."

But once the Chateau Montelena Estate Cabernet Sauvignon

2007 was ordered, Bernie Affolter, the owner and head chef, came out to greet them and do the honors himself.

Large and effusive, with meaty hands and a big friendly face, Bernie was over the moon about Sam's choice of wine.

"This has been sitting in our wine cellar for a good four years," Bernie enthused as he pulled the cork. "I'm thrilled somebody finally ordered it."

"We're so glad you hung on to it for us," Sam said.

"Now you're going to want to let this breathe a bit," Bernie said. "And I see you still have some champagne left, so that shouldn't be a problem."

"No problems tonight," Sam said. Then he sat back and looked pensive. "Well, maybe just one."

Really? Suzanne thought. *When everything seems so perfect?*

Bernie looked concerned. "What's wrong, Dr. Hazelet? How can I help?"

Sam reached over and grasped Suzanne's hand. "The lovely Suzanne and I are getting married next spring. And we were thinking about having our wedding reception right here."

"Yes!" Bernie exclaimed. He clapped his hands together gleefully. "We'd be delighted. And a spring wedding means we'll have plenty of time to work out all the details and plan a truly excellent menu." He directed his gaze to Suzanne. "Maybe even a farm-to-table menu using locally sourced produce?"

Suzanne nodded. "I love that idea."

Bernie held a finger to his mouth. "But I just had another thought."

"What's that?" Sam asked.

"Why don't you get married *here*! You know, we've got a beautiful garden out back."

Sam pretended to be surprised. "Oh really?"

Which sent Bernie rushing off to grab his book of photos.

Suzanne nudged Sam. "You were setting him up."

"Having a little fun. But, seriously, what would you think about having our wedding and reception right here?"

"It sure beats the Boom Boom Room at Schmitt's Bar," Suzanne said.

Anna came back and took their orders then, and Bernie popped by and left his brag book of event photos.

"This could be it," Sam said, peeking at a couple of the pages.

"It would be expensive," Suzanne said, trying to be practical. They hadn't quite gotten down to talking finances yet. But that conversation was definitely looming on the near horizon. She didn't have a lot of extra cash and neither did Sam, so they were going to have to draw up a guest list, figure out wedding expenses, and then make some difficult choices. Well, maybe not that difficult. Because when it came to the groom, that choice had already been made. So anything after that was a Lucky Strike extra.

Sam picked up the bottle of cabernet and poured two fingers of wine into her Riedel wineglass. "Happy, sweetheart?"

Suzanne snuggled closer to him. "You know I am."

"It feels like you're more amenable now to making some actual wedding plans."

"Absolutely I am."

"Am I going to see you in a long white dress and white cowboy boots?"

"Only if you show up in your blue scrubs."

They joked back and forth as they enjoyed their wine, Suzanne feeling relaxed and in the moment, but knowing she'd have to tell Sam about the missing horses. And how they'd ended up in Noah Jorgenson's secret barn.

When the moment was right, she would explain it all to Sam. And as she gazed lovingly at him, with crystal glasses sparkling in the candlelight and the fireplace snapping and crackling a few feet away, she decided that maybe this was the right time.

"Sam . . ." Suzanne began. But she'd hesitated a split second too long. And in that exact moment his phone rang. *Oh no. No, no, no.*

"Excuse me," Sam said. He pulled his phone from his jacket pocket and held it up. "Hello?"

Bummer, was all Suzanne could think. *Really bad timing.*

"What's that?" Sam said as he casually draped an arm around Suzanne's shoulders and gently massaged them. "Speak up, please. We don't have the best connection." He smiled encouragingly at Suzanne.

Suzanne leaned back and exhaled just as Anna set a wicker basket heaped with golden brown popovers in front of them. A tiny glass dish filled with elegant honey butter accompanied the popovers.

Suzanne reached into the basket and selected a popover. She could almost taste the sweetness of the honey butter as it oozed into the popover's doughy goodness.

"A fracture?" Sam said. "Wait a minute? Who?" This time he glanced directly at Suzanne as if she was somehow involved.

"What's wrong?" Suzanne asked. An alarm bell suddenly began to clang inside her head. Had something happened to Toni? Or Petra? A car accident or worse?

Sam dropped the phone from his mouth and gazed at Suzanne, concern evident in his eyes. "Ah . . . it's Junior. His shoulder is dislocated and his leg is broken."

"Junior?" Suzanne yelped. "Toni's Junior?"

Sam looked disheartened. "I'm afraid he's going to be *my* Junior tonight. It looks like he sustained a fracture to his right tibia."

"You're not going to set the leg . . ."

"No, but I'll have to line up a decent orthopod who will. And Junior's been asking for me . . ."

Suzanne tossed her popover back into the basket and sighed. "Of course he has."

THE ride back to Kindred was anticlimactic. Until they arrived at the hospital, that was. Toni was right there waiting for them, a tiny tornado dressed in denim and cowboy boots, rushing between the ER and the front desk. Her hair was gathered into a messy topknot, she looked utterly frazzled, and Suzanne figured she'd probably been driving everyone at the hospital stark raving bananas.

"You came!" Toni cried when she saw Suzanne and Sam hurry through the double doors that led into the ER. "Bless you! I knew you'd come!"

"How's Junior?" Sam asked.

"They keep telling me he's stable," Toni said. "But I don't know what 'stable' means. Is he back there playing pinochle with the staff or is he on life support?"

"It's a fractured leg," Sam said, sounding calm and in charge. "We'll take care of it. He'll be fine."

"Please take care of him," Toni begged. She was clearly worried sick.

"Let me go check on his status," Sam said. He gave a nod to Suzanne and disappeared down the hallway.

Suzanne put an arm around Toni's shoulders. "Come on, honey, let's go sit in the waiting room."

Toni staggered along with Suzanne and collapsed onto a beige vinyl couch. "Poor dumb Junior," she whimpered. "That stupid fool. He can never catch a break." Then she seemed to realize what she'd said and muttered, "Unless it's his leg."

"Just calm down and tell me what happened," Suzanne said. She figured Junior probably *had* done something foolhardy, like climb up on the roof of his trailer and fallen off. Once he'd even dangled over the edge of a highway bridge and spray-painted Toni's name inside a big red heart. Sweet but definitely misguided.

"I don't *know* what happened," Toni said. "All I got was a call from one of the ER nurses! I mean, here I was, sitting at home, watching a perfectly good bootleg copy of *Magic Mike* and munching a bag of Chips Ahoy! And suddenly I get this call." She mimicked a high, squeaky voice. "Mrs. Garrett, Toni Garrett? Your husband is in the emergency room and he's asking for you." She threw up her hands. "Can you believe it?"

"Yes, I really can," Suzanne said.

SAM was back with them ten minutes later, looking upbeat but guarded. "The shoulder is no problem," he said. "It was a subluxation—only partially dislocated—and the resident on duty already popped it back in place. But Junior's X-rays show that he definitely has a transverse fracture of the tibia."

"Is that real bad?" Toni quavered.

"It's actually fairly routine. I've got an orthopedics guy on the way—Dr. Bremmer, who was on call over at Fairdale Hospital—and he says he'll come by tonight." When Toni started to say something, Sam held up a hand and continued. "Not to worry, Junior's going to be fine. They'll do another X-ray to make sure the proximal tibia isn't involved and then put a cast on his leg."

But Toni was worried. "What happens then? How will Junior take care of himself?"

"Perhaps his insurance . . . ?" Suzanne said.

Toni shook her head. Suzanne wasn't sure what that meant, but she didn't want to delve into it right now. There'd been enough craziness already.

"Maybe you should come home with me," Suzanne offered.

"I think I better stay here," Toni said. "I could probably sack out on this grungy couch."

"There's nothing you can do here," Sam said in a gentle tone. "Best thing would be to go home with Suzanne and try to get some rest." He paused. "Do you have any idea what happened?"

Toni shook her head. "No. But knowing Junior, he probably did something really stupid."

"You're tired and overwrought," Suzanne said. "Come home with me. Everything will look a lot better in the morning."

"Promise?" Toni said.

"Of course," Suzanne said. "It always does."

CHAPTER 24

SOMEBODY was standing over Suzanne's bed and staring straight down at her. It was still dark, maybe six or six-fifteen in the morning and her first thought was that Baxter had crawled out of his dog bed and was begging for an early bowl of kibbles. Then the shadow hissed at her.

"Ssst . . . Suzanne. Are you awake?" It was Toni.

Suzanne's eyes opened slowly. "I am now."

"We gotta get to the hospital. Like, right away."

Suzanne sat up in bed so rapidly she practically saw double. She swung herself around until her legs dropped and her feet hit the cold floor. That woke her up a little more. "What's wrong? Did the hospital call? Did Junior take a turn for the worse?" She stared at Toni, who was clutching a borrowed pink robe to her chest.

"No," Toni said. "It's nothing like that. I just had a . . . a bad premonition, I guess you'd call it. That something might have happened."

"A vibe," Suzanne repeated.

Toni looked a little embarrassed. "It's probably nothing. I guess I just hit the old panic button." She waved a hand. "You should go back to sleep."

Suzanne blinked. Toni was still staring at her and now so were Baxter and Scruff. They'd heard the commotion and padded in to her bedroom to find out what was going on. So three pairs of beady eyes were locked on her in the shifting dull light of dawn. She hoisted herself out of bed. "Tell you what, I'll put on a pot of coffee. Then, as soon as we can, we'll head over to the hospital and make sure Junior's okay."

Toni brightened. "Suzanne, that would be fabulous."

But it took a while to get the gang rolling. Turns out Toni needed two cups of coffee to help kick her morning grogginess. Then the dogs had to be fed and let out into the backyard. And even as they sniffed about, Toni still hadn't gotten it in gear enough to run back upstairs and get dressed. Instead, she peered out the back window as she slowly sipped her coffee.

"What's wrong with your backyard? It looks like there's gopher holes all over the place."

"Not gophers," Suzanne told her. She was feeling comatose and sluggish, too. "Baxter and Scruff dug those holes."

"Those weren't just dug, honey, those were excavated. Like, the dogs did an archaeological survey and plotted them out. Maybe they saw that TV show about the lost treasure of Oak Island and wanted to see what they could dig up."

Suzanne yawned and looked at her watch. "Toni. Ten minutes, okay?"

Toni continued to stare out the back window at the dogs. "Yeah. Okay."

BY the time they arrived at the hospital, the morning routine was in full swing. Nurses bustled down the hallway with charts, big metal carts carrying food trays rumbled along, medications were being delivered, a few patients were taking creaky steps, helped along by nursing assistants.

"This is it," Toni said, stopping in front of room 316. "It's the room number they told us at the front desk, anyway."

"You think Junior's awake yet?" Suzanne asked. She hated to go crashing in on Junior if he was still woozy or resting. After all, the man had probably been given pain pills. Depending on the dosage, he might end up sleeping the entire day.

Toni put an ear to the door. "I can hear voices inside."

"That's always a good sign." Suzanne pushed open the door a crack and they both peered in.

Junior was sitting up in bed, two jumbo pillows propped behind him. He had an enormous white cast on one leg and a steaming breakfast tray had been placed in front of him. A young woman stood over him, smiling and seemingly enraptured.

"So you really own a car wash?" she asked. She was young, blond, and curvaceous-looking, even in her floppy blue uniform.

"I'm what you'd call your basic entrepreneur," Junior bragged. "A self-made man."

The nursing assistant poured orange juice into Junior's cup. "That's so impressive. Most of the guys I know just want to drink beer and race cars."

"After I did a hitch in the service, I hightailed it back here to Kindred and put my nose to the grindstone. Heck, I've even invented a few gadgets. Got patents pending and everything."

With a screech that would have put a vulture to shame, Toni rushed into Junior's room. Flailing her arms crazily, she descended on him like an avenging angel.

"What's wrong with you?" Toni screamed. "We're not even divorced yet and you're flirting with nurses?"

"Oh no," the girl said, flashing a smile and showing off her Chiclet-white teeth. "I'm technically only an assistant."

"Which means you're probably underage!" Toni screeched. She turned, her right hand already bunched in a fist. "Junior, you . . ."

Junior gaped in horror at Toni's outburst. Then, as if he'd just received a cue from an acting coach, he uttered a loud gasp, let his eyes roll back in his head, and flopped against his pillows in an exaggerated swoon.

"Junior, don't you dare play faker with me," Toni cried. Then she turned to face the young assistant. Gritting her teeth, she said, "And you, little girl, had better leave!"

Her harsh words sent the girl scurrying from the room.

Junior hesitantly opened one eye, then squeezed it shut again.

"Junior?" Toni said. She moved closer to his bed. "Junior?"

Junior's body twitched as if touched by an electric shock, and then he lay completely still. After a few moments, his lips twitched, one eye fluttered. "Who . . . wha . . ." he mumbled incoherently, and then pretended to lapse back into a coma.

Toni wasn't one bit fooled. "Doggone it, Junior, I know you're pretending. Open your eyes and face me like a man!"

Suzanne smiled. "He is kind of cute when he's playing possum. When his mouth isn't flapping a mile a minute." She knew that if Junior felt well enough to make time with a cute nursing assistant, he was probably out of the woods as far as any serious health concerns.

Toni grabbed a tube that snaked from under Junior's blanket and started to twist it. "If this is your oxygen supply," she said, "I'm going to rip it right out of the wall."

Junior continued to lie there, feigning unconsciousness. A fake rumbling snore filled the room.

"Junior," Toni threatened again. "I've been worried sick about you all night. I barely got ten minutes of decent shut-eye. So if you know what's good for you, you'll open your eyes and face me like a man."

One of Junior's eyes popped open. "You ain't mad at me?" he asked.

"I'm plenty mad at you," Toni said. "But I'm sick with worry, too."

Both of Junior's eyes winked open now. They weren't quite focused and were wavering slightly. "I ain't doing so bad," he whispered. "The doctors and nurses got me doped up pretty good. They've been giving me pain pills." A stupid grin washed across his face. "I feel all right."

"Just all right?" Suzanne asked.

Junior's eyes goggled in his head like a human pinball machine. "If you want to know the truth, the pills make me sort of giddy. Like I just knocked back three or four stiff drinks at Hoobly's."

"But without the go-go dancers," Toni said.

She'd calmed down enough to grab a spoon and start feeding Junior his scrambled eggs. But when a radiologist came in carrying Junior's X-rays, Toni burst into tears.

"I'm Dr. Helm," the doctor said, introducing himself. "I thought you might like to take a look at your X-rays."

"Why not," Junior said as the doctor slapped them up on a wall-mounted light box.

Suzanne studied the X-rays. "That looks like a fairly bad break," she said. "Is he going to need some rehab?"

A look of supreme horror crossed Junior's face as he spit out his eggs. "Rehab?" he blurted, yellow globs dripping from his lips. "You mean I gotta quit *drinking*? I gotta quit hanging out at Schmitt's and give up my blood clots?"

The doctor's face blanched white and he took a step back. "Sir, you have a history of blood clots?"

"No, no," Toni hastened to explain. "That's the name of Junior's favorite cocktail. A blood clot. It's your basic concoction of Southern Comfort and 7UP with a big shot of grenadine."

But Junior was bobbling his head, looking upset and still whining about going through rehab. "I don't wanna do no rehab," he whimpered.

"The doctor means *physical* rehabilitation, you dunderhead." Toni lifted her fist as if to slug Junior on his broken leg, then pulled back at the last minute. "He means you gotta learn to walk all over again."

"I can hobble pretty good now," Junior said. "All I need is a pair of crutches and I could probably bop-she-bop down the hallway. I could even drive my truck if I had a hunk of wood to jam in the clutch."

"Nooo!" Toni cried.

The young doctor frowned. "This broken leg seems to have upset all of you folks rather badly. I think it's best to give you some privacy." He was already backing out the door.

"Jeez," Toni said as the door swung shut. "That doctor couldn't get out of here fast enough. Are we really acting that crazy?"

"I think we're all under stress," Suzanne said.

Toni scooted a chair next to Junior's bed and sat down. "Junior, I know we don't always see eye to eye . . ." She stared at him for a few moments and then started to giggle. "Particularly right now, when you've got those wobbly eyes . . ."

"Go ahead, make fun of me," Junior mumbled. "A guy in a *hospital* bed. Forced to wear a dumb hospital johnny that's open in back."

"The thing is," Toni continued, "I'm still your legal wife."

Junior looked worried. "Don't be pulling any plugs on me. I know I can make a full recovery."

Toni patted his arm. "I'm sure you can. But right now I need a straight-ahead, unvarnished explanation of what happened. And I mean *down to the letter.*"

Suzanne leaned forward. She wanted to hear this, too. She hadn't been pulled out of bed on Sunday morning for nothing.

Junior rolled his eyes at Toni and grinned stupidly. "Heck, Toni, that girl didn't mean nothing to me. She was just plumpin' my . . ."

"I don't *care* about the girl," Toni hissed. "I want to know what happened to you last night. I want to know exactly how you broke your leg." She set her mouth in a deliberate scowl and said, "For some reason, nobody around here wants to give me a straight answer."

"It was an accident," Junior said. "Plain and simple."

Toni waggled her fingers. "Details, please."

Junior seemed to cower beneath his covers. "I was doing the two-step and my feet got tangled?"

"Very funny," Toni said. "The truth, please."

"I kind of hate to say," Junior said.

Suzanne stepped closer to the bed. "Junior, call me crazy, but I don't believe this was any kind of accident at all. I get the feeling that somebody did this to you." She hesitated. "Did a couple of guys beat you up?"

Toni clapped a hand across her mouth. "Oh no!" she moaned. She grabbed Junior by the neck of his hospital johnny and pulled him toward her. "Did somebody whack on you, Junior?"

"Yeah," Junior said. "But it's embarrassing."

Suzanne pressed on. "If somebody did this to you, Junior, we need to notify Sheriff Doogie."

"Here's the thing," Junior said. His shoulders hunched up and he looked nervous. "I was kind of investigating."

"What?" Toni cried. "You were playing James Bond when you were specifically told not to?"

"Go on," Suzanne urged. She figured the truth had to come out sooner or later.

Junior drew a deep breath. "I got to thinking about that guy Byron Wolf. The one I saw at the County Registrar's office. And I thought about how he was kind of a suspect in Mike Mullen's murder."

Suzanne nodded. "Because Wolf was dickering to buy the farm."

Junior aimed a finger at her. "And, like I mentioned to you guys, maybe he *did* buy it. So what I did was drive out to where that new shopping center was being built. Where the old Hy-Vee store used to be."

"Why did you go there?" Suzanne asked.

"Ah," Junior said. "I was poking around the Wolf Construction trailer."

"You went *inside*?" Toni asked.

"I might have," Junior said. "I was kind of looking for confirmation on the sale of Claudia's farm. But then a couple of goons saw me sneaking out of there and started wailing on me."

"Could you identify these men?" Suzanne asked.

Junior thought for a moment. "Well, they both wore hard hats and I think one of them was wearing Stetson cologne."

"That's it?" Toni asked. "That's all you got?"

Junior looked morose. "It all happened so fast."

"Knock knock," a voice sang out as a fifty-something woman peeked around the door. "May I come in?"

"The more the merrier," Junior said.

"Now what's wrong?" Toni asked. With every passing moment she was getting more stressed.

"A small matter of some paperwork," the woman said. She was a hospital administrator, plump and cheerful-looking, who looked like she enjoyed her job. Her hospital ID badge said her name was Mrs. Mickelson.

"Sir, I'm sorry to bother you," Mrs. Mickelson said, advancing toward Junior. "But do you have another form of ID?"

Junior's head lolled toward her. "Didn't I give you my ID last night?" he croaked. "When the EMTs hauled me in here all battered and bloody on a stretcher?"

The smile on Mrs. Mickelson's face slipped a little. "Sir, yes, that's true. But what you gave me was an expired fishing license. I'm afraid this hospital cannot accept a fishing license, even a current one, as a legitimate form of ID."

"Oh," Junior mumbled. "Sorry. I guess I was pretty out of it." One of his hands flopped toward the night table, where he started to paw through a rat's nest of car keys, Kleenex, gum wrappers, rubber washers, and old lottery tickets, looking for his wallet. "Just a second, ma'am."

Mrs. Mickelson relaxed. "Of course."

As Junior fumbled for his wallet, his hand bumped hard against the plastic water pitcher and sent it crashing to the floor. Everyone (except Junior, of course) jumped back to avoid the catastrophic spill.

"Oops," Junior mumbled. His hand settled on a black plastic wallet with brown lanyard laced around the edges. It looked like something he might have made at Boy Scout camp. His uncoordinated fingers plucked at a number of cards. Three came loose, two fluttered to the floor. "Okay, okay, just a minute." Junior flashed a woozy smile as he held up a card. "Here you go."

Mrs. Mickelson gingerly accepted the card. As she studied it, her face fell. "Sir, this is a membership card for Shooter's Pool Hall."

Toni dropped her head into her hands and mumbled, "Dear Lord."

THERE was only one thing to do. Let the chips fall where they may and exit the hospital fast.

"I'm gonna kill Junior," Toni fumed as she stormed down the hallway. "I'm gonna wait until he's all well again and then I'm gonna assassinate him. I might have to do ten to twenty years in a women's prison, but it'll be worth it." She dodged a food cart, punched a fist at a laundry bin. "If

Junior was on life support right now, I'd get down on my hands and knees and yank the plug out of the wall with my teeth."

"Take it easy," Suzanne said. "You've probably got low blood sugar or something and are having an adverse reaction. You just need something to eat."

"What I need is a baseball bat to beat some sense into my own head."

THEY ran into Sam on the first floor, just as they hopped off the elevator.

"Hey!" he said. "How's Junior doing?"

"About what you'd expect," Suzanne said.

"Grrrrrr," Toni said, practically baring her teeth.

Sam aimed an apologetic smile at Suzanne. "I'm sorry about ruining our dinner last night."

"Not nearly as sorry as Junior's gonna be when he has to face me!" Toni cried.

Which is when Suzanne decided to drive Toni back to her house for breakfast.

CHAPTER 25

"I'M an idiot," Toni said as she sat at the counter in Suzanne's kitchen. "Why do I even stay with that bumbling fool?"

"Technically, you don't stay with him," Suzanne pointed out. "You live in a cozy little apartment while Junior occupies a dinged-up trailer that's parked out by the town dump."

"You make it sound so charming," Toni said.

"I'm sure if Junior hung some nice harvest gold café curtains it would make all the difference in the world."

Toni chuckled. "Thank you, Suzanne."

Suzanne opened the refrigerator and pulled out a carton of eggs. "So . . . how do you like your eggs?"

"In a cake."

"Tell you what, I'm going to make us a nice batch of blueberry pancakes, okay?"

"That sounds good."

Suzanne whipped up her batter and added a cup of fresh blueberries. Then she dropped a dozen silver dollar–sized cakes onto her sizzling grill. Once they were golden brown on both sides, she served the pancakes with butter and plenty of syrup.

"You still love Junior, huh?" Suzanne asked as the two of them sat at the breakfast bar.

Toni set her fork down and ran both hands through her curls. "Ah, I don't know. Junior's like kryptonite to me. I get all worked up about dumping him and then he just sucks me right back into his orbit."

"Maybe you need a marriage counselor."

"First we'd need to have an actual marriage," Toni said. "And I just don't see that happening."

NOON came and went and still Toni was down in the dumps. She paced, scratched her head nervously, and generally fretted. She tried reading the Sunday paper but ended up just staring blankly into space.

"I've got an idea," Suzanne said.

"Huh?" Toni said. She was veering from nervous to listless.

"Let's go hit that White Elephant Sale that's going on in Founder's Park today."

Since its inception some ten years ago, the citywide rummage sale had grown to include hundreds of vendors, a dozen food trucks, and even live music.

Toni picked absently at her sweater. "Ah, I don't really feel like going out."

"You've already called the hospital three times and Junior's doing just fine. Come on, we've got our phones. If there's any change, the hospital will call. They've got our numbers."

"My hair's a mess," Toni said. "And I'm not wearing a speck of makeup. My poor face is bare naked."

"I've got hot rollers and plenty of makeup upstairs. Come on. Get dressed, pop open a button on your blouse,

do a five-minute primp, and let's boogie on out of here."
When Toni made no motion to get moving, Suzanne said,
"There are food trucks, you know. With really bad stuff
like Belgian waffles and chocolate chunk cookies and apple
crisp smothered in caramel."

Toni seemed to perk up. "Do you think there'll be fun-
nel cakes, too?"

"I don't know. We'd have to go to find out."

Toni hoisted herself up off the couch. "Girlfriend. You
always did know how to motivate me."

THE blocks surrounding Founder's Park were parked up
bumper to bumper, so Suzanne and Toni cruised down a narrow avenue until they found a spot some five blocks away.

No problem, because as they headed back toward the
tents and the White Elephant Sale, they serendipitously
passed a line of food trucks. Suzanne immediately gravi-
tated toward the fried cheese curds while Toni went wild
over a waffle cone filled with spumoni.

"Yum," Toni said as she licked her treat. "This is my
idea of good nutrition. Pancakes for breakfast, ice cream for
lunch. Just don't call the carb cops on me."

"Don't worry, I'm your partner in crime here, too."

"Whoa," Toni exclaimed when they finally arrived at the
park. "Look at this mob." There were hundreds of booths
selling antiques, vintage clothing, handmade crafts, used
books, homemade preserves, chocolate fudge, leather goods,
jars of honey, and quilts.

"Look at this gorgeous wedding ring pattern," Suzanne
said as she fingered a pink-and-cream-colored quilt.

Toni grinned. "And somebody I know will be getting
married soon."

"I don't think I could ever get Sam to agree to a pink
and cream quilt on our bed."

"Honey, I don't think Sam cares what's *on* his bed as long as you're *in* his bed."

Founder's Park was a riot of activity as they strolled the rows of booths. A multitude of black electrical cords lay like a giant spiderweb across part of the grassy lawn. In the center, an open spot had been reserved for music and dancing.

"Got some tunes cookin'," Toni observed.

A man with a long, gray ponytail and beat-up guitar banged out "Take It to the Limit," an old Eagles song, while a gaggle of preteen girls bounced and twirled in the grass. Off to the side, a woman who must have been the guitarist's wife sat at a booth selling her husband's CDs along with chunks of homemade lavender soap.

Toni was still being a trouper as she strolled along, but she was only half there—the other half was back in the hospital room worrying about Junior. She scanned the wares at the craft booths halfheartedly. "Do I need a spoon ring? No. Do I need a fringed leather halter top? No."

"Cheer up, will you?" Suzanne said. "Let's at least buy some homemade fudge or something." They strolled up to a booth and gazed at pans of fudge, toffee, and peanut brittle. "Maybe a half pound of this brittle?"

Toni gave Suzanne a nudge. "Do you remember that movie *Jurassic Park* where the *T. rex* was thundering through the jungle trying to lunch on the people in that Jeep?"

Suzanne lifted an eyebrow. "Uh . . . yeah?"

"Don't look now but something just as large and just as mean is heading our way."

Suzanne turned to find Sheriff Doogie lumbering toward them. He carried a bag of caramel corn, one big paw digging in repeatedly to toss handfuls into his mouth.

"Do you think if we stand perfectly still, he won't see us?"

"Did that work in the movie?" Suzanne asked.

Toni lifted a shoulder. "Not so well."

So Suzanne did the next-best thing. She put a pro forma smile on her face and said, "Hello there, Sheriff. Nice to see you."

"You look like a man on a mission," Toni said. She made a sweeping motion with her hand. "The mini donuts are that-away."

"Ha ha, very funny," Doogie said. He tipped his head back and poured another helping of caramel corn into his mouth.

"Are you here looking for antiques or did you come to arrest me for stealing Julian Elder's horses?" Suzanne asked.

"Why?" Doogie asked, chewing vigorously. "Are you ready to confess?"

"Certainly not to a crime I didn't commit."

With eyes that were cool and calculating, Doogie gazed at Suzanne. "But you know something," he said slowly. "And I'm gonna get to the bottom of it yet."

"Better you should be hunting for the guys who beat the tar out of Junior Garrett last night," Suzanne said.

"Yes!" Toni cried.

Doogie did a quick attitude adjustment. "I heard he was pretty messed up."

"Popped his shoulder and broke his leg," Toni said. She looked like she was ready to cry again.

"I take it the hospital notified you?" Suzanne asked.

"We got the call late last night, but they told us Junior was too out of it to give any sort of statement."

"But you're going to follow up on his assault?" Toni pressed.

"Oh yeah, hell yeah," Doogie said. "Driscoll's gonna drop by the hospital this afternoon, interview Junior, and write up a report."

"Just a report?" Suzanne asked.

"We gotta start somewhere," Doogie said. "Lord knows what trouble Junior got himself into this time. Amusing as he may be, the boy isn't the sharpest knife in the drawer." He nodded at Toni. "No offense, Toni."

"None taken," Toni said. "I know Junior sometimes dances along the fine line of incoherence."

"I realize your department is busy right now what with Junior getting beat up and those horses gone missing," Suzanne said. "But how's the investigation into Mike Mullen's murder coming along?"

"It's ongoing. We're sniffing around a couple of leads. Questioning a number of suspects."

"That sounds awfully vague," Suzanne said. She was about to say more, push Doogie a little bit harder, when his phone rang.

Doogie held up a finger. "Hang on, I gotta get this." He turned and stepped away from them for privacy's sake, then suddenly shouted, "Holy shit!" His bag of caramel corn flew out of his hands, the kernels bouncing everywhere.

People all around Doogie turned to stare, then moved away as he continued to jabber into his phone. Then he checked his watch, clicked off, and stuffed the phone in his breast pocket.

"Looks like we might be able to clear you after all," Doogie said to Suzanne.

"What's going on?" Suzanne asked. It looked like something big had just happened.

"Somebody just phoned in a tip about Elder's missing horses," Doogie said. "Apparently they're over at the Jorgenson place." He grinned and gave a thumbs-up. "We might have caught a real break here."

Suzanne suddenly felt sick to her stomach. "You're going out there right now?"

"Duty calls." Doogie slapped a hand against his holstered gun, spun away, and bulldozed his way through the crowd.

Toni stared after him. "At least he got a break in the missing horses."

"This is so bad," Suzanne murmured.

Toni frowned. "Why?"

"Because Noah's got those horses," Suzanne said. "He stole them out of Elder's pasture because he was afraid they'd be shipped to Canada for horsemeat."

"What!"

Suzanne gripped Toni's arm. "I've got to get out there and run interference for Noah. Because, sure as anything, Doogie's going to arrest that poor boy. Come on, I'll drop you off at my place."

"Are you kidding?" Toni said. "I'm coming along. No way I'm going to miss this!"

BY the time Suzanne and Toni arrived at the Jorgenson farm, it looked like a full-force police action. Doogie was hauling Noah out the front door with the boy's arms twisted behind him. Faith Anne dogged their progress, screaming like a scalded chicken. Her face was an angry snarl as her long gray hair streamed out behind her.

"Noah didn't take any horses!" Faith Anne cried. "He wouldn't do that!"

"Pu-please!" Noah shrilled as Doogie perp-walked him toward his cruiser, where the light bar pulsed red and blue.

"Holy cats, will you look at that," Suzanne said as she and Toni sat in her car, stunned by this bizarre turn of events.

"Maybe we should go over there and try to calm things down," Toni said. "See if cooler heads can prevail." She had just opened the passenger door a couple of inches when a second maroon and tan car blasted past them, almost clipping her door.

"Holy crap!" Toni yelped, pulling back.

The second sheriff's car slewed to a stop and Deputy Driscoll jumped out. He was followed closely by Todd Lansky, who, surprisingly, was sporting a sidearm and a shiny deputy badge on his chest.

"Look at Lansky," Suzanne said. "Doogie must have deputized him."

Toni nodded. "He said he was going to put on a couple more deputies."

"Now we really have to do something," Suzanne said. She hopped out of her car and ran toward Doogie, waving her arms. "Doogie, Sheriff Doogie."

Doogie saw Suzanne and frowned. "You *followed* me? What the heck do you think you're doing?" he barked.

"Let me explain things," Suzanne said.

"No, let *me* explain things," Doogie said. "This is official business, so remove yourself from this property immediately." He pulled Noah's arms back tighter.

Suzanne stood her ground. "I just need to put in my two cents' worth about the horses."

Doogie's head swiveled toward her again. "What did you say?"

"Tell him," Noah pleaded. "Tell him I was only trying to help!"

Doogie jerked Noah hard. "So you *did* take those horses, you little twerp. Two minutes ago you lied to me and said you didn't know anything about them."

"He didn't take the horses!" Faith Anne hollered at Doogie's broad back. "Why won't anybody listen to me?"

Sissy, Noah's black-and-white dog, suddenly lunged out of nowhere and nipped at Doogie's pants leg.

"Ouch!" Doogie screamed. "Somebody get that stupid mutt off me before I shoot it."

"No!" Noah cried.

"Sissy!" Suzanne shouted in her show-the-dog-who's-master voice. The dog hesitated, looked over at her, and wagged its tail. Then it trotted obediently toward her. Suzanne grabbed Sissy's collar and said, "Okay, can we all just take a nice deep breath here?"

Doogie glanced at Lansky. "Todd, will you escort Mrs.

Jorgenson back inside her house while I straighten out this happy crap?"

"Got it," Lansky said.

"No!" Faith Anne wailed as she was reluctantly led inside.

"Okay, kid," Doogie said. He released Noah and spun him around hard. "Start talking. Tell me exactly where those animals are."

Noah bowed his head and, in a hoarse whisper, said, "It's better if I show you."

CHAPTER 26

THEY trooped through the woods single file. Noah, Doogie, Driscoll, Suzanne, and Toni. Even though it was a gorgeous day—the fall foliage erupting in a riot of reds and bronzes—nobody seemed to notice.

When they arrived at the small barn, Noah opened the door and they all ducked inside.

"Hot damn," Doogie said when he spotted the four horses. Then he turned and glowered at Noah. "You stole these animals."

Noah shook his head vigorously. "No."

"Then how did they get here?" Doogie asked snidely. "Fly over here like magic?" He cocked an angry eye at Noah. "Kid, you better start talking. And I want the truth this time."

Noah crept forward and touched a small sorrel mare on her neck. "I didn't steal these horses, sir, I rescued them. Mr. Elder was treating them poorly. He gave them hardly any hay to eat and their water trough was dirty and scummy."

Noah worked up his courage to meet Doogie's disapproving eyes. "These horses were starving."

Doogie seemed to consider Noah's words. "That's a separate issue, Noah. There are legal protocols for reporting animal abuse. A complaint has to be filed, then a judge has to decide if a full investigation is warranted."

"Yes, sir."

Doogie kicked at a clump of hay with his foot and glanced over at Suzanne. One eye was half closed and she could see the wheels turning inside his head.

"Tell me why you're here, Suzanne?" Doogie asked.

"She's my friend," Noah said quickly. "She told me if I ever needed help that I should call her."

"That so, Suzanne?"

"We are friends," Suzanne said. She was relieved that Noah hadn't ratted her out. That he hadn't told Doogie that she'd known the horses were here all along.

Doogie glanced at Driscoll. "Are you buying this, Driscoll?"

Driscoll's lip curled. "I'm not sure, Sheriff."

Doogie put his hands on his ample hips and glanced around the barn. "Where'd you get all this hay, Noah? I see . . . what? Maybe two dozen bales stacked up over there?"

This time Noah remained silent.

Doogie moved closer to the stack of hay bales. "Did you steal this hay, too? Am I going to have to explain to some poor farmer how you . . ." Doogie stopped suddenly, his eyes practically bugging out. Then he leaned forward and yelped, "Holy Christmas!"

"What is it?" Driscoll yelled.

"Get me a pair of latex gloves. Quick!" A purple vein throbbed in Doogie's forehead and he looked like he was about ready to hyperventilate.

Driscoll knelt down and pulled a pair of gloves from his fanny pack. Then he handed them to Doogie.

Nervous, wondering what Doogie had found that was so

startling, Suzanne slunk forward. "What's going on, Sheriff? What did you find?"

Doogie pulled the stretchy gloves onto his meaty hands and snapped them neatly in place. Then he reached behind a hay bale and pulled out a long, dangerous-looking knife. "Will you take a look at this," he said, every syllable coming out clipped and harsh.

Suzanne gasped. Doogie was holding a machete!

"Holy crap," Toni muttered. "Maybe the kid did kill Mike Mullen after all."

"Don't you dare say that!" Suzanne cried. She knew this wasn't right. Noah had somehow been set up. But who would do such a thing? The real killer?

"Evidence doesn't lie," Doogie said. He said it in a smarmy, gloating tone, as if he was proud to have solved Mike's murder and the case of the missing horses all in one fell swoop.

"No way," Suzanne said. She was going to stick to her guns no matter what the cost. "This is a complete and total setup. That machete wasn't here yesterday."

"Wait just a minute," Doogie said. "You *knew* about this? You knew the horses had been stashed here and you didn't tell me?"

"I was just . . . trying to protect Noah," Suzanne said. Her argument felt lame even as she said it.

But Doogie had already dismissed her. "You're under arrest, Noah," he said as Deputy Driscoll snapped a pair of handcuffs around Noah's wrists. "You're under arrest for the murder of Mike Mullen."

"WHAT a mess," Toni said as they drove back toward town. "Now Noah's under arrest and Doogie's furious at you."

"Doogie can sit and spin for all I care," Suzanne said. "It's Noah that I'm worried about."

"So . . . you really knew he took those horses?"

Suzanne gazed straight ahead. "Yes, I did. I kind of figured it out after Noah left a little stuffed horse for me at the back door of the Cackleberry Club yesterday. He was sending me a coded message. Trying to see if I was really a friend and if I'd back him up."

"And you did."

"Not really. Mostly I feel like I failed him miserably. I mean, Noah's being carted off to jail."

"It's the county lockup," Toni said. "Not a federal penitentiary like Attica or Sing Sing. Junior's been in lockup a few times and look at him."

Suzanne glanced at Toni.

"Okay, so maybe that's not a stellar example."

"Junior's an overage juvenile delinquent who treats going to jail as one big joke," Suzanne said. "Noah's a kid who'll be severely traumatized."

"What can we do?"

"I'm trying to think," Suzanne said. She felt so desperate she wanted to bang her head against the steering wheel.

They drove along in silence for a few minutes. Then Toni said, "Where would you even get a machete?"

"No idea. I don't even know what you'd use one for. Clearing brush? Cutting down wild grapevines?"

"The only place I've ever seen machetes was in jungle movies," Toni said. "When greedy explorers were hacking their way through vines and stuff, trying to find a lost treasure."

"Or in war movies."

"Right. Like World War II guys fighting their way through the jungles of Burma or something."

"That's it," Suzanne said. "An army surplus store." She felt a little shot of adrenaline squirt through her. A little bit of hope.

"You think?"

"Let's see who might have bought one lately. Let's at least give it a shot."

* * *

ON the far side of town, a newly constructed industrial park included self-storage lockers, a commercial printer, scrapyard for reclaimed metal, and Sergeant Stan's Army Surplus. The surrounding streets were deserted. No cars, no pedestrian traffic, not even any frolicking squirrels. Probably because there weren't any trees.

But Sergeant Stan's Army Surplus was open.

Housed in an ugly, squared-off cinder block building, a red, white, and blue sign proudly announced Sergeant Stan's Army Surplus. Underneath in small print, World War II, Korea, Nam, Iraq.

"Looks like they've got all the conflicts covered," Toni said as they pulled into a parking space next to a dilapidated army-green jeep.

Suzanne had never been here before. Then again, she'd never been in the market for cheap, used army surplus.

The inside of the shop was as brightly lit as an operating room. Blaring fluorescents buzzed above mounds of dappled green uniforms, khaki packs, and strange-looking canvas bags. There were also folding shovels, pup tents, canteens, and combat boots.

"You could outfit your own army here," Toni said.

"Or at least your own band of guerrillas," Suzanne said.

"Help you find something, ladies?" asked a man who was standing behind a glass counter. He was barrel-chested and wore a black Don't Tread on Me T-shirt and camouflage pants tucked into lace-up boots. A jaunty watch cap covered his buzz cut.

Suzanne stepped closer to the counter. "Are you Stan?"

The man nodded. "That's me."

"I guess you were in the army, huh?" Toni said.

Stan nodded. "Supply sergeant."

"We're looking for machetes," Suzanne said. "Do you have any in stock?"

"Sure do. Boyfriend got on your nerves, huh?" Stan joked.

They followed Stan to the rear of the store where a line of locked glass cases stood next to a fire exit. Inside the cases were hunting knives, rifles, shotguns, and what looked like an old German Luger. He pulled a key chain from his pocket and unlocked one of the cases.

The machete Stan pulled out didn't look anything like the one they'd just seen back at the Jorgenson farm. This one had a grooved metal handle and a large hook at the end, almost like a bird's beak.

"This machete is the best one I carry," Stan crooned in loving tones. "It's got an eighteen-inch, corrosion-resistant blade. You can use it as an ax, machete, brush thinner, or knife. Comes with its own sharpening stone, too. Isn't it a beaut?"

"Do you have any with wooden handles?" Suzanne asked.

Stan shook his head. "Oh no. When you're talking wooden handles, you're probably dealing with a vintage model. Sheffield manufactured a really nice wood-handled machete. British commandos used them back in WWII." He nodded. "Those were the days."

"Have you sold any of those older machetes recently?" Suzanne asked.

"Nah. Those are pretty much a specialty item. But if you're interested, I could put the word out to some of the war relics collectors that I know."

"Thanks, but I think we'll pass for now," Suzanne said.

"Now what?" Toni asked once they were back in the car.

"Do you want to go back to the hospital and check on Junior?"

"Maybe I should just call him again?"

"You feeling okay?" Suzanne asked.

"Just a little blue."

"Let's go back to my place. Have a cup of coffee and call the hospital."

"You got anything to eat?" Toni asked. She gave a guilty look and said, "Sorry, but stress always kicks my metabolism into high gear."

"How about a cheeseburger? Or a French dip sandwich?"

"Be still my heart."

WHILE Toni called the hospital, Suzanne put in a call to Sam.

"There you are," Sam said. "I was wondering where you were."

"Toni and I went to the White Elephant Sale," Suzanne said. "After that, we got kind of sidetracked."

"What happened?"

"Oh, I suppose I'd better tell you. It's all going to come out anyway."

"Then you for sure better tell me."

Suzanne took a few minutes to explain the whole mess to Sam. About finding the toy horse, going over to Noah's and discovering the four horses in his back barn, then about Doogie storming in today and arresting Noah after he received an anonymous tip.

Sam exhaled a glut of air. "Did Noah steal the horses?"

"Yes, he did. But I can assure you he had a very good reason."

"Stealing is stealing, Suzanne. Those horses were not his property."

"But they were being mistreated. That guy Elder wasn't feeding them properly. If you could have seen how their hip bones jutted out . . ."

"I know you have a soft spot for horses, Suzanne. But . . ."

Suzanne was practically in tears now. "Elder was going

to ship them off to Canada, Sam. For horsemeat. Is that what you want? Poor, innocent horses being slaughtered?"

"Of course not. The problem is, they're not yours to interfere with."

"What if I bought them?" she blurted out.

Sam was momentarily taken aback. "If you bought . . . those horses? Come on, be serious."

"I am serious. As serious as a heart attack."

"What on earth would you do with them?"

"I have a barn, you know."

"And then what? You'll have four more hay burners munching their way through winter at six dollars a bale."

"I'll figure something out."

"Suzanne . . . please. The best you can do right now is to make an appeal to Doogie once he's cooled down. Maybe you can get him to . . . I don't know . . . drop the charges on Noah because he's still a minor. Maybe get a sympathetic social worker involved."

"Thank you," Suzanne said. "I'll try exactly that."

"Suzanne, you said something a little earlier that scared the crap out of me."

"What's that?"

"You said that Doogie received an anonymous tip."

"I guess the comm center did, that's right."

"So Doogie went storming out there, found the horses, and just happened to discover a machete."

"Yes! Because Noah was set up."

"Which means he had to have been set up by the murderer," Sam said, urgency coloring his voice.

Suzanne was quiet for a few moments. "That's exactly what I think, too."

"Sweetheart, you can't mess around with this anymore. You've got to stop investigating."

"I'll have to think about that."

"You're in too deep!"

"I'll be careful, I really will," Suzanne promised.

"You're going to keep investigating just like Junior did, aren't you?" Sam said in exasperation. "And look what happened to him."

For the first time in a long time, Suzanne didn't have a good comeback.

CHAPTER 27

THE sun had long since set and Suzanne and Toni still had no idea where that machete might have come from. They were sitting cross-legged on Suzanne's sofa, replaying their day.

"Maybe the machete was in Mike's barn all along," Toni said.

"Could have been," Suzanne said. "But then Mike's murder points to a crime of passion. There was a heated argument, a tremendous struggle, someone grabbed the machete."

"Crime of passion meaning . . . Claudia?"

"You tell me." Suzanne shivered. She hated the idea that Mike's wife could have been involved in his death, hated the idea even more that someone . . . the killer? . . . was trying to place the blame squarely on Noah's head.

"There's always Julian Elder," Toni said. "If he figured out that Noah took his horses, that gave him the perfect opportunity to shift the blame."

"And then there's Byron Wolf."

"Whose roughneck crew probably beat up Junior."

"Lots to think about," Suzanne said. "And it's terribly upsetting to think that Noah's sitting in jail right now. Makes me feel awful."

"We should do something," Toni said.

"What? Like bust him out of jail?"

"Nooo. I meant do something to take our mind off this stuff for a while."

"You could call the hospital and check on Junior again."

Toni waved a hand. "I've already done that ad nauseam. Junior says he's feeling great, he's watching TV and eating string beans and Salisbury steak. Even the gals at the nurse's station said he's doing fine. No, I meant we should do something that will give our prefrontal cortexes a much-needed break."

Suzanne thought for a few moments. "I kind of promised Joey that we'd check out his Haunted Forest."

Toni considered this. "I might have already had my quota of scary stuff for the day. Maybe for the week."

"Come on, Toni, it's for a good cause."

"Good cause? Those kids want to take a trip to Chicago. Do you know what happens on those class trips? Have you ever seen *American Pie?*"

"Toni. Really."

THE familiar rolling hills surrounding Catawba Creek cut crescents into the bright moon overhead. Moonlight partnered with giant cottonwoods to cast specters of shadows across the winding road while bright, shining eyes from the occasional whitetail deer observed their journey.

"Better slow down," Toni cautioned. "There's more mule deer on this road than cars."

Another quarter mile on and Suzanne fell into the queue of cars being waved into a vacant, weedy lot by a young man wearing a gorilla mask and an orange vest.

"Looks like we're in the right place," Toni said as they bumped across uneven ground, waved on by more kids with lanterns.

They parked the car and joined the crowd of people heading for makeshift wooden gates, curling woodsmoke, and loud screams. All of which emanated from a large copse of dark trees across the road. There, amidst frolicking masked monsters, flaming torches, and booths selling food and T-shirts, they bought a pair of tickets from a zombie in a letter jacket.

"I like your costume," Toni said.

The zombie leered at her. "It's not a costume," he hissed in a low, threatening voice.

Toni held up a hand and looked sideways at Suzanne. "Wait a minute. Are we sure we want to do this?"

"Come on," Suzanne said. "We walk along the trail, have a few laughs, and split. No big deal."

"Where's the trail? Oh, wait, I see it over there. With the balloons and fun bouncy house."

The zombie waved a withered hand. "That's just for kids ten and under." He licked his lips and grinned. "You ladies need to take the trail to the left and follow the pumpkin markers."

"Sure. Whatever," Suzanne said.

They headed down a path covered in woodchips until they came to a rustic wooden sign. It read Abandon All Hope, Ye Who Enter Here.

"Cheery," Toni said as they ducked under the sign.

The path snaked through a dense woods lit by more flaming torches and marked by fat orange pumpkins.

"What's that up ahead?" Toni asked.

"I think . . . more carved pumpkins," Suzanne said.

But when they got closer, they found extra-large pumpkins carved with smirking ghoul faces. Flickering red candles lent a malevolent feel.

"We should remember . . ." Toni began just as a screaming girl in a torn and bloodied hospital gown careened out
of the dark woods at them.

"Help me!" the girl screamed. "They're after me, every
one of them!"

Then, just as fast, she darted across the path and into the
woods.

"Holy crap," Toni said. "That was awfully realistic."

They'd walked only another ten feet before the howl of a
wolf pierced the air. Seconds later, a werewolf in ragged
clothing bounded out of the trees.

"No!" Toni threw up an arm to ward him off and the
werewolf disappeared. She cast a reproachful glance at
Suzanne. "I'm not really enjoying this."

"Stop worrying," Suzanne said. "It's kids playacting.
Where's your sense of fun?"

"Back home in my underwear drawer?"

They stepped up their pace but were immediately surrounded by a jostling pack of zombies. The zombies didn't
harass them, just gazed at them with dead eyes and envel-
oped them in a kind of zombie huddle.

As soon as the zombies fell behind, Suzanne and Toni
entered a cobweb forest where giant spiders trembled on
stringy, diaphanous webs. This was followed by a genuine
witch's hut, complete with a green-faced witch stirring an
outdoor cauldron, a squadron of giant bats dangling from
the trees, and Freddy Krueger showing off his recent man-
icure.

"I think I've had enough of this Haunted Forest," Toni
said. "Where's the parking lot?"

"I think . . . off to our left?" Suzanne said.

"If we see a trail heading that way, let's take it."

Suzanne was pretty much over it, too. "You'll get no
argument from me."

"Owwwww!"

Toni clutched Suzanne's arm. "What was that?"

Their old friend the werewolf was back for a return engagement.

"How do we get out of here, anyway?" Toni asked him.

The werewolf scratched his head and said in a youthful voice, "I'm pretty sure the trail splits off just ahead."

"Good enough," Toni said as she grabbed Suzanne and pulled her along.

And sure enough, they did come to a fork in the trail.

"Here we go," Toni said. "Let's beat feet out of here."

"That's not a marked trail though," Suzanne said. "There are no torches, no pumpkin markers."

"Who cares? It's our exit out of crazyland. What are you waiting for?"

They headed down the dark trail, walking single file, trying to avoid being whipped by tree branches or tangled up in vines that snaked across their path.

Five minutes later they still hadn't hit the parking lot and the woods felt darker, more oppressive.

Suzanne touched Toni's shoulder. "Let's pause and try to get our bearings, okay?"

A cool wind had sprung up. It swept through the trees, chilling Suzanne and Toni to the bone and rustling up piles of decayed leaves. Overhead, real-life bats dipped and dived.

"It's silent as a tomb out here," Suzanne said.

"Nice metaphor," Toni said. "Couldn't you have come up with . . . ?"

Not ten feet behind them a loud crack sounded, like a tree branch being split.

Suzanne instantly felt her skin prickle and her pulse rate jump. Primal instinct had just kicked in, the fight or flight response.

So what's it going to be? Fight or flight?

"It's probably Bigfoot," Toni whispered. "Even though he already got his own week on cable TV."

"No, Toni. I think somebody's really back there," Suzanne whispered. Her spider sense was kicking in big-time.

"Another kid in a stupid costume?"

"I don't know. I . . ." A dark shadow wavered just at the edge of Suzanne's vision, then slowly lumbered into view. Gradually, as if forming pixel by pixel, the shadow took shape. It was a man wearing a heavy, dark padded jacket. With something—she wasn't sure what—covering his face. He stood motionless as a statue, legs spread apart, head cocked to one side, as if listening. Or waiting for them to make a move.

Toni saw him, too. "Hello?" Toni said, her voice a dry whisper.

The man just stood there, his breath coming in long, hollow gasps.

"If you're lost," Suzanne said, in what she hoped was an authoritative voice, "the trail is right behind you."

Her words had no effect. The man continued to hover there.

"What's that thing on his face?" Toni asked under her breath.

"Don't know," Suzanne said.

Toni bent forward. "It looks like a . . ."

The man chose that moment to make his move. He stretched both arms out in front of him, let out an ungodly roar, and charged at them.

"Gas mask!" Toni finished as she and Suzanne took off running.

They sprinted down the narrow trail, dodging roots, jumping over fallen logs. Still the strange man careened after them, his breathing making a strange *ptu ptu* sound inside his rubber mask.

"Faster!" Suzanne cried. She put the flat of her hand against Toni's back and gave her a hard shove, willing her to pick up the pace. Her shoulder bag slipped off her shoulder and banged against her hip, branches whipped at her cheeks. Still she kept going.

"Who is that guy?" Toni cried as she pounded down the trail.

"No idea," Suzanne gasped. "But I can feel his hot doggy breath on the back of my neck."

"Ho boy!"

Suzanne's mind was in a turmoil. Was this some rogue performer from the Haunted Trail who'd decided to have some sick fun with them? Maybe. But this character looked to her like a full-grown man. A man who wasn't just out to scare them, but intended to do serious harm!

"Watch out," Toni called back over her shoulder. "It's muddy here."

Suzanne felt ooze suck at her shoes and then her right foot slipped out from under her. She crashed down onto one knee, tried to ignore the flash of stabbing pain, and stumbled on. Behind her, she heard the man getting all bogged down in the mud, too. Should she risk a glance? She couldn't help herself. She looked back, saw the dark man groping crazily for tree branches on either side of him as he slipped and slid through the mud. The gas mask still covered his face like some kind of reptilian Darth Vader. A hose swung down from the bottom of his mask like rubberized turkey wattle.

"I think we're almost there," Toni choked out. "Oh jeez, watch it!" Then she was clambering up and over another fallen log, Suzanne right behind her.

Ten seconds later, they popped out into the field where all the cars were parked.

"Keep going," Suzanne cried. "Don't let up until we get to the car." She fumbled for her electronic key fob, ready to punch it and unlock her doors.

"Hurry," Toni called as she slipped between a pickup truck and an SUV. "Oh thank God, there it is, there's your car!"

They tumbled into the car, punched down the door locks, and sat there, breathing like a pair of overwrought teakettles.

"I ask you," Toni said when she finally caught her breath. "Was *that* seriously part of the Haunted Forest?"

Suzanne shook her head. "I don't think so."

"That jackhole meant to hurt us," Toni said, slamming a fist down hard against the dashboard. "He was coming after us. Why would he do that?"

Suzanne folded her arms across her chest, trying to quiet herself as she gulped for air. "Why do you think, Toni? Why do you think?"

"Is it because of the murder? Because you've been investigating?"

"Has to be," Suzanne said.

"But you don't *know* anything! You haven't figured out who Mike's killer is."

Suzanne stared out into the darkness with anxious, searching eyes. "I guess whoever chased us didn't take that into account."

SUZANNE dropped Toni off at her apartment, admonishing her to lock the doors and turn on every light. Then she drove home.

Walking into her own house, Suzanne felt not one bit of apprehension. Probably because Baxter and Scruff, her trusty guard dogs, were there to greet her.

"Hey, guys." Suzanne got down on her hands and knees, accepted a few slobbery kisses (that was the love pact you made with dogs, after all), shook their outstretched paws, and scratched behind floppy ears.

The dogs followed her as she turned on lights all the way from the front hallway, through the living room, and into the kitchen.

"Want to go outside, pups?"

They all went outside, Baxter and Scruff immediately running for Suzanne's herb garden to sniff around. A small bunny—one Suzanne had secretly named Hazel—often hung out there. But there were no itinerant bunnies roaming around tonight. Just a silent backyard where cool winds whipped up leaves and tossed clouds across the sky.

Back inside with the dogs, Suzanne took a Motrin, since her knee was throbbing, and turned out all the lights except for the small light over the stove. She opened the refrigerator, took out a carton of milk, and poured herself half a glass.

She knew she was going to have to tell Sheriff Doogie about tonight and dreaded doing so. He'd scold and tell her to mind her own business. Something she really wasn't good at doing.

As Suzanne stood in the dark kitchen, gazing out into the backyard, she could hardly believe what a bizarre day it had been. Junior in the hospital, Noah hauled away in handcuffs, she and Toni getting chased by who-knows-what at the Haunted Forest.

Time for this day to be over. Time to pack it in.

Suzanne drained the last of her milk, turned toward the window, and blinked.

Had she just seen something moving outside?

No, it couldn't have been. Her eyes were playing tricks on her. Weren't they?

She dropped to her knees in the dimly lit kitchen and rested her chin on the window ledge. Watching. Waiting.

It took a few minutes to register, but there it was again. A shadow moving against the trees.

Suzanne clenched her jaw tightly. What was that? She waited some more, her heart doing little flip-flops inside her chest, her eyes feeling hot and dry from straining to see.

Maybe a critter come to call?

No. Just beyond a faint yellow crescent cast by a streetlamp, she could make out the shape of a man peering out from behind her crab apple tree.

Holy shit, was it the gas mask guy? The same guy who'd chased her and Toni like some hideous bogeyman from a childhood dream? Who'd made her heart race so wildly when she'd felt his breath on the back of her neck?

He followed her here to do what?

Spy on her? Break into her house? Do physical harm?

What to do? Call Sam? Dial 911?

Before Suzanne's jangled mind could make a decision, she saw the man move again. Right there. In her backyard. On her very own property.

Anger suddenly ripped through her like a stab of lightning. Someone had come to threaten her at home? How dare they!

Suzanne rose to her feet even as her hand crept across the counter and grabbed the biggest, sharpest butcher knife from the wooden block. It was a boning knife, ten inches of tempered steel, flexible enough for slicing right between bone and gristle. And for defending the home front.

But Suzanne was no foolhardy one-woman crusader. She was well aware she had other fine weapons in her arsenal. Actually, two weapons.

"Baxter, Scruff," she hissed.

Toenails clicked against kitchen tile as they came to see what their dear doggy mom wanted.

"Guard," Suzanne said.

The dogs wagged their tails. They knew the word "guard," knew that it tasked them with safeguarding the house. Which also involved thwarting unwanted intruders.

"Guard outside," she said.

Suzanne grasped the door handle, turned it, and kicked open the screen door, all in one fluid motion. Baxter and Scruff exploded out the door like circus performers shot from a cannon. Two furry bodies bounded across the yard, seeking, scenting, and quickly closing in on the man who was now cowering behind an arborvitae bush.

"Get him!" Suzanne screamed as Baxter rushed toward the man, teeth bared, tail down, hackles raised.

Then the man was kicking and whirling his way across the yard as the two dogs darted in to nip his legs, his hands, his butt. The dogs double-teamed him as he ran, attacking at will and yapping their heads off. The man—whoever he was—was scared witless, stumbling badly and falling down.

Suzanne was practically gleeful. The awful holes that Baxter had dug had tripped up her intruder!

Now the man was sprawled on the ground, kicking and struggling, making angry grunts, as Baxter dashed in to harass him, backpedaled away, and then rushed in again with snapping jaws.

"Get him!" Suzanne yelled again. But the man, kicking furiously, wiggled out of Baxter's reach. He clambered to his feet and, with a burst of speed, sprinted for the back gate. Zigzagging like crazy, he slipped through the gate and pulled it shut behind him with a loud *thwack*. In a split second, Baxter and Scruff were on their hind legs, paws draped over the top of the gate, barking furiously.

Suzanne walked out, looked around the yard, and went over to the gate.

"Good dogs," she praised. "Good guard dogs." The dogs jumped down and grinned at her. "You've earned your cookies tonight."

WHILE the dogs happily munched dog cookies, Suzanne called Doogie at home.

When he answered, she said, "Guess what?"

"Who is this?" he barked.

"It's Suzanne. I'll have you know that Toni and I got chased by a crazy man through the woods tonight. And then that same guy—at least I think it was the same guy— was just prowling in my backyard."

"Are you serious?" Doogie's voice rose in a squawk.

"I wouldn't interrupt your Sunday-night football if I wasn't serious."

"You want me to send somebody over there?" Doogie asked, as his To Protect and to Serve instincts kicked in. "Are you okay?"

"No. But I'm mad as hell," Suzanne said. "Somebody doesn't want me investigating. Somebody thinks I'm getting way too close to the truth."

"Huh," Doogie said. And this time he sounded almost thoughtful. "Maybe you are."

"I never thought I'd hear that coming from you." Suzanne hesitated for a few moments and then said, "We need to figure this out before somebody else gets killed."

"I hear you."

"Go over all the suspects again."

"Interviews, background checks, the whole ball of wax," Doogie said. "I'll get on it. And dang it, Suzanne, I am gonna send a car over to sit outside your house tonight. Just in case."

"Thank you."

"Your tax dollars at work," Doogie said.

"Noah didn't kill Mike Mullen, you know."

"I know the boy's innocent," Doogie said. "That's why I let him go home."

"You did, really?" The wire that had been stretched tightly around Suzanne's heart suddenly loosened a little. "Why?"

"Aww . . . I'm not a complete jerk, Suzanne. Besides, I saw those horses. I saw how skinny they were. That kid was just trying to help."

Tears suddenly oozed from Suzanne's eyes. "Thank you, Doogie. God bless you."

"Just doin' my job." There was a pause and then Doogie said, "You know John Casey?"

"The principal at the senior high?"

"Junior high, too," Doogie said. "Yeah, I called him at home and asked him about Noah."

"What'd he say?"

"That when the kids took the MMPI test, Noah scored in the upper percentile. He may have a touch of Asperger's, which can get in the way of his social skills, but the kid's plenty smart."

"Well," Suzanne said. "I think we already knew that."

CHAPTER 28

THE big Halloween party wasn't the only thing on everyone's mind this Monday morning. Toni had given Petra a blow-by-blow description of their chase through the Haunted Forest, and then Suzanne popped into the kitchen and scared the pants off both of them by relating her backyard intruder story.

"This is terrifying," Petra said from her post at the stove. She was dressed in a green Gumby costume, cooking up sausages and red peppers on the grill, keeping a watchful eye on a batch of eggs in purgatory, her special poached eggs in red sauce. "I hope you had the sense to alert Sheriff Doogie."

"I called him right away," Suzanne said. "Roused him out of his cozy armchair."

"What was his take on the gas mask guy?" Toni asked.

"Doogie says he's going to go over all the suspects again. Bring people in for questioning, get a lot tougher."

"If last night's story gets out," Petra said, "people are

going to be quaking in their boots. It means a stone-cold killer is still roaming free and . . ." She pointed a wooden spoon directly at Suzanne. "And it sounds like he was trying to tie up loose ends."

"Gulp," Suzanne said.

"You've got to stand down," Toni said to Suzanne. "Stay safe, let Doogie and his deputies do their job."

"Except they haven't done their job yet," Suzanne said. "It's been . . . what? Almost six days with not a whole lot of progress?"

"That doesn't mean *you* have to be the one to stick your neck out," Petra said.

"We love you, Suzanne, you're our fearless leader," Toni said. "That's why I think you should listen to Petra."

"I honestly don't know why she would," Petra muttered. "She never has before." She leaned forward and glanced through the pass-through. "Now, if we can move on, it looks like some folks in the café would like to put in their orders." She did a double-take. "Holy buckets, there's a fairy princess and a goblin sitting at table four."

Suzanne and Toni breezed into the café to wait on customers. Suzanne looking witchy in her long dress and pointed hat, Toni gussied up in a leopard-print leotard and jeans. About half a dozen customers were wearing costumes as well.

"Looks like the customers at Millennium Bank will be encountering a few interesting characters today," Suzanne said.

Janet Riesgraff, the fairy princess, smiled and said, "We're going all out at the bank today. Everyone's wearing costumes, we're doling out donuts and cider, and inviting the kids to stop by for trick-or-treating."

"Banker's hours trick-or-treating?" Toni asked.

Marlys, the goblin, ducked her head. "Well . . . sure. You don't think Don Morley, our manager, is going to stay one minute after four, do you?"

"No, I don't," Suzanne said. Morley had once turned her late husband, Walter, down for a loan and she knew him to be a stickler. A prickly stickler at that.

Suzanne poured coffee, brewed tea, and served up caramel rolls, rashers of bacon, and cheese omelets. When she wasn't hustling between the kitchen and the café, she slid behind the brass cash register whenever a customer wanted to pay his bill. It felt to her like the morning was flying by. So much so that she'd barely given more thought to last night's craziness.

Until Byron Wolf sauntered in.

Toni immediately greeted Wolf with a puckish smile and led him to a small table by the window. At which point Suzanne came by with a fresh pot of coffee, ready to take over.

"I got this," Toni said.

"That's okay," Suzanne said. "I'll take care of Mr. Wolf. I'm happy to, in fact."

A grin creased Wolf's handsome face. "Two gorgeous women fighting over me? What more could a guy ask for?"

How about rolling up your pants leg? Suzanne thought. *So I can see if my dog took a chunk out of your stupid leg.*

Instead, Suzanne poured Wolf a cup of coffee and said, "Our breakfast special today is eggs in purgatory, which is basically eggs in hot sauce."

"Sounds kind of wicked," Wolf said. "I'll take it."

Suzanne hurried off to put the order in and when she turned around, saw that another interesting customer had drifted in.

Julian Elder stood in the doorway, a scowl on his long, angular face. When he caught sight of Suzanne, he curled a lip and headed for a seat at the counter.

What to do? Suzanne wondered. But she knew there was only one thing she could do. Deal with Elder head-on.

"Mr. Elder," Suzanne said. She stood behind the marble counter, facing him directly. "May I offer you a cup of coffee?"

Elder gave a barely discernible nod.

Suzanne placed a ceramic cup on a paper napkin and poured his coffee. His hard eyes followed her every move.

"I think you and I have something to talk about," she said.

"You've been sticking your nose in my business," Elder said. But he didn't sound angry. In fact, he was actually quite conversational.

Suzanne drew a deep breath. "When a beloved member of our community is murdered, when horses are mistreated, when a young boy is traumatized, then it becomes all of our business."

Elder took a sip of coffee as he stared across the top of his cup. "Seems to me you're making some nasty accusations there, lady."

Suzanne shrugged. "I could go on, but then you'd probably say I was threatening you."

Elder's lips twitched. "I don't threaten easily."

"That's okay, I wouldn't go easy on you." She wondered if Elder had been the gas mask man. If Baxter's tooth marks were imprinted on *his* leg.

"You're a regular little spitfire, aren't you?" Elder said.

"Just trying to get to the heart of things."

"I heard that about you. That you like to . . . snoop."

Suzanne offered a thin smile. "Inquiring minds want to know."

"And what is it you want to know?"

"Did you get your horses back?"

Elder nodded. "That I did."

"Are they still for sale?"

"I suppose they are, for the right price."

"Care to name that price?" Suzanne asked.

Elder studied her. "Are you a serious buyer?"

"You bet I am."

"Got a pen?"

Suzanne pulled a pen from her apron pocket and handed it to Elder. He took it, wrote a number on his paper napkin, and slid it across the counter to her.

She glanced at what he'd scrawled. "Big number," she said.

He shrugged. "I'd need an answer today. Otherwise . . . well, I'll have to make alternate arrangements."

Suzanne thought for a few moments. "I'd need some time to pull things together. Could you drop by tonight? We're having our big Halloween party and . . ."

"I know all about your Halloween party," Elder said. He took a final sip of coffee and slid off his stool. "I'll see you then."

ELDER took off, Byron Wolf left some ten minutes later, and then, in what felt like a game of musical chairs, Sheriff Doogie came striding in. He sat down on his favorite stool and planted his elbows firmly on the counter.

Suzanne hurried over to pour Doogie a cup of coffee. She dearly needed to talk to him.

"I've been thinking about your high adventure last night," Doogie said for openers. "Dang, Suzanne, you sure set somebody's whiskers to twitching."

"Yes, but whose?"

Doogie dumped two sugar cubes into his coffee, stirred it, then added a third for good measure. "That's the million-dollar question, isn't it?"

"Two possible candidates have already been in here this morning."

Doogie lifted a furry eyebrow. "Who's that?"

"Byron Wolf and Julian Elder."

"Elder say anything about the horses?"

"Mostly that they're still for sale." Suzanne decided not to tell Doogie that she was contemplating buying them herself. Since she wasn't sure she could pull it off.

Doogie shook his head. "I'm gonna phone the county attorney. See if they can do anything to help those horses."

"And then there's Byron Wolf. If Junior got beat up outside of one of Wolf's construction trailers, it stands to reason it was done by a couple guys from his crew."

"But who were the guys?" Doogie asked. "We can't haul his entire crew in and question them." He pointed to the glass pie case. "I think that caramel roll has my name on it."

Suzanne put a caramel roll on a plate for Doogie, along with two pats of butter. "But you could question the guys who were last seen at that trailer."

"I doubt they're gonna fess up," Doogie said.

"And you can't beat it out of them. Innocent until proven guilty."

"Yup, that sticky little rule of law does get in the way sometimes."

"Have you checked to see if Byron Wolf has ever been popped?"

"You mean does Wolf have a record?" Doogie took a bite of sweet roll and chewed thoughtfully. "Wolf's had a DUI as well as a lien from a finance company placed against a leased Range Rover. And he's had an assault charge stemming from a bar fight."

"Did he do time?" Suzanne asked.

"Nope. He hired some hotshot attorney and the assault charge was reduced to a misdemeanor so he only had to pay a fine."

"But Wolf's no angel."

"Neither is Julian Elder. He's had his share of minor skirmishes with the law."

Toni suddenly ducked behind the counter to talk to them. "Guess what I did?" she asked.

"Finally divorced that no-account Junior?" Doogie asked.

"Nothing quite that drastic," Toni said. "No, I invited Byron Wolf to our Halloween bash tonight."

"You didn't," Suzanne said. "Wait a minute, did he say he'd come?"

Toni dimpled. "He said he'd try to make it."

"You're awfully flirty for a woman whose husband is still lying in a hospital bed," Doogie said.

Toni waved a hand. "I just talked to Junior again. He's being released at noon. His car wash buddy, Buggy Butters, is gonna pick him up and drive him home."

"That was a quick stay," Suzanne said.

Toni shrugged. "No insurance."

"That would explain it," Doogie said.

PETRA chuckled as she handed her menu to Suzanne. "You put this on the chalkboard and you'll get a few laughs," she said. "It's very Halloween themed."

Suzanne studied the menu. "I'll say. Egg Drop Dead Soup, Witch's Chicken Salad Sandwiches, Omelet with Voodoo Cheese Fondue, deviled eggs, and Skeleton Finger Cookies."

"You think I worked in enough Halloween?"

"And then some," Suzanne said. She flicked Petra's notes between her fingers and said, "I have a favor to ask."

"Sure."

"It's kind of strange."

"Well," Petra said. "I wouldn't want to do anything illegal."

"This doesn't involve horse rustling or anything like that," Suzanne said. "But what I'd like you to do is call Claudia Mullen and invite her to drop by tonight."

Petra looked a little taken aback. "You want her to come to the party? Why on earth?"

"I don't know. Call it a hunch. A weird vibe."

"It *is* weird," Petra said.

"The thing is, Toni already invited Byron Wolf and I kind of invited Julian Elder. If you invited Claudia Mullen . . ."

"Then all your suspects would be corralled in one single place," Petra said slowly. "Namely our place. You really think you can shake something loose?"

"It's a shot in the dark," Suzanne said. *After all, nothing else has worked.*

Petra eyed Suzanne nervously. "Eeny, meeny, miny, moe . . ."

Suzanne grinned but there was little warmth behind it. "Catch a killer by the toe."

AT quarter to twelve, just as the noon rush was beginning to build, Sam called.

"Suzanne?" Sam said. "Do you have something to tell me?"

Dang, Suzanne thought. *Somebody got to him before I could figure out how to sanitize my story.*

"I just ran into Sheriff Doogie over at Pilney's Pharmacy," Sam said. "And he said something about you and Toni being harassed by a guy in a *gas mask*? Is that true?"

"That happened at the Haunted Forest. Didn't I mention that Toni and I were going to the Haunted Forest?"

"Um . . . no. And I got the distinct impression from Doogie that this incident was unrelated to the students' event."

"I suppose you could say that . . . yes."

"This comes on top of you being present when Noah Jorgenson was arrested for stealing horses," Sam said.

"You know as well as I do that Noah was set up. Somebody left a machete in his barn in order to point the finger at him."

"Suzanne, we need to talk about this!"

Oh jeez, now Sam's mad at me.

"Are you really mad at me?" she asked

"Not entirely," Sam said. "But only because I don't have all the details about the Haunted Forest. Then I can work up some serious steam and indignation."

"Maybe we can talk at the Halloween party tonight?"

"Suzanne, I definitely think we should."

"Now Sam's mad at me," Suzanne said to Toni as they carried out bowls of Egg Drop Dead Soup and plates of Witch's Sandwiches.

"Sam could never be mad at you," Toni said. "He gives you that puppy dog look and comes running whenever you crook your little finger at him. You could probably get away with bloody blue murder and that man would still stick a wedding ring on your finger."

"No, this time he was really upset about the Haunted Forest thing."

"How could you tell?" Toni asked.

"Sam wasn't yelling. He was talking in a cool, controlled voice."

"Like the voice he uses when he tells some poor patient they need to have their gall bladder cut out?" Toni asked.

"That's right."

"Holy hiccups," Toni said. "Sam really is mad at you."

CHAPTER 29

SUZANNE was just putting a slice of apple pie in front of Gene Gandle, the *Bugle's* crackerjack reporter, obituary writer, and ad sales guy, when Junior came stumping in on his broken leg. His blue jeans had been slit up one side to accommodate his plaster cast and he was using crutches.

When Toni saw him, she came flying out of the kitchen. "What are you doing here?" she cried. "You should be home in bed resting."

Suzanne joined in the haranguing. "You should probably still be in the hospital."

Junior shook his head. "Too late for that. I already checked myself out and reserved a room at the Super 8."

Toni's mouth literally fell open. "What?"

"That doggone hospital charges almost two hundred bucks a night for a lumpy bed and bad food while the Super 8 is only thirty-nine bucks," Junior said. "Plus they got cable. HBO and Showtime."

"But . . . but . . ." Toni was so flabbergasted she couldn't spit out her sentence.

Junior held up a hand. "It's a room back by the Dumpsters, but the garbage truck doesn't haul away until Thursday so everything should be hunky-dory. As long as the trash don't pile up and stink too bad."

"Junior, you can't just skip out on your treatment," Suzanne said. "What about physical therapy? What about medication?"

Junior reached into his hip pocket and pulled out an amber prescription bottle. He held it up and rattled it. "That's all been taken care of."

"This is crazy talk," Toni said. "You need rest and recovery."

"I can't lay in bed all day," Junior said. He hobbled over to a chair and sat down heavily.

Toni threw up her hands. "This from a man who lays around in his underwear munching Doritos and watching *Duck Dynasty*."

"That's recreational laying around," Junior said. "This is medical. Medical laying around is boring."

"You hear that?" Toni said to Suzanne. "Junior's bored. His pea-sized brain is actually challenged."

"Maybe we should give him something to do," Suzanne said.

"Like what?" Toni asked.

But Junior was suddenly interested. He poked one of his crutches at them and said, "That's right. Put me to work. I'm happy to hang around and help out."

"Like you helped out before?" Toni said in an angry, accusing tone. "Snooping around that construction trailer and getting the stuffing beat out of you."

"Those goons caught me by surprise," Junior said. "I let my guard down. Otherwise I could have taken them."

"Instead you got taken to the hospital," Suzanne said.

"Do we gotta rehash this?" Junior whined. "You make me feel like some kind of wimp. Come on, give me something to do. I'll do anything you want."

"I suppose you could put together the trick or treat bags for the kids," Suzanne said.

Junior's face fell. "You're gonna make me do a *menial* task?"

"Okay," Suzanne said. "How about figuring out a macroeconomic stabilization policy for the country?"

"Huh?" Junior said.

"Have you even eaten yet?" Toni asked Junior.

Junior patted his stomach. "No, because that hospital grub was awful. It gave me a case of the burps." His chest rose and fell. "Oh, scuse me."

"Maybe you'd better feed him," Suzanne said. "We don't want Junior to keel over from hunger."

"I really should keep my strength up," Junior said. "Then I might be able to tackle those trick or treat bags after all."

"WAS that Junior I heard out there?" Petra asked when Suzanne walked into the kitchen.

"Newly released from the hospital," Suzanne said. "On his own recognizance."

"You think he's okay?"

"It's Junior, does that answer your question?"

"Got it," Petra said. She pointed to a couple bags of trash. "Could you carry those out?"

"Still worried about the opossum?"

"A little bit."

"Did you have a chance to call Claudia?"

Petra nodded. "She says she'll come. That she can get a ride over from Jane Breimhorst, one of her friends from church."

"Was she suspicious about why we invited her?"

"Not so much. I think she might have been a little bit pleased to get the invitation. She sounded kind of lonely."

I'd be lonely, too, Suzanne thought, *if I murdered my husband.*

On the other hand, Claudia might be completely innocent. Her only crime—and it wasn't really a crime—her anxiousness to sell the farm.

Suzanne grabbed the trash bags and carried them out to the Dumpster. She tossed them in and turned around to scan the woods, looking for the little opossum.

"Where are you, you little bandit? I bet if Petra knew what a sweet guy you really are she'd put out leftover donuts for you to snarf."

Suzanne stepped past her work shed and into the woods, where she was immediately surrounded by golden poplars, bright red sumac, and a clutch of pine trees. It was beautiful and peaceful in this little strip of woods that marked the border between her back parking lot and the farm field just beyond. Today, the recently harvested cornfield was playing host to a small flock of grackles that were carefully picking around for plump, dried kernels.

Friendly visitors passing through, she thought to herself.

But as she scanned the horizon in the direction of her farm, her eyes caught a quick flash of light from way across the field.

What was that?

Suzanne stood stock-still and continued to stare. There it was again. What was going on? She knew that Reed and Martha Ducovny, the couple who leased the farm from her, were out of town. Visiting their daughter in Sarasota, Florida.

Could someone be standing over there watching her through a pair of binoculars? Who would do that?

Feeling chilled, thoughts of gas mask man still swirling in her brain, Suzanne dashed inside.

*   *   *

"Telephone," Petra said as Suzanne flew through the door.

"Who is it?" she asked.

"I think it's that cheese guy."

Suzanne stared at Petra for a few moments before her brain finally caught up to Petra's reference. "The pushy guy from Claggett Foods?"

"I think so."

Suzanne grabbed the phone. "This is Suzanne."

"Suzanne," came Rick Boyle's booming voice. "Rick Boyle here. Glad I caught you."

Did you try to catch me? Suzanne suddenly wondered. *Was that you chasing me last night?*

"Mr. Boyle," she said in a crispy voice. "How can I help?"

"It's I who can help you," Boyle fake-chuckled. "We've just added three new cheese products to our line and I wanted to give you a heads-up."

"Okay." *Whatever.*

"I'm going to be in your neighborhood later on today and I thought I would drop off some product sheets."

"We'll be pretty busy later on—tonight's our big Halloween bash."

"Sounds charming," Boyle said. "I'll see you then."

Suzanne hung up the phone, trying to recall her impression of the guy who'd chased her last night. He'd been fairly tall and carried some weight on him. At least that was her general impression. Could it have been Rick Boyle? She supposed it could have been. Stranger things had happened.

"You invited him to our party?" Petra asked. She pulled up her green Gumby hood and was peering out of it.

"The more the merrier," Suzanne said.

"Know what I think?" Petra said. "The more the murderous."

* * *

WHEN Suzanne slipped into the café, Junior was sitting at a table working diligently. He was filling orange trick or treat bags, moving his lips as he counted out miniature candy bars, wrapped pieces of toffee, and lollipops.

He glanced up as she approached his table. "Suzanne, I have a question."

"Yes?"

"There are fewer Krackel bars than there are Mr. Goodbars. Do you think I should heavy up on toffee if a bag is minus a Krackel bar?"

"Just put eight pieces of candy in each bag," Suzanne said. "Don't stress over it."

Then Toni crept in with a roll of black netting draped over one arm. "Suzanne? My costume?"

"Oh right," Suzanne said. "I was going to help you with that, wasn't I?" She glanced around the café and saw there were only two tables of customers left. They were both finishing their coffee, ready to head out.

"You were going to help me fashion a ballet skirt," Toni said. "'Fashion' being the operative word."

"Let's give it a shot," Suzanne said. She turned over the sign on the front door that said Closed, then pulled Toni into the Knitting Nest and grabbed a needle and thread.

"I tried wrapping this myself," Toni said, unrolling her long piece of netting. "But I ended up looking like a sad tulip."

"Here, slip out of your jeans and let me figure this out. Okay, first we wrap two layers of netting around your hips . . ."

"For modesty's sake."

"Right. And then I'll take a tuck and secure it." Suzanne threaded her needle and made the necessary tuck.

"Don't stick me!" Toni cried.

"Not to worry. Now we'll kind of pooch out the fabric

just above your knees and take a few judicious tucks at your waist." Suzanne fashioned the netting into a semblance of a ballet skirt and then quickly did a running stitch around Toni's waist to hold it all together.

"This is looking seriously good," Toni said.

"Hopefully," Suzanne said. "Now, what you need to do is grab a spool of black velvet ribbon."

Toni hunted around, found the ribbon, and was back. "Whatcha gonna do with this?"

Suzanne snipped off a hunk of ribbon. "One piece gets cinched around your waist to hide the stitches. And this smaller piece will work as a kind of headband to tie your look together."

"Ooh, I like that."

Suzanne ducked into her office, grabbed a purple pen that had a tuft of black ostrich feathers on one end, and ripped off the feathers. "Then these feathers go in your hair." She tucked them into the headband. "*Voila*, you are now principal dancer with the Kindred Ballet Company."

That sent Toni scampering to a mirror. "This is great," she called back. "I love it!"

THE rest of the day was spent prepping for their Halloween party. Petra and Toni readied the brats and chicken wings, buttered the buns, and set out big jars of mustard, ketchup, and pickle relish.

At four o'clock a few kids dropped by to trick-or-treat and Junior, pretending to be terrified of all the miniature ghosts, elves, skeletons, and pirates, handed out trick or treat bags.

By five o'clock the trickle of kids slowed and Virgil Bannerman showed up with three enormous metal fire cauldrons and enough firewood to keep them roaring all night. Then Freddy from Schmitt's Bar showed up with two kegs of beer and three cases of apple cider. The Whistling Dixies, three guys in cowboy outfits and a girl singer in a fringed skirt, also arrived and immediately began warming up their banjos and guitars.

"It looks like the circus just hit town," Junior announced from his observation post at the window.

"It has," Suzanne said.

"Oh man, will you look at this!" Now Junior was hobbling back and forth on his crutches. "Horses!"

Suzanne peered out the window just in time to see Bud Nolden drive his team of Percherons into her parking lot. The giant horses were tossing their heads and snorting loudly as they pulled a large wooden wagon that was stuffed full of hay. Feathered hoofs rang out like anvil strikes against the pavement.

"It's gonna be a gas to ride in that wagon," Junior chortled.

"Don't you dare," Toni said. "You climb up there and you'll probably bust your other leg."

"I want to have fun, too," Junior whined.

"Then go back to the hospital and flirt with that nurse," Toni said.

"You're the only gal for me, Toni."

"Huh."

"Hey, Suzanne," Junior said. "Why don't you take some of that leftover black netting and wrap it around my cast? And then take another hunk and make me an eye patch?"

Suzanne stared at him. "And what would that accomplish?"

Junior grinned. "I'd be like Peg Leg Pete!"

CHAPTER 30

THE party was supposed to begin at seven, but their guests began arriving just after six-thirty.

"We're in for it now," Toni announced as cars began to stream in.

"You put the signs out so everyone knows to park across the road?" Suzanne asked. She'd moved her own car over there earlier in the day. "Because I think we're going to have a big crowd."

"Signs are up, we should be set," Toni said.

"Then let's go out and greet our guests."

Everybody came. In costume, no less. Lolly Herron and Ellen Hardy, a couple of teatime regulars, came bustling in. Lolly was wrapped in a Greek toga, Ellen wore a flapper dress. They were followed by WLGN's own Paula Patterson, dressed as a cowgirl, and Shar Sandstrom, a local baker, who wore her baker's whites and a chef's hat. Then the floodgates opened and at least another four dozen guests poured in. The fire cauldrons smoked and crackled, the band struck up a sassy, twangy version of "Red Dirt Road," and Mayor Mobley arrived with Byron Wolf in tow.

Toni sidled up to Suzanne. "Did you notice that Wolfy boy is here?"

Through the wavering heat of a fire pit Suzanne saw that Mobley and Wolf were already enjoying a glass of beer. "I did notice. Though neither of them came in costume."

Toni smirked. "Mobley's dressed as a petty bureaucrat and Wolf's in his sheep's clothing."

"And look," Suzanne said. "Claudia Mullen just walked in, too."

Toni rubbed her hands together. "I'd say things are getting mysteriouser and mysteriouser."

"Maybe," Suzanne said. She looked around, spotted Joey, their busboy, and waggled her fingers to get his attention.

Joey saw Suzanne waving and veered toward her, a big smile lighting his face. "Hey, Mrs. D, I heard you and Toni came to the Haunted Forest last night. What'd you think? Pretty cool, huh?"

"Pretty scary," Suzanne said. She wasn't about to spill the real details. "Do you know the drill for tonight, Joey?"

"You mean sticking close to Petra? Yeah. I guess she wants me to help with the food. Take care of grilling the brats and Bat Wings." Joey paused. "Say, they're not *real* bat wings, are they?"

"They're chicken wings dredged in batter and layered with seven spices," Suzanne told him.

"Like wing dings. Cool. So I should . . . ?"

"Head into the kitchen and check with Petra."

Suzanne's eyes fell upon two more guests coming her way. Oh no, it couldn't be! But Noah and Faith Anne were walking straight toward her and, praise be, Faith Anne actually had a faint smile on her face.

"Noah, Faith Anne," Suzanne said, greeting them warmly. "Welcome to the Cackleberry Club. Happy Halloween."

"I'll bet you didn't think we'd come," Noah said, ducking his head. "But here we are after all."

"I'm so sorry Sheriff Doogie hauled you away like that," Suzanne said. "It wasn't right."

"That's okay," Noah said. "I only had to stay at the Law Enforcement Center for, like, an hour. And they didn't even put me in a cell, just gave me a bottle of orange pop and let me sit in a regular chair."

"Sheriff Doogie even sort of apologized," Faith Anne said.

"Doogie told me that he felt awful about it," Suzanne said. "He knows Noah isn't any kind of killer. As for those horses . . . well, I'm still trying to work something out."

"Noah told me how nice you've been to him," Faith Anne said. "And I kind of want to, um, apologize for my behavior the other day. When the Yarn Truck was here."

"That's okay," Suzanne said. "I'm just glad you're here now, ready to enjoy the party."

Suzanne greeted another dozen guests and tossed a log into a fire pit. When the band played a pepped-up version of Garth Brooks's "Friends in Low Places," she even managed a twirl or two.

Then a red and blue light bar pulsed, a siren gave one low *brrrk*, and Sheriff Doogie pulled in.

Suzanne went over to greet him.

Doogie exited the driver's side of the vehicle, Deputy Driscoll hopped out on the passenger side.

"You're just in time for the food," Suzanne told them. "Petra put the brats on the grill two minutes ago."

"I like the sound of that," Driscoll said as he wandered off to join the party.

Suzanne faced Doogie. "What's up?"

"I was gonna ask you the same thing," Doogie said. His sharp, rattlesnake eyes skipped across the crowd for a few moments. "Isn't that interesting. I see Claudia Mullen and

Byron Wolf." He scratched his chin. My recollection is that you asked me to keep an eye on those two."

"That's right."

"Seems to me *you're* the one keeping an eye on them," Doogie said.

"It's a party. What can I tell you?"

"Nice try, Suzanne. But I think I'll stick around to see what's really going on."

"I don't know if anything is. Besides some Halloween spirit, that is." She'd just spotted Sam's blue BMW pulling into the lot, so she ambled over to say hello.

"Holy smokes, Suzanne, half the town must have showed up," Sam said as he climbed out of his car. He put his arms around her and kissed her. "You're a popular girl."

"Not half as popular as our beer and brats," she said.

"Ah well, beer and brats . . ."

"Sam, I wanted to ask you about Mike Mullen."

"Uh-oh, another murderous query. And on All Hallows' Eve at that?"

"It's about the machete."

"Mike wasn't killed with a machete," Sam said.

"What do you mean?" Suzanne could barely hide her surprise.

"Dr. Pope, the ME, issued a secondary report today. A kind of cuts-and-weapons analysis. He stated that the cuts were too deep and angular to be made by a machete. Dr. Pope suspects they were more likely from a hawkbill knife."

"How many people know about this?"

"Just myself and Sheriff Doogie. And now you."

"But the rumor all over town has been that the murder weapon was a machete!" Suzanne's words tumbled out. "I mean, a machete was even planted at Noah's place . . ."

"Yes, I'd like to know more about that."

"It's a long, crazy story, which I promise I'll tell you. But now you're saying the killer used a . . . what did you call it? A hawkbill knife?"

Sam's eyes narrowed. "That's right. And you're not to breathe a word of this to anyone, Suzanne. That knife is what you'd call exclusionary evidence. And for goodness' sakes don't start secretly scouring the countryside looking for that exact type of knife."

"Excuse me, excuse me!" a hearty voice rang out.

Suzanne and Sam both turned to find Rick Boyle steamrolling toward them.

"Suzanne!" Boyle held a clutch of paper aloft in one hand. "I've got those product sheets you wanted."

"Who is this turkey?" Sam asked under his breath.

Suzanne waited until Boyle was standing right in front of them.

"Dr. Sam Hazelet," she said. "This is Rick Boyle from Claggett Foods."

Boyle stuck out a hand. "How'd ya do, doc? I just came by to drop off some information for the little lady here." He handed the papers to Suzanne. "We're carrying a new blue cheese called True Bleu. I believe you'd like it." He looked around as if just noticing for the first time that a party was taking place. "This is some shindig you got going."

Suzanne indicated the grilling station for the brats. "Help yourself if you'd like. There's plenty of food to go around."

"Don't mind if I do," Boyle said, heading off toward the grill.

"What a weird guy," Sam said.

"Tell me more about the knife."

"There's not much to tell."

"So the final analysis of the knife wounds means that Noah's completely off the hook." Suzanne leaned closer to Sam. "Sheriff Doogie never did believe Noah was guilty."

"But Noah did steal the horses," Sam said. "Right?"

"I'm working on that angle," Suzanne said.

"Bad idea," Sam said. "You need to let this go, Suzanne. Like now."

"I hear you. But I also have a funny feeling that things might be coming to a head real soon."

THE punkin' chunkin' contest went off without a hitch, with top honors on distance going to Boots Wagner, owner of the Hard Body Gym.

"Probably because he's the one person in Kindred who works out twenty-two hours a day," Toni said to Suzanne. "The last time we went to his gym and did that core fitness routine I almost puked."

"You need a more positive attitude," Suzanne said.

"Even if I have a negative body?"

"How about you get that costume contest started?"

"I thought you'd never ask," Toni said. She fluffed her skirt. "Now if I can just avoid stepping in all the orange goo that's laying around."

Meanwhile, Suzanne had noticed a couple of new arrivals. Todd Lansky had pulled in with his pickup truck, probably still playing deputy for Doogie, and Julian Elder was prowling around in the shadows. She figured Elder was the one who required her immediate attention.

Suzanne cut through a line of costume contestants, skirted around Mayor Mobley and Byron Wolf, who both hoisted their beers at her, and headed for Elder.

"Mr. Elder," she called.

Elder stepped out of the shadows looking tall, sinuous, and slightly sinister. "Suzanne," he said in a gravelly voice. "Do you have my money?"

"Do we have a deal?" she asked.

"Eight hundred dollars for the lot."

"There's no wiggle room in that price?"

He cocked his head. "Take it or leave it."

"And then what?" Suzanne asked. "Then you get in another herd of horses? And another one after that?"

Elder shook his head. "Nope, this is it. I'm taking too much flack. It's tough to find horses in the first place, expensive to ship them, and there are too many activist organizations who want to rip my head off." He held up his hands in a gesture of resignation.

"Redemption," Suzanne said. *Or are you the killer we've all been hunting for?*

"Call it what you want," Elder said. "I'm wiping my hands of the whole business."

"Good. And I do want those horses."

"I thought you might," Elder said.

Suzanne worried her front teeth against her lower lip. "This is going to be a little tricky. Will you take a check?"

"Check works for me."

Suzanne turned her attention toward the party, which was in full swing. Music blasted, couples danced, brats hissed and spit on the grill. "I've got to take care of a couple of things. Can you give me fifteen minutes? I mean, you're welcome to mingle and have a beer and a bratwurst."

"Whatever," Elder said.

SUZANNE hurried back through the crowd, wondering how to pull off this deal. She had $200 in cash stashed in her car. If she cadged four hundred more from the Cackleberry Club account and wrote a personal check for two hundred . . . well, then she'd have it. It would be a squeaker to pay bills this month, but she could still manage.

Ducking into her office off the Book Nook, Suzanne hastily wrote out a check and stuck it in her pocket. When she came out into the café, Junior was sitting in a chair, looking morose.

"Wish I could join in the fun," Junior said.

"If I carried a chair outside, you could sit by a fire cauldron," Suzanne said.

"You'd do that for me?"

Suzanne picked up a wooden captain's chair. "Grab those crutches, Junior, and let's go join the party."

She deposited the chair near the fire cauldron, got Junior situated (he was given a bratwurst, but no beer) and headed for her car. As she passed the second grill, she saw that the Bat Wings were sizzling and that Joey was dousing them with gobs of Petra's hot sauce.

"Suzanne!" Bud Nolden called out. He'd just parked his hay wagon and was waiting for his passengers to clamber down. "Want to take a ride?" he teased.

"I'm just going across the road," she told him. "Have to grab something from my car."

"Hop in, we'll make it a short trip."

Suzanne, never one to turn down an opportunity to ride in a horse-drawn wagon, climbed up onto the wooden seat.

Nolden snapped the reins and the big horses rumbled off.

"This is so nice of you to bring your team to the Cackleberry Club," Suzanne told Nolden. He was one of those guys who loved to pitch in. Member of the Lions Club, helped with bingo at his church, drove grade-school kids on outings to the Logan County Historical Society.

"It's good practice for the team," Nolden told her as they clopped along, the big horses switching their tails as if in rhythm to the sway of the wagon. "We might even enter the two-horse hitch at the county fair next year."

"I bet you'd win."

They rolled along companionably through the night until Nolden pulled back on the reins. "This is as far as we go without clipping that red pickup truck."

Suzanne stood up, ready to hop down from the hay wagon,

when something sitting in the back of the pickup caught her eye. A large blue canister tucked in the corner with a single word printed across it in silver. The word was "Gleason."

The proverbial lightbulb fizzed on, flickered, and then exploded inside Suzanne's brain.

Gleason. Wasn't that the word Mike Mullen had scrawled in his calendar?

Suzanne leapt down from the hay wagon and peered into the back of the truck, certain she must be wrong. Positive she must have misread the label.

But no, the blue canister still read Gleason.

Her brain spun like an off-kilter merry-go-round, complete with dizzying sound effects. Whose truck was this anyway?

But she knew exactly who owned this truck. It belonged to Todd Lansky. She'd seen Lansky park it here around the same time Julian Elder had appeared.

Oh dear Lord. Could it be?

Like a woman possessed, Suzanne gathered up her long skirt, ran back across the road, and slalomed her way through the crowd of Halloween revelers. A werewolf loomed in front of her, a zombie offered her a glass of beer, but she kept going. And didn't stop until she practically collided with Sam.

"Whoa, whoa, Suzanne," he said. "You look like you just saw a ghost."

"It's . . . I saw . . ." Suzanne wasn't exactly sure what she'd seen. She drew a deep breath and said, "Did I tell you I saw the name 'Gleason' scrawled in Mike Mullen's calendar?"

Sam shook his head. "I don't think so."

"The thing is . . . I just saw that same name written across a weird-looking barrel-shaped container in the back of Todd Lansky's truck. But . . . I don't know what it means."

This time Sam offered her a strange, somewhat concerned look. "Gleason?"

"Yes."

"You're not referring to Gleason Sci are you?"

Suzanne grabbed his arm. "I don't know what that is."

"Gleason Scientific Medical," Sam said. "They're a chemical company. Labs use them. For ether, nitric acid, reagents, and buffers, that sort of thing."

Suzanne was incredulous. "You said *ether*? What would something like that be used for? I mean, if you were a guy from around here. A farmer, let's say. Why would you possibly need ether?"

Sam's brows pinched together. "I kind of hate to say this but . . . maybe for a meth lab?"

The pieces were suddenly tumbling into place for Suzanne. "And you'd need large tanks, too?" she asked excitedly. "The kind a dairy farm or a cheese shop might use?"

"I suppose so." Sam looked nervous. "Suzanne, tell me where you're going with this. Tell me everything."

"Mrs. D." Joey was suddenly at her elbow. "Petra wants to know if she should bring out the cake now."

Suzanne grabbed Joey by the shoulders. "Joey, I need to ask you something."

Joey suddenly looked twitchy. "What's wrong? What'd I do?"

"I'm going to point to a guy and I want you to tell me if you've ever seen him before."

"Huh?" Joey said. "What guy?"

"Just a minute." Suzanne turned to scan the crowd. "Okay, Joey, that man standing next to the band. You see him? He's leaning against the tree talking to that lady in the Snoopy costume."

Joey's eyes flicked across the crowded parking lot to Lansky. "Nah, I don't recognize the dude."

"Are you sure? Focus, honey."

Joey squinted at Lansky again. "Jeez . . . maybe I have seen him around. But it would've been . . . near the school?"

"Yes!" Suzanne said.

Joey frowned. "Yeah, I think he sometimes hangs out there. But I always figured he was a parent come to pick up his kid." His eyes flicked back at her. "Why? What'd he do?"

"Oh dear Lord," Sam said.

"Joey," Suzanne said. "I want you to go inside and wait in my office, okay?"

"Now?" Joey asked.

"Suzanne . . ." Sam said.

"What about the cake?" Joey asked.

"I'll take care of the cake. For now I want you nice and safe, okay?"

"If you say so."

Sam grabbed hold of Suzanne's arm. "You think Lansky's been cooking?"

"Yes, I do."

"Then you've got to tell Doogie about this. You've got to . . ."

"I will," Suzanne said. "And you go find Deputy Driscoll, okay?"

"Got it," Sam said.

Keeping one eye on Lansky, Suzanne circled around the perimeter of the party. Claudia Mullen was talking to Laura Benchley. Noah was handing his mother a plate of Bat Wings. Byron Wolf and Mayor Mobley were shaking hands with a newly elected city council member.

None of that mattered to Suzanne right now. Her eyes were focused on the khaki bulk of Sheriff Doogie as she homed in on him like a heat-seeking missile.

Doogie, no slouch at being cautious and circumspect, saw her coming. He took one step back into the shadows and waited for her.

"Problem," Suzanne said.

Doogie leaned in as Suzanne gave him a two-minute, CliffsNotes explanation that connected the single word scrawled in Mike Mullen's calendar with the canister in the back of Lansky's truck. Doogie interrupted only once to ask a question as Suzanne struggled to explain, trying to connect the dots that led to a probable meth lab. When Doogie had heard enough, he gave a hard-eyed nod.

"Stay back," he warned Suzanne. "Let me handle this."

"Be careful," Suzanne said. "Mike must have figured out the meth angle and confronted Lansky. And then Lansky got angry or frightened or whatever and killed him."

"I'll deal with it."

Doogie sauntered over to Deputy Driscoll, who'd been cornered by Sam. He added a few more gruff comments to their whispered conversation and then Driscoll hunched his shoulders and nodded.

Slowly, casually, the two officers walked toward Todd Lansky, who was now standing near one of the fire pits and holding a longneck beer.

Curious, Suzanne moved in closer, trying to look as unassuming and innocent as possible.

Doogie was talking to Lansky now, looking serious and nodding his head. His words floated across to Suzanne, a little jumbled, but she caught the gist of his conversation: ". . . received an emergency call . . . dispatch . . . need to roll out."

Lansky gave a grave nod and turned to follow Doogie. But as his eyes roved the crowd, they happened upon Suzanne. She was caught standing there, barefaced, listening to them, her posture almost rigid with nervous energy.

Lansky started to give her a half smile and then it slipped. He stared at her intently, the features on his face hardening. It was almost an acknowledgment that he knew that she knew.

And then, fast as greased lightning, Lansky bolted sideways, his bottle of beer flying out of his hand.

"Stop him!" Suzanne shouted.

Doogie spun around, pulled out his gun, and hollered, "Everybody down!"

People screamed and dove for cover as Lansky, running like a cornered jackrabbit, zigzagged madly through the crowd. As he veered toward the second fire cauldron, Junior Garrett, quick as a snapping turtle's bite, stuck out his crutch and tripped Lansky.

Lansky went down, sprawling face-first into a mess of orange pumpkin goo. Cursing, his eyes wild with fear, he slipped and slid, finally managing to get his legs back under him. Then Lansky was off and running, half limping as he picked up speed, pushing right through the startled musicians, headed for his truck.

Lansky threw himself inside and, two seconds later, the engine roared to life. His wheels spun crazily on the blacktop, trying to find purchase. His truck lurched ahead just as Nolden's hay wagon pulled right in front of him. Lansky's horn blatted wildly, causing the two draft horses to rear up in fright and paw the air. Then their front hooves, along with the tonnage behind them, smacked down hard on the hood of Lansky's truck.

Clunk, thunk!

Suzanne saw the look of panic on Lansky's face as he threw his truck into reverse, spun left, and hit the gas. Five seconds later his taillights were just a red blip in the dark night.

CHAPTER 31

DOOGIE sprinted for his cruiser with Driscoll stumbling after him. Suzanne was right on their heels.

As Doogie ripped open the driver's side door, he shouted, "You can't come with us," and dove inside.

Suzanne ran to the passenger side, stuck an elbow in Driscoll's gut, and hopped into the front seat ahead of him. "Please, I have to."

"Doggone it!" Doogie yelled as he cranked the engine and hit the gas. "You civilians just don't listen."

Driscoll was still pulling his seat belt across his chest, Suzanne scrunching between the two men as they roared out of the parking lot.

Doogie careened down the highway, driving one-handed, flipping switches like mad, lights and siren coming on full bore as they continued to pick up speed. "This is a really bad idea, Suzanne," he huffed as he tromped down hard on the accelerator.

"Sorry," Suzanne said. She wondered what Sam would

think, *worried* what Sam would think. But even as she sat tucked like a little mouse, knees bumping against her chin, she was jacked up on adrenaline. The dashboard of Doogie's car glowed like the control panel of a 747 and she was right in the middle of an honest-to-goodness, just-like-in-the-movies police chase!

They raced down the blacktop highway, whipping past All Saints Church, Bim's Discount Gas, Seifert's Used Cars, and the occasional house with its front porch light on. Ahead of them, cars heeded their siren and dove to the side of the road, allowing them to blast on by. But Lansky was still outdistancing them by at least half a mile.

"Get on the horn and call the comm center," Doogie instructed Driscoll. "Tell them we're in pursuit of a red pickup truck . . . uh . . . did anybody get the make and model?"

"I think it's a Ford F-150," Suzanne said.

"Got it," Driscoll said.

"Dang," Doogie said as he hung a left on Reservation Road. "He's heading right for downtown."

"Kids will be out," Suzanne said. "Trick-or-treating."

Doogie grimaced. "Our bad luck."

But just as Lansky hit Lawndale, the first cross street that marked the border of downtown Kindred, his brake lights flared and he slewed his truck into a screeching, rubber-laying right-hand turn.

"Where's he going?" Doogie muttered as he braked, cornered, and sped after him.

"Out Sawmill Road?" Suzanne wondered.

Lansky's truck was weaving wildly now, crossing into the oncoming lane, threatening to take out a parked car or two. And then he did!

"Holy smokes," Driscoll cried. "He just smacked a fender on that green Toyota! Ooh, and he just clipped an SUV. Insurance adjuster's gonna be hopping tomorrow."

They roared down the mostly residential street, where

home owners peered nervously out the windows of tidy little bungalows and Cape Cod homes, and into a suburban
area of newer homes. They were closing the gap now, running just two blocks or so behind Lansky, the engine of
Doogie's big Ford screaming like an Indy car coming down
the final stretch.

"Hang on!" Doogie warned as they squealed into a tight
S-turn, past a defunct oil change business, the Suds & Duds
Laundromat, Pickfair Garden Center, Hector's Automotive.
And then, suddenly, they were in open country. Rolling hills,
a hobby farm, mowed hay fields, woodlots here and there.

"Where's he going?" Driscoll wondered.

"Going to ground," Doogie growled through clenched
teeth.

"I bet he's heading for his farm," Suzanne said. "He's
going to try to make a stand."

"You know where that is?" Doogie asked.

Suzanne shook her head, but Driscoll said, "Yeah. He
rents the old Miller place. It's another six or seven miles
out, just past that country store and gas station that Dick
Webster runs."

"Hot dog," Doogie said. "Better notify dispatch again
and have them call in our reserve deputies. Then tell 'em to
contact the State Patrol and request backup."

"Got it," Driscoll said. He already had a finger on the
button and was connecting with the comm center.

While Driscoll snapped out instructions, Suzanne hung
on for dear life. Doogie, driving with an incredibly leaden
foot, had again narrowed the gap on Lansky. Now they
were tailing him by only fifty yards.

Like a miniature, high-speed convoy, they flew around dangerous curves, clattered over a one-lane bridge, and hit speeds
nudging one hundred miles an hour in the flat stretches.

"A meth lab," Doogie said, gritting his teeth. "And you
think Mike Mullen found out about it?"

"I'm positive he did," Suzanne said. "That's why Lansky killed him."

"We knew there was meth being sold around here," Doogie said. "Terrible to think it might be happening right under our noses."

"Disheartening to think we were pointing the finger at the wrong people," Suzanne said.

"Gosh darn it," Doogie stewed. "There he was, the little cockroach. Deputized by yours truly and sitting in on all our meetings."

"You couldn't have known," Suzanne said.

"None of us knew," Driscoll said.

"Hang on, hang on, Lansky's turning!" Doogie suddenly screamed. A burst of gravel hit their windshield, pattering like a sudden, intense hailstorm. Doogie cranked his steering wheel hard, churning after him, wheels screaming as he fought to maintain control through the turn.

They jounced along a bumpy, gravel road, the car's shocks being tested to the max as they pogoed up and down. Suddenly, Lansky's taillights disappeared completely.

"Where'd he go?" Doogie shouted. "Did we lose him?"

"Must have hit the ditch," Driscoll said.

Doogie punched the brakes hard, almost sending Suzanne flying through the windshield. Then Driscoll rolled down his side window and stared out into a night that was black as pitch.

"I don't see him," Driscoll said.

"Is this his farm?" Doogie shouted. "Are we close to his farm?"

"I think so," Driscoll said, but he didn't sound all that confident.

Suzanne strained to see in the darkness. She knew Lansky couldn't just disappear—poof!—in a puff of smoke. He had to be here somewhere. She put her hands to either side of her face to block out the interior light and help narrow her focus. And there, just ahead, she saw a dark shadow loom up.

"There's something up ahead!" Suzanne cried. "Some sort of silo."

"Maybe his farm?" Doogie said as he stomped down on the accelerator and rocketed forward.

It was Lansky's farm. But the place was silent as a graveyard. No lights were on in the house, none burning in the barn. His truck sat silently some forty yards in front of them.

"There's his truck," Suzanne said in a low whisper.

"I'll be damned," Doogie said. "Lansky is here." He rolled to a stop and sat for a moment, thinking, trying to appraise the situation.

"But where'd he go?" Driscoll asked.

"Doesn't matter," Doogie said. "We'll smoke him out. Pull your sidearm and we'll grab the other guns and gear out of the trunk."

Doogie and Driscoll scrambled out of the car. They slapped on bulletproof vests, grabbed a high-powered rifle and a shotgun. They acted like they'd done this a hundred times before, though Suzanne knew they hadn't.

Doogie stuck his head inside the car. "Suzanne, you stay put. No matter what happens, don't you dare move from here!"

"Okay." Suzanne was picking up on their stress and didn't have any keen desire to get involved in a gun battle or crazy standoff. But she did feel like she was a sitting duck.

Crouching low in the front seat, she watched as Doogie and Driscoll slowly approached Lansky's truck. Was Lansky sitting inside? Waiting for them? Was he armed?

They snuck up on either side of the truck, ripped open both doors, and poked their guns inside. No sign of him. So where was Lansky? Hiding inside his house?

Suzanne held her breath as Doogie and Driscoll had a

whispered confab, then turned and headed for the barn. Wasn't that dangerous? she wondered. If there was a meth lab inside, wouldn't Lansky fight to defend it? Or, since his cover was blown, would he be scrabbling around, trying to grab whatever was important to him—drugs or money—so he could try to disappear?

Nose pressed against the passenger side window, Suzanne watched the shadowy figures of Doogie and Driscoll as they stealthily approached the barn door. They were armed to the teeth, she decided, and professionally trained, so they must know what they were doing. With barely any wasted effort on their part, they slid open the door. It was a typical barn entrance, tall and wide enough to drive a tractor through.

Suzanne focused on their every move as they crept inside. Okay. So they'd probably assess the threat level, shout out their orders, and show their weapons. And that would be it. If Lansky had any sense at all, he'd surrender peacefully. No weapons would be fired. It would be a clean capture.

But that was the best-case scenario. And Suzanne knew plans such as that rarely went off without a hitch. Which was why she wasn't at all shocked when she caught a hint of movement and saw a shadowy figure slide around the far end of the barn.

What happened? Did Lansky clamber out a window or something? Oh dear, what if he slinks over to his truck and tries to take off? Or maybe he's got a second vehicle stashed somewhere.

But Lansky didn't do any of those things. Instead, he pressed himself against the outer wall of the barn and slowly, carefully, crept toward the gaping, dark hole where Doogie and Driscoll had just disappeared.

He's trying to circle round and sneak up on them!

Like a shadow man, a Halloween haunt, Lansky oozed his way along the length of the barn. Every couple of feet, he'd stop and crouch down, almost military style.

Suzanne's nerves were beginning to fray. *Please be careful, Doogie! Please watch your back!*

As Lansky rose to his feet and took another step, something long and thin poked out ahead of him.

Long gun! He's carrying a rifle or a shotgun!

But what could she do? Suzanne didn't have a weapon and she'd been ordered to stay put!

Without hesitating, Suzanne reached down and turned the key that Doogie had left in the ignition. She haphazardly flipped a couple of switches on the dashboard and the siren instantaneously poured out a shrill blat—*bwaaa, bwaaa, bwaaa.*

Alarmed by the noise, Lansky flattened himself against the barn. At almost the same time, Doogie came steaming out the main entrance, shotgun on his shoulder, fully cognizant that he was being warned.

Suzanne opened the car door a crack. "Watch out!" she cried. "He's got a . . ."

That's when it all went *kerpow* crazy!

A bullet struck the front fender of the cruiser, startling Suzanne and sending a surprised Doogie diving for the dirt.

Suzanne's brain registered the impact with utter shock. A bullet? Lansky had fired at her? Seriously?

She peeped out the window, her heart beating inside her chest like a wounded dove. And there was Lansky, clutching his shotgun as he negotiated a quick, shuffling side step, ducking and spinning away from the barn. The barrel of his gun was bouncing like crazy as he headed directly toward her!

What to do?

Suzanne did the only thing she could do. With lightning speed, she slid into the driver's seat and put the car in gear. Lights flashing and siren screaming now, she steered directly at Lansky, the cruiser bucking and swaying as it flew over uneven ground.

Lansky saw her coming and tried to leap out of the way.

No problem—Suzanne cut the car in Lansky's direction, fully intending to clip him hard and send him sprawling in the dirt. Instead, he spun away at the last second and swung the barrel of his shotgun around until it was aimed directly at her.

Holy shit!

Suzanne cranked the wheel hard right again, ducked down, and hit the gas. The car surged forward with all the fury of an Abrams tank unleashed. The reinforced front bumper—practically a cowcatcher—clipped Lansky at hip level and tossed him high into the air.

As her headlights caught Lansky in mid-tumble, Suzanne could actually see shock and pain register on his face. And then Lansky twisted in midair, almost in slow motion, and the shotgun bucked hard in his hands.

Boom!

Two feet of yellow flame belched from the end of the barrel. And then, like a scene out of a Vin Diesel movie, the nearby barn exploded in a quick succession of bursts. One side of the barn blew out, followed by an enormous explosion of orange and yellow flames. There was another rumble, like a freight train gathering speed, and then a fireball shot up and through the roof. It climbed three, almost four stories high, twisting and churning like the proverbial firestorm that had turned Lot's wife to salt. Chunks of flaming wood rained down upon the cruiser. Suzanne watched in astonishment as the explosion tossed Lansky ass over teakettle for a second time and blew the shotgun clean out of his hands.

Five seconds later, Driscoll was on top of Lansky, grappling with him, snarling orders, flipping him onto his stomach. Lansky wiggled and bucked, but Driscoll hastily subdued him. He pulled the man's hands behind his back and snapped on a pair of handcuffs. Then Doogie was yanking open the car door, screaming at Suzanne, "What did you do! What did you do!"

Suzanne blinked, as if waking up from a horribly vivid dream. "What do you mean?" she screamed back. "What are you talking about?"

Doogie was hopping up and down in a fit of excitement. "The barn. How did you set it on fire?"

Suzanne shook her head. "Lansky's shotgun went off. I think he shot his own barn."

Doogie stopped dancing. "He exploded his own meth lab?"

"When I hit him with the cruiser, he must have pulled the trigger. But the shot went wild. He must have hit something critical. Chemicals, I guess."

"Sweet dogs." Doogie swept his hat off his head in a show of victory. "Now that's what I call poetic justice."

CHAPTER 32

WHEN they got back to the Cackleberry Club, the party had long since ended. Guests had departed, candles guttered inside pumpkins, pumpkin grins had slipped sideways. Still, Suzanne's cadre of Cackleberry Club insiders were waiting there. Dying to hear what happened.

Doogie related the whole exciting scenario as Petra, Toni, Sam, Junior, and Joey stood there with their collective mouths hanging open. He detailed the chase to Lansky's farm, sneaking into the barn, Suzanne's ramming Lansky with his cruiser, the shot going wild, and the barn exploding.

"And then the ambulance and backup finally arrived," Driscoll added.

"Holy smokes," Sam said. "That really happened?"

"It sounds like a movie," Petra said.

"It kind of was," Suzanne said. "You could have filmed the whole thing frame by frame and ended up with an incredibly exciting action sequence."

"And Todd Lansky, the real killer, was hiding in plain

sight all along," Toni said. "While we were sneaking suspicious glances at Claudia and Noah and Byron Wolf and that horse guy, Elder."

Petra reached over and embraced Suzanne. "We were all so worried about you." She grabbed Deputy Driscoll and gave him a hug, too. "You, too, dear heart!"

Doogie stood there, looking askance. "What about me?"

Petra waved a hand. "Oh poop, you're just fine, Sheriff. You've probably been in more shootouts, ambushes, and car chases than *Smokey and the Bandit* and the *Dukes of Hazzard* put together."

Her words gave Doogie pause. "You really think so?" A silly grin spread across his broad face. He was pleased and bolstered by her words. "I like that." He let loose a hearty chuckle. "I certainly do."

"Wish I could have been in on the action," Junior grumped.

"Over my dead body," Toni said.

"Say, is there any food left?" Doogie asked. "'Cause we sure worked up a ferocious appetite."

"I'm sorry to say that the bratwurst and chicken wings are all gone," Petra said. "But there's cake."

Doogie brightened. "Cake?"

"Come on inside and sit down," Petra said. "Tell us some more!"

They all trooped into the Cackleberry Club, Junior stumping along and leading the way, waving his crutch like a bandleader with a marching baton.

Sam caught Suzanne's arm on the way in and pulled her aside.

"Are you okay?" Sam asked. "I mean, really okay?"

Suzanne gave a regretful smile. "I am fine, Sam. I'm just so sorry I took off like that. I'm sorry I scared you."

"More like terrified me," he said. "You're crazy and impulsive and a little too reckless for your own good." When worry and unease puckered Suzanne's face, he added, "But I wouldn't trade your wild ways for anything." He pulled her close and wrapped his arms tightly around her.

"Do you still want to marry me?" Suzanne asked in a muffled voice.

"Of course I do," Sam said. He was planting tiny kisses on her forehead, her ears, her eyebrows . . .

"Even though I might come with a little baggage?"

Sam stopped and peered at her. "You're going to buy those horses, aren't you?"

She took a step back from him. "Yes I am."

"How much money do you think you'll need?"

"About eight hundred dollars. I'm thinking now that I'll borrow half from the Cackleberry Club's account and get a cash advance on the other four hundred. You know, put it on my Visa card."

"You don't have to do that," Sam said.

Suzanne shook her head. "That's the thing you don't seem to understand, Sam. I *do* have to do this. It's important to me that I save those horses."

"No, sweetheart," Sam said. "That's not what I meant. I meant to say I'll *give* you the money. The eight hundred dollars for Elder's horses and whatever you need for Mike's horses."

"What?" Suzanne said in a whisper. She couldn't quite believe what she was hearing. Her voice caught in her throat as she gazed at him guardedly. "What?"

"I said I'll give you the . . ."

Suzanne waved a hand frantically in front of Sam's face. "No, no, I heard that part just fine. I guess what I meant to ask was *why*? Why would you do that?"

Sam touched a hand to her shoulder. "Because it's important to you. And if you're hurting over something, then so am I." He dipped his other hand into his jacket pocket and pulled out a wad of cash. "Here." He thrust it at her. "Take it."

Suzanne stared at the wad of fifties and hundreds. "For

gosh sakes, Sam. Where on earth did you get this kind of money? How much is here?"

He smiled at her. "I don't know, a couple of grand, I guess. Don't worry about it, okay? Just buy the horses."

"Sam, I really need to know where this money came from."

"I've been saving up."

"Yes, but . . ."

"Okay, if you really must know, I've been saving money to pay for our wedding."

Suzanne was stunned. "For our . . ." Tears welled in her eyes, a sob tore from her throat. She couldn't go on. Couldn't choke out one more word.

"You know, for the cake and flowers and things," Sam explained. "Our reception and a romantic honeymoon." He smiled at her, looking earnest and hopeful. "Just . . . wedding stuff."

Suzanne swallowed hard as she struggled to brush away tears and fought to find her voice. "But you told me that having a big ceremony and a fancy reception was important to you."

Sam leaned down and kissed her gently. "Sure, it would be nice. But it's not nearly as important as you are, Suzanne."

Suzanne threw her arms around his neck and sobbed. "Oh, Sam. I love you so much."

Sam hugged her back just as tight. "And you, sweet Suzanne, are my everything."

Recipes from the
Cackleberry Club

Suzanne's Chicken Pickin' Stir-Fry

3 whole chicken breasts
2 tbsp. oil
1 medium onion, diced
1 red pepper, chopped
1 green pepper, chopped
½ lb. mushrooms
⅓ cup your favorite stir-fry sauce
¼ tsp. crushed red pepper

Cut chicken breasts into 1" pieces. Heat oil, add chicken, and stir for 1 minute. Add onion and stir for 1 minute. Add 2 tbsp. water, then cover and cook for 2 minutes. Add red and green peppers and mushrooms and stir for 2 minutes. Add stir-fry sauce and crushed red pepper. Cook, stirring until sauce is heated and chicken and vegetables are coated with sauce. Serve over rice. Yields 3 to 4 servings.

Egg Drop Dead Soup

2 cups chicken broth
1 tsp. ground ginger
1 tbsp. soy sauce
2 eggs, beaten
2 small green onions, chopped finely
Salt and pepper to taste

In a saucepan, bring chicken broth, ground ginger, and soy sauce to a simmer. Slowly stream in beaten eggs while stirring soup in one direction. Add chopped green onions. Add salt and pepper to taste. Yields 4 servings.

Petra's Molasses Bread

2½ cups whole wheat flour
½ cup cornmeal
1 tsp. salt
1 tsp. baking soda
½ cup molasses
1⅔ cups buttermilk

Heat oven to 325 degrees. In large bowl, mix together whole wheat flour, cornmeal, salt, and baking soda. In separate bowl, stir molasses into buttermilk. Now pour liquid ingredients into dry ingredients and stir gently until just combined. Pour batter into a greased 9" x 5" loaf pan. Bake approximately 50 to 60 minutes, or until a toothpick inserted in center comes out clean. Allow bread to cool for 10 minutes, then carefully turn out onto a wire rack. Yields 1 medium loaf.

Harvest Pumpkin Soup

1 (15-oz.) can pumpkin
2 cups chicken broth
½ cup cream
½ tsp. pumpkin pie spice

Whisk together all ingredients in large saucepan and simmer for 5 minutes. Continue to whisk soup until ready to serve. Yields 4 servings.

Cackleberry Club Rice Pudding

1 cup rice, uncooked
1 tsp. salt
2 cups cold water
2 quarts milk
¾ cup sugar
2 tsp. vanilla extract

Place rice, salt, and water into a large saucepan. Cook over low heat, stirring occasionally until water is completely absorbed. Add 3 cups milk and cook uncovered until most of milk is absorbed. Add 3 cups milk and cook again. Add 2 cups milk and ¾ cup sugar. Cook until nice and creamy. Remove from heat and add in vanilla. Serve. Yields 6 servings. (Hint, top with raisins for dessert.)

Toni's Pumpkin Fudge

2 cups sugar
2 tbsp. pumpkin
¼ tsp. cornstarch
¼ tsp. pumpkin pie spice
½ cup Carnation condensed milk
½ tsp. vanilla

In saucepan mix together sugar, pumpkin, cornstarch, pumpkin pie spice, and Carnation milk. Cook on medium-high heat until mixture forms a soft ball when dropped into cold water. Add vanilla and let cool for 10 minutes. Beat until creamy, then pour into a buttered 8" x 8" pan. When cool, cut into small squares. Yields 12 to 16 squares.

Cheddar Breakfast Strata

6 slices bread
Butter, as needed
1 cup cheddar cheese, shredded
3 eggs
2 cups milk
Salt and pepper to taste

Heat oven to 350 degrees. Slice crusts from bread and butter one side. Place slices butter-side down into baking dish. Sprinkle cheese over bread. Beat eggs and milk together and pour over bread. Add salt and pepper to taste. Bake strata for 30 to 40 minutes until golden and bubbly. Yields 4 servings.

Suzanne's Cherry Cake Bars

1 pkg. white cake mix
8 tbsp. butter, softened (divided)
1¼ cup rolled oats (divided)
1 egg
1 (21-oz.) can cherry pie filling
½ cup chopped walnuts
¼ cup brown sugar, firmly packed

Heat oven to 350 degrees. In large bowl, combine cake mix, 6 tbsp. butter, and 1 cup of oats. Mix until crumbly. Reserve one cup of this dry mixture for topping. To remaining dry mixture add egg and mix well until blended. Press mixture into greased 9" x 13" inch pan to form bottom crust. Pour cherry pie filling over this crust. With reserved dry mixture, add remaining ¼ cup oats, 2 tbsp. butter, nuts, and brown sugar. Beat until thoroughly mixed. Sprinkle carefully over cherry mixture. Bake for 30 to 40 minutes or until golden brown. Allow to cool. May be served with whipped cream or ice cream. Yields 6 servings.

Apple Scones

2 cups flour
3 tsp. baking powder
2 tbsp. sugar
½ tsp. cinnamon
½ tsp. salt
6 tbsp. butter
½ cup apples, peeled and finely chopped
4 tbsp. apple juice or apple cider

Heat oven to 400 degrees. Combine flour, baking powder, sugar, cinnamon, and salt. Cut in butter. Add apples. Add enough apple juice to bring together a fairly stiff dough. Do not overmix. Roll dough out on a floured surface to ½" thickness. Cut into triangles and place on a greased baking sheet. (You can also use a scone pan.) Bake for approximately 10 minutes. Yields 10 to 12 scones.

Keep reading for a preview of
Laura Childs's next Tea Shop Mystery . . .

Pekoe Most Poison

Coming March 2017 in hardcover
from Berkley Prime Crime!

PALMETTOS swayed lazily in the soft breeze, daffodils bobbed their shaggy heads as Theodosia Browning stepped quickly along the brick pathway that wound through a bountiful front yard garden, and up to the polished double doors of the Calhoun Mansion. Pausing, she pulled back the enormous brass boar's head door knocker . . . nothing wimpy about this place . . . and let it crash against the metal plate.

Claaaang. The sound echoed deep within the house as the boar's eyes glittered and glared at her.

Turning to face Drayton, her friend and tea sommelier, Theodosia said, "This should be fun. I've never visited Doreen's home before."

"You'll like it," Drayton said. "It's a grand old place. Built back in the early eighteen hundreds by Emerson Calhoun, one of Charleston's early indigo barons."

"I guess we're lucky to be invited then," she said. Their hostess, Doreen Briggs, also known to her close friends as "Dolly," was president of the Ladies Opera Auxiliary and one of the leading social powerhouses in Charleston, South Carolina. Theodosia had always thought of Doreen as being slightly bubbleheaded, but that could be a carefully cultivated act, aimed to deflect from all the philanthropic work that she and her husband were involved in.

A few seconds later, the front door creaked open, and Theodosia and Drayton were greeted by a vision so strange it could have been a drug-induced hookah dream straight out of *Alice in Wonderland.* The man who answered the door was dressed in a powder blue velvet waistcoat, cream-colored slacks, and spit-polished black buckle boots. But it wasn't his formal, quasi-Edwardian attire that made him so bizarre. It was the giant, white velvet rat head perched atop his head and shoulders. Yes, white velvet, just like the fur of a properly groomed, semi-dandy white rat, complete with round ears, long snout bristling with whiskers, and bright pink eyes.

"Welcome," the rat said to them as he placed one white-gloved hand (paw?) behind his back and bowed deeply.

At which point Theodosia arched her carefully waxed brows and said, as a not-so-subtle aside to Drayton, "When the invitation specified a Charleston Rat Tea, they weren't just whistling Dixie."

IT *was* a rat tea. Of sorts. Drayton had filled her in on the history of the quaint rat tea custom on their stroll over from the Indigo Tea Shop, where they brewed all manner of tea, fed and charmed customers, and made a fairly comfortable living.

"Seventy-five years ago," Drayton said, "rat teas were all the rage in Charleston. You see, at the advent of World War II, our fair city underwent a tremendous population explosion as war workers arrived at the navy shipyard in droves."

"I get that," Theodosia said, "but what's with the rats specifically?"

"Ah," Drayton said. "With the increased populace, downtown merchants were thriving. Because they were so frantically busy, they began tossing their garbage out onto the sidewalks, which immediately attracted a huge influx of rats. The local public health officials, fearing some kind of ghastly epidemic, quickly spearheaded a 'rat torpedo' campaign. Volunteers were tasked with wrapping poisoned bait in small folded bits of newspaper and sticking them in alleys and crawl spaces."

Theodosia listened, fascinated, as Drayton continued his story.

"These rat torpedoes were so effective," Drayton said, "that prominent society ladies even held fancy 'rat teas' to help promote the campaign."

"And the rats were eventually eradicated?" Theodosia asked.

"Charleston became a public health model," Drayton said. "Several major cities even sent representatives to study our method."

THE blue rat at the door was nodding at Theodosia and Drayton as they stepped inside the foyer. Here, they were greeted by a second rat wearing a pastel-pink coat. This rat was equally polite.

"Good afternoon," the pink rat said.

"I feel like I've been drinking to excess," Theodosia said. "Seeing pink rats instead of pink elephants."

"This way, please," the pink rat said in carefully modulated tones.

They followed him down a long, red-tiled hallway where oil paintings dark with crackle glaze hung on the walls, and the hum of conversation grew louder with each step they took. Then the pink rat turned suddenly and ushered them into an enormous sunlit parlor where fifty or so guests milled about, and a half-dozen elegant tea tables were carefully arranged.

The pink rat consulted his clipboard. "Miss Browning, Mr. Conneley, you're both to be seated at table six."

"Thank you," Drayton said.

"Do I know you?" Theodosia asked the pink rat. Her blue eyes sparkled with curiosity and her voice was slightly teasing. She was a woman of rare and fair beauty even though she'd be the first to pooh-pooh anyone who told her so. But with her mass of auburn hair, English-rose complexion, and captivating smile, she certainly stood out in a crowd.

"I don't think so, ma'am," the pink rat said as he spun on the heels of his buckle boots and hastened off to escort another group of guests to their table.

"Who *was* that?" Theodosia asked, as her eyes skittered around the rather grand room, taking in the crystal chandelier, enormous marble fireplace, gaggle of upscale-looking guests, as well as tea tables set with Wedgwood china and Reed & Barton silver. "He sounds so familiar. The pink rat guy, I mean."

"No idea," Drayton said as he regarded the table settings. "But isn't this lovely? And what fun to stage a madcap homage to the rat teas of yesteryear." Drayton was beginning to rhapsodize, one of the most endearing qualities of this debonair, sixty-something tea sommelier, while Theodosia was suddenly fizzing with curiosity. Why had she been invited when she had just a nodding acquaintance with Doreen Briggs? And who were these white rat butlers, anyway? Professional servers shanghaied from a local catering company? Or actors who'd been hired to wear costumes and playact a rather bizarre role?

These were the kind of things Theodosia wondered about. These were the things that kept her brain whirring at night when she should have been fast asleep.

* * *

"DRAYTON!" an excited voice shrilled. Theodosia and Drayton turned to find Doreen Briggs closing on them like a five-foot-two-inch heat-seeking missile. She charged up to Drayton, rose on tiptoes to administer a profusion of air kisses, and then flashed an enormous smile at Theodosia. "Theodosia, she said. "So good of you to come." Doreen gripped her hand firmly, pumped her arm. "Welcome to my home."

"Thank you for inviting me," Theodosia said. "And I must say, you have a very lovely home."

"It is cozy, isn't it?" Doreen said. Her green eyes glinted almost coquettishly, her reddish-blond hair cascaded around her face in a forest of curls that didn't seem quite natural for a woman in her late fifties.

"We're thrilled to be here," Drayton added.

Doreen, who was stuffed into a pastel-pink shantung silk dress with a rope of pearls around her neck, waved a hand that was festooned with sparkling diamond rings, and said, "Don't you think this is jolly fun? The rat tea theme, I mean? Aren't my liveried rats just adorable?"

"Charming," Theodosia responded. Truthfully, she thought the rats—she'd seen at least four of them chugging officiously around the room—were a little strange. But this was a woman who supported the arts, gave money to service dog organizations, and was on the verge of bequeathing a sizeable grant to Drayton's beloved Heritage Society, so she was willing to cut her a good deal of slack.

"Where's Beau?" Drayton asked. "He's certainly here today, isn't he?" Beau Briggs was Doreen's husband, a self-professed entrepreneur who owned apartment buildings in North Charleston and was a partner in the newly-opened Gilded Magnolia Spa on King Street.

Doreen pushed back a strand of frizzled hair. "He's around here somewhere. Probably bending the ear of one of

our guests, talking about one of his pet business projects."
She put a hand on Theodosia's arm and said, "Isn't it cute
when men work themselves into a tizzy over business? I
love how they think they're masters of the universe when
it's really us women who run things."

"And a fine job you ladies do," Drayton said.

"Aren't you the most politically correct gentleman yet,"
Doreen fawned. "You'll have to indoctrinate Beau with
some of your fine, liberal ideas." She managed a quick sip of
air and said, "We're sitting right here." Then she waved a
chubby hand. "Your table is right next to us."

"I'm looking forward to meeting your husband," Theodosia said. She'd heard so much about the man who'd
helped create Gilded Magnolia Spa. Magazines had run
full-color spreads, health and beauty editors had rhapso-
dized about it in articles, and the ladies-who-lunch types,
who shopped at Bob Ellis Shoes and Hampden Clothing,
had been exchanging whispers about the spa's gold foil
facials and amazing electric-stimulation lifts.

"I imagine Beau will pop up any moment," Doreen said
as she glanced around the room. Then her face lit up and
she cried, "There he is." She waved a hand as bracelets
clanked. "Beau!" Her voice rose higher. "Yes, I'm talking to
you, hunky monkey . . . who do you *think* I'm waving at
like a crazy lady? Get over here and say hello to Theodosia
and Drayton."

Beau Briggs, who was forty pounds overweight, with
slicked-back red hair, the jowls of a Shar-Pei, and perfectly
steam-cleaned pores, came huffing over to join them.

"Dolly," he said. "What?" His pink sport coat was
stretched around his mid-section, the gold buttons looking
about ready to burst and go airborne. Theodosia decided
Beau might partake of his own spa's skin care regimen, but
not their low-cal smoothies and fruit salads.

"These are the people I was telling you about," Doreen

said. "Theodosia and Drayton. They run that lovely Indigo Tea Shop over on Church Street. You remember, they bake those chocolate chip scones that you adore so much."

Beau turned an expectant smile on them. "I hope you brought some along?"

Doreen gave him a playful slap. "Silly boy. You know our caterers are handling the scones and tea sandwiches today. Theodosia and Drayton are our guests. They're here to partake of tea, not serve it."

"A respite," Drayton said, trying to be jocular.

"Then sit down, sit down," Doreen said as the guests began taking their seats. "Oh!" She spun around to position herself at the head table, all the while looking a little scattered. "I suppose it's high time I get this fancy tea started." She glanced down, looking slightly perturbed. "Now where did I put my silver bell?"

THE tea turned out to be a lovely affair, albeit a trifle strange. The rat theme continued as everyone took their places and more liveried rats came scurrying out of the kitchen. They carried steaming teapots in white-gloved hands, pouring out servings of Darjeeling and Assam tea. By the time silver trays overflowing with cinnamon-and-lemon poppy seed scones arrived, Theodosia was well past her initial surprise. In fact, she was able to sit back and enjoy herself as Drayton did the heavy lifting, chatting merrily with all the guests as their table, most of whom she had only a nodding acquaintance with. Then again, Drayton was a stickler for politeness and decorum., and tended to be a lot more social than she was.

Let's see now, Theodosia thought, after they'd gone around the table and made hasty introductions. The two blonds, Dree and Diana, were on the board of directors for the Charleston Symphony. The woman in the fire engine red suit . . . Twilby . . . Eleanor Twilby? . . . was the executive director of . . . something. And then . . . well, she just wasn't sure. But the crab-and-Gruyère quiche she was digging into was incredibly creamy and delicious.

Doreen turned in her chair and tapped Theodosia on the shoulder. "Having fun?" she asked.

Theodosia, caught with a bite of food in her mouth, chewed quickly and swallowed. "This quiche is incredible!" She really meant it. "I'll have to get the recipe. Haley would love it." Haley was her chef and chief baker back at the Indigo Tea Shop.

"Carolina blue crab," Doreen said in a conspiratorial whisper. "Baked by Crispin's Catering. They're brand new here in Charleston and making quite a splash. We even tapped them to cater all the appetizers for our grand opening party at Gilded Magnolia Spa next Saturday."

"You have quite a large group here today," Theodosia said. "Are most of them spa customers?"

"It's a sprinkling of all sorts of people," Doreen said. "Spa members, media people, a few friends and neighbors, some business associates." She raised a hand to one of the rat waiters and said, "We're going to need a fresh pot of this orange pekoe tea for Beau." And to Theodosia. "It's his favorite."

"One of Drayton's recommendations?" Theodosia asked.

"Oh, absolutely," Doreen said. "I consulted with Drayton on all the teas we're serving here today. As usual, he was spot on."

"He's the best tea sommelier I've ever encountered. We're fortunate to have him at the Indigo Tea Shop."

"Watch out someone doesn't try to steal him away," Doreen said. She turned, held up Beau's teacup for the waiter to pour him a fresh cup of tea, and said, "Just set the teapot on the warmer please."

The pink rat leaned forward, set down the teapot, and, in the process, the edge of his sleeve brushed against one of the tall white tapers.

"Watch the . . . !" Doreen cried out as the candle wobbled dangerously in its silver holder.

But it was too late.

The burning candle bobbled and swayed for a couple more seconds, and then tipped onto the table. It landed, flame burning bright, right in the middle of an enormous, frothy centerpiece. As if someone had doused it with gasoline, a ring of dancing fire burst forth. A split second later, the decorator-done arrangement of silk flowers, pinecones, twisted vines, and dried moss was a boiling, seething inferno.

As the guests at Doreen's table began to scream, two people leapt to their feet and began beating at the crackling flames with linen napkins. Their efforts just served to fan the flames and set one of the napkins on fire. It twisted and blazed like an impromptu torch until the person waving it suddenly dropped it onto the table.

Beau Briggs, as if just realizing they might all be in mortal danger, suddenly jumped to his feet, knocking his chair over backward. "Somebody get a fire extinguisher!" he yelped as flames continued to dance and scorch the tabletop. Now everyone from his table was jigging around in a fearful, nervous rugby-like scrum, while people from other tables were rushing over to shout suggestions. Doreen, no help at all, put her hands on her head and let loose a series of high-pitched yips.

"Somebody do something!" a woman in a black leather dress screamed.

At which point Theodosia grabbed the teapot from her table, elbowed her way through the gaggle of guests, and poured the tea directly onto the flames.

There was a loud hiss as an enormous billow of black smoke swirled upward. But the tea had done the trick. The fire had fizzled out, leaving only the remnants of a singed and seared centerpiece swimming in a brown puddle of Darjeeling tea.

"Thank you," Beau cried out. "Thank you!"

"Good work," Drayton said to Theodosia, just as the blue rat arrived, fumbling with a bright red fire extinguisher. He aimed the nozzle at the table and proceeded to spray white, foamy gunk all over the remaining plates of food.

"Stop, stop!" Beau yelled at the rat. He lifted his hands to indicate they were all fine, that the danger was over, even as a few tendrils of smoke continued to spiral up from the charred centerpiece.

"Goodness," Doreen squealed, nervously patting her heart with one hand. "That was absolutely terrifying. We could have . . . all been . . ." She spun around toward Theodosia, a look of gratitude washing across her face. "Thank you, my dear, for such quick, decisive thinking."

"But your tea party's been ruined," Theodosia said with a rueful smile. "I'm so sorry." The head table, which had looked so elegant and refined a few minutes earlier, was now a burned and blistered wreck. The ceiling above was horribly smudged.

"We'll salvage this party yet," Beau said. Undeterred, he pulled himself to his full height and raised his hands, like a fiery evangelist, ready to address the upturned, still-stunned faces of all his guests.

"I don't know how," Doreen muttered.

"My dear friends," Beau said. "Please pardon the inconvenience." He pulled a hanky from his jacket pocket and mopped at his florid face as a spatter of applause broke out. He acknowledged the applause with a slightly uneven smile and continued. "Even though everything is firmly under control, I think it's best that we finish our . . . ahem, that we adjourn to . . ." Stumbling over his words, he halted mid-sentence as a tremendous shudder ran through his entire body. It shook his shoulders, jiggled his belly, and made his knees knock together. Then his eyes popped open to twice their normal size and he let out a cough, razor sharp and harsh. That cough quickly became a series of coughs that racked his body and morphed into a high-pitched, thready-sounding wheeze.

Doreen, looking properly concerned, held out a glass of water for her husband. "Please drink this, dear."

As Beau struggled to grab the water, his hands began to shake violently. He managed to just barely grasp the glass and lift it shakily to his lips.

"I just need . . ." Beau managed to croak out.

But just as he was about to take a much-needed sip of water, his head suddenly flew backward and he let loose a loud choke that sounded like the bark of an angry seal. The glass slipped from his hand.

Crash! Shards of glass flew everywhere.

"Beau?" Doreen said in a small, scared voice, as if she sensed something was catastrophically wrong.

Beau was waving both hands in front of his face now, gasping for breath and hacking loudly. "Wha . . . bwa . . ." He fought to get his words out, but simply couldn't manage it.

At least five sets of hands stretched out to help him, all holding water glasses. Instead of grabbing one of the glasses, Beau struggled to pick up his cup of tea. He managed to get his teacup halfway to his lips before his right hand convulsed into a rigid claw and the cup slipped from his grasp. As it clattered to the table, he clutched frantically at his throat. Eyes fluttering like crazy as they rolled back in his head, he managed a hoarse groan. Then, as if made of rubber, his legs gave way completely.

Bam! Beau dropped to the floor like a sack of potatoes, smacking his forehead on the sharp edge of the table on his way down.

In a frenzy now, screeching for help, Doreen bent over and tried to grab him. But Beau was so heavy and unwieldy that all she managed to do was bunch his shirt above his jacket collar. "He's not breathing!" she screamed. "Does anyone know the Heimlich maneuver?"

One man from a nearby table immediately sprang to his feet and came flying around to help. He knelt down directly behind Beau, wrapped his arms around his chest, and pulled him halfway upright. Then, locking his hands under Beau's sternum, the man pulled his arms tight, making quick upward thrusts.

Beau's eyes flickered open, then turned glassy, as white foam began to dribble from his mouth.

"It's working, it's working!" Doreen cried. "He blinked his eyes."

"Thank goodness," Drayton said. He sank into his chair as the Good Samaritan continued to thump and bump poor Beau Briggs.

"Is he coming around?" Doreen asked, in a tremulous voice, as Beau's head jerked back and forth spasmodically and then lolled to one side, as if his neck was made of Silly Putty.

"His color's looking better," the skinny woman in black leather cried out. "His face isn't purple anymore."

"That's good?" Doreen asked. Then, as if to reassure herself, said, "That's good."

Meanwhile, the man who was still administering the Heimlich maneuver was struggling mightily and beginning to lose steam. "If I could just . . ." he grunted out, trying to catch his breath, ". . . dislodge whatever he's got caught in his throat. Try to get him breathing on his own." He pulled and thrust harder and harder, his own face turning a violent shade of red. "Where's the ambulance?" the man gasped. "Where are the EMTs?"

"On their way!" the pink rat cried. "I can hear sirens now."

"Can somebody take over here?" the Good Samaritan gasped.

A man in a white dinner jacket sprang into action. He

employed a different technique. He bent Beau forward and thumped him hard on the back. But nothing seemed to be working. Beau's eyes, open wide, but unseeing, looked like two boiled eggs. His bulbous body was as limp and unresponsive as a noodle.

"I don't think that technique is going to work," Theodosia said in a quiet voice.

Drayton heard her and frowned, his eyes going wide with alarm. "Why would you say that? What do you think is wrong with him?"

"You see that white foam dribbling from his mouth?" Theodosia said. "You see his pale, almost waxy complexion? I think he's ingested some sort of poison."

"Poison!" Doreen suddenly screamed at the top of her lungs. "Don't drink the tea! The tea is poison!"

Watch for the next Cackleberry Club Mystery

Eggs Over Uneasy

When the Kindred Players hold their first dress rehearsal for *A Christmas Carol*, something goes terribly wrong and the star of the show is murdered. Even though Suzanne and Toni were backstage, working the curtains and moving sets, they didn't see a thing. Or did they play an unwitting role in this carefully staged tragedy?

And be sure to catch the new Scrapbooking Mystery, also from Laura Childs and Berkley Prime Crime

Crepe Factor

Holidays in the French Quarter of New Orleans bring candlelight concerts, a Winter Market, and bloody blue murder. Who on earth stabbed a nasty restaurant critic who reviews for the webzine Glutton for Punishment? And can scrapbook maven Carmela catch this maniac before he kills again?

Find out more about the author and her mysteries at laurachilds.com or become a friend on Facebook.

Writing as Laura Childs, this author has brought you the *New York Times* bestselling Tea Shop Mysteries, Scrapbooking Mysteries, and Cackleberry Club Mysteries. Now, writing under her own name of Gerry Schmitt, she has created an entirely new series of sharp-edged thrillers.

Little Girl Gone

an Afton Tangler Thriller
by Gerry Schmitt

On a frozen night in an affluent Minneapolis neighborhood, a baby is abducted from her home after her babysitter is violently assaulted. The parents are frantic, the police are baffled, and, with the perpetrator already in the wind, the trail is getting colder by the second.

As a family liaison officer with the Minneapolis Police Department, it's Afton Tangler's job to deal with the emotional aftermath of terrible crimes—but she's never faced a case quite as brutal as this. Each development is more heartbreaking than the last and the only lead is a collection of seemingly unrelated clues.

Available in hardcover from Berkley!